Megan Avery's biggest critique of modern media has always been "needs more kissing." She's taken it upon herself to make that happen by writing heartwarming and steamy romance novels. She loves coffee, dogs, and books—the bigger the better. On the rare occasion she leaves her home in Kentucky, she's most likely to be found at a concert or local restaurant with her husband.

Heart Racer

MEGAN AVERY

SPHERE

SPHERE

First published in Great Britain in 2026 by Sphere

1 3 5 7 9 10 8 6 4 2

Copyright © Megan Avery 2026

The moral right of the author has been asserted.

*All characters and events in this publication, other than those
clearly in the public domain, are fictitious and any resemblance
to real persons, living or dead, is purely coincidental.*

All rights reserved.
No part of this publication may be reproduced, stored in a
retrieval system, or transmitted, in any form, or by any means, without
the prior permission in writing of the publisher, nor be otherwise circulated
in any form of binding or cover other than that in which it is published
and without a similar condition including this condition being
imposed on the subsequent purchaser.

A CIP catalogue record for this book
is available from the British Library.

ISBN 978-1-4087-2480-4

Typeset in Carre Noir by M Rules
Printed and bound in Great Britain by
Clays Ltd, Elcograf S.p.A.

Papers used by Sphere are from well-managed forests
and other responsible sources.

Sphere	The authorised representative
An imprint of	in the EEA is
Little, Brown Book Group	Hachette Ireland
Carmelite House	8 Castlecourt Centre
50 Victoria Embankment	Dublin 15, D15 XTP3, Ireland
London EC4Y 0DZ	(email: info@hbgi.ie)

An Hachette UK Company
www.hachette.co.uk

www.littlebrown.co.uk

Content warnings: parental figure with terminal cancer, parental death (off-page), past sports injury (off-page); strained parental relationship (on-page), parents going through divorce, explicit language, explicit sexual content

*For my parents, who gave me roots
and wings to chase my dreams.*

*And for everyone still figuring it out. It might get worse,
but it gets better, too. Be here now and take a breath.*

"Have no fear of perfection;
you'll never reach it."

—MARIE CURIE

Chapter One
Keely

Sometimes, Keely Sinclair preferred to think about life in terms of atoms and cells.

They had perfectly definable expectations, ones she could look at and know instantly: pass or fail.

Atoms expected to remain whole, or to get that way as quickly as possible if they weren't.

Cells expected to grow, to multiply and divide in their natural cycle. Atoms made cells, cells made vitamins, and vitamins were going to be Keely's life's work one day. Her entire thesis revolved around artificial energy—namely how to have more of it when you needed to study late in the evening, and less when it was midnight and you had to be up at five the next morning.

Atoms. Cells. Vitamins. Easy. Predictable.

People were ... less so. She didn't know why Jeremy Chen had missed Theory and Application of Computational Chemistry this past Tuesday, when it was still so early in the semester, but she'd offered her notes anyway when he emailed the entire roster in a panic. Or why her neighbor Selina was going out of town midweek and needed someone to water her one single plant, but Keely agreed to that, too.

She didn't like not meeting expectations.

While the chromatograph ran, Keely fiddled with her to-do list, written in her favorite Paper Mate Flair pen. She liked it because it was permanent, no room for errors. On the off chance she *did* make a mistake, she had to start over, as many times as it took to make it perfect. And also, secretly her main reason, they came in fun colors. Magenta for tests, blue for study groups, and the almighty Ruby Red for absolutely-important-do-not-forget tasks. Today's list was filled with red.

- ~~Biochem II — review notes before study hall~~
- ~~Histology — Chapters 4–6~~
- ~~Thesis Work — book lab~~
- ~~TW — draw blood~~
- TW — Check caffeine levels (use chromatograph this time?)
- ~~TACC — Send Jeremy notes~~
- Selina — water plant on the way home

"Keely!"

Keely jumped, accidentally drawing a line straight through the last to-do on her list: *go to bed early and re-run labs in the morning*.

That was about right.

"Sorry, Lori." Keely sat up, dropped her pen, and flexed her hand. Her phone lay on the page, still glowing brightly. She'd been syncing up her planner with her digital calendar, and a timer ran in the background, counting down the precious seconds to the end of her experiment. She only had five to seven minutes to add the dye after the test stopped, and seven was pushing it.

She spun on the stool, giving Lori a full grin alongside her attention. "What were you saying?"

Her lab partner's mouth was drawn into a straight line.

They didn't have much in common. Keely's default was *smile*, and Lori's was *frown*. Keely's hair was golden brown, claw-clipped in a style that took her exactly twenty-three seconds to perfect each morning. Lori's hair was box-dye black, unbrushed, and it often fell in her eyes. Lori had a hoop through her septum and Keely cried when she got her ears pierced at thirteen. Whereas Keely lived with her best friend in a glorified closet masquerading as a two-bedroom apartment, Lori lived in a house off-campus with her boyfriend. Keely was from the East Coast, grew up a little under five hours away outside Richmond; Lori's parents resided in downtown Portland, Oregon. More than that, Lori's parents were still together. Keely's were *not*.

But her and Lori's final thesis projects were complementary, so their advisor stuck them together last year when they declared their biochemistry tracks. Proximity had made them friends, but shared extracurriculars made it stick. That was sort of how it went by the time you got to spring semester of senior year: the same faces, in every lecture, day after day.

"I'm heading home." Lori swiped her student ID off the desk where she'd been working, then her scarf from the back of her chair. "It's almost eight."

Keely wiped at her eyes, wishing *her* final thesis cared about trivial things like clocks or bedtimes. She wondered if the vending machine on the second floor still had the caramel apple energy drinks stocked from fall. "I've got a few more hours left, I think."

Lori's mouth pinched, her septum piercing skewing sideways as her nose followed suit. "I can hang out if you want company."

"No, no. You go home. Eat food that isn't from a vending machine." *Cuddle with your boyfriend. Have a life outside the lab.*

That garnered a small smile. "I'll see you tomorrow, right?" Lori slung her backpack over her shoulder. When Keely didn't nod, Lori's dark brows inched up her forehead as she tugged the zipper of her coat. "For Olympiad training at lunch?"

Keely nodded, subtly flipping to tomorrow's page in her planner. "Of course. I'll be there." If it was written down—and it was—Keely was legally obligated to not only attend but to give it her all.

She really hoped tonight's experiment would tell her how to do that, over and over again.

Maybe she'd discover some incredibly rare phenomenon where she could multiply herself, do everything she needed, then merge back. Cells did it all the time, no problem.

Oh, to be a cell in a biochemistry lab.

After Lori had left, Keely checked the countdown on her phone. It'd be close, but she could run and grab something from the vending machine to tide her over.

Davidson Hall was built to accommodate massive lecture rooms, and since the college wasn't big enough—or endowed enough—to have a separate lab building, her thighs suffered every time she needed to be on the second floor.

A few other students lingered, escaping from late-night labs or huddled in study groups, the first major tests of the new semester on the horizon.

"Keely, hey." Sam Mabry, her friend from Inorganic Chemistry, waved her over to a table tucked in the alcove behind the vending machines. "My savior. Please help me. Do you remember where this coefficient goes when the special conditions are met?"

Keely glanced at Sam's notebook, though she really shouldn't ask. Her test had *maybe* five minutes remaining when she left, and she'd used two of them already. Plus she could hardly breathe from the impromptu StairMaster exercise.

"What are the special conditions?" she asked anyway, because it mattered, and because she couldn't leave someone in the lurch. That was an expectation, and well—

As Sam explained his predicament, she reached in her lab coat pocket to peek at the timer. It was empty, save an old peppermint wrapper. Her phone must still be tucked between the pages of her planner.

She didn't love handing out the answer, but time was of the essence. She scanned his paper more thoroughly. "Oh, this is a trick question. There's no heat factor here." She pointed at the variable. "So it wouldn't react anyway. The entire coefficient becomes zero."

"Oh, duh. That was the last chapter, wasn't it?"

"Two chapters ago, I think."

"Thanks, Keel." Sam held up his hand for a high-five. She returned it, along with his genuine smile. She really did love helping people. It gave her a little ... *boost*. "Hey, are you going to Jamie's party this weekend?"

"I'm not sure yet. We'll have to see how this lab goes." She grimaced. "We should get coffee soon, though."

Maya Maldonado, a friend from Keely's multiple science-based extracurriculars, leaned over the arm of her wheelchair to grip Keely's elbow. Her study materials took up the other half of Sam's table. "*Please*. We can go after Olympiad practice tomorrow?"

"I've got yours, Keely," Sam chimed, grinning. "For saving me with this analysis." He sent Keely on her way with a two-finger salute to his temple.

She ignored the little voice in her head saying, *if you go to sleep right now, you'll* still *only get six hours and thirteen minutes*. And the vending machine was, in fact, out of caramel apple energy drinks.

The chromatograph wasn't spinning when she came back, her phone chiming with the alarm alert between the pages of her planner. She ran over to it, even though rushing *now* was futile. She shouldn't have stopped to help Sam but couldn't bring herself to regret it—at least she would have achieved *something* today.

After silencing her alarm, Keely dropped the dye in half-heartedly. This experiment was as good as failed.

Yet, despite her pessimism, as she watched and waited for the results, blood rushed to her cheeks. Her fingertips tingled. Her toes too, no matter how much she wiggled them in her shoes. She always got this way right before an experiment finished, jittery with anticipation and adrenaline. Who needed caffeine, anyway?

Keely's brain spun like the machines tucked along the wall, running overnight tests for other students. Was there weight behind that random thought? Adrenaline? Is that what she's been missing in all her previous research? That made sense. Adrenaline had a crash like sugar or her beloved caffeine, but was also naturally produced.

She grabbed her phone to jot it down, for poring over later when she inevitably couldn't sleep.

An email preview waited on her screen, and it derailed her train of thought. Her everything.

Your most recent loan application status

Keely was onto something with the adrenaline thing, because she didn't hesitate to open it, the way she normally did with important emails. This time, she ripped off the Band-Aid.

And started bleeding out.

> Dear Keely Sinclair,
> Thank you for your recent application for a continued education loan with Valley View Bank and Trust. After careful review of your application and supporting documentation, we regret to inform you we are unable to approve your loan at this time in line with our internal credit policy, and your application has been denied.
> We understand this may be disappointing, and we encourage you to address any factors that may improve future applications, such as having a co-signer.

No, no, no ... There must be some mistake. Her application had been watertight. She frantically skimmed the rest of the email but always came back to the word *denied*. It may as well have been bolded and in bright red.

Her heart plummeted. She couldn't afford grad school without a loan—she'd worked her tail off to keep her full ride scholarship all four years—and her parents weren't an option to co-sign. Keely's mother had considered taking out a second mortgage just to pay for the divorce lawyer. She couldn't afford Keely's debt too.

Some of the programs Keely had been accepted to weren't feasible without funding, and some of the others were so outlandish her acceptance was contingent on the loan itself.

Caltech—her dream school—was the latter.

And she'd failed to secure it.

She looked down at the data the lab computer spat out in crisp black lines. The coefficients, the very ones she'd helped Sam with upstairs, were all off. Her hypothesis had been disproven.

That had failed, too.

Pressure, dense and dark, made a home on Keely's chest. Rerunning the test tonight wasn't an option. It would take four hours, and that was assuming she had enough sample to retest, which she wasn't sure she did.

If she didn't find a way around the loan problem, her final thesis wouldn't matter anyway. She couldn't be a biochemist without a master's degree. It would be like a doctor using a toy stethoscope.

Numbly, Keely packed up. Her planner. Her pens. The sheets of data, tucked neatly into their assigned folder.

She tugged on her winter coat, blinking the sting from her eyes, and began the walk home.

Tears weren't on her to-do list today.

・・・・・

When Keely made it back to her apartment after watering Selina's plant, a few of those tears had managed to slip free anyway. She told herself it was the frigid winter air.

Her roommate and best friend, Zoey Lamb, stood at the stove, dark curls wound unnaturally tighter from the steam of whatever was simmering. Her phone, propped in an open cabinet, was on a video call. Zoey's Italian-American family lived in Boston, but that didn't stop Zoey's mom Rina from trying to ensure Zoey never went more than a week without authentic Italian, even if it meant watching her like a hawk on FaceTime while she talked Zoey through step-by-step instructions.

Zoey looked back at Keely, eyes rounding out in a silent plea. "I need to go, Mamma."

A voice floated over the bubbling sauce. "Is that Keely I see trying to sneak in behind you? Put her on the phone."

Mustering up a smile for her adopted second mother, Keely slipped off her jacket and placed her backpack in a dining chair. "Give me a second."

"I tried," Zoey mumbled.

Keely staunchly ignored her, stepping into the frame. "Hi, Rina."

"Look at you! Your nose is all red. It's too cold for you there," Rina said. "Good thing California is so much warmer."

At this, Keely's eyes watered again. California was still going to happen.

Wasn't it?

Zoey's gaze narrowed as she clocked Keely's mood. "Time for Mom to go," she hissed at a volume only Keely could hear. She turned back to her phone, reaching for the screen in mock panic, shouting "oh *no*" as her thumb hit the end-call button.

Despite the heaviness on her shoulders (and in her email inbox), Keely managed a tiny smile at the staged theatrics. "Won't she call back, like, immediately?"

The phone was buzzing already, but Zoey left it, waving a hand in dismissal. "I'll say I dropped her in the sauce."

"Naturally," Keely said flatly.

Zoey grabbed the sauce spoon and held it out for Keely. "What's wrong? Why were you crying?"

"I was only tearing up a little." Keely sipped at the spoon and a garbled noise left her throat, the hearty flavors knocking the truth free. "My loan application got denied."

A glob of sauce fell on the floor between them as Zoey's hand wobbled. "For Caltech?"

Keely nodded. "It will be fine." *Probably. Maybe.* "They said I can reapply. Or get a co-signer." She swiped a rag from the sink and cleaned up the mess. "I'll figure something out."

Zoey chewed her rose-pink bottom lip. "Why don't you go see your guidance counselor tomorrow? Isn't it her job to help you figure this stuff out?"

Of course. Dr. Goff would know how to help Keely. Other loans to apply for, ways to boost her application. Keely could bring her coffee as a pre-emptive thank you.

"You're a genius," Keely told her best friend.

Zoey preened and gathered the homemade pasta from the wooden drying rack. "Technically a few points shy, but I'm going to test again at the end of the year." She winked. "Can you grab the garlic bread from the freezer?"

Keely feigned a gasp. "Storebought bread? What would Rina say?"

"Just wait until she finds out I like Olive Garden. I'll be disowned."

As they finished dinner, some of the tension eased from the base of Keely's spine. Zoey was right. This mess was easily sorted, especially after pasta and a good night's sleep.

Chapter Two

Max

More. More. More.

Max Simmons's heart pounded, sweat trailing down his throat and dipping beneath the neckline of his emerald-colored crew-neck sweatshirt. His ear warmers kept the moisture on his forehead from dripping into his eyes, but didn't completely keep out the chill. Bitter-cold mountain air did that.

Just because it was January in Virginia didn't mean he had the luxury of sprinting *indoors*. They saved that for Division One schools. Instead, he and the rest of the track and field team started every other winter practice scraping snow from the track when the maintenance department forgot to put the covers on.

Coach said it didn't count as a warm-up, and Max was inclined to agree.

Faster. Don't drag your left foot, carry through with your right, tighten your abs. Controlled breaths as you—no, not like that. You made that mistake last time.

Max increased his speed, pushing against the perpetual bite of air from the nearby Ash Mountains and into the valley where his university was nestled. It was more hills than real mountains, he thought, but Ash Hill University didn't have the same ring to it.

He surged forward, closing his eyes against the wind. He didn't need to see the finish line—it was something he felt in his marrow, in the deepest recesses of his brain.

Which is how he knew, when he'd crossed it, his times still hadn't improved.

"Fuck," he gritted out, slowing from a sprint to a jog, hands on his head. His lungs hurt in the best way, sweet, hard-earned pain lancing his chest. When he looked at Coach Miller and Coach looked away without making eye contact, Max muttered another, more heartfelt, "*Fuck*."

Most of his teammates were already either in the showers or home for the evening. Max would have preferred those places over this one, but he was here still, the altitude biting at his lungs alongside the last vestiges of alcohol-induced regret.

It was two beers, *days* ago. Two and a half, maybe. And it had been Coach's birthday. It wasn't often Coach blurred the lines with the team, so when he agreed to go out, Max did too. He'd hoped to pick Coach's brain uninhibited, dig into the secrets of how to improve his times.

How to improve everything, really, so he wouldn't screw up so badly anymore.

But Coach hadn't had time to talk to Max with everyone else vying for his attention, and Max was left alone in a room full of people. When someone offered Max another round, he took it, desperate to feel something.

He wouldn't make that mistake again—the beer *or* the feelings.

Alcohol worked differently in his athlete's body, disappeared from his blood but lingered in his mind like cigarette smoke in a thrifted shirt.

"Hit the showers." Coach's voice echoed over the track and cut off with a crackle of static.

There were two other people out here, but Max knew the comment was meant for him. No one else pulled that specific color of disappointment from Coach's voice. The girls he passed, high jumpers, waved at him. One of them blushed, which made Max's face go hot in turn. Girls were a distraction, one he couldn't afford, so he pretended not to see her wave him over.

Fifteen minutes later, too-hot water stung his frigid skin as he replayed his sprints in his head. Right before take-off, he'd adjusted his left foot on the block. Had he been back in position when the tone went off? One of his spikes was a little loose this morning. Or maybe it was the ear warmers. His sweatshirt was a little bigger than his normal sprinting unitard and had way more wind resistance. And there was a lot of wind tonight.

He was standing at the mirror, dragging a towel over his chest and through his hair when Coach's voice bellowed through the room, bouncing off the walls and hitting Max square in the chest again. "Simmons. My office, once you're dressed." Coach coughed and muttered, "Please and thank you."

Max saw this coming. The same way he could tell when he was doing his best, he also had an aptitude for pinpointing the exact moment he'd let others down. He'd take the verbal lashing, or the wind sprints, or whatever other punishment on the chin. No way Coach was madder at him than he was at himself.

He watched his reflection in the mirror, steam rising from his head. His chest and neck were still red from the cold, the physical exertion of running in the dead of winter, and his scalding shower hadn't helped. His brown hair hung in clumps, but it would dry to soft waves, overdue for a trim. He scrubbed his hands down his face, letting out a slow, heavy sigh.

"Hey, Simmons." In the mirror, Nolan Aghil's sable eyes met his tawny ones. "Doin' okay?"

Nolan was on the relay team; he was the second to Max's anchor. Nolan was the one who'd invited him to Coach's birthday party. To most places, come to think of it.

Max tried not to be angry at Nolan for that. It wasn't *Nolan's* fault Max had over-imbibed and was still paying the price. No, that all fell firmly on Max's own shoulders. Like he said, he was the anchor.

He was used to the extra weight.

"Fine." Max shrugged. "What's up?"

"My roommate got his hands on the new GTA. Was gonna grab some food from the Q and check it out, if you're interested." Nolan shifted on his feet. "It's been a while since we hung out outside of practice. And I think they've got the grilled wraps today."

The wraps were pretty good. Max's favorite, if he thought about it hard enough. Did Nolan know that? They'd eaten enough of them in sophomore year, when they weren't so worried about being cut from the team that they followed the dietician's instructions to the letter.

Max glanced in the mirror again. Chest still bright red, lungs still tingling from the earlier exertion.

Exertion that hadn't been enough.

"Some other time?" He swallowed. "Coach called me to his office."

A cop-out, and they both knew it. Nolan's shoulders dropped, but

Max told himself it was a trick of the light, the flickering one in the corner, plus the steam from the showers messing with his perception.

"No pressure," Nolan said, except Max didn't know what *no pressure* was supposed to feel like. Nolan hefted his emerald-green, track-and-field-branded backpack onto his shoulder by one strap. "I'll catch you tomorrow at practice?"

Max dipped his chin in a nod.

Once Nolan was gone, Max stared at himself again. At some point during their conversation, he'd taken to gripping the porcelain sink, and his knuckles nearly matched now. They cracked when he let go.

With a fierce shake of his head, Max dried off and got dressed. Time to face the music, even if it was a funeral march.

Coach Miller's office was tucked in the back of the locker room, and Max had to dodge extra hurdles, a bin of shot-put balls, and, randomly, the head of the mascot costume. Beady bug eyes followed him as he approached the door. Max shuddered.

Night had fallen while Max was in the showers, Coach's office now softly backlit with the desk lamp he preferred over the stark and unforgiving beam of the strip light overhead. As Max sat across from his mentor, he watched the last of the day slip below the Ash Mountains.

If he'd known his hope was going with it, he would have stared longer.

Instead, he turned his attention to the man currently watching him with an unreadable expression. Max was used to those, too, though he didn't necessarily like them.

"I'm going to cut to the chase." Coach cleared his throat. He glanced away briefly with a small shake of his head, then looked Max square in the face. "Your funding's been cut."

It took a few seconds for Max's brain to catch up, because—

His brow furrowed. "That's impossible. It's airtight."

"It was," Coach drawled. The yellowing lampshade caused an illusion of sweat on Coach's dark brown forehead. "Until your sponsors caught wind of what those shitheads on the football team have been up to."

At the beginning of the fall semester, nearly half the football team's starting lineup was cut after mandatory drug testing. They'd tested positive for the hot new street version of human growth hormone. The AMU rumor mill's working theory was that they thought it was new enough not to be detected on the standard drug test.

Coach was right—they absolutely *were* shitheads.

"My tests came back negative," Max protested, his pulse picking up like he was still on the track. "I can test again right now, if you want."

"I appreciate that, son—"

Son? This was worse than Max thought.

"—but I've already tried, and they're not having it. They don't want the bad press."

Max rubbed the back of his neck. Whatever good his hot shower had done to relax his muscles was becoming undone the longer this conversation stretched.

That sponsorship was the only reason the word *Olympics* was on the table.

A dull pang thudded in his chest, a dampened gong of hurt. He wouldn't let something as inconsequential as football dopeheads stop him.

He *couldn't*. Not when his dad needed this as much as Max did. Dad's cancer was aggressive, but Dad was a fighter, and so Max had to be, too.

Max straightened in the chair. "What are my options for new funding?" It came out as less of a question, more of a barked demand.

It stiffened Coach's spine as well. "I'm not sure we have any." If Max was in a laughing mood, he might have found it funny, the way Coach slipped into *we* because he was so used to it on the track. This wouldn't change anything for Coach, but everything for Max. "It's too late in the year. Everything's already allocated."

"So, what? That's it?" Max struggled to keep the anger from his voice.

Coach sat back in his chair with a violent squeak. "Don't come at me for this, Max." His tone held a warning. "I know you've worked hard to get here. After last year ..."

Max looked away. He stared at his hands instead, clenched over his chair's armrests. His knuckles were white again, his nails leaving half-moons in the wood.

Last year wasn't somewhere he let his mind wander often, and on the tail of such a horrible training session *and* bad news, it was painful to go there now.

Coach's voice was softer when he spoke next. "You may be able to talk to your career counselor."

Max didn't realize he *had* a career counselor. He vaguely remembered monthly emails from a Dr. Griff or something that he deleted unopened. "And you think that's something they'd be able to help with?"

"I think they'd be able to offer more help than I will." Coach's mouth pressed into a tight line beneath his mustache. "Maybe they've got some extra cash hiding in the woodwork over there."

He was joking, but Max still wasn't in the mood to laugh.

"I'll go first thing in the morning," Max vowed.

Coach nodded like that was exactly what he wanted to hear. Max wished people would tell him what *he* wanted to hear, instead of everything wrong in his life.

Not fast enough.

No funding.

I'm sick, Max.

Max ran home after Coach released him, because there were a thousand thoughts on his mind at any given time, but they were muffled when his shoes pounded pavement.

But tonight, the voices didn't quit.

Which, it turned out, was the least of his problems.

Chapter Three

Keely

Four hours and seventeen minutes: the final amount of sleep Keely's phone told her she'd got last night.

Zero hours and two minutes: the amount Keely felt like she'd had.

Forty-two minutes: how long she waited for Dr. Goff to show up at her office this morning.

Keely had been to the career counselor's office once a month for the past three and a half years, since she was a baby freshman with the world at her feet, not knowing whether a concentration in general chemistry provided more opportunities, or if she should declare a specific track.

Because Ash Mountain University was so small, students were assigned counselors based on last name. Dr. Goff had students S through Z. It meant she was a little less versed in the inner workings of the biochemistry department than Keely would have liked, but beggars and choosers and all that. The first time they talked,

Dr. Goff hadn't even known the biochem graduation rates compared to the national average and had only stared blankly at Keely.

Dr. Goff wore that same wary look now, her navy blazer wrinkle-free over her white button down and jeans. An enamel pin winked from the collar—Abe the emerald ash borer, the school's mascot. Why a school would use an invasive species as the mascot, Keely would never know.

"Good morning, Keely." Dr. Goff checked her watch as she unlocked her office door. "I didn't have you down on my schedule for another week and a half."

Once inside, Keely handed over one of the two coffees she was holding. "I know, but I'm having a bit of a crisis."

Dr. Goff hung her coat on a rack by the window before getting settled behind her desk. She took a long swallow of coffee, eyes closing. When they opened, she looked considerably more chipper, which gave Keely hope, especially when the next words out of her mouth were, "I'm assuming this is about your loan application getting rejected."

"Oh, good. You got my email."

"The one you sent me at ten o'clock last night with the subject line 'URGENT REQUEST, PLEASE READ IMMEDIATELY'?" Dr. Goff's chin dipped, her mouth quirking to the side. "Yes, I got it."

"There has to be something we can do," Keely continued. She crossed her ankles, though her winter boots didn't facilitate much grace. She ended up tipping sideways. "Something *you* can do, Dr. Goff. Linda, if I may."

Dr. Goff spluttered, her silver-blonde pixie cut bobbing as she covered her mouth with her hand. "Well, if you *have*—"

"Because otherwise everything we've been working toward for

three years is ruined." Keely blinked, hard, then cleared her throat and took a dainty sip of her own beverage. "Basically."

Dr. Goff nodded slowly, eyeing Keely's cup. She turned to her computer and logged on. "I don't know the specifics of this particular loan program, but you can always appeal the rejection."

"*Yes*. Great. Let's do that immediately." Keely had known the loan committee was wrong, anyway. She'd appeal, they'd see the error of their ways, and she'd be back on track in no time.

"You can definitely get it started." Dr. Goff's voice slipped into something conciliatory, and Keely didn't like that very much. "But it will take a while, and there's still no guarantee they'll accept it the second time around."

No certain success, Keely heard. She bit her lip. "Are there other loans?"

"Yes, but I think this late in the day you'd run into the same problem anywhere." Emails pinged as the computer connected to the internet, splicing through the sirens going off in Keely's head. "Unless you had someone who co-signed the loan. Most students use their parents, but it can be any adult with established credit history."

Dread snaked through Keely's veins and turned oily. She could hear the conversation between her parents now. Or the shouting, rather, as they inevitably placed the blame at each other's door. Her mom would be too worried about her ever-rising divorce debt, something she wouldn't need to take on at all if dad were a "half decent person." Her dad would undoubtedly find a way to bring it back to the proposed division of their assets and why, as "the breadwinner," he deserved more, and Mom would say something like "there's more to life than money, Jason," and he'd say, "then why do you want so much of mine?" and Keely couldn't very well ask for money *then*, could she?

All of it would leave Keely torn down the middle again, feeling like a burden to them both.

Keely stared at her hands, clutching her coffee like a life raft. "That's not an option."

Dr. Goff leaned back in her chair, a noise catching in her throat. "I see."

Over her shoulder, Keely studied the pictures lined up on the windowsill: Dr. Goff standing arm in arm with a woman under the Eiffel Tower. Dr Goff and that same woman in ski suits, the Northern Lights visible in the background. More photos sat behind them, in locations Keely didn't recognize. The frames hung off the ledge, there were so many.

An unfamiliar pang struck Keely's chest. She chalked it up to sleep deprivation and lingering disappointment over last night's failed experiment. If she had time left when she was done with today's to-dos—she nearly snorted; when did that ever happen—she'd dig into the data and figure out what went wrong, aside from missing the dye window.

"You could always wait a year to start grad school," Dr. Goff offered. "This fall's scholarships may be full, but next fall's haven't opened yet. You'd almost certainly be able to nab a slot with the next cohort."

Dr. Goff may as well have slapped her across the cheek. "I can't *wait* for grad school," Keely said. The computer dinged with an incoming email, distracting Dr. Goff from the pure horror pinching Keely's face.

She needed to go to grad school *next* year, in order to graduate four years after that. She had different tracks for if she chose academia or went on to pursue her doctorate, but either way she'd still be in her forever job by twenty-nine at the latest, married by thirty-one, and well on her way to taking similar pictures to the ones on the windowsill. A perfect life for the perfect daughter, who made things as easy as possible for her parents. "I have a five-year plan, so it's imperative that—"

She cut herself off, because it sounded sort of lame, when she said it like that.

She sat forward in her chair, hands pushing into the mess of papers scattered across the desk. "There has to be something, Dr. Goff." Keely was not above begging. "Maybe I could—"

Dr. Goff held a finger up. "Hold, please."

Keely's mouth snapped shut.

The five seconds it took for Dr. Goff to look at Keely again may as well have been a millennium.

"Sorry." Dr. Goff smiled, and Keely forced herself to return it; it wasn't Dr. Goff's fault she was teetering on the edge of catastrophe. "I needed to make sure I was reading my email correctly. We just had a student drop out."

Keely really was tired. Tired enough to imagine *joy* driving Dr. Goff's words. "And that helps me ... how?"

The smile on Dr. Goff's face grew. Keely didn't add frivolous things like *make my guidance counselor smile* to her to-do lists, but she checked it off mentally anyway. "It helps you because that student was a recipient of the Pursue Your Passions Scholarship, and their absence means there is exactly one extra slot."

I want it.

Across the desk, Dr. Goff's graying eyebrow tipped upward. Keely must have said that aloud. She pursed her lips. Placed her coffee on the desk and sat on her hands for good measure.

"Do you want to know what it's about?" Dr. Goff prompted.

"If it will help me get into grad school, I'll learn the Phoenician alphabet," Keely said, and Dr. Goff laughed but it wasn't a joke. Keely nodded. "Yes, please."

A few more clicks on the outdated computer, and Dr. Goff swiveled the screen. The page was decorated in AMU's signature emerald and gold, *Pursue Your Passions* scrawled across the top. Keely was sure she knew of—and had applied for—every possible scholarship, so she wasn't sure how she'd missed this one.

Until Dr. Goff said, "It's dedicated to helping students bridge the gap post-graduation. Aimed at supporting them through the first steps after school, whatever that looks like."

No wonder Keely hadn't applied. She already knew what her next steps were.

Or she did, until last night. That dirty word—*denied*—filled her brain again, and she had to blink a few times to clear it away.

"I'll take it," Keely breathed.

Dr. Goff chuckled, a hint of bemusement behind it. "It's not *quite* that simple, unfortunately. You still need to apply, and it's a more robust application than you're used to. Grades and extracurriculars, of course, which shouldn't be a problem for you—"

Keely tried not to smile. She'd founded her region's Science Olympiad. She was president of AMU's Women in Science Society, too, and that position was elected. Popularity had to count for something.

"—but also volunteerism outside of your area of study, and a written essay to show why you, above others, should win," Dr. Goff finished.

So this wasn't as in-the-bag as she'd hoped. Keely's heart fell again, then picked up, faster than before. She probably should switch to decaf after this. Maybe forever.

The essay part was fine—she'd managed two required semesters of English essays with little problem, and she wrote peer reviews and research abstracts all the time. Her brain was already pulling items over from her resumé, drawing parallels between the work she'd done on campus and her plans for grad school, the specialization that would someday help others become more fully functioning members of society, ones who could still sleep at night.

It was the volunteerism part that might cause issues.

Keely grabbed her laptop from her bag and propped it on the corner of the desk, throwing the lid open to find her running to-do list. She'd make time. Her Friday nights were still free, and Saturdays, plus Sunday afternoons. And that forty-minute window between class and lab on Wednesday nights where she usually scarfed down a turkey wrap. She could totally pick up garbage and eat at the same time.

The biologist in her shuddered at that.

Dr. Goff took a noisy sip of coffee, then shuddered too. "Is there an extra shot in this?"

Keely shrugged, but nodded. "I got two of my usual."

"That explains it," Dr. Goff murmured.

Keely bit her lip. She should *definitely* cut back on the caffeine.

"The deadline to apply is May first. Right before finals week starts, so you'll have plenty of time to get things sorted. And remember, the key word here is p ..."

Keely tuned her out, because she already had it all sorted. Here, with her color-coordinated calendar, her brain calmed from the state of buzzing it had been in since last night. She could do this. This scholarship was hers. If she left right now, she had an hour before her first class. She would rearrange the little boxes of her life until everything fit *just so*.

She rose, not bothering to slide her laptop in the designated pocket of her backpack. She was half-typing as she zipped it shut. "Thank you, Dr. Goff!" Scooping her coffee off the desk, she walked backward out the door.

Which is why she didn't see the jock with an invasive, bright-green cartoon *bug* on his chest until it was too late. She threw up a hand to stop the collision but knocked against something cold and wet instead.

The smoothie in his hands exploded all over them.

Chapter Four

Max

If Max was a list-making person—which, gross—this would be number one on the *Things I Don't Have Time For* list.

This, of course, being his chocolate-peanut-butter protein shake dripping into his eyes. Why was it *burning?* He blinked, but that only made it worse. He wiped a hand across his face and tried to clear his vision. That didn't work, either. It was in his eyebrows, too, and maybe his mouth?

He ripped his headphones off, letting them fall to their usual home around his neck. "I'm—"

"It's all over my laptop," a voice squeaked, then groaned, and he could have sworn he'd heard it before. His mind blared warning signals, but he couldn't place it.

He tried to look up, but more goop stuck to his eyelashes, dripping from his forehead. "It's in my nose."

"It's in my *hair*," she whined.

This was ridiculous. He wasn't going to argue with a girl while he had puréed banana dripping down his front. He used the hem of his sweatshirt to wipe his face and blinked slowly until the spots started to clear.

By the time he could see again, she had turned away and was swiping her hand across the keyboard of her expensive-looking laptop, flinging brown goo into the garbage can against the wall. Her fingers were nimble, capable, with ink smeared alongside her left pinkie.

That little ink blot did funny things to his pulse, made it stumble a step.

Before his gaze tracked up the rest of her distinctly feminine body to her face, she was gone. He hadn't even gotten a chance to apologize. But there she went, ducking around the corner in a fury of golden-brown hair, and he was left standing in her peppermint-scented aftermath, wondering what the *fuck* just happened.

This was why Max didn't come to the career center. Far too many highly strung academics for his liking.

"Hi, there," someone said from inside the office. "Can I help you?"

Max took one more glance down the hall, but that girl clearly wasn't coming back. And neither was his protein shake—half of it was still seeping into the carpet.

He shook his head clear. He didn't have time to worry about the mystery girl, anyway. He was supposed to be at the gym five minutes ago to meet his relay team for an impromptu weight session between morning practice and their first classes, and if he stood Nolan up again, Max wasn't sure he'd receive another invitation.

Hesitantly, he stepped over the threshold. The office was homey, warm and comfortable, which for some reason went against Max's expectations. He'd always imagined these places to be clinical, or look like his high school one, with motivational posters and magazine stands full of brochures about *Your Next Step*. This ... wasn't that.

Pictures lined the windowsill, and sunlight shined through the window behind the desk, making the greenery in the corner deeper and more vibrant. Max wondered if there actually *was* hope to be found here, like Coach had suggested.

It wasn't like things could get worse.

"Are you Dr. Goff?" he said. He'd searched through his email's garbage folder for five minutes this morning while getting ready to find the right name.

The woman behind the oakwood desk stood and extended her hand. Bracelets jangled, sliding down to cover her dainty wrist bones. "I am. I don't think we've met."

"Max Simmons," he offered after a beat, and it was hard to miss the recognition that flashed across the counselor's face as they broke their handshake.

Yeah. He was *that* Max Simmons. Record-breaking state champion. Total embarrassment. People might not know his face, but they sure as hell knew his name.

Dr. Goff put on a smile, but it was too early in the morning, and Max didn't know her well enough to discern whether it was genuine. "Well, Max, what can I do for you today?"

She gestured to one of the chairs across from her, and he took off his backpack, setting it in the empty seat. Once he was settled, she handed over a roll of paper towels.

"Thanks," he muttered, tearing off a sheet and wiping his face again before dabbing at his sweatshirt. "So, Coach told me last night—"

"Coach ...?"

Oh, great. She was one of *those*. If she knew who Max was, she should also know his coach. "Coach Miller," he amended, trying not to grit his teeth. "From the track team."

"Right. Go on."

"Coach Miller told me last night my funding was cut. And he suggested you might—" he shifted in his chair "—that you might have some options for me."

Her mouth quirked as she studied him. She turned to her computer without another word.

"You can do that, right?" Max's hand twitched toward his backpack before he curled it into a fist around the used paper towels. "Because, if not, I really need to—"

"What's your funding for?" Her voice was calm, soothing some of Max's jumping nerves. She typed on her keyboard. "You're a senior. Surely, it's not this semester's tuition?"

"No." He shifted again. "It was a private athletic fund aimed at helping promising athletes go pro. It covered my continued training and expenses for two years."

"Why did it get cut?" She sat back and took a drink from her travel coffee cup.

"Football dopeheads," Max muttered, then winced. He wasn't supposed to say that out loud.

Dr. Goff spluttered, and a few drops of coffee landed on the desk in front of Max. "Right. I heard about that." Wiping her hand across her mouth, she looked at her computer again. "So, you're looking for something to fill the space after graduation? Assuming you're on track, no pun intended? What's your major?"

Everything this lady said came out as a question. Then again, maybe Max wouldn't be as overwhelmed if he didn't have to cram four years of advisement into one twenty-minute session.

"I'm on track, yeah. Exercise science." Max wasn't so short-sighted as to not have a plan for after he finished racing for good.

Based on recent events, if he didn't get his act together, *after* would be here before he knew it.

Dr. Goff nodded, alternating between glancing at him and her screen. "I have a fabulous idea." She spun her monitor around for Max to see.

"'Pursue Your Passions?'" Max read aloud. "What's that?"

As she explained the scholarship, the caveats and stipulations, Max's mind whirred. It sounded perfect—one year after graduation to get his act together. He could find an agent, secure a brand deal. Nothing major, but something to tide him over until the next Olympics season kicked in.

"It won't be easy, though," Dr. Goff said, eyes sparkling with something Max couldn't place. Mischief, perhaps? "It's going to be competitive. Other students have already expressed interest." She glanced at the door.

It took him a moment. "You mean that ... *girl*?" he said, for lack of a better word. "The one who ran into me?"

"From where I was sitting, it seemed to be a mutual running into."

"How is that relevant?"

Dr. Goff coughed, used the tip of her index finger to straighten one paper on her desk swimming with other crooked packets.

"She's got a very impressive resumé," Dr. Goff said, and he couldn't tell if it was in confirmation or defense. "Your application will need to be airtight to stand up to hers. How do your grades look right now?"

A heaviness pressed on Max's chest, making his next breath

harder to come by. It was only two weeks into the semester, and only based on a few assignments. And maybe he'd missed a few classes in favor of training sessions, extra laps, more stretches and weight reps.

If his grades really were the deciding factor to his future, he was well and truly screwed.

"They're alright," he said, not meeting her gaze, and gave into the urge to reach for his backpack. He slung it over his shoulder. "I'm sorry to waste your time. I need to get to practice."

"It's not a waste of time, Max. My door's always open if you want to talk something through. I'll email you the details of the scholarship." Dr. Goff smiled, that same sparkle in her eyes. "Deadline's May first," she reiterated.

He replaced his headphones on his ears, but didn't turn on music.

May first, Max chanted in his head instead as he made his way across campus to the Quad to grab a replacement breakfast, since his protein shake was clinging to the front of his sweatshirt.

His phone vibrated in his pocket. The message had him gritting his teeth.

Nolan

> grabbed us a bench in the back corner

Max typed out a response saying he couldn't make it. His thumb hovered over the send button. He'd be letting Nolan down again, and how were they supposed to team-bond if Max never showed up?

But he'd already missed half of their session, and Nolan

probably expected him to bail. It'd been Max's default setting for over a year. Alex was a better spotter anyway.

Max pressed send. If he only had three and a half months to secure his future, he needed every spare minute he had.

Chapter Five

Keely

My dedication to uplifting women within the science community is my greatest passion. Between being president of Ash Mountain University's Women in Science Society and co-founder of the Mid-Atlantic Regional Science Olympiad, my—

She backspaced.

I...

"I have nothing else to offer," Keely muttered to the empty Friday-morning library the following week, then groaned. She was supposed to be working on her essay, but it was turning into a resumé, and she already had one of those.

She navigated to the bookmarked scholarship website again, then unstuck the enter key for the fifth time today. She'd had to take a special trip into town to see if the tech store could save it after that rude guy at the career counselor dumped his smoothie on it, and the fan still made funny noises when she typed too fast. Not to mention it smelled like a rancid garbage can.

With her free hand, she flipped to the page in her planner she'd dedicated to the scholarship.

Keely was due to start her community services today. Services, plural, because she didn't know how to do things by half measures. Of course, she needed three. What if the first two opportunities didn't work out?

Each Friday afternoon, she'd be reading at a local elementary school. On Saturdays, she was set to grocery shop for an elderly woman named Matilda and sort her daily medicines. And Sunday, Keely had her first shift volunteering at a local animal shelter.

When she was going to work on her still-struggling thesis or help Zoey plan the charity auction for Women in Science, Keely didn't know. But she'd find time. Like now, when she had exactly an hour between Chem 547 and her once-weekly genetics lab. Or tonight, when she was supposed to be sleeping. Why was Q Coffee open until midnight if not to foster late-night studies, anyway?

She sighed and closed the lid to her laptop, knowing it would stick together when she tried to open it next time. This essay wasn't happening right now. She'd learned through years of perfecting her concentration: if she tried to force something when she wasn't in the zone, she'd just have to redo it later.

She decided her time was better served fueling up before lab, so she packed up.

January in the Virginia mountains was crisp, cold, with snow clinging to the mountaintops and fluffy gray clouds dimming the blue skies overhead. Keely much preferred it to the humid and sticky air of summer, when she couldn't move without sweating, or the horrible allergies of fall and spring, when she couldn't breathe without sneezing.

She ducked her chin further into her scarf as she headed to the Q.

Ash Mountain University was nestled within its namesake range, and if they didn't have one of the best in-state biology programs, Keely may have chosen it for the views alone.

Campus itself was arranged in a circle, with the Q—officially, the Quad—at the center. It was the hub of campus, a large glass-walled food court and coffee stall. The walls sat on tracks, so on temperate days it became an open-air patio, seating impossible to come by unless you knew the right people.

Draw a straight line out from there to the edges of campus and you'd find dorms and upperclassmen apartments, named for their cardinal direction. Keely and Zoey lived in East Tower.

Everything else—Davidson Hall (the STEM building, named after a white man who probably didn't do enough to earn the honor), Ed (the education building), Humanities (creatively called Humanities), and Libby (the Liberal Arts building, which housed what was left)—sat more or less in between. They were connected with a mix of worn cobblestone and well-trod dirt paths students decades before Keely's time had carved.

She'd already decided to come back one day, after making an Important Scientific Discovery, and rename Davidson after herself.

Thankfully, the line at the Q was short enough to grab coffee *and* have time to drink it before lab started. They weren't allowed water bottles at their stations, much less a staining dark liquid. Keely loved the severity of it all.

She was pulling out her wallet to pay for her drink when someone else's card appeared over her shoulder.

"Add a medium Americano, please." Sam Mabry smiled at Keely's bemused expression. "And two eggwiches."

Keely grabbed his forearm. Between her gloves and his coat, it was mostly fabric. "Hey, you don't have to—"

"Nah, I got it." Sam grinned. "Told you I owed you. You saved my ass on that assignment last week."

She wanted to argue, but she didn't have time. With a playful eye roll, she relaxed, tucking her wallet back inside her bag. "You passed?" she said.

"Not only did I pass. I got an A."

She beamed at him, holding up a hand for a high five, which was cringey for half a second before Sam returned it and grinned wider.

They moved to the side to wait for their coffee, and her stomach twisted. Keely really hoped one of those eggwiches was for her. "How are things otherwise?"

Sam shuddered. "My parents are on my case about figuring out post-grad. I've applied at a few different jobs, but nowhere has called me back yet, and a lot of the science gigs want a master's degree. I'd need to work for a while to afford it, and they say the longer you're out, the harder it is to go back in."

Her stomach grumbled, louder this time, and Sam glanced over, mouth quirked. Her neck warmed beneath her scarf.

"I'm right there with you," she said. It wasn't the whole truth; unlike Sam, Keely knew exactly what she wanted and how she was going to get it, but the part about parental pressures? She knew that all too well. "There are special scholarships for gap years," she murmured, watching the barista slide two eggwiches into paper sleeves. Then she fought a flinch as she realized what she'd said. As much as she liked Sam, she really didn't need more competition.

Sam was nonplussed. "Like Pursue Your Passions? Yeah, I heard about that."

Shoot. If he'd heard about it, other people likely had, too. "Oh, yeah?"

"Yeah, but I'm not applying. I heard one of the jocks has an eye on it, and I don't know. Seemed like a waste of time going up against that." Sam shrugged, and when the barista called his name, he stepped up to grab his haul.

One of the jocks. "A football guy?" Keely pressed, shifting her weight. She'd take crumbs at this point—literal or figurative.

"Football *player*," Sam corrected, handing over a coffee and, to her utmost joy, a sandwich. "But no. One of the track stars. Apparently, he's heading for the Olympics."

"The Olympics were last year." She took a sip of her blonde latte. It was scalding, a little too heavy on the steamed milk and a little too light on the espresso, but it would do. She cleared her throat. "Weren't they?" she asked when she realized she didn't know for sure.

Sam snorted around a bite of his sandwich. "They don't just train for three months, Keel. It's an ongoing thing. Like how you practice chemical reactions for *fun*, even in the summer."

"I don't do that," she lied, and she could tell she was getting a little hangry. She slid the eggwich from its sleeve. The first bite cleared her mind enough to realize Sam was teasing. "Are you heading to Davidson?"

"Home," Sam said. "I'm gonna make lunch."

Keely eyed his half-gone sandwich. "Of course you are."

He grinned and bumped her shoulder with his. Was he flirting with her? She checked her stomach for butterflies, her pulse for racing, her cheeks for blushing, but there was nothing.

It wasn't that Sam wasn't cute—he had chin-length brown hair, sparkling green eyes, a nice smile. But hard as she tried, she'd never been able to care about dating or sex more than she cared about the unchecked boxes on her to-do list. Sam, as much as she valued his friendship, was no exception.

Keely pushed open the door.

The wind ripped it out of her hand, hard enough for her teeth to slam together and her sandwich to fall from her grasp, landing on the doormat. The one that thousands of students walked across and wiped their feet on daily.

She stared down at the dismantled sandwich and pretended she was teary eyed from the chilly breeze.

"Bummer," Sam said. "I'll grab you another one."

Her phone dinged with a reminder: ten minutes until lab. "No time, but it's fine." She scooped up the sandwich and threw it in the garbage. It landed right next to her hopes of eating while the sun was still up.

"Here, take mine." Sam held out his sandwich, maybe four bites left in total, but sniffled in the same breath, and she eyed it warily. Keely Sinclair did *not*, under any circumstances, share food.

She waved Sam's concern away and said her goodbyes.

She was halfway to Davidson when her stomach gurgled again. Her one bite did more to tease her than anything.

Lab was only two hours. She could grab something quick from a drive-thru on the way to the elementary school. And, after that, she'd be one step closer to winning the scholarship out from under the mysterious track star.

He probably wasn't even that fast.

Chapter Six

Max

There was a notification on Max's phone screen when he parked in front of the animal shelter on Sunday. He was terrified to click through. His Prevention and Treatment professor had posted the results of this week's quiz. The one he hadn't studied for. The one he'd figured he'd be safe from until at least Monday morning, when the world sucked anyway. He thought wrong, obviously.

Max tapped his screen—and winced.

He knew his grades were bad. He hadn't realized they were in the toilet.

Were they all this way? He honestly couldn't say, so he clicked out and poked around his other classes. Two Cs, a B minus. One A in Strength and Conditioning because the only assignment in there was a syllabus acknowledgment. It was amazing he hadn't been benched yet.

He shifted in the driver's seat and fought the urge to bang his head on the steering wheel. This scholarship application was going to be the death of him. Volunteerism and extracurriculars wouldn't matter if he was on academic suspension. He'd have to do the majority of the work there, in class and on tests, to come anywhere close to the mystery girl Dr. Goff seemed to favor.

Sighing, he stretched his neck and caught a glimpse of the clock.

"*Shit*," he said, and rushed inside.

He'd been spending his Sundays at the animal shelter since freshman year. He felt closer to his dad, who'd been a dog groomer until recently, when he was doing something they both loved. Home seemed a little closer when Max was parked in the back lot of Ash Mountain Shelter and Rescue.

It didn't matter if Max's life was falling apart: rain or shine, he was here every Sunday. Dogs always made it better.

Before the dogs, though, he had to go to the back room to check in with the lead volunteer, Tricia.

A pale woman in her early fifties, Tricia's face showed signs of life lived outdoors. Life *lived*, in general. Sunspots and freckles on what was visible of her forehead, crow's feet reaching for her hairline. Her shaved blonde hair was obscured by the bandana of the day, paw-print patterned.

The familiarity tugged up the corner of Max's mouth, lifting his spirits after the peek at his grades.

Tricia greeted Max with an outstretched fist.

He bumped it. "Sup?"

"Gonna be a fun shift for you." Tricia eyed him, leaning back in her chair. It creaked loudly. The shelter hardly had money to cover vet expenses, let alone new office furniture. "New volunteer."

Max grunted. Tricia knew he hated new volunteers, mostly sorority girls who wanted to pose with doodles for Instagram while simultaneously fulfilling their community service requirements.

They usually lasted two weeks—or one, if they stepped in something unsavory. "Can't wait."

Her smile lines smoothed out as her head tilted the slightest bit off center. "You doing okay, kid?" Hesitation colored her words. Sadness, too.

Pity.

Max hated pity most of all.

"Been better, been worse, here now." It was something his dad said. Max hadn't realized he'd adopted the habit until now. Warmth flooded his veins, and a smile tugged at his mouth before he forced it away and shrugged. "How are things looking today?" If anything could distract Tricia, it was talking shop.

She glanced at her computer. "I'll need you to take inventory later. I'm making a bulk order soon. For now, the new girl's out in the dog run if you want a laugh. Make sure you bring them all in when you're done, though. It's too cold right now to stay out much longer."

Max could picture it: the latest Nikes stepping in piss, fur Velcro-ed to $90 lululemon leggings. His day was looking up already.

He took his time on the way to the dog run, stopping in to see his favorite long-term rescues. Champ was an aging mastiff with no teeth, which meant he required a special extra-wet diet that stunk to high hell. He was also a spoiled little baby, which meant if he saw a human at all, he would only entertain that extra-wet food if it was hand-fed to him.

Farah Pawcett, on the other hand, was a Chihuahua with an attitude problem and wasn't allowed out in gen pop or near new volunteers until they'd been fully briefed. Max gave her a wave. Farah bared her teeth and growled.

It was good to be back.

Biscuit, a one-eyed bulldog-boxer mix and unabashedly Max's favorite, wasn't in his pen, which meant he was probably out in the run with the new volunteer. Max would pay money to see that. Biscuit was a bit of a terror who chased anything that moved, especially shiny things. And then he'd slobber on it, hump it, or fall asleep on top of it. Sometimes all three within the same minute.

Max let himself out the side door and waved to Georgie, one of the other volunteers. They opted for a jerk of the head as opposed to removing their hand from their pocket to wave back. Max couldn't blame them. The cold bit at his skin and made him regret leaving his heavier winter coat at home.

Most of the dogs were inside—their barks echoed for half a mile—but a few played out here with miscellaneous toys scattered across the patchy, dead grass. A new golden he hadn't gotten a chance to know yet, two mixed breeds he couldn't distinguish from this far away.

And Biscuit, exactly where Max hoped he would be: causing problems for the new girl.

She crouched, wrestling her shoe from Biscuit, and Max heard the commotion even over the barking and whistling wind.

"No, actually, if you wouldn't mind, that's my—okay, you can have it."

Georgie stifled a laugh against their shoulder, and Max fought a smile of his own as Biscuit whipped the tennis shoe back and forth.

When Max's toes started to tingle from the safety of his thickest socks, he figured enough was enough.

He whistled, and the dogs came running, Biscuit included. The shoe still dangled from his mouth. He'd probably been drawn to the metallic emblem on the side. Max deftly stepped out of the way of the stampede, grabbing the shoe when Biscuit dropped it to barrel through the doggy door.

The slimy, frayed lace smacked against Max's wrist. They weren't the brand-new Nikes he was expecting. Paint speckled the toe box, and the midsole was stained fresh-grass green. While they wouldn't win any sprints, couldn't jump hurdles, they were good for this.

Georgie gestured to the shoe with an elbow, hands still shoved in their pockets. "Want me to take care of that?"

Max shook his head. "I've got it."

With a nod, they headed for the door, but turned back at the last second. "Remember the rule about hazing."

"Don't get caught?"

Georgie grinned. "Exactly." They jerked a thumb over their shoulder as they crossed the threshold. "Don't keep her out here too long. She's been alright so far."

Max looked to the field again. The new volunteer hobbled over, head ducked against a strong blow of wind. The breeze hit Max in the face too—then stiffened his spine. Biscuit had serious digestive issues.

When she was within speaking distance, he figured now was as good a time as any.

"Hey," he said, except it came out a little too harsh, because he recognized the ink-blotted pinkie dangling at her side. The wind blew again and he only smelled *her* now—peppermint.

The girl from the counselor's office.

His competition for the scholarship.

He clenched his teeth so hard one of them clicked. Of all the volunteer opportunities in town, she *had* to pick this one.

Not only would he have to see her here every week—he'd

probably have to listen to her talk about how perfect she was, too. How everything had gone exactly right for her since the second she'd been born, how Max had no chance.

Fan-fucking-tastic.

She looked up then, her golden-brown waves of hair catching on the wind. He took in her heart-shaped face, her big round eyes, and—

Familiarity reached its fist into his lungs and stole his breath.

"*Keely?*" he rasped. She was ten years older, but he'd know her face anywhere. The last time he'd seen it, she was standing at his seventh-grade locker with wet lashes, clutching an algebra book to her chest. He remembered thinking he'd do just about anything to ensure that look never crossed her face again.

Of course Keely was going out for Pursue Your Passions. The overachiever vibe fit her perfectly. The only thing surprising about the situation was that someone like Keely—with her color-coordinated notebooks and folders, her class schedule memorized on the first day of school, her outfits picked out the night before—would wait until the last minute to secure a scholarship. She seemed the type to have things figured out well before they were relevant. Her backup plans had backup plans.

But what did he know? Maybe she'd changed in the years they'd been apart.

Keely blinked at him, and her blue-speckled eyes went wider and rounder. The tip of her nose was pink.

He didn't know why he noticed that.

He coughed. "I'm not sure if you remember—"

"*Max.* Of course I remember you."

For a stretching second, they only stood there, staring at each other from ten feet apart. The sharp breeze kept blowing her scent his way. Seriously, why did she always smell like peppermint? Did she keep them tucked in her jaw or something?

It doesn't matter.

Pushing his tongue into his cheek, he held up her shoe. "I believe this is yours?"

"Thanks," she said, walking over, gaze trained on the ground. "Um, hi, I guess. It's been ... forever."

She took her trainer, wobbled as she slid it on.

He shoved his hands deep in his pockets. "Feels like it."

To her credit, she only winced a little at Biscuit's damage. If they were Max's shoes, he'd be buying new laces. When she stood again, a new determination lit her face.

Or an old one. He remembered it on every version of her.

The first time they'd met, some hazy, undefined day in fourth grade when their teacher stuck them together on a math assignment and she'd finished the entire thing before he had time to read the third question.

In fifth grade, on the second day of school, when they'd decided each other's presence was preferred to sitting alone at lunch. When Max traded his pudding for Keely's chips, and they kept a shared pack of floss in his locker when they got braces within two weeks of each other.

Their sixth-grade year, once they'd moved to middle school. She joined the science club and he started enjoying gym class, the one subject he excelled at. It was the beginning of their end, but for a while, it was nice. At the very least, it gave them something to talk about besides who was holding hands or, God forbid, *kissing*.

By seventh grade, he was gone, and she stayed, and they weren't friends anymore.

The girl who stood before him now wasn't a girl at all. Her body had filled out to soft, sloping curves, and even though she was almost an entire foot shorter, she still had the uncanny ability to look down her pink-tipped nose at him.

Was she cold?

"Would you rather talk inside?" he asked.

She studied him for a second, then shrugged one shoulder beneath her thick winter jacket. "Sure, thanks."

The ever-present fist around Max's lungs eased its grip. "No problem." She settled in place beside him as they walked to the door. "It kinda worked out that we're volunteering together. I'm glad we've got another shot at reintroductions, especially after last week."

Keely skidded to a halt. "Wait. What happened last week?" Her words were drenched in accusation and mistrust.

Shit: apparently he'd stepped in it.

He turned to her. It was probably best to get this out in the open. Maybe she'd laugh about it like he wanted to, and they could start making up for lost time. *Small world, right? Would you want to get coffee?*

He was still gathering his words when her eyes transformed from baby blue to deep ocean, the skin around them tightening in turn. Her lips, rosy like her nose, pressed tight and flat.

"At Dr. Goff's office. That was *you*." She let out a sharp laugh, mumbled something that sounded an awfully lot like *of course it was*, and crossed her arms, her jaw set in a hard line. "You dumped your smoothie on my laptop."

"It was a protein shake, actually, and *you* knocked it out of *my* hand." He rocked back on his heels, a spark catching and igniting in his bloodstream. "And I never got a chance to apologize."

"I don't need your apologies, Max." Apologies, plural? Did he owe her more than one? "I *need* to do this community service. You know, I think I changed my mind. I'd rather not talk at all." She beelined toward the door and pulled it open so hard the spring recoiled.

He wrapped his palm around the edge before it hit her in the face.

He wasn't sure where her hostility was coming from, but he wasn't an asshole. Not completely, anyway. "Look, does the laptop not work or something? I can replace it." It would dip into his nonexistent funds, but he didn't want this weird tension hanging over them for months to come.

But she only mumbled, "It's not about that," and stepped into the chaos. It did little to help him make sense of anything, least of all why Keely *despised* him.

He caught her lightly by the elbow, and she turned to him with murder in her gaze. Across the room, Tricia and Georgie watched them. The dogs noticed them and danced around their ankles, twining between their legs. He needed to choose his next words carefully.

"What is it about, then?"

Her pupils telescoped in the bright lights, lips parting the tiniest sliver.

"Forget it," she murmured, stepping backward and nearly tripping over Lucette, a Boston terrier with a severe underbite.

He reached for Keely again, but she pulled away this time, rubbing at her arm. She slipped around the perimeter of the room, avoiding the dogs—Biscuit, namely—with a wide berth. He watched her until Lottie and Milo, a bonded pair of German shepherds, bounded over to him.

"I'll forget it if you will!" He raised his voice as a tug-of-war started and dogs vied for his affection. "I'm here every weekend!"

"Well, great." Some of the color had receded from her face when she looked back. "As of today, so am I."

Great indeed.

Chapter Seven
Keely

Keely Sinclair's a nerd.

Sometimes, when she was having a particularly vicious case of the Sunday Scaries, she replayed that scene from seventh grade.

The one where Max Simmons, in the middle of a crowded hallway, laughed at her for liking science.

She'd been coming into herself, more comfortable in her own skin—metaphorically, of course; maybe her thesis should have focused on finding a cure for pre-teen acne—and Max, her best friend, had abandoned her in favor of the other guys who also thought PE counted as a class.

The absolute audacity of men.

Keely somehow managed to avoid him for a week, and then he moved schools, which she was glad for. She hadn't wanted to look at his miraculously pimple-free face anymore.

She didn't want to look at it now.

Which meant having to share space with him at the animal shelter once a week was going to be its own painful form of community service. At least she was alone for now, tucked in the laundry room.

How did an animal shelter amass so many towels? She tried not to think about what had been on them *before* the rinse cycle.

Being back here served multiple purposes: she could avoid Max *and* review the latest notes from her thesis advisor. Something in her calculations wasn't working, and she'd already tried two other methods. She'd ask Zoey to look at it when she got home. Zoey was an anatomy major and helped pull Keely's head out of the cells-and-atoms level of detail she normally existed in to see the bigger picture.

Keely flipped the page on her notes, then cleared the lint trap again. How did the dogs have any fur left? Surely it was all in this trash can. And stuck to her pants. And possibly in her bra?

The door behind her opened, and though she wanted more than anything for it to be Tricia, telling Keely the shelter's never seen such a wonderful first-time volunteer and offering a letter of recommendation on branded letterhead, she already knew who it would be.

"Can I help you, Max?" she said without turning.

"Yeah, actually." His steps grew closer, and if the hairs on Keely's arms stood on end ... well. Static electricity, probably. She'd tell Tricia to buy more dryer sheets. "Biscuit needs his anal glands expressed, and it's a two-person job. I'm tagging you in."

She spun on her heel, and her shin banged the open dryer door. "*What* are you doing to Biscuit?"

"Kidding." He wasn't smiling exactly, but there was an uneven tilt to his mouth that made more than Keely's shin throb. "I just wanted to make sure we're on the same page. Clear the air." He pulled his wallet from his back pocket and held it out for her. "You can order a new laptop if you want."

He seemed sincere, which stabbed little knives into all of Keely's exposed skin. He was acting like their history was inconsequential.

Maybe she should do the same. Move on, focus on the community service and winning the scholarship. Worrying kept her awake at night, and she needed every ounce of sleep she could get.

"My laptop is fine," she admitted.

He slid his wallet back in his pocket with a firm nod. "So, we're good?"

"Whatever." She was so, so tired. "We'll stay out of each other's way. That's my best offer."

His mouth tipped up. "Cool," he said. "With the scholarship and everything, I figured—"

Keely's mind skidded to a halt, and because it had been going well over a hundred miles an hour, she jolted. "Wait. What *about* the scholarship?"

Max took a half step back, tore his gaze from hers. But something in his posture, the way he carried himself, the strong lines of his arms...

He had a runner's body.

One of the track stars, Sam had said.

No. It wasn't *one of* the track stars.

It was this one.

"*You?*" she spat out. "*You're* the jock going out for Pursue Your Passions?"

He sniffed, one corner of his mouth going up with his nose. "We prefer the term 'student athlete.'"

Touchy subject, the word "jock." She stuck that in her pocket. "There's no way you have the grades to win."

It was a guess, but an educated one. She knew jocks tended to skip class for practice, meets, games, and because they celebrated too hard when they won and were hungover.

Her gamble paid off.

Max pushed his shoulders back, puffing his chest. Keely cursed the part of her brain that noticed his shirt gliding over his muscles. "And you clearly don't have the community service hours," he said. "If you're here."

"You can't possibly know that." *Can he?* "And besides, I've got three killer extracurriculars." Two, but what was a little exaggeration between rivals?

He shifted and looked away. "Well, then, I run four events."

They were basically even, then.

Which meant Keely needed to appeal to a different part of his conscience.

"Max," she pleaded. His name felt funny in her mouth when she said it that way, a familiar word in a foreign language. "I need this scholarship." She reached out, but what was she going to do—touch him? She pulled back and made a tight fist behind her back, hoping it would stop the sinking in her stomach.

This was something she hadn't planned for, something she couldn't strangle into perfect lines of control.

Max Simmons was a variable she hadn't considered.

"I won't be able to afford grad school without it," she tacked on. The tears that sprang to her eyes were surprisingly genuine. She blinked them back.

"I don't need it any less than you," he said. Something deep and cutting flashed on his face, before a shutter came down and sealed it away. "I lost my funding, too, in case you hadn't heard."

Her brows pinched, and she leaned against the dryer. "You do track, though. Not football."

"I *run* track," he corrected, his jaw ticking. "But my investors don't care. And it doesn't matter. If I want a shot at the Olympics, I need all the help I can get." His Adam's apple bobbed.

"Do you have a shot?" She'd meant it as a jab, but she was a little curious as to exactly how good he was.

She, under no circumstances, would allow herself to look up his race videos. If his *face* was that well defined, with its sharp cheekbones and strong nose and brow ridge, there was no telling what the rest of him looked like. Imagining it sent something like nausea shooting through her stomach.

"I have a shot," he confirmed. Was he being too confident, or underselling his abilities?

It doesn't matter. The less she thought about Max Simmons, the better off she'd be.

She tried her last-ditch effort. "I ... I want it more."

Another beat of thick silence. "There's no possible way you can scientifically prove that." He tilted his head. "Can you?"

"Well, no, but—"

His mouth quirked. Was he *still* teasing her?

Time did not heal all wounds, because her face burned with embarrassment the same way it had ten years ago.

This feeling, she could work with. Could mold it into something useful, productive. She rearranged, sorted, and slotted details into place.

She turned back to the dryer. "This is a waste of time."

"Agreed," Max said, and Keely relished the uncertainty coloring his voice. After a few seconds, he leaned against the washer. "So where does that leave us?"

She shrugged, threw an air of innocence over her features. Stuck out her bottom lip the tiniest sliver. "I'm sure the person most deserving will earn the scholarship fair and square."

Max's gaze narrowed. "Fair and square?"

She blinked and gave him a small shrug. "May the best person win," she said.

But cogs were already turning in her mind. After all, she wouldn't be a scientist if she didn't put something in place to control the variables.

• • • • •

"Change the signature," Zoey said through a bite of her eggplant parm. Keely had come home tonight to another family recipe, passed down from Zoey's great-grandmother. Zoey pointed at Keely's screen and left a grease smudge behind. "His students call him The Waz."

Keely snorted. "That cannot be true." She reached for a mozzarella stick (storebought, because balance) before deciding against it. Introducing more grease and crumbs to her already precarious laptop situation was a bad idea; she had a hypothesis Max's good will wouldn't last past the email she was about to send.

All it had taken was Keely cashing in an owed favor, and she had Max's class schedule. He was an exercise science major, so unoriginal for a jock.

Keely took a small sip from her water bottle. "And your brother's sure this is untraceable?" Zoey's brother was in grad school at MIT, and had set Zoey up with a private VPN so she could watch K-dramas unreleased in America. Keely was just ... borrowing it.

Student and faculty emails were in an open directory and therefore public record. This sort of thing probably happened all the time.

This was harmless.

Right?

"Promise." Zoey plucked Keely's abandoned mozz stick off the tray. "Do it already. We need to study for the Olympiad."

Keely sunk her teeth into her bottom lip as her mouse hovered over the *send* button. "But is it a good idea?"

A glob of marinara dripped onto Zoey's thumb. "It's grad school, Keel. Our future's on the line." She gripped Keely's sleeve, taking care not to touch her with the red sauce. "The *sunshine*. The *surfers*."

They'd had the plans to go to Caltech since freshman year, eager to swap out Virginia's hills for California's waters and waves. It was the farthest Keely could feasibly go to get away from her parents, and she needed that desperately. Needed to go somewhere she couldn't hear their shouting.

Zoey was right.

"Okay." Keely nodded. She took in a large gulp of air and held it while she pressed send, then blew it out in a single, strong gust. "Okay. It's done."

Zoey threw her head back and laughed, and Keely joined in. Max wouldn't know what had hit him.

All was fair in scholarships and sabotage.

> From: Angus Wazlockowski (angus.wazlockowskii@amu.edu)
> To:
> BCC: Max Simmons (mbsimm01@amu.edu)
> Date: Sunday, February 1
> Subject: Classes Canceled Week of Feb 2
>
> All sections of class canceled this upcoming week. Bad stomach bug. As an aside, please take caution when dining from the taco truck that frequents the west side of campus.
> Sincerely,
> The Waz

Chapter Eight

Max

Max lived in North Tower, supposedly one of the best housing complexes on campus for its views of the mountains.

Unfortunately, Max's apartment faced west, and the only thing visible was the Athletics facility. No matter what window he looked out of, he saw the track. He couldn't escape it.

Not that the view from *inside* was much better.

His roommate, Yoon, had a nasty habit of hoarding dishes in his room, which Max was expressly forbidden from entering, and bringing them out in the dead of night every few weeks, once Max inevitably texted him that it smelled worse than the bottom of the locker room's laundry hamper after a late-summer practice. The dishes would sit unwashed in the sink for another few days—at *minimum*.

Today, the first Wednesday in February, was one of those days, and he gritted his teeth as he nudged cups to the side to wash his hands.

Max pulled glass Tupperware from the fridge, glad his meal prep days and Yoon's whenever-the-fuck dishwashing days rarely overlapped. He popped his bowl in the microwave, and his phone dinged.

Nolan

Gym in 30?

Eager to make up for bailing last time, Max liked the message. Since his Adaptive PE class was canceled this week, he had the free time. It'd be better served doing sprints with Nolan than avoiding the mold growing in the bottom of Yoon's cereal bowl.

Maybe Keely Sinclair could sample it. She'd probably discover a new species.

He rolled his eyes and scarfed down his food.

Nolan was already at the gym when Max got there. Other people milled around—they always did in Athletics—but since this was scheduled class time and not practice, Max didn't recognize any of them.

"I was thinking after we stretch, we'd spot on the bench press," Nolan said. "Then run intervals outside?"

"Sounds good." Max threw his duffel beside Nolan's and pulled off his hoodie.

They didn't talk while they stretched. Max should have tried to contribute something, anything, but he didn't know where to start. Didn't know Nolan's major, if he had a significant other or roommate, where he grew up. And he couldn't ask now—they'd been teammates for four years. He should already know the answers.

He opened and closed his mouth a dozen different times before deciding the quiet was way less awkward than putting his foot in his mouth. Shoes scraped the rubber floor whenever they changed stretches; aside from the person on the treadmill in the back of the room, it was the only sound.

"Classes going okay?" Nolan asked after they moved to the weight bench.

Scratch that. Max would have rather physically put his foot in his mouth than talk about class. Improving his grades seemed more impossible with every returned assignment, and being off for Adaptive PE this week wouldn't help any. Waz would probably combine assignments or knock a unit off from the end to make up for it, and neither option helped Max. He needed *more* opportunities, not fewer.

"Is it spring break yet?" Max muttered in answer as he lay back on the bench and wrapped his hands around the bar.

Nolan let out a quiet chuckle. "I wish. You got plans?"

Max grunted. "Pretty far away to make plans."

Nolan started a sentence but bit off the end of it. Didn't try again.

Max did a few reps in silence, steadying his breath the way he did on the track. The metal bar dug into his hands, and he focused on the ceiling instead of Nolan's looming presence over his shoulder. He didn't know how to talk like this. So casually.

If Keely's reappearance in his life had taught him anything, it was that Max really didn't know the first thing about having friends.

The bar slipped and rushed for his chest.

Hands immediately landed beside his own, taking the weight off Max so he could get situated again.

I don't do this. Max didn't mess up a simple warm-up repetition on the bench press. Didn't try to make nice with his teammates or talk about plans for a vacation he couldn't take anyway.

"At this rate," Max said, shaken from his near drop, "I'll probably be studying on spring break." Which wasn't the worst idea he'd ever had. He flexed his fingers.

Nolan was steadfast, waiting to let go of the bar until Max signaled he was ready. "Dude, tell me about it. I thought Waz was gonna throw me out of class the other day."

Max huffed a mix of a laugh and a snort. "I didn't know you were in Waz's class."

"I have him for Methods in Secondary." So Nolan was an exercise science major too. "Monday's pop quiz was brutal, but he drops the lowest one, so—"

Max faltered, the bar wobbling in his grip again. "Wait. Monday?"

Nolan set it back in its cradle this time. "Whoa. You good?"

Max ducked out from under the bar. "Sorry, go back for a second. What do you mean, Monday? This Monday?"

"Yep."

"That's not possible." Max bounced his leg. "Waz canceled class this whole week. He has a stomach bug."

Nolan shrugged. "Seemed fine when I saw him."

"No, because that would mean my class is . . ." Max checked his phone. "Right now. Dammit. Sorry, I have to go."

He grabbed his bag, but he still saw Nolan's shoulders fall, his jaw taking on a hard set Max hadn't seen in a while. One more item on the list of things he'd messed up.

It would be getting long now, if it existed.

Good thing he didn't make lists.

He skidded into Adaptive PE as his classmates poured out, and he cursed himself for the hundredth time since sprinting across campus from Athletics. At least he'd gotten a workout in after all.

"Max," Waz said wryly. He didn't stop packing his bag. "I understand this class isn't a priority for you, but there's no need to come in and make a scene about it. I told you weeks ago: if you skip, your grades will reflect your effort."

Some students lingered; others whispered.

Max put his back to all of them and focused on his professor. "I didn't mean to miss it, though. Someone sent me an email saying you'd canceled."

"I've heard a lot of excuses over the years, but that has to be a new one." Waz scratched his ear, smoothed a hand over his balding, curly head of hair as he studied Max's face. He must have seen something honest there, because he tipped his chin and sighed. "Show me the email, then."

Max handed over his phone, canine sunk into his bottom lip.

Waz stared diligently at the screen, then let out a surprised, delighted laugh. "You got phished."

"*Phished*?" Max repeated.

"Scammed. Bamboozled. Had the wool—"

"I know what phishing is." He couldn't fathom falling for it, though. He'd learned about it in middle school, for crying out loud.

Waz tapped the screen twice with his thumb. "Extra 'l' in the sender email. Pretty clever; easy to miss. Probably one of your friends playing a prank." He held out Max's phone.

Impossible. The only people Max remotely considered friends were his teammates, and it didn't benefit them for his grades to slip.

So who *did* it benefit?

His stomach flipped as one singular face came to mind. Blue-speckled eyes. Ink smears. Knowing smirk.

"If you want, you can open an investigation with Tech Support.

They'll trace it back to the sender and you can file a complaint with the school board. That's about all I can offer you, though."

He didn't know what game Keely was playing, but he knew the stakes, and he wanted to up them on his terms.

"I'll think about it," Max said, but there wasn't much thinking to be done. Not now, after Keely had already fired the first shot.

Oh, it was so, so on.

· · · · ·

Max bounced on the balls of his feet early Saturday morning, waiting for the tone to sound. Every time they ran a relay, he tracked his teammates' strides, their handoffs, their arms and their breaths. Knew them like extensions of his own body. They had to be, if they were going to act as a cohesive unit. If they were going to win.

Alex Harmon, a walk-on sophomore from Texas, was in first position. It had been a toss-up until a few months ago which of them would anchor and which would start. But Alex was steady, rare for someone so unseasoned, and got great distance with his strides. He pulled it out, and always had a flawless handoff. The perfect first position.

Nolan was second, and his left thigh held more power than both of Max's combined. He wasn't the fastest in their quad, but he could push harder than anyone, dig deep where it counted, and propel himself forward by pure will.

Their third, Jazz, got excited, and sometimes grabbed the baton off-rhythm, but she made up for it when she flew through the curve. She wore shorts in the winter, as most of them did, and every muscle in her long legs shifted as she drew closer. Max counted her strides as he readied himself and started jogging. He knew exactly what position he should be in when she passed the three-fifty marker, when to throw his arm back, the easiest way to grab the baton and where his fingers would meet when wrapped around it.

And then Max got to do what he did best—*run*.

Maybe it was genetic. His dad had been a runner, something that propelled Max more than his muscles ever could. All he wanted was for Dad to see him win, achieve the dream he'd given up starting his family.

Most everything Max knew, he'd learned from his father. Picking his brain on early-morning runs in the summer, watching scraps of race tape from his time as a competitive dasher.

What would his dad say about his form right this second? *Open chest, straightened spine, give your knees more bounce.*

If Max didn't pull his grades around, didn't pull his head out of his ass and stop worrying about how to get even with Keely, he wouldn't win Pursue Your Passions. And without Pursue Your Passions, there was no guarantee Max could keep racing long enough for Dad to see him win gold.

No guarantee Dad would see him graduate, not with cancer eating at his body from the inside out—

He shut it down. Poured all his frustration and anger at the unfairness of life into his strides, his breathing.

And wouldn't you know it.

It still wasn't enough.

Coach looked up from his iPad. "Distracted today?" he monotoned, because he already knew *Max* knew why he'd screwed up.

Max didn't bother commenting, just jogged back to his starting position.

Forty minutes later, Max's times weren't improving. He would have screamed, if he were alone. Instead, he took another scalding shower to thaw his frozen body, scrubbing hard enough to turn his skin pink.

To his surprise, his relay squad was still in the locker room when he finished. Normally if they had a Saturday practice with no meet, they'd scatter off to enjoy the rest of their weekend before being dragged back bright and early Monday morning.

Even Jazz, who wasn't supposed to be in here, straddled one of the benches, laughing at a joke Max wasn't in on. Which didn't bother him. He was used to it.

"We're grabbing breakfast," Alex said, patting his stomach. "Wanna come?"

Max shouldered his bag. "I was going to head to the library." Waz had taken mercy on him for the fake email and allowed him to make up the quiz he missed. Hopefully it would help.

"Grab some fuel for the road, then." Jazz popped up, bouncing on her heels. While Max had changed into his favorite joggers, she was still wearing shorts. She was constantly moving, burning energy, so it made sense.

Max didn't really want to be around people, though, and would have cooked breakfast at home if Yoon's dishes weren't still fermenting in the sink.

Maybe he'd grab a protein shake after all.

"Whatever, yeah." He tugged his headphones over his ears. He'd walk to breakfast with them. He didn't have to participate in their conversation.

Max followed his teammates out of Athletics and onto campus, winding their way to the Q. The walk would take a normal person seven minutes or so; it took their group only four.

Campus was usually a dead zone on the weekends, but Davidson Hall, the STEM building Max hadn't entered since freshman year for a required math elective, was abuzz with activity. Bright banners in AMU's emerald and gold flapped in the breeze, but he couldn't read them from this angle. Students milled around outside, laughing and smiling despite the February chill. There was still *frost* on the ground.

He pulled his headphones down and jerked his chin. "What's going on over there?"

"Oh, I heard about that," Jazz said, switching her bouncing stride to deep, knee-to-ground lunges. "A science bowl type thing. Some kind of competition."

Max raised his eyebrows. "Huh. No kidding."

An idea formed in his head too quickly to be a good one. This couldn't possibly work.

A shrill laugh bounced off the cobblestone and ash trees, and even though he didn't see the source, he could have sworn it was *her*. She'd probably laughed like that when she sent the fake email.

Just one little stroll around the building . . .

"You know what?" Max patted his pockets. "I forgot my keys in the locker room."

"We can go back after we eat," Alex offered.

Max put on a wince. "My ID's attached."

"I'll get your breakfast," Nolan said.

But Max was already shaking his head, jogging backward. "I'll catch up on Monday at practice."

"Bright and early!" Jazz redirected her lunge into Alex's path. He wasn't paying attention and stumbled, catching himself in a full-on plank position. They all laughed, momentarily drowning out the sounds from Davidson.

Max would just peek inside the building, switch Keely's room assignment or something and make her a few minutes late. That was a fair trade for missing two full classes and a pop quiz. She deserved worse, to be honest.

Once his team was out of view, he headed straight for the conference.

Mid-Atlantic Science Olympiad Spring Scrimmage, the banner read.

"She has her own Olympics," Max muttered, rolling his eyes. "Cute."

With one more quiet breath, he pulled the door open.

He didn't get very far; there was a table directly inside the entrance. A girl with kinked black hair and dusky-tan skin gave him a bright smile. Her name tag read *Zoey*. "Can I help you?"

He obviously didn't belong here, but it stung a bit that she could tell by looking at him. For all Zoey knew, he was in the Science Olympiad too.

"I'm in the Science Olympiad," Max blurted, then cursed mentally. Why didn't he say he was here for a study group or something?

One of Zoey's brows twitched toward her hairline, but she still sat forward in her chair, pulling the stapled packet of paper closer to her. "Perfect. Name?"

"Sim—" He coughed. "Smith." That was generic enough.

Zoey nodded slowly, giving him a blank look. "*School* name."

"Oh." *Think, Max.* "Rutherford." It was their biggest rival for track; hopefully it was the same for their science programs.

From the way Zoey's gaze now dripped with undisguised contempt, he'd guessed right. With a heavy sigh, she flipped through the packet. "Zane Smith?"

"That's me." Max smiled at her. Or grimaced.

Zoey, pointedly, did not smile back this time. She grabbed a highlighter, pulled the cap off with her teeth—sort of aggressively, actually—and slashed a bright orange line through Zane Smith. She pointed at a pile of name tags and Sharpies. "We ask that you add your pronouns in addition to your name and school."

"Sure thing," he said, moving to the corner of the table to scribble his new identity. *Sorry, Zane Smith from Rutherford (he/him). Bet you would have killed it today.*

He slapped the badge on his plain black sweatshirt and made sure to spin so Zoey wouldn't see his AMU bag. Then he pulled open the stairwell door to his left and *bolted*.

It took him a few tries to find what he thought was the right place, but he still wasn't sure. Students with goggle lines on their faces wore lab coats, but others were dressed in regular clothes like him. He passed a guy wearing flip-flops. He didn't remember a lot from high school biology lab other than almost throwing up on dissection day, but he was pretty sure that was a giant red flag.

He had no idea how this event worked or what the goal was. Were there medals? Prizes? Was it even a competition? Maybe all these amateur scientists got together to trade formulas on index cards or something.

Studying was a better use of his time, but his mind was snagged on Keely, how she'd looked so innocent at the shelter Sunday afternoon and stabbed him in the back by dinnertime. So he'd mess with her in return. She couldn't list this on her scholarship application if it blew up in her face.

Just when he was about to give up, head to the Q with another lie about finding his keys in his backpack, he saw a flash of gold ahead. Keely, coming out of a room. He shrunk back behind a corner, poking out just enough to track her.

He hadn't thought she'd be wearing a lab coat, but there it was, every button done, the lower hem hitting above her knees. She, at least, was wearing closed-toe shoes. Her hair had been clipped back the few times he'd seen her, but she wore a perfect low bun now, not a strand out of place.

When she ducked through a doorway, Max took the only chance he'd get. He sprinted for the room she'd come out of.

It wasn't empty.

A girl with severe black eyeliner, blunt bangs, and a hoop through her septum sat on a stool, staring at the worktable. *Lori*, according to her name tag. She looked him up and down, disgust pulling at her mouth. "Can I help you?"

"Um," he said, blanking. "Keely ... asked ... for you?"

She frowned harder. "Why?"

"Something about—" He looked around and skimmed the poster on the wall. "Newtonian physics." That wasn't going to work. There was no way she would believe—

She cursed under her breath. "Did Jeremy fall down the stairs again? It's those stupid flip-flops."

And Lori left the room, leaving Max all alone.

Two beakers on individual hot plates housed bubbling liquid, steam rising from the mouths. In a stand on the right, three vials of dry white powder. A notebook lay open to the left side. Complicated chemical equations, timestamps with observations scribbled next to them in thick black ink. *No wonder she has ink smears.*

"Enough with the ink smears," he mumbled.

He had no idea how much time he had. Lori or Keely could come back any minute.

Max dove for the glass-walled cabinet with stoppered vials inside. He dug around for something that looked like what was on the station, barely reading the names—he couldn't pronounce them anyway. He wrapped his fingers around what looked the most similar to the powder in the vials.

This was harmless, right? The way her email had been "harmless."

Still, he searched the chemicals on his phone quickly. He didn't want it to *actually* blow up in her face. Beyond that, he didn't really care. She'd look fine with one eyebrow.

When he confirmed none of the chemicals on the table or in his hand were toxic, he swapped the vial on the right with the one he pulled from the cabinet, carefully peeling the labels away and pressing them down again on the other tube.

At the door, he hesitated, but only for a second.

What was done was done, and if he lingered, he'd get caught for sure, whether by Keely or Lori or the real Zane Smith, who could still show up and cause a mess for Max.

He hurried away, taking a turn and then another to distance himself from the scene of the crime.

He ducked into a back stairwell as a scream sounded from down the hall.

Chapter Nine

Keely

Blue.

Max's little prank had turned her hands Smurf-skin blue.

She'd figured out pretty quickly someone had switched the glucose at her station with dry benzoyl peroxide. It was the only thing that explained the corresponding explosion. The blue coating on everything—her hair, her lab coat, her hands, which had gotten the worst of it—was from the methylene blue.

At first, she thought either she or Lori had made an honest mistake, though Keely's lab notes were meticulous, and she simply didn't *make* mistakes.

But they put the pieces together—first with Lori, who rushed in right after Keely screamed, and Zoey, who mentioned later that Zane Smith from Rutherford showed up late but his name had already been marked off.

"What did he look like?" Keely had pressed, hands under the

hot water in the bathroom with Zoey sprinkling baking soda over them. Lori squirted dish soap.

"Tall. Curly brown hair. A really smug expression, even though I could tell he didn't belong here."

Keely had run through the likely suspects in her head until she hit a brick wall. Her blood froze. "Was he wearing athletic clothes? And a green backpack?"

Zoey had caught Keely's eye in the mirror, eyebrows rocketing toward the ceiling. She'd nodded.

And Keely had cursed.

This had Max's name written all over it.

But Keely couldn't publicly claim her experiment had been tampered with, not when she'd organized the event. Admitting a problem would all but ensure AMU wouldn't host again. It would discredit the hard work she and Zoey had put in, and it was no one's fault but Max's.

The good thing about the Olympiad, about science in general, was that failed experiments were simply viewed as opportunities to learn. And because it was a scrimmage, it didn't count toward or against AMU's overall ranking for the year.

She'd apologized to Zoey profusely no less than seven times when she'd entered the lab and caught Keely quite literally bluehanded, but her best friend did what any best friend would do: grabbed a pair of blue latex cleaning gloves, made a joke about them matching while trying to keep a straight face, and got to work on clean-up.

Besides, Keely thought wryly as she parked in the animal shelter lot the next day, dogs didn't care what color the hands that fed them were.

Last week, Max had shown up after Keely, but he was here bright and early now, perched on the corner of Tricia's desk. Not a care in the world.

Keely kept her back to them as she hung her coat on the hook. Dreaded the moment when someone would ask—

"I heard through the grapevine that you had a little ... accident yesterday." Innocence blanketed Max's snide tone, even as his gaze dropped pointedly to her hands. The corner of his mouth twitched before it smoothed away. "Keeping those gloves on?"

She wanted to shove said gloves down his throat. With her fists still in them. "I have a hangnail."

"On all ten fingers?"

She turned. An emerald-green AMU hoodie and black joggers hugged his body. He was somehow devoid of the dog hair floating through the air in clumps.

That made the most sense out of anything, when she thought about it. Keely didn't imagine anything would *want* to cling to Max Simmons.

She crossed her arms. "I'm also a little cold."

Tricia made a noise of dissent, shaking her head. "The dogs will tear those to shreds. Better ditch 'em. I'll crank the temperature up a few notches."

Keely's stomach sank.

"I'm sure once you get moving," Max offered, "you won't even feel it." His tone was neutral now, but there was a shift to his eyebrow, maybe the angle of his mouth, that let her know he meant the exact opposite.

She didn't want to do this. It would invite endless teasing, and she'd got enough of it from Zoey at home last night. But Max and Tricia were staring, waiting, expectant.

Inhaling a breath and holding it, she peeled off her gloves, one at a time, then stowed them deep inside her bag.

Tricia's eyes shone with mirth. "Oh! Poor blue—you," she corrected, then busied herself with her computer.

Max morphed his chuckle into a cough, and Keely turned away from his glee when her cheeks started to burn.

Out in the dog pen, Keely tried to sweep the kennel floor, but it was a lost cause. Half the dogs followed her around wherever she went, and the other half stopped her in her tracks, muddy and dusty paws on her knees, nipping at the broom.

"Down," she said, but her voice was meek, and didn't carry over the barking or the clatter of nails on concrete or the whoosh of tails. One of the larger breeds—she only knew a few of the dogs' names so far—jumped, putting its front paws directly into her stomach, and she buckled.

The dog lathed her hands with its tongue, and while the sensation wasn't unpleasant, the odor coming from its mouth was enough to have Keely's breakfast threatening to reappear.

"Down, Lottie."

Max appeared over Keely's shoulder, grabbing the broom.

She'd take it back in a second. But first, she walked to the trough sink across the room and scrubbed fiercely at her hands. She'd done this twenty times in the last twenty-four hours, but maybe the soap here was stronger.

She should use a paint stripper and be done with it. Her cells would regenerate in a few weeks, anyway.

Cleaned of drool—but still not dye—Keely marched back to where Max was using the broom to play with Lottie and grabbed it from him.

He grabbed it back. "I've got this. Go organize the front desk or something."

She pulled, but he held firm. Damn muscles. Why did he have so many? Weren't runners supposed to be beanpoles? "I had it *first*."

"Reverting to kindergarten playground tactics?" His smirk made Keely's eye twitch. "I thought we'd grown up by now. Must have only been me."

She snorted, letting her hands fall away. "Yes, it's so mature to sneak in somewhere, lie about your identity, and sabotage an important science experiment. That just *screams* 'I'm a fully-fledged adult.'" Biscuit bumped her palm with his nose, and she crouched to scratch behind his ear. "Don't you think, Biscuit?"

He barked, and she looked back up at Max, head tilted to the side. "Exactly."

Max blew laughter through his nose. "You're so ..."

"So *what*?" Her lungs burned. "Finish that thought, I beg you."

His eyes flashed. "Do a lot of begging, Keely? Down on your knees?"

"No," she quipped, fire sparking along her tongue and lashing out at him. She stood. "But you would."

His chest expanded on a deep inhale as Lottie and another German shepherd bounded right through the pile of hair Max had swept up.

She jerked her chin at it. "You missed a spot."

• • • • •

Play time became "try to eat Keely's hand" time, so she was relegated to the front desk after all.

She hadn't been there five minutes when the door to the lobby opened, and a harrowed-looking guy with a baseball hat pulled low over his eyes carried a box inside.

Surely, she could accept a package. She smiled brightly. "Delivery?"

"Sort of," he said, looking away.

The box barked.

Keely stifled a gasp as the visitor pried the box open. A fluffy white head popped out.

"Puppies," Keely said faintly, trying not to squeal.

"Four of them," the guy said, handing the box over.

One of the puppies stuck out its snout and let out a yowl. Zoey made that same noise when she was hungry.

"Are you surrendering them?" Keely asked, catching the box as it nearly toppled from the weight.

"They're not mine," the guy insisted. He held his hands up, like he was preparing to shove the box away if Keely refused it. No worries there. She wasn't letting him lay a finger on it again.

He inched toward the door. "I found them."

Keely tilted her head. "Where?"

"By that Valero near the highway?" He wouldn't meet her eyes, and now it wasn't the shelter's cats making her nose tickle but the pungent, lingering scent of tobacco.

She propped the box on the desk so she could grab a notepad and pen. "Have you fed them anything?"

"No," he gruffed. He pulled his cap down further over his brow. "Look, is that all? The internet said this was a rescue. So—" he threw a hand with yellowing fingernails in the direction of the noisy, shifting box "—rescue them."

Keely leaned her hip against it to keep it from sliding off the desk. The puppies climbed all over each other, heads popping out of the box like whack-a-mole. She tried to pet them all. "Yes, but I'd love to get some more—"

The word *information* was swallowed up by the ding of the bell over the door as he slipped back outside, sans the four puppies he'd come with.

Naturally, that was when Max and Tricia found her.

"We have some new friends," Keely said weakly. One of the puppies licked her hand. Another gnawed on her sleeve. A third popped its head over the side of the box and used it as a vault, half crawling, half jumping onto her chest and settling into her arms.

Max and Tricia stared. She was used to attention, but not this kind, where her skin crawled with fear that she'd do or say something wrong.

Like when she went home this past Thanksgiving and the word *divorce* was passed alongside the mashed potatoes and gravy.

The last puppy sat on the desk, milk teeth trying to embed into the flesh of Keely's thumb. "I don't understand why this keeps happening."

"Dogs see blue better than any other color." Max was practically *giddy*. "It's why they've been all over you today."

She pursed her lips. Of course he'd know that.

Tricia gave her a weary smile as she walked around the desk, gently prying the dogs from the various parts of Keely's body and placing them back in the box. "Why don't we stick you in the back room for the afternoon? We had a lot of deliveries this morning."

Keely's mouth popped open. "But who's going to take care of the puppies?"

"Max can handle it," Tricia said, trying to smile again. A concerning vein popped out in her forehead.

Over Tricia's shoulder, Max was extra smug.

Which Keely took very, very personally.

Chapter Ten

Max

After Max's shift was over, he walked out to the parking lot and was completely unsurprised to see Keely standing by his car, blocking the driver's door. He figured a confrontation of some sort was coming, especially after he'd got to spend his day socializing *puppies* while Keely stocked *cat litter*.

"This was too far," she started, holding up her ungloved, still-blue hands.

He wanted to laugh, but had a feeling if he did, he'd be leaving this parking lot in Keely's trunk.

He swallowed his amusement. It went down thick. "I didn't mean for that to happen." He shoved his hands into his pockets and popped a hip against the quarter panel of his Trailblazer. "How was *I* supposed to know it would turn your hands blue?"

She scoffed, mirroring his posture on the fender. "Why did you mess with the Olympiad in the first place?"

"Why did *you* send an email saying my class had been

canceled?" This time, he did let his laugh out, a dry, sardonic one. "From where I'm standing, you started all of this, Keely. I'm only following your lead."

Jaw tight, she looked away, and he watched her watch the darkening sky.

"Did you need something else?" he snapped. He didn't know how to handle this new version of Keely, one that challenged him, bit back.

She was unbothered by his tone—or more bothered by something else, judging by her teeth sunk into her bottom lip.

"Those puppies ... he just *left* them." She rolled her eyes, but they were shining.

This was her first abandonment since she'd started. Max still remembered his; he also remembered how much he'd cried when that bully was eventually adopted.

His heart softened a fraction. Maybe it was the poorly hidden fear in her gaze, glinting against the streetlights.

Or maybe he was hungry.

He shrugged it all off. "Don't worry. The puppies always go really fast. As soon as we can get them up on the website, basically." He tried not to notice the way the corner of her mouth lifted. Tried not to notice how he kept talking, just to see if it would go higher. "And it's good for some of the longer-term strays too, because people don't fall in love with them until they're here for the puppies. I mean, you could see how Biscuit wouldn't photograph well."

Her mouth twitched. A breeze shifted a lock of hair into her face, and she brushed it back. When she caught sight of her blue hand, they both froze.

Then she huffed and spun on her heel toward her own car. Max dug his keys from his coat pocket.

She pulled open her door and gave him a blue-tinged wave. "Have a great week, Max," she called.

Before she got in, she made a point to blow air in her hands and rub them together menacingly. She held eye contact the entire time.

That wasn't ominous at all.

* * * * *

For half a week, Max looked over his shoulder in anticipation of Keely's retaliation. He'd see her ducking around corners outside his apartment, slipping into the back of his classroom to embarrass him in front of his peers, tying his shoes together right before the tone went off.

But it was his imagination, fear playing tricks on his mind. She wasn't anywhere. Nothing happened. Things were fine.

And that worried him more than anything.

Thursday, Max had a meeting with Dr. Goff to touch base on his scholarship application. He spent ten seconds talking about his stagnant grades and ten whole minutes trying to gain intel on Keely.

"How am I looking in comparison to the other applicants?" he said, fidgeting in his chair.

Dr. Goff raised an eyebrow. The arch was sharp enough to still him instantly. "While I can't speak on others' academics, of course—"

"Of course," Max agreed, nodding emphatically.

"—I *can* say your work is cut out for you." She pulled open her desk drawer. "If I were you, I'd look into a tutor." She slid a card across the desk. "The sooner, the better."

So, basically, he was screwed.

After his appointment, he made his way across campus, heading for the gym.

He made sure to avoid stepping on Abe the emerald ash borer, the school's mascot overlaying the bricks in the sidewalk intersection nearest the Q. Rumor had it, if someone stepped on him, his spirit would be crushed and AMU would lose the next sporting event. Didn't matter what sport or what part of Abe's body. Max wasn't superstitious, per se, but there had to be a reason it was the least worn part of the sidewalk. He took a wide berth around the mascot to be safe.

A sudden chill went up his spine, and he checked over his shoulder for the dozenth time today.

Still no sign of Keely.

Maybe she'd given up. He'd nailed her pretty damn good with the experiment. She probably didn't want to risk escalating things.

Which was fine. He needed to focus on his own application, anyway. Find a tutor to pull his grades up from six feet under.

His phone buzzed with a call in his pocket, and the name on the screen made his heart skip a beat.

"Dad," he said, worry sharpening a knife along his ribs. "Is everything okay?"

His father let out a chuckle, and it eased the sting in Max's chest, but only marginally. "How would you like it if I answered your call every time with 'is everything okay?'"

Max grunted. "I see your point." He cleared away the rock in his throat, but it lodged near his heart instead. "What's up? Is that better?"

"Much," Dad said. Max *heard* his smirk. "How's your season so far? Race day this weekend."

At the start of every semester, his parents printed out AMU's track and field schedule and magnetized it to the refrigerator door. Put the dates in the family calendar. While most of it was taken up by his father's treatments and appointments, his parents tried to come to his races when it was feasible for Dad. When it wasn't, they streamed them on an iPad propped up at the end of the hospital bed or on the living-room television.

The rock in Max's heart had to be blocking something major. He pressed a fist there and massaged. "That's right."

"How have your times been this week?"

Max's jaw ticked. "PR this week was eleven point eight on the dash, and a minute-six for relay."

His dad made a thoughtful noise. "Decent for this early in the season. What about your hurdles?"

The word sent a shiver down Max's spine the same way Keely Sinclair did. "Coach thinks the dash is the safe bet for this weekend." It was a non-answer, but his dad knew how to read between the lines.

"Well," he said after a beat, "I have no doubt you'll do your best. And there's plenty of season left. Plenty of career."

Max's chest tightened again, and he pulled at the fabric of his sweatshirt, trying to get some air. The problem was Max's best wasn't good enough. It wasn't good enough last year at Olympic trials, when he'd fallen on his face and tweaked his knee. Wasn't good enough to keep his funding for postgrad so he could try again in three years. Wasn't good enough to win the scholarship outright, or to have decent enough grades so he had a fighting chance.

There wasn't a single aspect of his life where he wasn't treading water in a thunderstorm, trying to keep rain out of his eyes and saltwater out of his mouth.

"Gain any weight lately?" Max asked, desperate to take the spotlight away from his failings.

"Five whole pounds, I'll have you know."

Max let out a whoop, and other students threw him curious looks. "Five more next month, yeah?"

His dad chuckled. "How about you run your race, and I'll run mine."

They talked until Max reached the gym, catching up on what new recipes Max's mother had tried recently, which ones made his youngest brother Jacob gag and which ones Duck and Goose, his family's bonded golden retrievers, begged for the most. What his other brothers, Thomas and Henry, thought about their favorite sports teams' seasons so far.

By the time he hung up, Max had almost forgotten about Keely's blue hands and the fact that last night he'd woken from a nightmare in which they were wrapped around his neck.

Only almost, though.

And he still made sure the door was firmly latched behind him when he went inside.

Chapter Eleven

Keely

When Keely walked through Mrs. Kershaw's classroom door that Friday, the teacher visibly relaxed. "I really didn't think you were coming back."

Volunteering with children had a steep learning curve, something Keely experienced firsthand last week. It was a student's birthday, so her reading time was overshadowed by the opportunity to eat massive amount of sugar and crush juice boxes like red solo cups. Her throat had been hoarse for the rest of the day, and more than a few children ended up in tears. The teacher might have also been crying.

Now, Keely laughed, one among many in the bright-colored room. She sat her bag down next to her stool. "What you don't know is that this is the best part of my week."

And she wasn't kidding. Fridays were slowly becoming her new favorite day. Being surrounded with all the childlike wonder really helped to calm her nervous system, despite the constant chaos. The kids asked more questions than she did, which was a surprising change of pace.

She'd spent an hour at the library last night searching for the perfect book, something she couldn't afford to do every week if she was going to stay on top of the scholarship application. She'd been about to give up and grab a random one from the shelf when she remembered the kids' tiny faces. They expected Keely to read an amazing story, and Keely wasn't exempt from their expectations, even if they were only three feet tall.

The teacher instructed the kids to sit on the crayon-printed rug. Keely watched as one kid wiped their nose with their palm, then wiped it across the carpet. She gagged, just a little.

Once they were settled, she held up the book for them to see. "Today, we're going to read one of my favorites from when I was a little girl."

"You were little?" one of them asked. Keely was still learning names.

"I *was* little, just like the main characters of this book. This is *Frog and Toad Together*, by Arnold Lobel."

• • • • •

That night, Keely and Zoey went on their own *Frog and Toad* adventure as they peeked around a corner of the Athletics building.

Keely should have been studying. Or sleeping. Memorizing chemical reactions. Literally anything else.

Instead she was here, getting the upper hand on Max again. He'd be so mortified he'd stop coming to the shelter each week or drop out altogether. The scholarship would be hers for the taking. That's how it played out in her head, at least.

This was a building so far removed from Keely's normal sphere, she didn't even know where it was on campus. Zoey had led the way here and around the corner, pulling open a side door once her student ID card granted her entrance.

"How did you do that?" Keely whispered.

Zoey ducked her head inside, and waved Keely in behind her. "You remember the swimmer I saw casually during sophomore year?"

"How could anyone forget Broughton Stockard III, heir to Stockard NFT Holdings, LLC." Keely's voice was flat enough that her joke landed, and Zoey's snicker set off her own.

"Well," Zoey said, "he gave me blanket access so we could hook up after his swim practice and forgot to remove it when we stopped. I've been using the sauna for two years."

"Zoey Lamb, you are a genius."

"Tell me something I don't know."

Keely thought for a second. "Lise Meitner was a physicist who helped discover nuclear fission, but her name wasn't included on the Nobel Prize, so she wasn't credited for the discovery at the time."

Zoey blinked at her. "Everyone knows that."

Keely snorted. Maybe everyone in their circle of friends did, but Keely highly doubted Max Simmons knew fusion from fission, much less the scientists who discovered both.

"Cut me some slack. I'm too nervous to think straight." Keely eyed the dimly lit corners, then the security cameras blinking down at them from the ceiling. "What if we get caught?"

Zoey wrapped her hand around Keely's and gave her a tug. "We'll say we didn't know, and if they didn't want us in here, they should monitor who has access." She stopped halfway down the hall, fingers still glued to Keely's. "Don't tell me you're second-guessing this."

Keely balanced on the sides of her tennis shoes. They were the same ones she wore to the shelter, an old pair she'd never been able to throw out just because they were dirty and stained. They were her volunteering shoes now. And her sneaking shoes. Her *sneak*ers, if you will.

"This feels different than the email. That was passive. Mostly harmless."

"And then Max upped the ante. You could have been seriously hurt, Keel. He deserves to pay for that."

The security lights glinted off Zoey's dark brown eyes and made them glow. It was a little scary.

"Has anyone ever told you you're massively vindictive?" Keely asked her.

Zoey preened and said, "Broughton Stockard III, heir to Stockard NFT holdings." Keely grinned. "Now, for real. Let's get in, get this done, and get out."

They still weren't sure exactly what they were doing; only that Max had a race tomorrow and, to quote Zoey, "needed some messing with." The plan—flimsy as it was—was to poke around and see what trouble they could stir up.

Which, in Keely's opinion, was not really a plan at all.

Finding the right locker room was the easy part, given each room was labeled with a plaque beside the door.

Zoey whistled low under her breath. "I know where the money is."

"These lockers are bigger than our fridge," Keely agreed. They were maybe three feet wide and tall enough to stand in. She peeked inside one and spotted built-in shelves and hooks, plus a mirror. "And we have to share Bunsen burners," she grumbled.

None of the lockers were padlocked, probably because support staff had to place freshly laundered and starched gear before tomorrow's meet, but they weren't labeled either.

They started on opposite ends of the room, quietly checking uniforms and locker decorations.

Keely adjusted the claw clip sliding down her hair, then opened the sixth locker in the row.

This was his. This was Max's locker.

It smelled like him—and she hated that she'd noticed his smell during the handful of times they'd interacted.

But it was the picture taped to the back that gave it away for sure, a dated family portrait, and she didn't need her phone's flashlight to confirm she knew the second face from right.

Sure enough, when she unfolded the uniform on the top shelf, *SIMMONS* stared back at her in goldenrod-yellow block letters.

"Over here," she said, and her voice echoed in the empty room. She spoke louder than intended, jarred by what she held.

Held between *blue hands*. Almost an entire week, and the dye had only just started fading.

Zoey was right. Max deserved to pay.

The laundry room was so state of the art, it took Keely and Zoey, two esteemed burgeoning scientists, a full ten minutes to figure out how to do a simple dryer cycle.

"Extra hot," Zoey said, spinning the knob. Her brows furrowed at the machine. "At least I think that's hot."

Keely threw in the uniform, and Zoey shut the door.

The machine started.

Keely looked over. "Now what?"

"Now," Zoey said, "we wait."

Thirty minutes later, after they'd passed the time by

brainstorming for the Women in Science spring auction, Keely pulled Max's freshly laundered unitard from the dryer. It was very small.

She swallowed, holding it up between them. "Will this fit him, do you think?"

"Uh, babe." Zoey snorted, then covered her mouth. "That's sort of the point."

"Okay, but I still wanted it to cover his *penis*," she hissed. "This won't even cover a testicle."

A smirk overtook her friend's mouth. "Interesting how that's where your mind went just now. And the scrotum is the sack. You can't physically see the testes."

Keely made a noise of protest. "Shut *up*." Her cheeks flamed. "Now is not the time for an anatomy lesson."

Zoey pouted. "But the male anatomy is my favorite."

Back in the locker room, Keely couldn't remember which locker exactly was Max's. They opened a few. Too loudly, apparently.

"Hello? Is someone in here?" Zoey said, except—her mouth wasn't moving.

Panic spiked in Keely's bloodstream, and color leached from Zoey's face. They passed the uniform back and forth a few times as the steps grew louder.

A tall, lanky Black guy with a towel around his waist rounded the corner from the showers. Keely slid the unitard behind her back.

He stopped short. "Uh, hi."

"Hi," Keely squeaked. If her face didn't give it away, her voice definitely would. They did not belong here. They were going to get caught, thrown out, and then *she'd* be the one who wouldn't need the scholarship.

The guy crossed his arms over his bare chest. "I don't think you're allowed to be here." He didn't sound certain, or maybe he didn't have the authority to kick them out.

Zoey and Keely shared a look. They could work with this. There might still be a way to survive with their dignity intact.

But first they had to get the uniform back in the locker without this guy seeing.

"Is this not the gym?" Zoey asked, and Keely wasn't sure exactly what was about to happen, but she was along for the ride.

"Uh, no." He shifted, adjusting the knot of his towel. "Well, it is, I guess, but just for athletes. The campus gym is near South."

"Whoops. Silly us. It's our first time here, obviously. We'll get going." Zoey turned away, then spun back. "Didn't you say you needed to pee?"

Keely blinked. "I—yeah." It was a lie, but she was still buzzing with nervous energy and bouncing on her feet, which added to the ruse that her bladder was about to burst. The uniform burned in her hands. "Really badly."

"Around the corner," the guy said, jerking a thumb.

Keely did a side-step toward where he indicated. At the last second, she spun, hopefully keeping the uniform hidden until she was out of sight.

As the stall clicked closed, Zoey said, "So, I heard a rumor that they keep the mascot costume here."

"Yeah," he replied. "It's back by Coach's office."

"Ooh. Can you show me? I've always wondered what material they used to make him gleam like that. I'm Zoey, by the way. And my friend with the small bladder is Keely."

"I'm Nolan. And I would, but I'm not exactly dressed for the occasion."

"*Pleaaase*," Zoey pleaded. "I graduate in a few months. This might be my only chance to see Abe up close! I'll be quick, I promise."

A deep sigh. "I guess while we're waiting, I can show you. You can't touch it, though."

"Oh, pinky swear, Nolan. Hands to myself."

Footsteps echoed and then faded as they went farther into the locker room.

Once Keely was sure they were out of sight, she let out the breath that had been beating inside her eyelids and quietly unlatched the stall door. She threw Max's uniform back in his locker and went to wash her hands so her alibi would hold up when Zoey and Nolan came back.

Neither the guilt nor the blue dye came off.

· · · · ·

Keely woke up the next morning well before the sun. Even on weekends, she couldn't sleep in. Her mind wouldn't let her, not with her to-do list a mile long.

Today, for example, she needed to squeeze in a few hours of Inorganic Chemistry equations before heading into town to grocery shop for Matilda. She also needed to check her favorite research database for new articles on vitamin and caffeine interactions. The ones she really needed didn't exist—because she was supposed to be writing them.

She sighed until she ran out of air, then pulled herself out of bed.

Their apartment was nothing special—the furniture was cheap and the carpet was so thin it was practically nonexistent, but it got the job done. If nothing else, it was somewhere to plug in her coffee pot.

She still hadn't switched to decaf.

Three hours later, after an abstract-induced eye twitch, a shower, and a change of clothes, Keely headed for the grocery to pick up Matilda's standing order.

Matilda Hargrove was ninety-seven years old and lived on the first floor of an assisted living community. She had four children, fourteen grandchildren, and eleven great-grandchildren so far.

Even now, a few weeks in, Keely still wasn't sure whether the woman liked her.

Which Keely, decidedly, did not like.

"I called in the refills of your medications last week, so we'll get that sorted while I'm here," Keely called, unloading the bags onto Matilda's wrought-iron, glass-topped kitchen table. "But I still don't like you on the hydrochlorothiazide. I think it's why you're having so much acid reflux. And I'd like to get you on a better multivitamin. I did some research."

Matilda grunted from her spot in the living room. "The one I'm on is fine."

Keely hadn't seen her out of her recliner aside from the first day, where she *had* to answer the door in order to give Keely a spare key. She wouldn't be sure Matilda ate the food Keely bought if she hadn't seen the remnants in the garbage can. She made a mental note to take out the trash when she left.

"Not all vitamins are created equal." Keely pulled out the items Matilda had requested—saltines, mostly, plus Earl Grey tea, a few ill-advised freezer meals, and apples. Each week so far, Matilda had requested exactly three of the latter.

But there were still three apples in the bowl from last week. She grabbed two, testing their softness, then went to show Matilda. "You didn't eat these."

"They're hard to eat," she mumbled. "With the dentures."

Keely worked to tamp down her smile. She could fix this. "Oh, no problem. I'll cut them for you and pop them in the fridge."

Matilda frowned. "They'll go brown in an hour."

"Nothing a little lemon juice won't fix." Keely went back to the kitchen and rooted in the cabinets for a cutting board. "I think you have a bottle in the fridge. Fresh is better though, so next week I'll grab a lemon, too. With my own money, of course. The citric acid helps prevent oxidation."

"You sound like a textbook," Matilda grumbled under her breath.

Keely poked her head around the corner. "What was that?"

Matilda grunted again.

"Back to the vitamins," Keely mused as she chopped the apples, a content smile rounding her cheeks. "You should really take something with extra vitamin D, and collagen wouldn't be bad either."

Matilda groaned. She must have *wanted* Keely to hear her.

Groceries put away, apples sliced, medications sorted, Keely locked Matilda's door on her way out.

She yawned. That eye twitch from earlier wasn't getting better, but one more cup of coffee wouldn't hurt. Especially if she was going to be in the library all afternoon, marking up research article after research article.

She'd no sooner sat down, fresh chai from the Q at her side, than her phone buzzed with an incoming call.

"Hey," Zoey said. "What are you doing right now?"

"About to study. I'm over on the third—"

"Come to the stadium."

Keely uncapped a pen (purple, for taking notes). "I have to study."

"Don't you want to see your handiwork in action?" Zoey's tone was more than suggestive, and Keely could picture the way her eyebrows bounced.

Max's outfit would be ill-fitting regardless of whether she was there to see it, and she didn't have time. "I don't kn—"

"Please?" Zoey said. "Pretty pretty please, with enzymes on top?"

Keely looked over her study plan wistfully.

All she wanted was five minutes. Five minutes for her thoughts to slow down, for her chest to be able to fully expel one of the thousands of breaths she took each day.

But the thought of Max's strong-angled face framed with embarrassment made that breath come a little easier. The uniform would probably be way too unflattering for him to step foot in public. And the idea that he'd be too embarrassed to compete at all ...

That, she had to see.

"I'm bringing my study stuff," Keely warned, sliding her still-sticky laptop closed again.

Chapter Twelve

Keely

Keely heard the crowd well before she saw it—as soon as she left the library, really.

It was Valentine's Day, which explained why all the signage at the entrance of the stadium was decorated with red and pink hearts instead of the usual emerald and green. Even Abe the ash borer wore a pink sweater and held a bow and arrow, Cupid style.

Keely hadn't been inside the stadium—or attended an athletic event in general—since her freshman year when some of the girls on her floor dragged her to a football game. It had been cold, and rainy, and the nachos were twelve dollars and served with artificial cheese.

She wasn't much of a sports girl in general, but especially after that.

Now, after paying for her discounted student ticket, she made her way across the rickety bleachers toward the location Zoey had texted. She spotted her, along with some other familiar faces.

In the bottom row, below Zoey, Jeremy and Maya snuggled up

to each other, her wheelchair folded and tucked out of the way. They'd been casually dating since the fall. Keely wasn't sure how they found the time. Maybe their to-do lists weren't as long as hers. Maybe they were *on* each other's to-do lists.

Keely slid into the row behind them and hurried under the garish yellow fleece blanket Zoey held up for her. Rubbed her hands against her thighs, which she could no longer feel.

"You're just in time," Zoey said. She spread a paper program across their laps and pointed at it. "Max's relay is on deck."

Keely's brows knit together. "I thought he was a sprinter."

"Are you talking about Max Simmons?" Jeremy turned his head, then leaned back into their bubble. "He does *three* events. Hundred-meter dash, the four-by-one-hundred relay, and one-hundred-ten-meter hurdles." An inordinate amount of awe colored his voice.

"And that's ... good?" Keely guessed.

Jeremy looked at her like she had two heads. Whatever. *Keely* wasn't the one who wore open-toed shoes to lab. "Two events is above average. Three is basically unheard of, especially at the collegiate level." He glanced at the track. "I mean, it makes sense. He almost went to the Olympics last summer."

Nerves jumped under her skin; Sam had mentioned that too. She'd figured Max was good, based on the way he carried himself, and how he really, truly believed he had a shot at the scholarship.

The Olympics were better than good, though, and she had a hypothesis that the better Max was, the worse her chances were.

Zoey gasped, knocking her knee into Keely's. "There he is."

Sure enough, down on the track, runners in myriad colors jogged to their starting positions, dipping into lunges or twists as they went.

And there, wearing the uniform Keely had tumbled extra-hot the night before, was Max.

Zoey's elbow dug into Keely's ribcage.

She barely felt it.

"What—" She swallowed. "What did we do? He's not supposed to look..."

"Hot as fuck?" Zoey blurted unhelpfully.

The thing was, she wasn't wrong.

Keely always thought runners were supposed to be lean, with sinewy limbs and smooth, too-flat torsos.

But Max had muscles—plenty of them, in lots of creative places. Even from this distance, Keely distinguished the curves of his shoulders, the sweeping expanse of his broad chest. His shrunken uniform did little to hide the definition of his stomach. In fact, it highlighted each individual ab. And the angles of his obliques and the dips at his waist were two lines converging on what was, by Keely's calculation, a very impressive package.

If he looked this *defined* from far away, she could only imagine what he looked like up close.

Not that she'd ever want to be close enough to him to find out for certain.

The other AMU runners stopped at various distances as the announcer listed details and team member names. She recognized Nolan from last night; he stopped a quarter way around the track. Max kept going, though, toward the end. The last position.

Then he bounced on the balls of his feet, which shifted every single muscle poured into that polyester suit.

Quite rude of him, if you asked her.

Keely couldn't move. Her body wouldn't let her, and her brain was busy whispering that she was a *traitor*. She wasn't supposed to find her biggest competition attractive.

And yet, when the tone sounded, her heart suspended in her throat. She should have been watching the runners with the baton, but she could only watch *Max* watch them, his body stilling the closer they came.

Of the runners in the last position, Max didn't receive the baton first, but it didn't matter. Once it was in his hand, he was a blur, easily catching the few runners ahead of him. One, then the other, with methodical, practiced ease.

He was flying.

She didn't blink, didn't breathe. Only focused with rapt attention as Max sprinted toward the finish line, all the muscles and dips of his body working in tandem to create something *magical*.

Her hands came up to her chest, clutching her coat closed and giving her something to hold onto.

She'd been wrong before—he *was* that fast. Faster than she'd thought possible. No wonder the Olympics were on the table. No wonder he had a shot at the scholarship.

No wonder he carried himself the way he did.

Max won the relay for his team. The entire thing lasted under a minute, and Keely felt every beat of her heart, pumping blood through her energized body.

Adrenaline, she thought weakly. Maybe there really was something to that hypothesis.

As the runners slowed and caught their breaths, times flashed in bold white numbers on the jumbotron. AMU was first. On the right side of the screen, SIMMONS appeared. That must have been the individual times. First again.

She shouldn't be sitting here ogling muscles. She should be

studying. Working on her thesis. Figuring out why Max always seemed to have the upper hand.

"I'm going back to the library," she said to Zoey. To herself.

At the bottom of the stairwell, a strong gust of winter wind blew Keely's hair into her face, and she lost sight of where she was going.

"Oof," she wheezed, hands splaying wide in front of her as she ran into a brick wall. A brick wall that sort of smelled like ... sweat?

Keeping one hand planted, she swept the hair from her face and craned her neck up—and up—and up.

This wasn't a wall at all.

It was Max Simmons, and Keely's hands were all over him.

His uniform was slightly damp with perspiration under her fingertips, and the rhythmic thump of his heart sent shockwaves through her palm and up her arm. All the way down to her toes, which made no sense at all.

He stared down at her, a brown curl hanging over his forehead. He tilted his head down. "Hey there." His voice was scuffed at the edges, amused.

Her jaw unhinged, and another slight breeze deposited a lock of her hair into her mouth. She spit it back out and realized she was still holding onto him. Her fingers had started curling into the fabric of his uniform. His racing bib brushed the sleeve of her coat.

Keely snatched her hand back and immediately shoved it into her pocket. Then took a giant step back.

He clocked her movements. And winked.

Max winked.

At her.

If her face hadn't been beet red before, it was now. She burrowed into her coat, hoping her collar would hide it, or maybe he'd think it was windburn.

Now that he was closer, his outfit wasn't just tight. It was *devastating*. Painted on. Running naked wouldn't have revealed more.

And she'd been touching it.

Been *feeling him up* in it.

She spun around without another word, putting as much distance between them as possible.

"Keely." That same raspy, gravel-rough voice. Did he always sound like this after a race?

Against her better judgment, she looked back. His gaze was laser focused despite the expanse of ten or so yards between them. She shot him a fake, closed-lip smile. "Yes, Max?"

He grinned right back, wicked and wide. "Thanks for the upgrade." He ran a hand over his chest, down his torso, stopping with fingers splayed below his belly button. An image flashed of him making that same movement. Of *her* making that same movement, with no fabric between their skin.

"And happy Valentine's Day," he tacked on, winking again.

She swallowed, and, unable to think of a sufficient retort, settled for leaving as quickly as she could.

This was just ... a basal urge. She'd watched him win, defeat his competition handily, and evolution proved winners get ahead. She was probably ovulating.

It didn't have anything to do with Max himself. Or that tiny, ungodly tight outfit. She plucked the memory from her brain before her neck flushed again, and headed back to the library.

• • • • •

The following day at the shelter had been surprisingly uneventful. Keely had dutifully showed up for her shift, her hands mostly cleared of their blue tint.

She'd come prepared for the worst of Max's wrath. Surely, he'd retaliate after the uniform fiasco.

But he hadn't bothered her. Didn't put dog slobber in her water bottle or tie her frayed shoelaces together or try to talk to her outside of their normal duties. He'd hardly looked at her at all.

She'd certainly avoided looking at *him*, now that she knew about the body hidden under Max's pitch-black hoodies and joggers.

But her guard hadn't dropped. She'd still watched, waited for him to relocate one of Biscuit's, erm, *biscuits* into her bag. Or stuff catnip in her pockets right before she emptied the litter boxes.

When he didn't, she'd tucked those ideas in her back pocket instead. She had others too, progressively more unhinged, in case Max ever decided to raise the stakes.

Maybe when Max bested her at her own game, it voided the rest. Which was fine, because she'd had too much to do this week to think too hard about it. Olympiad practice on Wednesday, Women in Science yesterday, a biochem test this morning, and a hundred or so hours of thesis work in between everything. She'd been at the lab until midnight last night, working and reworking equations to see what could be tweaked.

The official title of Keely's thesis was "Drug and Vitamin Interactions with an Emphasis on Adaptable Energy Levels." While there were plenty of supplements out there that boosted energy—vitamin D, B12, good old-fashioned caffeine—there were far fewer that put you to sleep, and fewer still that did both consistently and across multiple metabolisms and body types.

Keely wanted to find the perfect cocktail, whether it be natural substances, artificial, or a combination, that would provide just the right amount of energy, readily available, whenever she needed it.

Whenever *someone* needed it. This wasn't just for her.

But she sure as hell would benefit from it now, trudging into Mountain Ridge Elementary School Friday afternoon.

After stopping in the office for her visitor's pass, she wound through the halls. This was only her third week here, but she already knew her way around. Like the staff bathroom at the end of the hall, which she had full access to.

She was about to walk into said bathroom when her phone buzzed in her pocket. She had a few minutes, so she answered.

"Hey, Dad. I can't talk long."

"Hey, punk." Her dad's nickname for her, an inside joke between them because Keely had never, in her life, done anything rebellious. "Just need to run something by you."

Keely's ribs closed over on her lungs like one of her claw clips. "Sure," she said, trying to keep the wariness out of her voice.

"So, ah. When you come home ..." Dad cleared his throat and started over. "I finally nailed down a more permanent place." Her father had been pushing the boundaries of his short-term rental since the fall, when her parents officially started the divorce process.

"That's great, Dad." She meant that—didn't she? Even if her throat had gone a little raw. "I can't wait to see it."

A beat of silence. "You won't have a room there."

Her heart crashed inside her chest. Had he somehow found out her grad school acceptance hung in the balance? With her parents separating finances, assets, lives, Keely thought her problems would slip by unnoticed. She'd hoped to have a solution in place before she presented them with another problem. Another point of contention. Another stick of dynamite to implode an already-crumbling house.

It must have been too much to ask for.

"Oh," she breathed. Except, not really. She had to work to get oxygen into her chest to ease the tugged-under sensation.

"Sorry, kiddo," Dad continued, not hearing the catch in that single syllable. "Two bedrooms were significantly cheaper than three." Keely knew her parents were still working out what Vince's schedule would look like, what days he would spend where. It made sense that Vince would have a permanent spot with their dad. She'd just thought she'd have one as well. "And with you being in grad school, I figured you'd stay with Veronica when you visited." Since when had he started calling her mom *Veronica*? Even her closest friends didn't use her full government name.

Maybe Keely should just tell him. Get it over with, rip off the bandage again. The last time she did that, though, it didn't work out well for her.

"Dad, about grad school—"

"Don't worry. We can work something temporary out for summer if you're not already in California by then. Well at least I can. I'm not sure if Veronica is ready to be that civilized yet." Under his breath, he mumbled, "She'd probably expect me to pay for it."

Keely's chest burned now, searing inside the deepest chambers of her heart. "Dad."

"I supported her for years before you were in school. You remember, right?" Keely didn't remember, but it was apparently a rhetorical question. "*She* must not. Last week her lawyer asked my lawyer if she could have an extra forty dollars a week for Vince's after-school robotics program. Obviously I'm going to pay for his robotics. But I don't want her to have it. I'll mail the check myself."

This was what always happened. Whenever Keely so much as *thought* about one of her parents while in the presence of the other, the conversation ended at the same place. Hatred, accusations, choking out all Keely's air.

Would there ever be a good time for her to bring up her problems?

Jury was still out.

"I have to go, Dad." She swallowed. "Can you text me if you need anything else?"

If he noticed how raw her voice had gotten during their short conversation, he didn't let on. "You got it. Talk soon."

She shoved her phone into her backpack and left it on a table outside the bathroom—because, gross.

She took a second to tidy her hair in the mirror. Press cool, wet fingertips to her ruddy complexion in an attempt to alleviate the redness. Cup the back of her neck. It felt like there was sand in her eyes, remnants of tears she couldn't afford to shed.

Keely took a deep breath and shoved it all down.

She'd figure out how to tell her parents later. What was one more item on her endless to-do list, anyway?

In the mirror, she practiced a kid-friendly smile, which looked demonic in this lighting and with her bloodshot eyes. She grimaced and said, "You've got this," under her breath. After one quick adjustment of her top, she grabbed her backpack from the table outside—had it always been this heavy or was the extra weight of her deception piling up? —and made her way to Mrs. Kershaw's classroom.

The teacher was, as always, incredibly gracious to Keely for showing up. She always got the impression that Mrs. Kershaw would kiss the ground Keely walked on if it meant half an hour where she didn't have to say *please remove your hand from your pants, Samson*. Keely could turn it into a drinking game, if she wanted.

The desk phone rang, and Keely knew as soon as the teacher hung up that it wasn't good news.

"I need to pop to the office," she said. "I'll be back as quickly as I can. And the TA is right next door."

"We'll be alright," Keely said, assurance flooding her bones and replacing the ever-present anxiety. "Won't we, kids?"

She got settled on the too-small stool at the front of the room. The children bounced on their knees and butts, hands shooting pre-emptively into the air. The volume reached earsplitting quicker than ever.

"Who's ready," Keely half-shouted over the noise. She reached into her backpack. "To learn about Frankie the Fish and all his Fin-Tastic Friends?" The children's cheering could have broken glass. Keely pulled the book from her backpack. Except—

"This isn't Frankie," she murmured.

"What's condom mechanics?" one of the girls sitting near the front asked.

"*Quantum* mechanics," Keely corrected gently, despite her mind blanking out. She hefted her bag onto her lap, opening it wider. It didn't make sense; this wasn't her textbook.

None of these were her textbooks. *Biological Anthropology. Particle Physics. Genetics.* Did she grab someone else's backpack by mistake?

No, her Women in Science button was still pinned to the front pocket, next to one Zoey had gifted her last Christmas that read *I periodically make bad science jokes*.

These books didn't even *go* together. This is what would happen if someone walked through the science section of the library and chose books blindfolded.

As she flipped to the front of the book, desperate to find a clue, a note fluttered out.

> Keely,
> Happy reading—hope those first-graders like science as much as you do. Maybe you can teach us all something we don't know.
> All my love,
> Max

Her head snapped up, and her gaze caught on someone, out in the hall. She'd know that cocky grin anywhere.

Oh, he'd learn something today—Keely could handle her science.

Chapter Thirteen

Max

Max overestimated how long it would take Keely to connect the dots and realize he'd swapped out her books. He wouldn't do that again.

This had been one of his longer cons, and the payoff was so, so sweet.

Keely had left her planner open one of her first Sundays at the shelter, and Max snapped a picture of the color-coordinated chaos to study at a later date. It had taken half a week—and an online catalog of AMU's biochemistry course offerings—to discern what classes she was taking, let alone her extracurriculars.

She also tracked her period, caffeine intake, and sleep. She had a severe deficit of that last one.

Getting into the school was a little trickier until he'd asked around to some of the other people in track and field. Jazz told him she'd given talks at local schools before, a peek into life as a collegiate athlete. It sounded like pulling teeth, but it would be a one and done thing. He didn't need to come back after this, and he could use it to bolster his chances for Pursue Your Passions. It was still only late February, but the sooner he could get his application in shape, the better he'd feel.

A few emails later, he was in. The fourth graders were stoked to hear about the branded swag he received (just enough to make sure his drawers didn't close all the way), the traveling he did (mostly regional), why he didn't make the Olympic team (because he'd been distracted). The teacher was onto him, but the kids ate it up.

And it was all worth it to see this look on Keely's face now. To watch her choke, get embarrassed, get up and leave and ultimately scratch this out in her perfect little planner.

But then she just ... shifted, right before his eyes. Pushed her shoulders back, calmly set her backpack on the floor again, and smiled.

Not at him. He wasn't that lucky.

*Un*lucky.

Whichever.

Keely smiled at the children crowding into her personal space. Had to ask them a few times to quiet down. And none of it seemed to bother her. She kept her gentle grin as she answered questions about the book she hadn't read yet. What was her plan, anyway? Was she just going to pretend this book was *Frankie the Fish*?

She held up the textbook, flipping through a few pages to display the diagrams and graphs. "This is *Quantum Mechanics*, which is a really fancy way of looking at the amount of something—or how much space something takes up—versus the frequency it emits. Because atoms are the building blocks of life, but they also have energy which is constantly emitting wavelengths."

The kids were dead silent. Maybe this would work out in his favor after all.

"Change of plans." She snapped the book shut. "Does anyone want to come up and help me with a demonstration?"

Almost every hand in the room went up.

He bit back a scoff. Did she have to be so good at *everything*?

Keely selected three kids as her volunteers and lined them up at the front of the room. She instructed the first kid—a girl with severe French braids lining her head—to stay as still as she could. The second was told to bounce up and down, which got a giggle out of everyone.

"What about me?" the third kid asked, eager as he stared up at Keely with hearts in his eyes.

"I want you to do both."

He licked his lips so thoroughly, Max saw the saliva from here. "What do you mean?"

"Be totally still, but bounce up and down," she instructed.

He tried, bouncing, then freezing midair once he realized he wasn't supposed to move.

"I can't," he said, looking down at the floor. "I'm sorry, Miss Keely."

She crouched to his level, giving him a kind smile. Max really needed to stop noticing her smiles. "You don't need to be sorry, Reid. That's exactly what I wanted you to say."

Reid looked up. "So I didn't make a mistake?"

"Not at all. You helped me make my point. We as people can't do that, but there's something in our bodies—something in everything on earth—that can."

"Is it boogers?" one of the other kids shouted.

"Good guess, but it's actually *atoms*." Keely gave weight to the word, as if it mattered more than anything else. She let the kids go back to their seats and took up a spot at the whiteboard and uncapped a marker. "Atoms are so small, we can't even see them."

"Like boogers," the same kid said.

"Smaller," Keely responded.

Shock and awe filled the air. Max heard one kid gasp.

Keely commanded the room, asked leading questions, drew funny cartoon images on the whiteboard, and the kids ate right out of her palm.

She was left-handed, something one of the kids pointed out with reverence. She stopped what she was doing to give him a high-five.

As her hand worked to keep up with her mouth, some of the writing and diagrams smudged. No wonder ink smeared on her hand so often. But she didn't let it stop her. The longer she talked, the more excited she became.

She was a natural, the way she was at everything, and it spiked his blood pressure. How was he supposed to win when he was up against perfection?

He stayed for her entire presentation, half enraptured, half trying to work out a way to best his biggest competition once and for all. He'd be late for strength and conditioning, but that was glorified weightlifting, and basically the only class he wasn't concerned about.

"Next week," Keely said as she packed her bag, "I'll bring Frankie, but maybe we can also talk about vitamins. I bet you all take some to make sure your bodies and brains are healthy and strong."

"Mine are shaped like strawberries," one kid said.

"Mine are dinosaurs!"

"I want dinosaurs," wailed a third.

Their teacher swooped in, effectively dismissing Keely.

Max held his breath, bracing for impact.

Keely shut the door behind her, threw him a nasty look, and marched toward the front office.

He fell into step beside her. "Fancy meeting you here."

"Why did they let you into this school?" she hissed, hiking her backpack up higher. "Did you even pass a background check?"

He sneered. "I'm a *jock*, not a criminal."

She glared right back, craning her neck. God, she was short, five two or five three. Wait, she probably measured everything in *metric*.

"Yes, Keely," he monotoned. "I passed a background check, same as you. And I'm so glad, because I got to witness whatever *that* was." He jabbed a thumb over his shoulder. "Anyway, sort of full circle, don't you think? Us, ending up back in a classroom together. Sweet memories and all that."

Keely barked a humorless laugh. "For you, maybe."

Her words held so much raw emotion, he jerked to a stop. "I—what?"

"Just forget it, Max." She pulled open the office door. It was the same tone she'd used that day at the shelter, when she said she didn't want his apologies, plural.

He followed her lead, tearing off his visitor badge and handing it back to the office administrator.

Outside, the February chill smacked him in the face. The forecast was calling for snow this weekend, and the dark clouds overhead promised that would hold true.

"What do you mean? I thought we had fun in school. Back when we were friends. *Best* friends." They had been, hadn't they?

Keely beelined toward her car, a tiny blue coupé. "I *said*, forget it."

"I ..." he started. Maybe he was making a mistake, pushing too close when she was already nursing an invisible wound, but his brain wouldn't let it go.

When she spun around, he was right there. Close enough to see her pupils battle against the bright daylight. Close enough to watch the vein in her neck throb.

Close enough to count her eyelashes.

His swallow got caught in his throat.

"Fine. Can we call a truce now?" he said. "As far as I'm concerned, we're even. You got me, I got you, you failed to get me back and so did I."

Her jaw ticked, and he had the strange, sudden urge to feel it with his mouth.

He took a step back, and another when he could still smell her. "Well?" he rasped.

Keely's gaze searched his. Her pupils had adjusted to the light and now consumed the blue color rimming them. A pink blush bloomed near her temples. "I don't know," she said softly. "It's a long time until May first."

The deadline. Right. "Thanks for the reminder. Plenty of time to break all your Bunsen burners and send your laptop to an early grave for real."

Her eyes flashed with hurt and, maybe, a little fear. "You wouldn't do that to me."

He wasn't sure why the addition of "to me" at the end of that sentence changed it for Max. But it did.

"No." He licked his lips. "But there's a lot I *would* do to you, Keely."

They caught the innuendo at the same time. The flush from her temples spread to her cheeks. Max's neck went hot, and he quashed down the rampant thoughts that barreled to the forefront of his mind.

Keely crossed her arms and cocked her head to the side, a lock of hair falling into her face. He tightened his hands into fists so he didn't brush it away.

"Anything else?" She was breathless. Hoarse. "I have somewhere to be."

He spun for his own car, on the other end of the visitor's parking lot. "Better bundle up," he threw over his shoulder. "They're calling for snow this weekend."

On cue, a snowflake hit him in the eye. Another landed on his neck, melting down into his collar.

But the cold water did nothing to cool his blood.

• • • • •

The flurries turned constant on his drive back to campus. By Sunday morning, Max's world was covered in white.

Growing up, it would have meant an impromptu snow day. While his mom couldn't take off work, his father was a dog groomer and had such a loyal clientele that he set his own hours. Customers rearranged *their* schedule to fit.

So at least once every winter, Dad shut down the shop, and he and Max and his brothers would spend all day outside. Snow forts, snowball fights, snow angels, snow cream. They'd tried it all.

Nostalgia tugged at his heart, so he FaceTimed his dad, ready to show him the late-winter wonderland.

Max knew instantly it was a bad day: the gray pallor of his dad's face; dark, sunken circles beneath his eyes. A wracking cough that started as soon as he opened his mouth to speak.

"What's—" Max remembered their last conversation and corrected himself. "What's going on, Dad? Is now a good time?"

His dad finished coughing, then wiped at his mouth and nose with a wrinkled tissue. He was in their living room at home, stretched out in the recliner that overlooked the front yard. Max was just glad he wasn't in the hospital again. "Always a good time to talk to you."

Max flipped the camera to show his dad the snow outside—and also so Dad couldn't see Max's eyes mist over. "Check this out."

"Whoa. We didn't get that much here. You're not running today, are you? Make sure you bundle up if you do."

"Nah." Aside from his ritual morning and night stretches, done like clockwork in the middle of his floor, Max took rest days seriously. "Just the shelter in a bit."

Would Keely be there again? Ash Mountain got snow often enough that it wasn't an excusable absence, but part of him hoped she'd skip anyway.

Another part of him hoped she didn't: he was unsettled by how they'd left things Friday after the book swap gone wrong, and their parking lot conversation left him with more questions than answers.

If she showed up today, if they had a moment alone, he could dig into why exactly Keely Sinclair hated him. He was starting to suspect it was about more than the scholarship.

"Stayin' out of trouble?"

Just blowing up science labs. Swapping books. Racing in two-sizes-too-tight uniforms when a girl washes them. A girl with a smile in her eyes for everyone else but fire in her eyes for him. The usual.

He hesitated long enough that his dad caught on. "I see. Well, does this trouble have a name? A girl's name, perhaps?"

For some inexplicable reason—maybe the furnace kicking

on—his cheeks heated. "I—uh." He scratched the back of his neck and glanced out the window again. "Funny story. Do you remember Keely Sinclair?"

"From middle school?" His dad nodded. "Wow. I haven't heard her name in years. Did you reconnect with her?"

"I wouldn't call it that, exactly." He couldn't tell his dad about the scholarship. Max worried about it enough for both of them, and any extra stress would only exacerbate his father's symptoms. "We realized recently we both go to AMU."

"Small world," Dad said, voice dripping with glee.

"We're just—" They weren't friends. Not really. "We've been running into each other recently." *That was one way to put it.*

"Well, if you run into her again, make sure you're protected. I've got enough grandchildren for now. No need to rush things."

Max accidentally-on-purpose hung up the call.

An hour later, Keely and Max arrived at the shelter at the same time. Clumps of snow clung to her shoes and the cuffs of her jeans. Her hair was covered by a fluffy white hat with a ball on top, and when she pulled it off, some of the strands stuck straight up, frizzing out at odd angles.

He stifled a smile, but she still clocked it. She opened her mouth to say something—or to bite off his head, if he was placing bets—but Tricia walked through the door, effectively ending the conversation before it began.

As Max logged his clock-in time on the cork board, he watched Keely in his periphery. She was up to something.

"Tricia," Keely said solemnly. "Can we talk in private? I need to tell you something."

Wait. Was she actually quitting?

And wasn't that what he wanted?

His pen broke through the paper. He pulled back, dropping it in the cup once again. "I'd like to hear this," he mumbled, but it was loud enough that they all heard it.

Keely looked down at her feet, and he would have thought she was seriously upset, if she hadn't glanced at him the split second before her mouth opened. Mischief danced in her eyes. *If you insist,* that look said.

Her gaze redirected to Tricia. "Max was the one who dyed my hands blue." She took a deep, steadying breath, like it was some massive secret she'd been carrying. "It was all his fault. I just needed you to know."

Something in his chest eased. This was more of her antics. She was grasping at straws, and he suspected she knew it. He bit his lip so he wouldn't laugh.

Tricia looked similarly amused. "Right." She turned toward a cabinet and didn't say anything else.

Keely choked. "Aren't you going to—to discipline him?"

Tricia shrugged, messing with her dog-bone printed bandana. "Didn't happen here. Your business is not my business. What you two do together—" her tone dripped with suggestion "—outside these walls is none of my concern."

"We're not *doing* anything—" Keely started, nearly drowning out Max's own cry of, "Tricia, you know it's not like that."

But Tricia just grabbed a roll of paper towels and left them alone in the office.

Keely stood there, her cheeks flushed and her chest heaving beneath her sweatshirt.

And that, for some reason, really pissed him off.

He closed the space between them. "What was that about? What are you trying to do?"

He'd been expecting her to take a step back, but she held her ground. It put her much too close to him. An eyelash rested on her cheek, near the curve of her nose. He wasn't sure why he noticed that, when his blood was still boiling. Like that day at the stadium when the wind had carried her scent to him—like every time he stood too close to her—peppermint filled his senses.

And his mouth fucking watered.

Max ground his jaw, continuing before she could say something else that would derail him. "You're not going to make her hate me, Keely. I've been coming here for years."

Pink smeared itself across her cheeks, and her gaze narrowed. "I'm not giving up," she said.

"I wouldn't expect you to." *Or want her to*, he realized.

This competition was spurring him toward ... something. He just didn't know what.

What he did know, though, was that sooner or later, this dangerous energy sparking between them would finally catch.

And there would be no survivors.

Chapter Fourteen

Keely

Keely stared intently at Dr. Goff the Wednesday following her and Max's weird showdown at the shelter, studying each individual eyebrow lift or jerk of her mouth, every subtle nod. How fast her eyes jumped across the page and when she flipped to a new one.

This was Keely's third attempt at an essay for the scholarship application, and she already knew it wasn't going to cut it. She sat back and waited for the blow.

"Better," Dr. Goff said eventually, dropping the paper back on the desk.

"'Better' doesn't win scholarships, Linda," Keely sighed, shoulders slumping. When Linda gave her a pointed look, she tacked on a rushed, "I mean, Dr. Goff. Respectfully."

The counselor peered at her. "Your application overall is strong. And the addition of your new community service will look great alongside your campus involvement."

The essay was still terrible, was what she didn't say.

"I don't know how else to write it." Keely rubbed at a knot in her neck. "It's missing something, but I don't know what." Unease stirred in her belly.

Though if Keely was being honest, she'd been a little uneasy all week, waiting for Max to retaliate. Or was it still her turn? Wires were getting crossed, failed attempts merging with successful ones until the entire thing was a mess. It was too big to write on her checklist, too many colors to label as any one thing.

"If I can speak frankly ..." Dr. Goff clicked her red pen open and closed a few times on her desk. It drove Keely crazy. She didn't want her essay to warrant a red pen in the first place. "I think your essays—all *three* of them—" she coughed "—have been fine enough, but what they're lacking is passion. And that's the entire point of the scholarship."

"I have passion. So much!" Keely tried to smile, but it felt waxy and forced, and it showed in the wince Dr. Goff couldn't stifle quickly enough. "I love science. I love the potential. It's the study of life at its most basic form, finding ways to improve upon what centuries of people before us have learned and discovered."

She should write that down.

"I believe you, but I'm not on the committee. And the people who are will only see this." Dr. Goff tapped the paper. "If you have the chance, you should ask to read Max Simmons's essay. It's the strongest part of his application, and I don't want to freak you out, but it alone puts him in contention."

Well that was *horrible* news.

"What I'll do is mark this up more thoroughly for you, pull out some areas you can expand on your passion for science, learning and discovery. All the things you told me about just now."

More essay edits. More sleepless nights. More checkboxes in her planner, with no additional time to check them.

"Thank you." Keely's phone beeped with a calendar reminder for study group. Quickly, she pulled up her texts. The one she'd sent her mother last night: *do you have time to talk?*, her mother's response of *I'll call you later*, the call that never came.

Blowing out a breath, Keely gathered her things.

Dr. Goff watched her. "I mean it." The essay was slid into a desk drawer out of Keely's view. She immediately wanted it back. "Talk to Max. Learn from each other."

The snow outside had all but melted, only dirty gray clumps lingering in the shadows, but Keely still wanted to tell her there was a snowball's chance in hell of that happening.

She spent the next several hours bouncing around campus. Somewhere between classes, study groups, and fighting with the sample incubator during her thesis work block, she also decided she absolutely did not need to read Max's essay.

Keely was passionate. She was *so* passionate it kept her awake at night, made it so her brain didn't turn off and wouldn't stop ruminating on issues until they'd been solved. If she weren't so passionate, her heart wouldn't ache with the threat of failure, and her stomach wouldn't twist with the possibility of her life not working out the way she had planned since she'd learned what planning meant.

She needed to buckle down, try harder, concentrate more, focus on Max Simmons and his infuriating face *less*. And if she did it well enough, she'd show Max and her parents and Dr. Goff and *everyone*—maybe even herself—she was meant for this after all.

So, hours later, after the janitor had practically picked up Keely's feet to vacuum under them, she trudged back home.

She loved this apartment. It was one of her safe spaces, alongside her designated table in the library and her bedroom back home—until recently, at least. She and Zoey had moved here for their sophomore year and never looked back. While it was humble (and always smelled vaguely of dust, no matter how many clearance-section candles they burned), they'd taken care to decorate it as best they could with cheap thrift store finds, gifts from birthdays or holidays.

They were still scientists at heart, though. Below the TV, instead of a gaming system or DVDs, they'd stacked Keely's biochemistry textbooks, Zoey's multiple editions of *Gray's Anatomy*. The books they shared, advanced calculus and differential equations. They referenced them *regularly*. One singular spider plant hung in the corner, above their anatomically correct model skeleton affectionately named Seeley Booth.

And above the television, which they had to wipe dust from on the off chance they turned it on, hung art prints of women in science, their icons and inspiration.

For Keely: Barbara McClintock, Dorothy Hodgkin, Katherine Johnson. Katherine's book was on Keely's nightstand, even if she hadn't had time to read so much as a page since the semester had started.

For Zoey: Isabella Cortese, Rita Levi-Montalcini, Anna Morandi Manzolini, the Italian women Zoey looked up to and idolized from within her own Italian-American family.

For both of them: Marie Curie, the original badass Woman of Science herself, right in the center.

On the couch, Zoey hunched over her notes, but she straightened when Keely dropped her bag in a chair. "Where have you been?" Her words carried an unusual bite.

Keely had never been caught sneaking in after curfew, but she imagined it a lot like this.

"I had biochem lab until eight," she said around a yawn. "I stayed after to work on my thesis for a bit." And got next to nowhere. At this rate, it wouldn't matter if she won the scholarship. Caltech wouldn't take her if she couldn't defend her thesis.

Zoey pushed her shoulders back, and her spine cracked like dry pasta. "I thought we were going to start planning the auction for Women in Science tonight."

Keely's stomach did a free fall. "What? That wasn't tonight." Had she—had she *forgotten* something? Something as important as this?

She pulled her planner from her backpack and flipped to this week's spread. *Sccchick*. A paper cut on her middle finger. It didn't sting as much as the threat of disappointing her best friend. "Oh, here it is. I wrote it down for tomorrow."

Keely looked up to arched eyebrows and a pinched mouth.

"But you have thesis lab tomorrow," Zoey said. "We can start now."

A laugh flew from Keely's lips. "Zo, it's nearly midnight. I'm about to pass out. Can we do it tomorrow, please? We've got a WIS meeting at lunch anyway."

Zoey slid the notebook on her lap shut. "Cassie's presenting her picks for this year's Nobel Prizes. She's had it scheduled for weeks. Everyone's really excited."

Unticked checkboxes flashed in Keely's mind, each one louder and bigger with every blink.

Box one: the fundraising for Women in Science's spring auction. It covered administrative costs and floated anyone who couldn't swing the fees coming into a new semester. It was how they were able to allow access to everyone, regardless of income levels. They never turned anyone away, and the group was richer and more diverse because of it. Keely had implemented it her first semester.

Box two: her thesis, which needed exponentially more hours in a week than she had access to.

Box three: her essay, which *lacked passion*.

What she needed was to lock herself in her room, put on her noise-canceling headphones, and hammer out another, much more passionate draft.

But there wasn't time for that, either.

Keely persisted. "Friday night, then. I don't have plans." She dug for a pen to block out the evening.

"I'm flying home tomorrow after class. It's Great Aunt Lucia's birthday." Zoey sighed, stretching her legs in front of her. "That's why we decided on tonight, remember?"

How had Keely screwed this up so badly? Her arms fell limply to her sides. "I'm so sorry."

"I know, Keel." Zoey picked up her notebooks and computer. "I'll see you in the morning." Without further fanfare, she went down the hall to her room, throwing a half-hearted "goodnight" back to Keely, where she stood frozen by the table.

For about five seconds, before she swayed against it. If her back didn't meet her bed in ten minutes, she'd fall asleep standing up.

Exactly nine minutes and thirty seconds later, she was out cold, the to-do list she'd been updating in her phone notes still glowing on her screen.

• • • • •

The next morning, Keely woke with an angry headache from lack of sleep. By Saturday afternoon, her entire body pulsed with that same anger.

She'd shown up bright and early to Matilda's, only to be greeted with a grunt. "I don't need you anymore."

Keely had blinked. Then she'd spread her smile wider, made sure it lit up her eyes and crinkled the skin of her nose. No one could resist that. "Of course you do. How else will you get your groceries?"

Matilda, it seemed, *could* resist. "I thought someone would have called you."

Called about what? Keely had shifted on her feet. "Is something wrong?"

Matilda had gasped and snapped shut the footrest of her recliner, so swiftly Keely had feared the old woman would fall. "Not at all! I'm better than ever." To Keely's shock, Matilda's mouth had spread in a slow smile, one of the first Keely had seen from her. "Especially since that handsome young man stocked me up so nicely."

"Handsome ... young ... man." Keely's lungs had deflated. She didn't need to ask—she knew exactly who was responsible—but the question still slipped through. The name, the one that had been occupying his very own bullet on her checklist: *"Max?"*

Everywhere she went, his name followed her. He was a ghost she couldn't banish, a shadow she couldn't shake.

Matilda had nodded fiercely. "Take a look for yourself."

In disbelief, Keely had walked to the pantry. Multiple varieties of trail mix, pudding, and applesauce cups, two loaves of bread, a sleeve of English muffins. Two packages of iced oatmeal cookies. There were several boxes of Raisin Bran, plus single-serve packets of Benefiber, and children's water bottles next to an easy-grip opening tool. *She should've thought of that.*

No question about Matilda's bowel health. But what about her emotional health? Did Max even know what she *liked*?

Keely had looked in the fruit bowl on the counter, but it was empty. Her brows furrowed. "What about your apples? Will he cut them for you every week?"

Matilda's response had been downright *giddy*. "Check the crisper."

Keely pulled open the fridge and had to bite her tongue to keep a nasty curse from slipping out. Everything was here: the prebiotic yogurts, low-sugar protein shakes to help keep some weight on in the right places, individual cartons of milk with a long shelf life.

And in the crisping drawer, *pre-sliced* apples. Enough bags to last well past the semester. They'd go bad before Matilda ate them all.

Keely shut the fridge but held white-knuckled onto the handles. "Your prescriptions," Keely had called. "Who's going to fill up your pill organizer?"

That had seemed to stump her. "I hadn't . . . oh, I hadn't thought of that. Hmm."

So Max wasn't amazingly wonderful at everything. He wasn't Midas after all.

Keely wiped the smugness from her face before she went into the living room. "I'm happy to keep coming on Saturdays and—"

"My nurse!" Matilda had interjected. "My nurse already comes once a week for physical therapy. I'll ask her to do it while she's here. Save you a trip." She opened the footstool on her recliner again and it snapped into place.

"I really don't mind." Keely tried her winning smile again, but she did not feel like a winner.

And when Matilda held firm, kindly demanding Keely leave her key on the counter on the way out, she was pretty sure this was the first time in her life she could be considered a sore loser.

She had to do something to even the playing field, to weasel into Max's mind and life the way he had hers.

But Keely didn't want to intentionally put herself in his path, give him more ammunition to throw at her. Seeing him once a week at the shelter was bad enough, and now that he'd started showing up in the other areas of Keely's life—the elementary school, ruining things with Matilda—nowhere was safe.

Even hours later, after she'd brainstormed for the fundraiser to uphold her promise to Zoey, she couldn't go two minutes without his face popping into her mind. Where was he now? Was he plotting some new ingenious way to crawl under her skin like a bug?

She literally locked herself in her apartment alone, but she was half convinced he would somehow set off the smoke detectors so the sprinkler system would ruin her fastidious outline for her essay—this newest version was so, *so* passionate!

What did he know about passion, anyway? And was his essay really that great? He probably used the wrong they're/there/their.

Her blood boiled again as she remembered Matilda's absolute glee. Why had he done that?

Weren't they supposed to be in a truce? It didn't look like it from where she sat, striking through the section on her essay that listed *volunteering with the elderly.*

Max wasn't her only distraction. Her phone kept buzzing, and she peeked into the group chat around eight, when her empty stomach started stabbing her with a knife, demanding food.

Sam

Party tonight?

Maya

Where?

Sam

> Off campus. Wait a sec I'll drop the address

Jeremy

> Ohhh that's over by the football houses. Those parties get CRAZY

Maya

> That's THIS party?! It's gonna be full of athletes since it's a campus-wide bye week

Sam

> That's weird. Why? Keel, do you know?

Maya

> Midterms. They want us all to be studying.

Jeremy

> IJBOL. Studying. Funny

Jeremy

> Count me in tho. I heard Max Simmons will be there

Maya

> No wonder you want to go LOL. Cookout after??

Sam

> @Keely your read receipts are on. Stop ignoring us

Keely cursed under her breath and scrambled to type back:

Keely

> Not ignoring! Thesis-ing. Trying to get ahead before midterms. Probably out for the party though. Maybe next time!!

With Zoey back home for the weekend, there was nothing to distract Keely from her intrusive thoughts, no noise to drown out the feeling that there wasn't enough time, that if she didn't get everything *just right* she wouldn't get the scholarship. And if she didn't get the scholarship, if she didn't have an ironclad plan when she went home for spring break in a few weeks, her parents would press and poke on the carefully laid house of cards that was her future until the entire thing came tumbling down.

Her last semester of undergrad wasn't supposed to go like this. Everything had started going off course when she shrank Max's uniform. It was supposed to make him too embarrassed to compete. But instead, she'd been the one who couldn't meet *his* eyes. It was her who'd been frazzled and fumbling, flipped upside down in an undercurrent she couldn't find her way out of.

She scrolled back through the group chat.

Max Simmons will be there.

Max was going to a party, while she was stuck here, in her bedroom, working on her application. It should make her feel better—if she hadn't already known she was the more diligent candidate, this left no doubt.

But why should he get to have all the fun? This was her senior year, too. What was it they said? "If you can't beat 'em, join 'em?"

Not that she wanted to *join* Max Simmons anywhere. Gross.

Keely sat up straighter as an idea took shape in her head. *If you can't beat 'em, join 'em*. If Max wanted to keep playing dirty, why couldn't she? And where better to do so than at a party where his guard would be down?

She might even get a chance to grill him on his stupid essay. And if nothing else, she could find new ways to get under his skin, the same way he'd burrowed under hers. See who he hung out with, what his weaknesses were.

Better yet, she'd get momentary relief from the stress of this semester. She'd recharge her social battery, let down her hair for one single night, and leave her essay and textbooks at home. She could always come at it with fresh eyes tomorrow.

Hopefully it would help.

She needed it to help.

Decision made, she typed out a message in the chat. Then she went to her closet.

Chapter Fifteen

Max

Max didn't want to be here. These kinds of parties always got too rowdy too fast, and you couldn't walk to the bathroom without bumping into people making out. The music was so loud, his teeth clicked in time with the bass ... and forget trying to understand the lyrics.

This wasn't his usual scene.

Which explained why his relay team was surprised he accepted their invitation. Jazz got so excited she thrust her cup at him when he showed up. It spilled all over his hoodie. Now he smelled like beer, and he wasn't drunk enough to find it funny.

He wasn't drunk at all.

But almost the entire track and field team was here, along with most of the basketball and soccer teams. Some of the football players too, but they were still largely scared to show themselves after the doping scandal.

Max stood off to the side of the fenced backyard with Nolan, who drank from a yellow Solo cup. Jazz had disappeared into the bowels of the house, probably to find hard liquor or someone to drag home. And Alex was near the keg—because what was an all-American college party without one of *those*—challenging people to keg stands.

"My money's on the freshman," Nolan muttered as another of Alex's unsuspecting victims emptied his pockets and unbuttoned the top of his shirt in preparation.

Max snorted. If there was one thing that outweighed Alex's enthusiasm for the track, it was beer foam. "Not a chance."

"Wanna put twenty on it?" There was a playfulness to Nolan's tone Max didn't recognize.

Or maybe it'd just been a while since he'd last heard it.

It was jarring to realize he didn't really know the person he at one point considered his best friend. More jarring to realize Nolan was no longer the only person he could say that about.

"Uh, no," Max said, which effectively killed the conversation.

He welcomed the distraction of the back door sliding open. "Pong and bongs!" one of the guys who walked through yelled, and a few people standing near the folding table by the fence chanted back.

Max vaguely recognized some of the newcomers, but he couldn't place them. Nolan did, though. He clapped the tallest one on the back, then gestured with the hand holding his cup.

"Max, this is Sam. We were the only two guys in women's and gender studies freshman year." Everyone but Max laughed, something he was well acquainted with. "And his friends, who I don't know...?"

"Jeremy and Maya," Sam supplied.

"Max is on the relay team with me," Nolan offered. "He's fast as hell, in case you weren't aware."

"Oh, we're well aware." Jeremy listed forward before Maya stuck a hand into his back pocket and towed him beside her wheelchair. "Big fan," he said anyway, wrapping a gangly arm around his girlfriend's shoulders.

"They're playing Mario Kart inside," Sam said with wide eyes. "It looked intense."

Nolan chuckled. "It can be. They do tag team matches, where you're on a pair and every lap you have to switch off. If you're not racing, you're chugging. We should snag a game if we can." He looked at Max. "You in with that?"

Max cleared his throat. He didn't know how to do this. How to make small talk, have friendships the way other people did. It took discipline, attention, focus. Lately, he only ever focused on *running* that much.

Well, running and—

"Max."

The voice simultaneously dropped icicles down his shirt and ran hot claws over his stomach.

Slowly—as if it would make a difference—he turned.

Keely. Keely was *here*. At this party, where guys were drunk and horny and had little else on their minds.

And wearing... whatever *this* was. Painted-on dark jeans, a red tank top that crissed and crossed just enough to throw shadows in interesting crevices. Mascara rimmed her eyes. Gloss coated her lips. Her hair hung in shiny loose waves down her back, no clip or ponytail holder in sight.

"Nolan," Keely greeted, but she looked at *him*, studying Max the same way he studied her. "Hey."

"Good to see you again," Nolan said. "Let me know if you need me to show you the bathrooms or anything. I've been here a few times, so I know where they are."

Max couldn't tell from the dim lighting in this part of the yard, but it looked like Keely's cheeks flushed to match her ruby-red top. "Um, yeah, maybe. Thanks," she murmured, looking at her feet for a second.

"Is your, uh, friend here?" Nolan scratched the back of his neck. "Zoey?"

This question, weirdly, seemed to put Keely at ease. Her shoulders fell away from her ears, and she gave Nolan a smile that scrunched her nose. "She's back home this weekend."

"And ... where is home?"

"Boston?" Keely ran a hand down her arm and shivered.

Which was when Max realized she wasn't wearing a jacket. It would be March tomorrow, but it wasn't warm enough to go without, especially at night. Not when snow still capped the Ash Mountains and he could see his breath.

"Can I talk to you inside?" Max muttered. "I'll ... get you a drink."

Keely's gaze returned to him, and it narrowed. "I'm good, thanks."

"You know him, Keel?" the tall one—Sam—said. He took a half step forward, angling his body toward hers.

Keel. The familiarity with which this Sam guy used the nickname turned Max's stomach into a pretzel.

And what kind of nickname was that anyway? *Keel?* She wasn't a boat, for God's sake. It made him want to *keel* over.

"I do. We're tag-teaming Matilda's shopping." Her eyebrow arched, a promise and a threat. "Apparently."

Ah, hell. He knew he shouldn't have done that. He'd set it in motion after she tried to ruin things with him at the shelter.

All he wanted was to get ahead, have a second to breathe around her.

But that seemed unlikely now. There was something that looked like hurt, just behind the playfulness sparkling in her eyes, and he was the one who'd put it there.

"Don't worry, Sam." Her razor-sharp glare didn't move away. "I can handle him."

Her tone was teasing enough that her friends laughed, but he knew she was serious. He shifted on his feet, searching her ice-cold exterior for a sliver of vulnerability, a way past her defenses, and instead found himself noticing how golden her hair looked in this light, catching the glow from the Edison bulbs strung up over the patio.

All he could think to say was, "What are you doing here, Keely? For real."

The rest of their group read the change in temperature and scattered around the yard, muttering about more drinks or snacks or watching that video game thing after all. So her friends were just as smart as she was.

She threw her head back and laughed, and her hair cascaded and dipped into the curve of her lower back. "I'm here to have a good time, Max. Same as you. Nothing nefarious."

He didn't believe that for a second, but he could play along.

"Cooler's over there." He pointed. "In case you can't tolerate me sober."

She tipped forward, peering into his cup. Peppermint assaulted his senses once more. His jaw tingled. "What are you having?"

Sprite and nothing else, but what Keely didn't know wouldn't hurt her. "Vodka," he lied.

That same eyebrow arched again, dancing along her forehead. "With carbonation?"

"Vodka tonic," he corrected.

"Tonic water at a college party?" She walked to the cooler and dug out a cherry-flavored hard seltzer. "And here I thought it was all kegs and Fireball."

"Fireball's inside by the Mario Kart." He jerked his chin. "Keg's over there. It's the thing your friend Jeremy is currently trying to make love to."

They looked over, and Max wasn't sure *what* the guy was doing, but his description wasn't far off.

Keely took a heavy sip of her seltzer, then hid a burp behind her hand. "Excuse me."

It was obscenely cute. He downed the rest of his soda and wished it were ninety proof.

They stood in silence long enough for Alex to conquer another two suckers with his keg stand tournament, one of whom proceeded to throw up everything he'd chugged.

Keely's amusement played out across her defined features. Her cheekbones were accentuated with shimmer, and the tip of her nose kept catching the light—and therefore Max's eyes. He forced them away *again*.

"So," he mumbled. His voice was low, for her ears only. "You and that Sam guy."

That Sam guy was currently glancing over every sixty seconds or so, probably to make sure they hadn't moved any closer.

One of Keely's arms was crossed under her chest, her other elbow resting on it. She held her seltzer to her neck like she was hot, but goosebumps dotted her skin. Her head cocked, those same stars from earlier dancing in her vision. The patio lights, probably. "Does it matter?"

"No," he growled, sharp and immediate. Who was he trying to convince?

Keely gasped under her breath, which made everything worse.

He cleared his throat. "No," he repeated in a lighter tone. "Just trying to make civil conversation. But I guess we don't know how to do that."

She made a noise in the back of her throat, but didn't comment otherwise.

Sam must have had enough of watching them, because he made his way over. To Keely specifically. He wasn't looking at Max like that with stars in his eyes.

"I haven't seen you around much lately, Keel," Sam said, nudging her with his elbow. Max's jaw clenched.

Keely shrugged, sliding a hand in her back pocket. "You know how I get before midterms."

"I thought that's why you weren't going to come originally. So what changed your mind?" Sam shot Keely a blinding smile, and Max tried very hard not to let it bother him.

He didn't know why Sam wound him up, especially when he didn't usually feel anything but indifference toward guys like Sam.

Maybe it was how he looked at Keely.

"Nothing specific," she said breezily, and maybe it was the lights, but Max swore she glanced at him. "I just remembered it's my senior year, and I want to have at least one crazy memory to show for it."

A roar went up across the yard. One of the other partygoers was upside down atop the keg, chugging, doing a half-decent job.

Keely gestured to them. "Like that."

"*You*, Keely Sinclair, doing a *keg stand*?" Sam snickered, elbowing Max like he was in on the joke.

Max staunchly ignored him, choosing instead to study Keely's reaction. Her eyes narrowed at the challenge.

"Why is that so hard to believe?" She sniffed. "I could do a keg stand."

Sam snorted around a drink of whatever was in his own cup. "Sure, and I could take off my clothes and sing 'The Star-Spangled Banner' on top of that table over there. I'm not gonna do it, though."

Keely raised her chin. "It can't be *that* hard."

"Can't be that hard," Sam echoed. "Wanna bet?" *What was this guy's deal?*

"Keely." Max's jaw ached from how hard he was clenching it. "You don't have to prove anything to—"

Keely silenced him with a look. Then her mouth quirked. "Just watch me."

· · · · ·

What a disaster.

Alex was *giddy* that someone else wanted in on his game, and he'd gathered everyone he could from the party. Maybe some neighbors, too. The result was approximately fifty people in a half circle around the keg.

"Ladies first," Sam said, gesturing.

Alex explained the rules to Keely, who listened intently, tucking her tank top into her jeans. Max, once again hanging out on the periphery, got one too many glimpses of smooth pale skin for his liking.

Keely gripped the edges of the barrel. "Is someone going to hold my legs?"

Across the circle, Sam took a step forward. Which—no.

"I'll do it," Max muttered. Sam rolled his eyes, but Max ignored him. He tipped his head down, so his words were only for Keely. "No pranks right now. Promise. Fair and square."

She bit her lip. Was that still her lip gloss, or was it from her seltzer? And why the hell was he thinking about that right now?

Her gaze searched his face. "The same way our little game is fair and square?"

He gritted his teeth. The onlookers were getting rowdy, and the attention stiffened his shoulders. "Do you want to do this or not?"

"I'll hold your other leg," Nolan offered. "As an impartial third party."

With a sigh, she nodded. "You only live once, right?"

Did she just—

Keely grabbed the rim of the keg, kicking off the ground, and Max grabbed one of her legs. His grip was firm on her ankle, his thumb brushing the smooth skin between her jeans and sock. Heat flashed at the base of his spine.

"My first keg stand." She whooped.

Her friends cheered in response. Jeremy started a chant of *Keely*.

As they hoisted her upside down, Max and Nolan shared a look.

Yeah, this was going to end horribly.

Keely, surprisingly, didn't puke. Not at first. She chugged like an athlete would, breathing through her nose while downing the beer in slow, steady beats. He tried counting in his head, but lost it around twenty seconds, when the cheers of the crowd got too loud.

Max tried not to notice how her jeans hugged the curve of her ass. How these weren't her shelter shoes, or the normal, cleaner sneakers she wore on campus, but pristine red Keds that matched her tank top.

And just when Max realized how weird it was that he kept noticing, of all things, her *shoes*, someone yelled, "Spit or swallow, Keely!"

Keely's stomach spasmed with a choked-back laugh.

"She's gonna hurl," Nolan murmured, and they lowered her.

On instinct, Max's hand found the dip of her waist as she came right side up and the blood rushed back to her extremities.

For a split second, Keely looked up at him with something other than animosity in her eyes. Here, in the moonlight, with music so loud it rattled his bones, she almost looked ... thankful. A drop of beer slid down her chin and he wasn't thinking when he reached to wipe it away.

"You okay there, Key?"

Her lips parted, eyes widening; they *danced* in the fairy lights. Max's heart kicked up so hard, he felt like he'd just finished a sprint. The nickname had slipped out before he could stop it. Looking at her now, he didn't know if he *wanted* to stop it.

Then Keely covered the bottom half of her face as white foam spewed out from between her fingers and out her nose. It sprayed over his chest, dripped onto his neck and across his skin. She doubled over, coughing and gasping for breath.

Oh. That look of hers made more sense now.

The vibe died pretty quickly as people floated off and were reabsorbed to the rest of the party. Aside from Jeremy, who was taking a video. His girlfriend shoved his arm down and muttered, "Be so for real right now, Jer."

Max scooped his near-empty drink off the ground and held it out to Keely. Her face and neck were bright red. She shook her head, pushed him away, but he persisted. "It's just Sprite. Drink it, Keely."

She wrapped greedy hands around it and gulped it down. Her mascara was ruined, globbed around her eyes and in tear tracks down her cheeks.

He wouldn't let himself wipe it away this time.

Instead, he slipped off his flannel, the one he'd found in his car earlier after the *first* round of alcohol had found its way to his shirt. Thrust it at her. "Here."

Over her shoulder, near the porch and the drinks, Sam watched them. Max cocked an eyebrow.

Sam just shook his head and went inside after his friends.

"I'm not cold," she said through chattering teeth. She wiped her forearm across her face, and more mascara smudged toward her temple.

"Well, I don't have a towel, so—" He waved his shirt in front of her again like a white flag. Is that what it was? A surrender?

No.

This was a temporary ceasefire, until she wasn't on the verge of passing out. Until she wasn't looking at him like this anymore. So small, and yet so dangerous.

She took the shirt, wiping it down her chest, across her arms, everywhere sticky beer clung to her bare skin in fat drops.

Max looked away with a thick swallow. Someone turned up the music, and it helped drown out all the thoughts Max wasn't supposed to be having.

Keely handed him back his shirt and empty cup. "Um, thanks." She burped again, louder. Her hand came up too slowly to cover it, and she swayed a bit.

He had a sinking suspicion that Keely Sinclair was a lightweight.

"I'm gonna sit," Max said. "And I would encourage you to do the same. Only so you don't fall down."

Her gaze narrowed as she followed him to a hanging bench. "Any whoopee cushions on your person?"

"Nah," he said, sitting and patting the spot next to him. He didn't start swinging until she was settled. "I'd rather make you throw up after the keg stand."

"Har, har." She wiped the back of her hand across her mouth. "I've never done that before."

"*No*," he gasped, deadpan.

She shoved his shoulder. "I meant throw up after alcohol, doofus."

"There's that crazy college memory you wanted." The music switched, and he threw his head back on a grumble. "God, this song sucks."

Her nose wrinkled. "I love this song."

"Of course you do." But he chuckled, and she smiled, and his heart suddenly had a stitch in it, the way his side did on distance days if he didn't stay focused on his breathing. Sharp and uncomfortable, but he relished the sting.

"Do you like to dance?" she said.

Max looked out at the other partygoers. Even the people who were supposedly dancing were just grinding on rhythm.

"I took a ballet class freshman year," he blurted. He hadn't had a single sip of alcohol—he hadn't since Coach's birthday—so he wasn't sure why he was being so vulnerable, giving her more ammunition to kill his chances at the scholarship.

She didn't laugh like he thought she would. She nodded thoughtfully, something akin to appreciation tugging at her mouth. "A lot of professional athletes take ballet. Yoga, too. It helps to use your muscles in a different way. Focuses on flexibility and fluidity instead of strength and speed." She burped to punctuate her sentence. Her hand came up. "Excuse me."

"You're sort of drunk." He was halfway joking. "You called me a professional athlete."

This time, she bumped his shoulder with her own. Their arms settled close to each other. Body heat radiated off her in waves.

"Don't get used to it, jock. By tomorrow morning I'll be back to normal."

Somehow, he doubted that. He certainly wouldn't be.

The bench creaked as they rocked in a gentle back-and-forth, nothing that would further upset her stomach. But it gave him something to do with this restless energy. The same one that cropped up whenever Keely was around.

"Why are you here tonight? I didn't take you for a party girl."

"I've been to parties," she said, resting her head on the back of the swing. "It's been a while, though. I've been busy."

"Perfecting your application?"

"More like wondering what the point is."

Exactly how much alcohol had she had? He eyed her seltzer and clocked the condensation line.

Her chin hit her chest as she murmured, "My parents are getting divorced." Her hair fell forward and created a wall between them.

Max ran straight into it. That had to be why all his air snagged behind his ribs. "I'm sorry. That really sucks."

"It does." She took a glug of seltzer. "Especially when I never told them I didn't have grad school locked down. Now there's no good time, and we graduate in two months, and I have even less space to figure it out than before."

His heart squeezed in his chest. He should get that looked at. He shifted on the bench, and his foot knocked against hers. "That's a lot of pressure."

"No, pressure is force over area. This is ... an equation. I'll figure it out soon enough."

She looked over at him, tucking her shiny hair behind her ear. Her earrings were little stars, except they had six rounded points instead of five, with a gemstone dot in the middle.

Atoms, his brain supplied. Her earrings were atoms.

The song changed, and with it, her mood shifted. The threat of tears was gone, replaced by alcohol-fueled excitement. "Do you want to dance now?" she asked, scooting forward to the edge of the bench. "Not with me or anything. Just like, generally. Out there, with everyone."

He arched an eyebrow, his heart still fumbling a bit in his chest. "Do *you* want to dance?"

"I *wanted* to buy Matilda's groceries." She leaned over to poke him in the solar plexus. "But you took it away. It won't count on my application now." She took a deep breath. "Pre-sliced apples are horrible for the environment, by the way. They increase carbon—"

He grabbed her wrist, returning her hand to her side of the swing. "I'll talk with you about this when you're sober. And I'm not dancing."

"I'm *totally* sober." She fluttered her eyelashes. "Please?"

A deep sigh bubbled up from his lungs. "I don't dance."

"You don't have to. Just—" she gestured wildly and he ducked out of the way "—stand there."

"Stand there," he repeated.

She nodded fervently, teeth biting at her plump bottom lip.

Her *perfectly normal bottom lip*.

He gestured to the yard, rolling his eyes. The sooner he got this over with, the better.

She hopped off the bench, grabbing his hand. "Come on."

After a detour to grab another seltzer, she joined the bodies moving to the music.

The tentative sense of peace didn't last long. Two of the guys near them were drunk, stumbling, and they bumped into a girl. Her seltzer fell and splashed all over Keely's pristine shoes.

"I'm *so* sorry," the girl said, her eyes welling.

"Don't worry about it. Here," Keely said. "Take this one. It's not open."

The tears in the girl's eyes morphed to stars. "That's so nice. Thank you."

The girl was barely out of earshot before Max muttered, "You didn't need to do that. The cooler is right there."

Keely shrugged. "It's a seltzer, not a brand-new car."

"You're so ... *sweet*. To everyone, all the time." *Everyone except him.* "It gives me a toothache."

She craned her neck and blinked up at him. "There's no sense in being mean for the sake of it, Max. The world has enough of that already."

The song changed, the tempo slowing into something sultry and languid. The bass was just as heavy, but instead of warring with Max's pulse it blended with it. He buzzed with energy.

Especially when someone bumped into Keely this time, and her hips fell in line with his. He reached to steady her and met soft and gentle curves that were oddly right in his rugged hands. This wasn't like when he'd caught her coming down from the keg, or anytime they'd brushed against each other at the shelter.

This wasn't accidental. He'd made a fully conscious decision to put his hands on her, and he'd have to live with the consequences.

"Max," she murmured. Licked her lips. "I—I don't know what's going on right now."

He tracked the movement of her mouth. It was all he could do. "I don't either."

The corner of that mouth twitched as she stood on her tiptoes, splaying a palm on his stomach to brace herself. Her lashes fluttered, her mouth opening a sliver to reveal the wet pink tongue nestled inside.

Keely was going to kiss him.

He shocked himself with how much he wanted it. How much he wanted her mouth on his, to taste and see if she was spicy when she wasn't spitting insults at him, too.

But she was well past tipsy, and if the amount it took her to get that way was any indication, she didn't get this way often.

He turned his head, and her pillow-soft lips landed on his jaw instead. He let himself have it for three heartbeats.

One for the past version of him, the Max from middle school who only wanted to be looked at by this girl, even if he didn't know why.

One for the version of him tomorrow, who'd have to pretend this hadn't happened.

And one for the version who stood here now, with Keely's mouth on his skin and her hand on his stomach.

He stepped back, prying her hand away from him for the second time tonight. "We can't do this."

She blinked in half-speed, yet another sign he'd made the right call. Her bottom lip trembled. "I'm sorry, I thought you—" She shook her head, hair flying out at all angles. "Never mind."

And his heart crashed onto the ground. "Keely," he murmured, wrapping his palms around her shoulders. She shivered again. "It's not that."

He didn't know what it was, didn't have a clue, but wanting Keely wasn't the problem.

"Come on," he said. "Let's get you home."

• • • • •

Keely wasn't drunk enough not to remember where she lived, so twenty minutes later, he found himself standing in Keely Sinclair's bedroom.

It was tidy, naturally, with a light blue comforter and pillows propped up pristinely against the headboard. He spotted a bottle of lotion on her nightstand and thought he'd finally solved the peppermint mystery for a second, before reading the label and discovering the lotion was unscented. Odd disappointment crashed in his chest.

Her desk was organized but functional: textbooks stored vertically near her computer, a few cups of pens organized by color family. While Keely tumbled onto her mattress, he swapped an orange and a green.

Just to keep the status quo.

"Max," she whined, propping herself up with her palms. "My feet are too tight."

He pursed his lips to smother a smile. "You mean your shoes?"

"Yes." She hefted one leg, waving her foot in his face. "Take it off, please."

He did what she asked.

"That tickles," she said, jerking out of his grasp.

Gritting his teeth, he gripped her other ankle more firmly and ripped off this one quicker.

"Hey." She frowned. "Easy." Her eyelids drooped. She was fading fast. "Pants next."

His pulse skyrocketed and he let out half-hearted chuckle. "You're on your own for that one, Key."

She groaned and shifted before blowing an exasperated huff of air. "Whatever." Her face twisted, and even with her features distorted, she was still stunning.

"What are you doing?" he asked.

She relaxed her face and gave him a lazy grin. "That was my impression of you. Because you're so grumpy all the time." She could barely keep her eyes open. "I'm so sleepy," she added, nestling into her pillow, hair splaying out in a golden halo. "Aren't you going to tuck me in?"

He glared at the ceiling like it might hold answers—or an escape hatch.

"This is the last thing," he said. "And then I'm leaving."

"Promise." She nodded resolutely.

"C'mon then, lift up."

Keely arched her back, all sleek curves, and Max gritted his teeth and stared hard at the blue fabric of her bedspread. He pulled the blanket out from underneath her, then back up over her prone body.

A lock of golden-brown hair hung in her face. He ran his fingertips over his palms before deciding to smooth it behind her ear, over her shoulder.

His thumb brushed her little atom earring.

Then, for absolutely no reason he was ready to investigate, he leaned down and pressed a kiss to her forehead.

"Goodnight, Key."

She was already asleep.

Chapter Sixteen

Keely

Keely groaned into her pillow.

Her head pulsed, and she cursed her past self for never investing in blackout curtains because her "circadian rhythm worked better with the natural state of the sun." She was rethinking that philosophy now.

She burrowed deeper under the covers to hide from the light, the world.

And then her scheduled alarm went off.

She blindly reached for her phone and grabbed—*wet*?

A full glass of water waited for her on the nightstand, dripping with condensation. It sat next to a bottle of headache relief medicine and half a sleeve of crackers. She blinked at them, unseeing.

Nothing made sense this morning. She blamed the keg.

Though she'd gone to parties before, she hardly drank and she *never* got drunk. She didn't know how she got back to her apartment or managed to fold herself into bed. She hadn't brushed her teeth or—she wiped a finger along her lash line—taken off her makeup, so she highly doubted she'd had the forethought to put *Excedrin and crackers* on the bedside table.

The last thing she remembered was spewing beer foam all over her top when someone had yelled something inappropriately funny about swallowing, and she'd looked behind her to see an upside-down Max Simmons, his gaze trained intently on her face.

Was he the one who—?

Nope. No way. Max would never bring her home. He didn't even know where she lived.

But then why was she in her bed versus crashed out on a cheap secondhand futon, surrounded by strangers' bodies and discarded cups?

It must have been her friends. She opened the group chat.

Keely

> Thanks for bringing me home last night. Killer headache and the sun is the devil. Status report for everyone else?

Jeremy

> Bringing you home??? I can't even leave the bathroom. Literally still at the party lol HELP

Maya

> You are so dramatic. But unfortunately telling the truth. On Jeremy and Pepto duty all night. Not me

Keely

> @Sam that leaves you

She held her breath when typing bubbles appeared. Disappeared. Reappeared.

Sam

> Wasn't me. From what I could tell there was only one person allowed to go near you last night

Her head pounded with her exhale. Was she too young to vow to never drink again?

Hours later, she was less miserable. Marginally. The crackers helped.

Also marginally.

If asked, though, she would credit her lukewarm shower, non-sweat-and-beer-smelling clothes, and today's freshly inked to-do list.

Which included a task she absolutely detested, but had to do, nonetheless. She wouldn't be able to sleep tonight otherwise, and the Sunday Scaries were at their worst when she couldn't sleep, anxiety and self-doubt creeping in to whisper her bedtime stories.

At the shelter for her Sunday shift, the growing sense of dread loomed over Keely like a raincloud. Most of the dogs were in the open play area, so she and Max had been tasked with cleaning out the kennels, sweeping and mopping when necessary, refilling water and discarding ragged toys. He hadn't looked her way all morning, which made what she had to say only slightly more tolerable. It still took her a few minutes to figure out the shape of the words.

"Erm, thank you," she said. She didn't need it hanging over her head any longer. That hurt enough all on its own. Every time a dog barked—so, constantly—she winced.

Max grunted. "For what?"

He didn't even look hungover. How was that fair? His eyes were their normal shade of light brown, sans dark circles underneath. She'd had to use half a tube of concealer this morning.

"For getting me home last night. The water, the crackers, taking off my shoes ..." She rested her hip against the kennel he was working on, ducked her head. "It was very thoughtful of you, Max."

He still didn't bother looking at her. Instead, he grunted and reached into Champ's kennel. He pulled out a slimy blanket, shredded to pieces. "Don't know what you're talking about."

"Really?" Keely's tone was flat, accusatory. She crossed her arms.

The blanket dropped into the garbage, and he shrugged. "Really. Not a clue. Wasn't me." But he still wasn't meeting her gaze.

Something in her heart turned tender, throbbing in time with her temples, but the pain was sort of ... sweet.

"Well." She kicked off from the cage. "If you figure out who it was, let them know I said thank you."

They worked with minimal noise, which was to her benefit.

Even the sound of the broom on the floor was too much for her sensitive head.

"If I did know who it was," Max murmured out of nowhere, so low Keely struggled to hear him. "They'd probably say you should consider electrolytes next time." He coughed and scratched the back of his neck. "They're good for hangovers."

"I'll take it under advisement. And thank you—"

He looked away. "I told you, it wasn't—"

"To that person," Keely finished. She rested her chin on the broom handle. "Whoever and wherever they are."

They were wrapping up in the kennels when Tricia came through, a smiling Biscuit at her side. His tongue lolled from his mouth. Drool dripped onto the spot Keely had mopped five minutes prior.

"Biscuit needs a walk." Tricia threw a flat look down at the dog, sitting happily on his hind. His tail moved faster than some windshield wipers. Certainly the ones on Keely's car. "He's amped up today. Think it's the weather."

This would be great for Keely's essay, an example that showed exactly how *passionate* she was about volunteering. "I've got it." Keely jolted forward, then swallowed down the stomach bile rising in her throat. She could use some fresh air.

"Are you sure?" Max stopped sweeping. "He's a lot to handle sometimes. Especially if he sees—"

"Max," Tricia said. Her tone was still neutral, but a warning lifted the edges.

Keely preened, following Tricia out through the side door.

She handed over the lead, a bone-shaped container of green waste bags hooked near the hand hold. "Usually we go to the end of the road and back a few times. You'll know when he's done."

Biscuit tugged on the leash, straining toward the sidewalk he must have been familiar with. "Won't one or two be enough?" Keely asked, tapping the waste bags.

Tricia shook her head. "You never know with him."

That was mildly concerning.

Steeling her spine, Keely gave a nod and let Biscuit pull her down the sidewalk.

They fell into a pattern of stop-and-go, Biscuit-runs-and-Keely-follows-miserably. Every blink hurt out here in the sunlight, and with each jolt her stomach turned over.

Definitely never drinking again.

"Let's stop here for a second," she pleaded. She bent over, resting her hands on her knees. There was a very real possibility she was going to vomit.

And, with her luck, Biscuit would eat it and then *also* vomit.

As if in confirmation, he let out a loud howling bark. The fur on his neck stood at attention, which pricked her own in turn.

She saw it all in slow motion: a squirrel, running across the sidewalk, with an empty candy wrapper in its mouth. Biscuit, distracted by the shiny new object and bolting after it. The leash slipping from her hand, her only tether to the dog in her care.

Panic flooded her limbs and spiked in her chest as she raced after him, calling his name. Whenever she got close, he would change direction, go back the way he came, or slide right past Keely's reach.

She was well off the path now, brambles and sticks shooting up from nowhere, scraping her legs and palms. Between her hoarse cries for him and the freshly blooming allergens being stirred by their chase, her throat was raw. Her breaths sawed in, in, in, but never out.

After the fifth near miss, Keely realized this wasn't going to work. She had to get help. Someone who knew what to do in these emergency situations, because that surely wasn't her.

Hangover or not, she sprinted back to the shelter. She could vomit later.

Though crying—she did that now.

She burst through the nearest door. "Help," she wanted to scream, but it came out as a yelp instead.

"Is someone there?" a familiar voice called. *Max.*

Of course it would be him, the logical part of her brain whispered. *It's always him. It's always going to be him who sees you at your most vulnerable, isn't it?*

Snippets of their conversation from the porch swing last night flooded back to her. God, she'd told him about her parents, hadn't she? It wasn't everything, but it was enough for him to use it against her, to dangle it in her face every time she let her guard down.

He rounded the corner. "Keely?" As he took her in, his jaw hardened. He picked up speed. "Are you—what happened?"

"Biscuit—he saw a squirrel—and it had—and he—took—" Her breaths were gasping, ineffective. Her words were no better.

Somehow, Max understood her anyway. "Hey, hey." Max took her face between his hands. Her head pulsed again, that same sweet pain as earlier. "Slow down," he continued. "Breathe. It's alright, Keely. We'll get him." There was a weird light to his eyes that stirred up her barely settled stomach.

She tried to pull away, but his fingers were gentling along her cheekbones, and she was suddenly too weak to do anything but stand here and stare up at Max Simmons. "This isn't funny."

"I'm not joking." He gulped, releasing her face. He rubbed his palms on the front of his jeans. "I'd never joke about this. I promise. We will find him."

Keely nodded, wiping her tears with her hands. Max ducked into the back room and came out with another lead, a bag of treats, and a squeak toy.

They took off.

She led Max to where Biscuit had gone off leash, pointed out where she'd last seen him. Her throat quickly went hoarse from calling his name, but Max made up for her fatigue. He was louder, his voice carrying farther through the trees. He squeaked the toy in intervals.

Keely shook the bag of treats, hoping Biscuit had worked up an appetite with all his running. "Has this ever happened before?"

"At the shelter? No."

Her lip trembled, and his eyes went wide.

"But it's happened back home," he said. "One of our goldens loves being outside. She'll do whatever it takes to spend all day out there, and if it's sunny? Game over. Once, right before I left for college, she got out. We couldn't find her. It really messed with my summer training that year. I couldn't concentrate on anything—" He glanced over at her, pressed his tongue into his cheek, and cut off the rest of his sentence.

"Did you find her? And if the answer is no, just—lie to me a little longer. I need hope."

He held a large branch out of the way, then paused on the other side of it. Was he waiting until she got closer to release it, so it'd hit her smack in the nose? "We're going to find him."

Tentatively, she stepped forward. It wasn't until she was well out of the way that he let go.

"And to answer your question, yes. Goose came back after two weeks with a horrible sunburn," he continued. "Do you know how rare it is for a golden to get a sunburn? We ended up having to shave her to treat it. But she was home." A small smile lifted the corner of his mouth. "Henry said it must have traumatized her too, because she hasn't run away since."

"Henry, as in your brother Henry?" They'd never had this long a cordial conversation, and Keely chalked it up to the lingering alcohol in her bloodstream.

Another item on her Reasons to Never Drink Again list.

He nodded. He gave the toy another squeeze and called for the dog.

"How *is* Henry these days?" Growing up, Max's brothers had been annoying extraneous distractions from her best friend, but she supposed they were men now—not unlike the one standing in front of her. Something inside of her jolted at the acknowledgment that Max was a *man*, and she tried to force the thought from her mind. "And the others ... Thomas and Jacob, right?"

"Right." The corner of his mouth twitched. "They're good. Thomas is married with a kid if you can believe that. Another boy in the family."

"So many *boys*," she murmured.

At Keely's half-amazed, half-disgusted expression, Max laughed.

They used to laugh together all the time in school, both at and with each other, but Max had barely entered puberty back then. This one now was somehow both softer and harder, lower pitched. It wasn't a bad laugh, as far as laughs went.

A *bad* laugh wouldn't make Keely's stomach churn with more of that same sickly-sweet pain.

His elbow brushed hers. "A totally different story in the Sinclair household, Miss Only Child."

"Not quite." His eyebrows shot up, and she laughed. "Vincent is eight. He was a complete surprise, obviously."

"Is he a genius, too?"

"If by genius you mean 'builds working model rockets from parts he finds at garage sales,' then yes, he is also a genius."

She shook her head and the treat bag as they stepped over another log. "*Biscuit! Tr—argh*!" She tripped on something hidden beneath the dead brush.

The bag of treats went flying, and her face was seconds away from scraping against the rough bark of an ash tree when hot, firm hands came around her waist. She wasn't falling anymore, but her stomach didn't get the memo.

"Careful," Max snapped as he spun her around. He sounded... not mad, but definitely not happy. His hands swept down her arm, fingertips running over her knuckles and palm. "You're so cut up. Is this from earlier, or the keg stand last night? Keely, you should have—"

"Max." Her heart was suspended in the space between beats.

"I'm serious," he muttered. "These are *bad*. You'll need some antiseptic, maybe gauze."

Her free hand—the one he wasn't holding—came up to grip his wrist. "Max. Listen."

"Keely, we need to—"

She gave up getting him to stop talking and did it for him by pulling her hand from his, placing it over his mouth instead.

His gaze snapped up. The tree cover doused them in shade, which explained why his pupils swallowed the golden flecks in his brown irises. His breath was hot on her palm, and while it *was* tender, it didn't hurt anymore.

He blinked, his eyelashes fanning over his cheek. His mouth moved against her skin. Like he was going to talk again.

Or kiss the center of her palm.

Listen, she mouthed. She didn't trust herself to speak. Not when they were more tangled than the brush along the path. Her hand was on his wrist, his mouth, and it was all too much.

Up ahead, she heard it again. The sound that had stopped her in the first place.

The faintest little bark.

As one, they took off running, down a hill, around one final curve in the path.

And there sat Biscuit, with his leash snagged on a downed tree, that shiny wrapper dangling from his smiling mouth.

They collapsed at his side, her knees sinking into the wet moss and grass.

She buried her face into Biscuit's fur, right at the back of his neck. His fur absorbed some of her tears.

Max was similarly emotional, words rough around the edges. "What were you doing out there, dude? You have a stuffed squirrel back home." He scratched behind Biscuit's ears, throwing Keely a carefree grin.

She found herself smiling back, just for a second. Max's pupils dilated further in the dim light.

Keely broke the moment, threading the leash onto her wrist and looping it around twice for good measure. As her pulse slowed, her body went heavy, limbs taking on twice their weight.

"Adrenaline's wearing off," she said, standing up. Then she groaned, because that meant the pain in her head and stomach would return soon too.

The three of them walked in silence to the shelter, and Max's mere presence seemed to calm Biscuit's frantic energy.

She wished the same could be said for her.

Most of the dogs were in the outside run when they got back, and Keely veered that way. When Max didn't immediately follow, she paused. "Aren't you coming?"

He shook his head. "I need to talk to Tricia about something."

Panic scratched at Keely's ribs. Max was going to tell Tricia what had happened, that Biscuit got loose, and Keely wouldn't be able to count this toward her scholarship application either. He'd already sabotaged her once with Matilda. Several other times, actually.

Maybe that was the entire reason he'd helped her: to watch her screw up. If he kept collecting little bits and pieces of her failures, eventually he'd have enough to complete the whole picture.

"Sure," she said weakly. She took a half step away from him.

It didn't feel far enough.

Chapter Seventeen

Max

"Your essay is flawless," Dr. Goff commended. "It's one of the best I've ever read, application or otherwise. I don't think you need to touch it." His stapled essay fluttered to the desk, landing next to another that was covered in red writing. *Ouch.* He strained to read the name, but Dr. Goff straightened it into a stack and it slipped out of view.

A clear sign to keep his eyes on his own paper.

"Really?" Max shifted lower in the chair. He was still getting used to coming to the career center. Everything was decked out in school colors, down to the free pencils waiting in a cup by the door like the condoms at the student health center.

After he'd spoken with Tricia on Sunday to tell her he'd be heading home for spring break, he realized he needed to stop in at Dr. Goff's, too. Mostly to see if he needed to stress about the scholarship while he was home, or if he could worry about something else instead.

Like his father. No one would tell him how bad things were, and Max had gotten so good at catastrophizing as of late that his mind wouldn't be able to settle until he saw it for himself.

"Really." Dr. Goff nodded. "And your track season is looking okay."

Okay was generous. His times were still sub-PR, and while he didn't subscribe to the harmful notion of needing to shave milliseconds with every race, he would have liked to be running faster than he was in *freshman* year. But the team overall was ranked well, upper middle of the pack, and Coach was pleased for now.

"Let's talk about your grades," she continued.

Max swallowed a groan. "What about them?"

One of Dr. Goff's silver-tinged eyebrows tipped upward. "You know I can *see* your grades, right?"

"Have they gotten any better since the last time I looked?" he asked wryly.

Her mouth pressed into a line, which Max took to mean no. He ran a hand over his hair. His mom would probably make him get a haircut while he was home.

"It's frustrating." He hooked a hand over the back of his neck and squeezed out some honesty. "I'm doing my best, but it doesn't feel like enough."

"Did you look into tutoring like I suggested?"

"That's not for me." This time, both of her brows went up, and he found himself continuing practically against his will. "I'm not morally opposed to it or anything. My little brother has dyslexia, and his tutors keep him afloat. It just ... I don't know. It always felt like cheating or something."

"Tutors don't just help you memorize the material, Max." She dug around in her desk and produced a pamphlet. "They provide study methods you haven't been exposed to before and help find what works best for you. 'Teach a man to fish,' that kind of thing."

She hovered it over his essay.

"I'll start after break," he said, and she made a happy little noise as she dropped it on top of the others and smoothed them into a pile.

And he meant it. If this was his only shot at the scholarship, and therefore fulfilling his dad's dreams, he would do whatever he needed to.

This way, when he saw his father in a few short days, Max could tell him the truth:

He was doing his very fucking best.

"Why wait?" Dr. Goff slid a paperclip in the shape of an airplane onto the stack. "They probably have some slots left today."

"I have practice," Max said. "Last one before break."

"Are you heading home?"

He nodded, his chest squeezing. He still had evening practice, the four-hours-and-change drive home, but clearly his heart was already there.

Chapter Eighteen
Keely

Your essay is flawless ... one of the best I've ever read.

It was all Keely had wanted to hear since the semester started. Longer, probably.

Only, Dr. Goff wasn't talking to Keely.

She peeked through the door again.

And yes, that was one Max Simmons sitting in the guest chair.

Did he have to be good at *everything*?

Keely hadn't meant to eavesdrop. She hadn't had this little detour on her to-do list at all today, but Dr. Goff had emailed this morning to let her know she'd finished marking up Keely's essay, and Keely wanted to grab it before campus shut down for spring break. She'd already informed her parents this would be a working vacation. She hadn't received a response.

She'd known Max's essay was decent—Dr. Goff wouldn't have suggested she read it otherwise. But from this glowing review, it *carried* Max's application. They were still well matched in extracurriculars (for now; if Max had ratted her out to Tricia like Keely suspected, she hadn't been disciplined for it yet) and as the counselor sang the praises of the tutoring center, Keely inferred she still had him beat in grades.

So they were basically even.

Which was not good.

Basically even meant she couldn't control the outcome. It would be in the hands of the selection committee instead of Keely's white-knuckled grip.

This was a problem Keely couldn't fix.

She either needed Max to *stop* being the school's track star—his sculpted uniform-clad body popped up in her mind and she wrote that off as highly unlikely—or she needed to get her essay on par with his.

If you have the chance, you should ask to read Max Simmons's essay, Dr. Goff had said, probably thinking Keely would do just that: *ask*.

Keely would rather have a hangover for a week than admit to Max's face that his essay was better than hers. Honestly, she was half tempted to call up Zoey's MIT brother again, have him swipe the essay from the cloud or wherever else it resided besides Max's laptop.

Keely's head tilted.

Now there was an idea.

One she could implement right now, if she was careful.

She wouldn't steal the laptop, of course. Just the essay. To see how he'd organized it, note where he was finding passion she wasn't.

In the office, a chair scraped the ground, and Keely ducked behind the corner. She caught the word *practice*.

Of course. She could follow him there, wait for him to change and head to the field, duck into the locker room with the all-access card Zoey had bequeathed to her for occasions such as these, *email herself the essay*, and sneak out unseen.

Easy as Pi.

She had too much to do today to have any other option. She was catching an early afternoon bus home. Her car had started making a weird noise on the way back from the shelter on Sunday, and she didn't trust it to carry her three hundred miles without stranding her on a lonesome mountain highway.

She checked the calendar on her phone one final time, slotted *ML* into the empty space (for Max's laptop), and tucked it in the side pocket of her backpack before slinking after him.

Keely trailed Max across campus at a respectable and unassuming distance, a familiar tickle forming at the base of her throat. The weather was turning, which for Keely meant she had maybe one more good week before springtime allergies decimated her ability to breathe through her nose. She added a note on her mental to-do list to preemptively start taking Claritin in addition to her vitamins.

Max scanned into the building, and she waited behind a large ash tree outside for thirty minutes to make sure the locker room had emptied.

Get in, email the essay, get out.

The halls weren't empty, but she didn't recognize any faces. It didn't stop her from holding her breath as she turned each corner, fully expecting Max to have somehow read her intentions and catch her in the act once again.

But she made it unseen and ducked her head into the locker room. The door squeaked on the hinges, and she winced.

"Hello?" she whispered. No answer, but maybe she should try

speaking at a volume someone could realistically hear. "Hello?" she called, a little louder.

The coast was clear.

She padded to Max's locker on silent feet. She'd expected him to put a padlock on it after the uniform shrinking, but it was thankfully still unlocked. His backpack hung from one of the built-in hooks. Seriously, why were these lockers so spacious? She pulled it down and unzipped it.

A change of clothes and spare socks, loose papers and one unlabeled notebook. Did he—a shudder rolled down her spine—use the same one for every subject? And she didn't see a planner *anywhere*, just crumpled protein bar wrappers and an empty (but thankfully clean) shaker bottle, eerily similar to the one that had tumbled over her laptop.

She pulled his computer from the insulated pocket and shoved the backpack onto the shelf at the top where more clothes rested. *What was he wearing right now?*

"Get it *together*, Keely," she muttered.

She threw open the laptop lid. Max's school email was on the page, and she scanned quickly for Dr. Goff's name, or **READ MY ESSAY HERE** in bold letters. Of course it wouldn't be that easy.

She blew out a breath so noisy it rattled the lockers.

Except—the rattling didn't stop when she did.

It took her a few seconds to register the noise from the hallway. Heavy footsteps coming closer, heading right toward her. Practice wasn't over already, was it?

Panicked, Keely looked for somewhere to hide. The laundry hamper was big enough, but empty. Not to mention the bacteria. The showers might be safe—emphasis on *might*—but she was out of time.

Gritting her teeth, she stepped forward into Max's locker and shut the door behind her.

Noises were somehow both muffled and amplified within this tiny space. She couldn't distinguish the voices other than that they belonged to two guys fighting about who forgot to grab the foam rollers.

Every footstep made Keely's pulse jump as they searched and found the sought-after equipment. But eventually they left, heading back to practice, and Keely was alone again.

She pressed forward.

The latch held.

"No," she gasped, pushing and pounding at the door. "*Nonononono*. Seriously. Come *on*."

She stuck her finger through the hole closest to the lock, but she couldn't reach the release.

Keely was stuck.

In Max Simmons's locker.

Her head fell forward, taking up a rhythmic *bang-bang-bang* against the metal.

Phone. Where was her phone? She tried to grab it from the side pocket of her bag, smushed against the back wall, but her elbow hit the side. She whimpered but persisted, curling her arm farther.

Her fingers gripped the edges of her phone. She tugged up and—

Lightning shot down her arm as her ulnar nerve met a metal wall hook at the exact wrong angle.

Her phone clattered to the bottom of the locker and landed near her foot, which was tingling from the aftershocks of hitting her funny bone.

Keely blew out hot air and rubbed at the tender spot. She could have planned this better.

Or at all.

Her breath turned the cramped space hot and humid. The holes in the door were big enough that she wasn't worried about suffocating, but small enough that she was getting mildly claustrophobic. Her legs cramped, and she lost sensation in her toes for how tightly her knees were locked. Which was not promising for rescuing her phone.

She persisted, and had worked it up to her ankle by the time the thundering started. This one was much, much louder.

Practice was over.

Dozens of jocks filtered into the room, voices twining and overlapping, shouting, laughing, cursing.

Footsteps drew near, and her throat closed. She shifted, and her head bumped the upper shelf. A panicked yelp slipped free.

The movement outside the locker slowed, shadows shifting like someone had touched the latch.

She bit her bottom lip hard enough that her teeth broke the skin, the metallic tang of iron filling her mouth.

Light flooded her hiding place as the door swung open.

Max stood in front of her.

And Keely was still clutching his laptop to her chest.

For a second, he just blinked at her.

In that second, she saw the full glory of a post-practice Max. A darkened strand of hair stuck to his forehead with sweat. It beaded at his hairline, glistened against the exposed skin of his neck, down the fronts of his arms. Even the darkened fabric beneath them didn't *completely* disgust her. His chest heaved slightly. He'd clearly worked hard.

Max tilted his head, his hand curling around the edge of the locker. Her stomach pitched, fingers tightening on the laptop.

He clocked it, his gaze dropping there. She spotted a flash of tongue as he licked his lips.

For some reason, heat flooded her cheeks.

Beyond Max's shoulders, voices got louder. He stepped closer to block the locker—and her—from view. The door shut a few more inches.

Her ribs constricted around a tight ball of panic. He wasn't going to leave her in here, was he? Surely that was illegal.

More illegal than sneaking in and stealing the laptop in the first place?

He didn't pull her out, divulge her breaking and entering or expose her to most-likely-naked men.

Instead, he pushed the door closed another inch.

Keely started to say the word *please*, but his head jerked in a quick shake.

No, he said without words. She would stay right here until he'd decided how to deal with her.

Right before she lost sight of him, he cocked his head to the side. It was the same playful movement she'd seen a dozen times. At the shelter. Outside the classroom, when her books had been swapped.

It was Max's challenge face.

Which meant this was very, very bad.

The locker snicked shut.

· · · · ·

Keely was completely at Max's mercy.

All she could do was wait and hope he was decent enough not to leave her in here overnight. Right now, she should be packing her last few essentials, grabbing road trip snacks from the convenient store by the bus stop, texting her mom her ETA.

Instead, she listened in on conversations, gauging noise levels to estimate how many team members had left the locker room. Which ones lingered.

Finally, after her toes were fully numb and she'd adjusted to her less-than-ideal oxygen saturation, the noise faded, and the locker room was empty.

Nearly. One single set of footsteps drew closer.

She readied flimsy explanations—they accidentally swapped laptops at the shelter this weekend and she only noticed today, despite having used it since then. Or she wanted to reimburse the cost of his ruined uniform, but she didn't know where to leave it so she tried to slip it through the slots but it got jammed.

When the door swung open and she was once again face to face with Max, she had absolutely nothing.

She stepped out and to the side, clutching the contraband laptop to her chest.

Max's eyes dropped there, and hers dropped...

Everywhere.

Aside from the bleached-white towel wrapped around his waist, he was *naked*. This was so, so much worse than post-practice Max.

Water clung to his chest, rippling over his smooth skin and dipping into the grooves between his muscles. And there were a lot of grooves—a lot of muscles. Pectorals, obliques, abdominals... others she couldn't think hard enough to remember right now.

She gulped. "You're..."

"Confused," he supplied, crossing his arms over his chest. His *bare* chest. "What were you doing in my locker?"

She couldn't answer. Her tongue weighed ten thousand pounds.

His eyebrows arched. "I'll ask it a different way. Why do you have my laptop?"

She tried meeting his eyes but got as far as his neck. She could *see* his pulse, a wild flutter at the base of his throat. Her tongue darted out as if to taste it.

"Keely," Max rasped, dark edges at the beginning and end of her name that scraped a Microplane over her nerves. He stepped closer. "I'd like an answer, if you don't mind."

"I—I was—" Her back hit the locker next to his open one, as much as her backpack would allow. She smelled him: sea salt, cedar, vetiver, something distinctly *Max*. As disarming as it was, she lifted her chin. "I was borrowing it." She gulped. "For research."

Max's hand splayed behind her head. His skin sliding over the metal sent a corresponding shiver down her spine. "For research," he repeated.

She nodded, and her hair snagged on his knuckles. He frowned at it, even as he gave it a light tug.

"Very important scientific research," she breathed. "Because I'm a scientist."

A noncommittal sound vibrated his throat as he drew closer. Closer.

"As a scientist, Keely, didn't anyone ever teach you ..." His mouth hovered over the hinge of her jaw. She bit her lip to stop her moan and tasted blood again. Max curled his other hand around Keely's hip. Which meant there was no longer one on his towel. "Not to touch what isn't yours?"

This was different from their normal pranks. His breath had never misted over the petal-soft skin below her ear before, and his mouth hadn't been this close to hers. To *her*.

If he'd been playing this dirty the entire time, he probably would have won.

Which reminded her.

"You—you're touching me right now," she argued, even as she let go of the laptop with one hand so her palm could hover over his stomach.

"I—" He tensed and stepped back. "Should've asked first. Sorry."

"Don't be." The words burned on the way out, the same way her skin did when he grazed it. "I was just going to say it seems a little—contradictory."

He tipped his head to the side. "You don't want me to stop?"

Her stomach tilted. "No," she whispered, the fingertip of her index finger brushing the groove in the middle of his torso. "You could even come closer, if you wanted."

He stepped forward again, pressing her into the locker with his body, and she gasped.

He was ... hard.

Max Simmons was hard for her, Keely Sinclair.

A whimper escaped her lips. She smashed them together but it was too late.

He hummed. His towel had to be coming loose, didn't it? "What was that, Key?"

Key.

She shook her head as heat soared up her spine. Her fingers climbed his chest, toying with the sharp jut of his clavicle right next to her mouth. She could lick it.

What would he taste like?

"Well, then," he murmured. "What if instead of asking you what you were doing here, I asked you not to leave?" Bright red splotches bloomed on his neck. He wetted his lips while staring at hers. "What would you say to that?"

What would she *say*? She couldn't *think*. Her mouth moved over words that wouldn't form.

He tsked deep in his throat. "Cat got your tongue? Color me surprised." His voice dragged over her skin and dropped into her lower belly. It was easy enough to imagine other scenarios in which he might also talk this way. Early in the morning.

Late at night.

His gaze traveled every peak and valley of her face, the lines and slopes. It may as well be his fingers, his tongue, for how vividly she felt it.

"You always have something to say. This little pink mouth of yours ..." He touched his thumb to the center of her bottom lip, gentling over the teeth marks she'd made earlier. His brows furrowed. "Drives me crazy with how much it moves."

The tip of her tongue flicked forward infinitesimally to make contact. She did taste him then, over the iron and over her fear.

"*Please.*" It sounded like her voice, but breathier, more desperate.

She couldn't distinguish his next noise from a growl or a groan or a grumble, but it spiked her blood pressure and turned her limbs to melted butter. She sagged against the lockers, and the hand that had been learning her lower lip wrapped around her instead, winding up under her bag to press against her back. Fingers slotted in the spaces between her ribs.

Something sharp dragged along her earlobe, quickly smoothed over with something softer. His teeth; the inside of his bottom lip. "Please, what, Keely?"

"Anything, anywhere, just—" She squirmed. Somewhere in the back of her mind, she vaguely registered the towel coming loose from his waist and fluttering to the ground. She was on fire. "*Please*," she said again.

"You want me to kiss you?" His nose bumped hers now, sliding up, back down until their mouths were millimeters apart. "Touch you? Strip you down like you stripped me?"

Max, her body whispered.

"Max? You in here?" The locker room door whooshed open.

Keely froze.

"*Don't come in*," Max called. His voice was hard as granite. As hard as he was, pressed into the soft flesh of Keely's hip. "I'm— we're not decent."

"Oh, uh." *Nolan*, Keely's brain supplied. "Got it. I'll … keep watch?"

Keely's head thunked forward onto Max's collarbone, face flaming hot. She tried to center herself, but her entire body pulsed, her underwear uncomfortably wet.

"I, erm—" she murmured into his chest. "I'm not really sure what that was."

"Same." He cleared his throat. "I need my towel."

"Right. Let me just—" She shut her eyes.

Her other senses came alive. The rustling of the fabric, the rasp of his breathing. Her heartbeat, loud and fast in her ears. What had they done? This wasn't on any list she'd made. Something she hadn't expected.

"I'm good," Max said.

She didn't give herself time to look him over too closely, lest she continue what they'd started. Instead, she shoved his laptop into his chest, scooped her phone off the floor of his locker, and got as far away from him as possible.

Chapter Nineteen

Max

Nolan rounded the corner, hands shoved into his jogger pockets and a shit-eating grin on his face.

"We're not gonna talk about it," Max muttered into the cavern of his locker. Fucking *peppermint*.

Still half-hard, his pulse rocketed violently through his body, memories replaying at warp speed every time he blinked.

Keely tucked into his locker, anticipation shining in her eyes.

Keely's hair scraping his knuckles.

Keely gasping against his neck.

He'd had her right here, pinned beneath him, his mouth raking across the velvet skin of her ear, the tiny hollow behind it.

He would have had *all of her* right here, if not for—

Nolan's smile widened. "Talk about what?"

Max's jaw clicked. "Thanks."

Nolan waved a hand to dismiss him and leaned against the wall.

Max dug for his backpack at the top of the locker and slipped the laptop into the pocket. Keely was obviously aiming to get her ink-painted fingers on his essay, probably to erase all traces of it and make him start completely over. He pushed aside images of that ink-painted little finger dragging over something *else*. Shoved it deep into the back of his brain, for examination at a later hour. Or never.

Max freed his briefs from his backpack and put them on. Modesty didn't exist in the locker room, and Nolan had seen it all before anyway.

"Did you need something?" Underwear in place, Max pulled the towel away and rubbed it over his hair.

"Oh, yeah. I wanted to see if you had spring break plans. We're going to Myrtle Beach. There's an extra spot in my car with your name on it."

What was Keely doing for spring break? Figuring out more ways to wreck his life, probably. She'd nearly done that earlier, when she'd moaned in his ear.

"I'm good." Chest tight, Max dropped the towel on the floor. "And you don't have to keep checking in on me every week. I'm a big boy."

Nolan pushed off from the locker, his shoulders bowing the slightest bit.

It was a sight Max was too familiar with.

For some stupid, unknowable reason, Keely's voice popped into his head, quiet and slightly husky from the alcohol at the party. *There's no sense in being mean for the sake of it, Max. The world has enough of that on its own.*

He cleared his throat and tried to be the opposite of mean as he pulled out a black T-shirt.

"Thanks, though. My..." He stared down at the fabric crumpled in his fist, then let it fall limply at his side and looked Nolan straight in the eye. "My dad. Is sick."

It came out choppy, raw, which might be because he'd never spoken the words out loud to anyone besides Coach. They tasted wrong. Bitter and sharp all at once.

Nolan's mouth tipped upside down, and his throat shifted with a swallow. "That blows. I'm sorry. I didn't know."

"I don't really talk about it." *With anyone.*

Raw emotion lit Nolan's eyes before it was gone again, smoothed over to a blank mask. "I hear you. Whatever you need, man. I'll follow your lead."

"I'm ..." Max searched for the right words. "I'd be okay if you asked about it. Sometimes." Nolan had reached out a hand to Max over and over and *over.* Max couldn't not take it anymore. It took more energy to fight him off.

The guy was *persistent.*

"You let me know if that changes." Nolan's nod was firmer this time, to match his words. "Even just a thumbs-down text or something."

"Thanks. For the invite, and for ..." The words were right there, straining against the cage of his teeth. Instead, he focused on the rest of his clothing spilling out from his backpack. "I just need to be home this week."

The drive between Ash Mountain and his hometown was four hours and thirty-eight minutes. Every time Max made it, he watched the clock and worried it would be the last time he'd see his father ambulatory. Awake.

Alive.

He should have been on the road already. Should have never left in the first place. Shouldn't have to come back a loser, with no secured funding and no chance at living up to his father's desires for him.

Dad had given up everything to raise Max, including his dreams. He'd ripped them out of his heart and planted them safely in Max's.

So Max would keep them safe. He had to.

It was his father's dying wish.

Which meant he needed to shove the encounter with Keely, the flushing on the bridge of her nose and just below her glowing eyes, somewhere deep down where it couldn't distract him.

He picked up his towel, crammed it into the wash bin, and shut the lid as firmly as he could.

· · · · ·

Visiting hours were technically over by the time he pulled into the hospital parking lot, but his mom had called ahead to the nurses' station, and one of them waited to sneak him back.

Dad was propped up in bed, cannula fitted snugly to his nose. Headphones hugged his ears. Probably listening to the *Red Rising* series on audiobook again. He tugged them off, smiling as he pushed himself up. Max resisted the urge to surge forward and help. His dad hated that, feeling broken and weak.

Max got *that* from him, too.

His dad coughed, but it wasn't wet or heavy. It sort of sounded liked a laugh. "I'm not gonna break, Max. Come hug your old man." There was color to his cheeks, more than on their last video call.

Max didn't hesitate anymore. He took three large steps across the room, slung his backpack onto the floor, and clutched his father in a fierce hug.

"I thought Thomas was supposed to be here," he muttered into his dad's shoulder. His oldest brother had moved his family closer for that exact reason, to alleviate some of the burden on their mother. They tried to time it so someone was always here, especially for overnight stays.

Max's dad clapped him on the shoulder before giving a firm squeeze. "He left when you called your mom. Between you and me, he needed a shower. And to spend time with his lady. Speaking of which ..." The suggestive tone clued Max in to where his dad's mind went.

So he changed the subject as he dropped into the chair beside the bed. "Home tomorrow?" Max hoped aloud.

Dad rolled his eyes, and Max couldn't help but notice the way the skin around them sagged. A tired you couldn't erase with enough sleep and sunlight. It went deeper.

All the way to the bone.

"Let's sure hope so." Dad lifted his arm, and an IV tucked into the back of his hand followed. "Do you know how annoying it is trying to sleep when this thing's pulling at you all night?"

Max snorted. "I can imagine."

"How was practice?"

One question led to dozens more, and they talked for close to an hour, catching up on Max's times and recent race results. At one point, Dad made Max retrieve a tablet from his bag and pull up the footage so they could review it together.

More often than not, Max forgot to watch the footage and instead focused on his dad, searching for any hint of his thoughts on Max's performance. Every twitch of the mouth or shoulders, watery blink or squinted eye was catalogued for Max to dissect later.

Whenever his dad tried to broach the topic of girls, even if he never mentioned any by name, Max steered it away. He wasn't ready to talk about Keely yet.

If it was the only mercy he received today, he'd take it gladly.

A few times, Dad talked his way into a coughing fit, and Max guided a cup with a lid and straw to his father's hand. Or offered tissues when some of it dribbled onto his chin anyway. If the wheezing persisted, he could hit the oxygen button to deliver more fresh air. Dad had that privilege now. Most patients in the oncology wing did.

Max had thankfully missed hospital dinner, and the fast-food cheeseburger he'd downed hours ago was long gone. So he raided the vending machines, letting his dad steal Hot Cheetos while Max flipped through channels. It settled on ESPN, and the rolling commentary between them became spare, choppy sentences before his father finally fell asleep.

Only then, with the lights of the hospital dimmed above him, did Max let his tears fall.

Chapter Twenty

Keely

Keely woke violently from a dream about Max Simmons. A particular *kind* of dream, one that picked up right where they'd left off in the locker room. Some sort of alternate universe, where they'd never been interrupted and Max followed through on his promises. Or were they threats? In the morning light of her childhood bedroom, she wasn't quite sure.

The violence itself arrived in the form of her little brother, Vincent, whose knobby knee was currently threatening to rupture multiple internal organs.

"Keely! You're here!" He bounced on her again, and she groaned, rolling out from under his weight. Vince was only eight, but gravity worked the same at any age.

"Vincent!" she croaked back, matching his inflection if not his volume. "You're yelling!"

Keely had made it to her childhood home last night just before midnight, so she hadn't had the chance to greet her little brother. She thought she was going to wake the whole house when she stepped into the dark hallway and stubbed her toe on a box.

He plopped down beside her. "Can we spend the *whole* weekend together?"

He already wore his school uniform, khaki shorts and a navy collared shirt. At least he didn't have his shoes on yet. He looked so eager, his tongue trapped between his still-growing-in teeth, hair sticking up in a cowlick their mother could never tame, eyes sparkling with childlike wonder.

"I'll be here all week," she told him, and his pure adrenaline was contagious, working almost as well as a cup of coffee.

An angry shout filtered through Keely's open door.

"It doesn't matter, Jason. Your lawyer was supposed to send the final draft over to my lawyer last week."

Keely and Vincent shared a look, and wordlessly, she lifted her covers so he could crawl in with her. She tugged the blanket over their heads. It didn't do anything for the noise, but they'd gotten used to drowning that out on their own.

She nudged him with her elbow. "I'm sorry I can't be here with you when they're fighting."

Vince's little shoulder, pressed against hers, gave a weak shrug. "It's not as bad since he moved out."

"Do you like his new apartment?"

Another shrug. "It's close to my friend Eli's house. We get to ride the bus together when I stay at Dad's."

"That's really cool," Keely said.

Downstairs, their mother's voice rose, words like *alimony* and *new girlfriend* flying over Vince's head and stabbing right through Keely's soft middle.

Her parents' marriage had never been perfect, and if she was honest with herself, this divorce was long overdue.

Growing up, Keely had known what was important to her parents by what they showed up for. It wasn't ballet recitals or soccer games but for awards ceremonies, honors programs, science fairs.

It was the only time her parents ever got along. They were so focused on her for one presentation, for one posterboard, for one single night, they stopped hating each other for a bit.

She swallowed. Would it be better or worse for Vincent, this way? "Mom's not being too tough on you, is she?"

"It's fine," he answered, which splintered Keely's heart into tinier pieces. After a second, he added, "Do you have to move to California?"

Tears filled her eyes, and she shut them, even though it was dark under her covers. "I love you, Vince, but, yes, I have to." Was that true? "I'll still visit all the time." Was *that*?

He nodded and rested his head on her shoulder. "I love you back. Can I come see you there? I wanna go far away sometimes, too."

"Of course. Where else would you go, if you could go anywhere in the world?"

And they talked about dreams and plans and faraway places—life outside of these four walls—until the yelling stopped.

Once it did, when they emerged from underneath the safety of Keely's covers, she got a whiff of coffee and shoved her brother off the bed to get to it faster.

So, naturally, he wrapped himself around her ankle, and she was required to carry him out of her bedroom and to the kitchen like that.

It was a *journey*. Boxes stacked precariously in corners, windows naked aside from the blinds. Shadowed impressions of paintings hung on bare walls, and it made every footstep, every breath, sound twice as loud in Keely's head.

Their mother stood at the counter in a cream-colored loose linen shirt, tucked into boyfriend jeans with fraying ankles. Her makeup was perfect, her jewelry minimal but effective to highlight the long lines of her face and neck, even if the skin around her eyes was red-rimmed after the shouting match.

Keely had inherited her dark blonde hair, the cerulean shift of her eyes, her petite frame. Keely's mother was the blueprint by which Keely measured her own success. Sometimes just looking at her made Keely's heart ache for how beautiful she was, how put together even as her life was torn apart.

How unlike Keely.

"I see your brother was successful in his mission." Mom took a sip of coffee. Her voice was hoarse.

"If his mission was to rupture my appendix, then sure." At a sharp pinch, she peered down. Vincent tried to pluck out another leg hair. "It's good to be home," she deadpanned.

"Vince," her mom chided. "The school bus will be here soon."

Keely grabbed a mug from the under-cabinet hook and poured herself a cup. Mom set out Keely's preferred creamer and slid the sugar canister across the counter. The movements were so practiced, she felt for a millisecond like she belonged.

Her phone chimed in her pocket, one of today's many reminders. The sooner Vince was at school, the sooner her mother was tucked into her office for work, the sooner Keely might finally be able to breathe.

"You don't have to wait around for me," she said.

Mom sipped at her coffee leisurely. "I took the day off."

Keely's heart skipped a beat. Was the fight with her dad that bad? "Why?"

Her mother gave her a sad smile. "It's been a while. I wanted you all to myself today while Vincent's at school."

Amidst Vincent's protest, Keely's mind whirred. An entire day of her mother's undivided attention, when they were both already tender? She wouldn't survive. She'd turn into a diamond from all the pressure. All the lies. "That's really not—you don't have to."

A finely manicured hand sliced through the air. "I insist," her mom said. "Now go get ready." Ronnie James-Sinclair didn't take no for an answer—even from her daughter. Was she keeping the Sinclair? Keely hadn't asked. "We'll get breakfast and grab boxes so you can pack your room."

Keely glanced down at her body, which now featured a red patch near her ankle thanks to Vincent's ministrations. She'd been planning to stay in her pajamas, a Woman in Science T-shirt and oversized joggers, all day. "What's wrong with this?"

"Nice try," her mom said, shooing her away. Keely didn't even get to go back for her coffee.

· · · · ·

Keely's parents had entertained the idea of divorce for years.

She remembered the yelling, the holidays and family dinners where Keely shrunk into herself because if she was small, quiet, likeable, a *good* kid, they wouldn't have anything to fight about.

The afternoons and weekends she spent at Max's were a reprieve. The noise in his house was laughter instead of shouting, and if something broke it was on purpose, or maybe it wasn't, but it was never from a place of anger.

Then Max moved, took Keely's safe place away, and she was alone.

Her parents discussed it seriously around that time, when Keely was thirteen, but it didn't stick. Ten months later, when Vincent barreled feet-first into their family, Keely understood why.

It became *when Vincent starts daycare, when Vincent starts grade school, when Keely finishes high school*, then *when Vince does*.

Now there was a sold sign in the front yard of the only home she'd ever known. It had been four months since Thanksgiving, when she and Vince had learned her dad was moving out. His things were gone before Keely went back to school, and her mother hadn't tried to fill the spaces. There were gaps in their family, and Keely didn't know how to fill those, either.

At least she could put off packing her childhood bedroom for a bit longer and focus on avoiding high school acquaintances in the grocery store instead.

She was pulling a box of Cinnamon Toast Crunch off the shelf when her mom laughed in disbelief. "No way. Small world, huh?"

Keely looked up and the cereal dropped from her hand. She may as well have swallowed an entire box of wheat squares *dry*. Because who else was at her hometown supermarket but the person who had her pinned to a locker the day before?

The same hand that had gripped her waist, her hip, caught a wisp of her hair with his knuckles, lifted to wave at her and her mother from the other end of the dry goods aisle.

She considered diving into the shelf to hide. Instead, she bent for the cereal box and fumbled it three times before it landed in the basket.

Mom tapped Keely's elbow with a sleeve of English muffins. "It's your old friend, Max. You used to be thick as thieves in middle school."

Max shoved his hands deep in his pockets. *Good*. She needed them out of sight, especially if—*why the hell was he walking over here?*

"How are you, Mrs. James-Sinclair?" He tipped his head to her mom. It shouldn't have done anything that he remembered his mother's hyphenated name. So *what?* But it made Keely wonder—did he remember how Keely used to hate it because it meant her middle name was a boy's name? Did he remember teasing her with it over and over again? *Keely James, Keely James.*

"Keely," he said.

She expected a smirk, but he didn't look capable at present. Purple smudges under his eyes, a shadow to the very edges of his jaw, messy strands of hair in all directions like he'd been pulling at it... Between last night and this morning, something had changed. Something was wrong.

"Just Ms. James now," Keely's mom said.

Max's gaze flicked to Keely. Her face went instantly hot. "I'm sorry to hear that."

"I'm not." Her mom snorted, and Max's mouth twisted like he wanted to match the expression but couldn't quite manage it. "You still run track?"

"Yeah." Max glanced down at his shoes. "Thanks for remembering."

"What school again?"

"Ash Mountain." Max gestured down to his hoodie. The cartoon bug that had been haunting Keely for months stared back at her, mocking.

"AMU? Small world," her mother repeated, nudging her. "That's where Keely ended up, too. About to graduate with a biochemistry degree."

Did she even need to be here?

"You don't say." Max licked his lips. They were colorless and dry, like he'd spent the morning pressing them into a firm line until all the blood had fled.

"Keely's headed for Caltech in the fall," Mom said. "She's already got a place lined up."

Sweat beaded on the back of Keely's neck. She still hadn't found a good time to tell her parents about the loan application. They were always fighting, or making passive-aggressive comments about the other, and she couldn't tell them separately, because whoever she told first would gloat, and whoever she told second would get their feelings hurt. She wanted to tell them together, but they weren't ever together these days. And, if she was really honest, she still wasn't sure she could face the horror of watching herself become another thing they fought about—another asset to be divided. And so the cycle went.

But for some reason the way Max was looking at her felt almost... encouraging? Maybe this *was* her chance to come clean. She didn't relish the idea of doing it right here in the cereal aisle, but she knew if she let this window of opportunity close, she'd find it impossible to open up again. Before she lost her courage.

"Actually, Mom—" Keely started.

"She's going to do great things. She takes after me, obviously. Not her sad excuse for a father," her mom continued, steamrolling right over Keely's attempted confession. Keely felt flattened out. "She's got so much potential."

The pressure on Keely's shoulders intensified, and she saw stars from the diamond she was becoming.

Potential.

In science, potential referred to the possibility of action. The split second before a boulder fell off a cliff, the last inch of a stretched rubber band. It stored all the stress an object was under, waiting for just the right conditions to release, to move, to fall. Currently unrealized energy saved for a later date.

But if there was a later date for realizing *her* potential, Keely worried it would never come. Her energy was already actualized. This was the best she could do, the thinnest she could stretch before ripping apart.

And it still might not be enough.

Max watched her closely. Was he going to rat her out, twist this around into some way to come out ahead? Later, she could deal with that. Just not right now. She shook her head, a silent plea.

His mouth twitched but remained shut, and rare gratitude pulsed behind her ribs.

Then she went and ruined it by saying, "I thought you lived in Elmwood."

"The Simmonses moved back last year," her mom interjected, a set of wrinkles appearing around her pinched mouth. "I thought I told you."

She pointedly did not. Keely would have remembered. Would have ... girded her loins or something.

Max coughed behind a clenched fist. "It's closer to St. Francis than our old place."

The hospital? Keely's gaze shot up, but he wouldn't look at her. Max's dad was a dog groomer and his mom was a bank manager. Did one of them have a late-in-the-game career change? And somehow squeezed med school, residency, and boards into the ten years they'd lived elsewhere?

"Dad had to close his grooming business," he added, and Keely's confusion deepened. Maybe his dad was working at the hospital now, but it didn't feel right. He'd *loved* those dogs, *all* dogs. She could still remember him coming home with a huge smile on his face day in, day out, telling them wild stories of his craziest clients. Max and his brothers used to fight over who'd get to lint-roll his clothes free of pet hair before they went in the hamper, because his mom refused to clog the washer with it. "So it was nice we could come back to a place everyone already knew, instead of having to start over."

"Of course." Her mom gave Max a sad smile. "How's he doing, by the way?"

"He's, ah …" Max kicked at a scuff on the linoleum, and his throat bobbed. "He's alright. I'm coming from there."

Coming from where? Keely had missed a vital piece of the equation. A big piece, if the yawning hole in her understanding was anything to go by.

Her mom's face softened. "I'm sure they take wonderful care of him."

"The nurses are great," Max agreed, voice hoarse. "And his doctor's really confident in this new treatment."

"Today's chemo is top of the line."

Her mother continued speaking, but all Keely heard was a high-pitched buzzing as the final bit of that equation slotted into place.

Chemo.

Chemo = cancer.

Cancer.

Max's dad had cancer. Or if *not* cancer, something equally as taxing and damaging that required chemotherapy treatment. She'd done a whole unit on cancer last year in biochem. Every data point from those research articles, five- and ten-year survival statistics buried in academic papers, tightened a binding around her heart.

"Well, we won't keep you." Her mom gave Max a quick hug, then bumped Keely with her elbow and gave a polite, under-the-breath cough.

"Nice running into you, Max," she murmured, crossing her arms against the sudden urge to give him a hug of her own.

His head tilted again, but he nodded. "See you around, Keely."

She stared unfocused at the shelf in front of her but tracked him in her periphery until he rounded the corner.

"Keely," her mom murmured. "Go grab some extra ground beef. We'll make them a casserole and you can take it over later."

The worst part was, Keely couldn't even be mad.

Chapter Twenty-One

Keely

She'd never been to the Simmonses' house. Not this one, at least. The one she'd visited a handful of times for pizza parties and birthdays was on the other side of town.

In middle school, when Max moved, it plucked him from her school. And his crude comment about her being a *nerd* had plucked him from her life.

Apparently, though, their mothers had stayed in touch—enough for Facebook friends and Christmas cards and an updated address now plugged into Keely's phone.

So here she stood on Max Simmons's new front porch, clutching a casserole dish to her chest like armor against her dumbest decisions. Her mom's car was parked on the curb, and she would have left it running for a quick getaway if she didn't know so much about carbon emissions.

She hadn't let herself think about what she would do if someone other than Max answered the door. She tried to avoid thinking about him at all, if she could help it.

Which she absolutely could.

Most of the time.

When she wasn't standing on his doorstep.

The door swung in, and Keely blanched. "Mrs. Simmons."

Faint lines—the same ones that graced Max's face whenever Keely weaseled especially far under his skin—bloomed at the corners of her eyes. "Virginia, please."

Keely pressed her mouth into a line; Max's mother, however, did not try to smother her own smile.

"No, no, it's okay. You can laugh. A woman named Virginia who *lives* in Virginia?" She rolled brown eyes the same color as Max's. "Original, I know."

Keely pulled the casserole more firmly into her chest. She needed to get this over with. "I'm not sure if you remember me, but—"

The sound that left the woman's pale, flat mouth was almost a scoff. "Don't you dare try that, Keely Sinclair. Bring your ass in the house."

Compared to the mid-move disarray of her own home, Max's was near pristine. Or maybe just lived in. Shoes kicked off by the mat, blankets hung precariously over the back of the couch. There was art on the wall, rugs underfoot, an air freshener tucked away somewhere doing its very best to mask the subtle scent of *dog* she recognized from the shelter.

Keely followed Virginia to the kitchen and sat the casserole on the counter. "My mom and I made this for you. It's a lasagna bake." She pulled the recipe card from her back pocket and sat it on top.

Was there something else she was supposed to say, an

explanation of sorts that she shouldn't have to worry about dinner when her husband was in the hospital?

But Virginia only nodded, letting Keely off the hook as she moved toward the refrigerator. "That's very thoughtful. We'll have that tonight."

When she pulled open the door, half a dozen other casserole dishes were stacked like little soldiers on the shelf.

Virginia didn't need Keely to explain something she knew better than anyone. She shut the fridge with her hip and dusted off her hands. "Now."

Now? Now, what? Keely hadn't expected a *now*.

Max's mom closed the space between them, throwing her arms around Keely for a hug.

Then the front door slammed, and Keely's teeth clanged against Virginia's collarbone as she jumped back.

"Mom. Whose car is that?"

Max.

Her pulse kicked up. If she'd come ten minutes earlier, she could have missed him altogether. And if she left now, it'd be obvious she was avoiding him.

Max came into the kitchen. He stopped short when he saw her.

"Mine," Keely said. "Well, my mom's."

Any hope that his sallow features were because of the poor grocery store lighting died out. He looked worse than yesterday; though his cheeks were still pale, more color rimmed his bloodshot eyes, and the stubble around his mouth was thicker.

He threw a set of keys onto the counter and propped a hand on his hip. "What are you doing here?"

"*Max*. Keely brought a casserole," his mom said, a warning clear in her tone. Outside, dogs barked in tandem long howls, and Virginia blew out a huff. She pointed at Max. "Make her feel welcome. And you—" she bopped Keely on the chin "—make yourself at home."

Max snorted under his breath, which set off Keely's alarms. If his mother found out about their ... animosities, it was only one step away from finding out about the scholarship. And Virginia might tell Keely's parents.

That wasn't an option.

So she improvised.

Keely smiled at him. The one she gave people who made her laugh or held the door open for her. Sincere and wide and showing far too many teeth.

For a second, Max only blinked, sluggish, like whatever was making him look that tired on the outside had started working on his insides, too. His throat bobbed. Then he came back to himself, giving his head a little shake as he looked away. "I need a shower."

"I can wait," she said in her most convincing tone. The one that, more often than not, got her whatever she wanted.

It worked this time too. With a sigh, Max flicked his gaze to his mother, then nodded. "Five minutes," Max mumbled.

As Max thundered upstairs, Keely found her way to the living room. A television was nestled inside light-gray built-ins, a talk show rerun playing on low volume with trinkets and coffee-table books tucked into the open spaces. On a higher shelf, one single trophy glinted in the sunlight. Max's, no doubt.

"He thinks he's so good," she muttered, then threw a glance over her shoulder to make sure she was still alone. She didn't know where the other Simmons brothers were, but in a family this big, people could appear out of thin air.

Framed photos stylized the remaining open spaces. One that looked like Max from here caught her eye, and she stepped closer to get a better look.

Her hand flew to her mouth. It *was* Max, fifteen-or-so years younger, running into the arms of someone Keely instantly recognized as Wade Simmons.

Zoey would classify Max's father as a DILF. Keely didn't let herself think about him in those terms, because the conventionally attractive features of light brown hair and a wide, sturdy set of shoulders were the same ones Max had inherited. He was the perfect amalgamation of his parents, two gorgeous people who had created, if she were being completely honest, another gorgeous specimen.

That was biology, and she respected the hell out of good genes.

She looked for more evidence Max hadn't always been so … how he was now. Max, posing with his brothers. Wade and Virginia's wedding photo, which Keely vaguely remembered from the other house when she was younger.

And Max mid-race, one muscled thigh stretched out in front of him, the other kicked back, timed in a way that made him look like he was floating.

But this wasn't Max. The photo was too grainy, taken before today's high-resolution cameras. The build was off, the shoulders not as defined as Max's.

Not that she knew Max's shoulders by heart. They were just fresh on her mind because she'd seen them earlier.

She took a step back, eyeing the lone trophy on the shelf above it. She went to her tiptoes to read the inscription:

1994 USATF NATIONAL CHAMPIONSHIPS
100-METER DASH
3rd PLACE
WADE SIMMONS

The truth smacked Keely in the face so hard, she gasped.

Max's dad ran track. At one point, his body had been honed like Max's, carrying him across finish lines.

And now it was killing him.

Memories slotted into place, recolored until they were the shade of a violent bruise, deep and dark and tender. *I don't need it any less than you*, Max had said about the scholarship.

He was telling the truth.

This was likely Max's only chance to show his dad that he'd followed in his footsteps—literally.

As she ran her fingers over the engraving, Keely's heartbeats pounded out in heavy thuds, almost rattling the foundation.

"Please don't touch that."

She snatched her hand back, curling it into a fist over her heart. Max stood in the open archway, wearing an expression she'd never seen before. A black T-shirt stretched over his chest and arms, and dark gray athletic shorts hugged his thighs and cut off several inches above his knees.

His hair was damp. It made her think of the water droplets that slid down the side of her face in the locker room, the ones Max followed all the way to the curve of her jaw. His mouth, his lips—

Neck hot, she stared at the floor. "I'm sorry."

"It's fine," he said. "Just . . ."

"Just what?" she prompted. There was an entire living room between them, and she couldn't decide if it was too much space or not enough. Every time she blinked, the last time they were alone together flashed behind her eyes.

"What are you doing here, Keely?"

His tone was still biting, and she grabbed at her opposite elbow to rub some warmth back into her suddenly chilly skin. "Your mom told me to make myself at home."

He remained unblinking. "And?"

Wasn't that enough? "And—I don't know. Could we talk for a bit? Just until she loses interest and I can sneak out."

His face was completely unreadable, and Keely, who'd been reading since age three, was more upside down than ever.

She bit her lip, then released it. It was still tender from the locker room yesterday.

Max blew out a slow breath. "Whatever," he said, jerking his chin toward the couch. "Sit down, I guess. We'll … *talk*. You're freaking me out standing there like that."

She sat on the end of the brown sectional closest to her. A little tuft of dog hair floated in front of her face.

Max plopped down with only a cushion between them, which was smart. Virginia might suspect something if he were any farther away. One eyebrow inched up his forehead. *You wanted to talk*, it seemed to say. *So talk.*

"Were you at the hospital with your dad?" she asked, then regretted it. Of all the topics, she had to pick the most uncomfortable.

A quick dip of his chin was all he gave her at first. She tried to convey her sincerity with her eyes, and he shifted on his cushion. "I've been staying there at night," he said eventually. "We usually take turns."

"You and your brothers?"

"Mom, too."

Her brows scrunched. "Weren't you coming from the hospital yesterday when we saw you at the store?"

He glared at the ceiling. "And?"

"And ..." Her mouth dried, and she tried to swallow. "That means you're taking *everyone's* turn at the hospital. Not just yours."

Through a breath, Max lifted and dropped his head on the back of the couch a few times, probably wishing it were a brick wall. "How did I ever forget how intuitive you are?"

She rolled her eyes at his implied insult, but something in her chest tugged all the same.

His head lolled to the side. From this angle, the sunlight turned his irises the color of hot, fresh caramel. It melted her into the couch.

"He ran track," she offered softly. She didn't have to specify. "When he was younger."

"He did a lot of things when he was younger. Healthier." Max's throat bobbed.

This was uncharted territory for them, a rubicon that Keely was terrified to cross. But she couldn't help it. Not when Max looked like he was on the verge of tears. "What happened?" she whispered. "I mean, how did you find out?"

He stayed quiet so long, she thought he wouldn't answer. "I'm sor—"

"A pain in his left knee," he said over her apology. "Do you know how often runners get those? How often *I*—" He sucked in a breath, ran a hand over his damp hair. She thought she heard his jaw click. "He ignored it. Thought it would go away on its own, with enough ice and Advil and stretching."

Keely blinked new moisture from her eyes.

"Then the pain moved to his hip, which again, is ..." Max

stared at his hands. "Not an immediate cause for concern when those are the two joints that take the brunt of the damage, anyway. Mom finally made him go to the doctor after six months of near-constant pain.

"They weren't planning to tell us anything until they knew for sure. Didn't want us worrying over nothing. Thomas's wife had just had the baby, and I was doing Olympic trials. They wanted me focused on that instead."

His voice dropped off. She wanted to pick it up, hand it back to him alongside the peace she wasn't sure she was actually offering.

"Max?" she prompted. "We don't have to keep talking if you don't want to."

He shook his head, and a drop of water from his hair hit her on the side of the neck. She pressed her fingers there.

"They were staying in the same hotel as me. For the trials. I'd gone down to meet them for breakfast that morning when I overheard them talking about it. It wasn't aches and pains. It was chondrosarcoma." Max said the word like it should have meant something to her. She wanted it to. He sounded so *sad*, so angry. Confused. "Bone cancer. It affects the cartilage around the bones. Hips, knees, shoulders ... all the places that already ache for runners. Even retired, out-of-practice ones."

"Is that why you didn't qualify?" As soon as the words were out, she wanted to snatch them back. This wasn't her business; he'd shared more than she'd expected already.

To her surprise, though, Max simply nodded. "I ... I couldn't get out of my head. Couldn't stop hearing that word. *Cancer.* Couldn't stop thinking about what it would be like if I made it to the top and he wasn't there with me. I lost my timing on the hurdles. Tripped. Fell. Busted my knee. Screwed my chances and his."

"I'm ..." She swallowed and swiped trembling fingers under her eyes. "I'm so sorry, Max."

He stared unseeing at the space in front of him. "Yeah," he rasped. "Me too."

Her body ached, her heart most of all. "He was good?"

Max let out a dry chuckle, but she didn't detect any humor behind it. "He could have been the best if he'd gone pro. But ..." He closed his eyes for maybe ten seconds, and Keely waited, studying the lines of his jaw as it flexed. When they opened, Keely swore his lower lashes were wet like hers. "My mom wanted a family. And Dad wanted Mom."

Warmth filled in some of the tender spots inside her chest. "That's sort of romantic."

His face twisted, clearing of any lingering emotion. "That's *ridiculous*," he countered. "He was about to reach his prime, about to be one of the *best* in the *world*. And just—gave it up. And now he'll never get there." He scoffed, rolling his eyes.

"I'm not sure either of them sees it that way," she said gently.

He flinched, and she murmured an apology. They did have a line, apparently, and she'd crossed it.

Awkward silence filled the room, and she was about to heave herself off this heavenly sofa when he said, "I can give him another go. By winning the scholarship."

"'Give him,'" she echoed, sitting up straighter. "Max, that's not your responsibility."

"Isn't it?" His chest heaved beneath his T-shirt.

She pointedly did not look.

He rested his forearms on his knees and took in a deep, shaking breath. "I have to do this for him." He spread his palms. "He's my *dad*."

His voice broke.

So did her heart.

Before she could talk herself out of it, she leaned over and squeezed his knee. Electricity still lingered between them from the locker room, but she didn't mean this as anything other than a show of support.

He stared up at her from under charcoal lashes. At this angle, all she could see were the sharp lines of his face, his nose. She recalled it skimming the space behind her ear and shivered.

Max's pupils expanded.

This was a mistake. The party, the locker room, coming here today.

She'd vilified Max for so long in her head—from the start of the semester, if not longer—but he was becoming a person again before her eyes. And Keely wasn't mean to people. She was never deliberately harmful or hurtful. It wasn't in her nature.

Which meant Keely had some capital-T Thinking to do for the rest of spring break. She'd be sure to pencil in some time between packing up her childhood bedroom and figuring out how to win the scholarship if she couldn't destroy her biggest competition.

She pulled her hand away and smoothed it over her thigh.

"I think your mom is plenty distracted by now." She stood up. When had her knees turned to jelly? "I should go."

Max stood too.

She held up a hand. "You don't have to walk me out."

He mimicked her hand gesture. "Don't flatter yourself. I'm getting water." He was still hoarse. Water would be good for him. But there was a tilt to his lips that hadn't been there before. He inhaled, his lips parting.

A cacophony of sound cut him off. "*Duck*," Virginia yelled.

Keely, as instructed, ducked.

And Max—Max threw his head back and laughed.

She was thankful she hadn't heard the sound before, because she wouldn't have gotten nearly as much studying done this semester. Her stomach tightened, her skin too. Her heart might burst right out of it soon.

"What?" she hissed, looking up to make sure nothing was about to knock her out.

He swiped a finger through his tears of amusement. "Nothing, it's just, Duck is—"

"Duck! Heel!" Virginia yelled from the kitchen, but it was no use. What sounded like a dozen paws skidded across the hardwood, and Keely tried to smother her smile as two fluffs of sunshine rounded the corner, hopping over each other to reach Max.

And then they saw *her*.

She was enveloped in graying fur, rough wet tongues. A sharp pain pinched her heart. She missed the shelter dogs, every last slobbery toy and ruined shoelace. Farah Pawcett, who had literally eaten out of Keely's hand last week. Even Biscuit, with his vanishing acts and rancid odors.

"Duck. Goose." Max hooked a finger in the blue collars peeking out of the shiny golden coats. "Easy, or she won't come back."

Did he *want* her to come back?

There were more pressing questions. "Your dogs' names are *Duck* and *Goose*?"

"Give me some credit. I was obsessed with *Top Gun* when we got them." He looked at her, his lashes throwing more shadows on the skin beneath his eyes. "I'll keep them back, if you still want to leave."

She did. She definitely did. "I'll see you around?"

"Only if you're lucky," Max said back.

Keely rushed out before he saw her smile.

• • • • •

Keely was going to die. Death by a thousand cardboard box cuts.

She should have started packing sooner. She should have driven her own car home. At least then she'd have an escape plan.

Mom had instructed her this morning that anything left here when Keely went back to school would either be put in storage or thrown out, at her parents' discretion. So Keely now had the logistical nightmare of trying to figure out her save-in-a-fire items, what she could squeeze into her suitcase and duffels and take on the bus with her.

Currently, her entire bed was covered with save-in-a-fire items.

She pulled the cork board off the wall above her desk. She'd have to disassemble it, tuck her photos and ribbons inside her textbooks for safekeeping, and trash the rest.

Something fluttered to the floor, probably a paper or pamphlet that had started in a corner and got shoved to the back over time. She didn't often let things fall through the cracks this way, but there was a first time for everything.

She picked up the picture. Her heart catapulted into her throat.

A younger version of Keely stared back at her, arm looped around the shoulder of a boy with a gap in his teeth and mischief in his smile. This was taken at Max's old house, near the backyard creek where they wasted sticky summer afternoons. Ice cream speckled the tip of her nose, no doubt placed there by the owner of that mischievous look.

They were so *young* then. Things were so much simpler. It made her sad for the version of herself who stood here now, who couldn't honestly remember the last time things were easy.

Tears stinging her eyes, she tossed the photo toward the garbage.

Chapter Twenty-Two

Max

Max understood how Keely had felt standing on his front porch the other day. His legs twitched with the urge to run, to keep campus Keely and hometown Keely in two distinct boxes in his mind.

But her mom had made his family a casserole, and his mom sent him back with the dish the next evening. Who the hell uses glass bakeware? Everyone knows you're supposed to—

The door swung in, and Keely blinked in surprise.

"Use disposable next time," he barked, thrusting the dish at her. "So I don't have to bring it back."

She didn't take it. Instead, her lips pressed into a line so flat, the color disappeared. "Disposable is bad for the environment."

A dry, humorless laugh slipped out. "Yeah, well, ease of use is generally preferred over environmental impacts when someone's dying, so..."

Her gaze shuttered. "Max, I—"

"No." He shook his head fiercely. Told himself that was the

reason he saw stars when he looked back at her. "No, don't apologize. That was on me." He blew out a heavy breath. He still wasn't used to being this vulnerable with anyone, let alone Keely. "I thought my dad might get to come home for a bit between treatments. It was supposed to happen while I was off, but his doctor thinks it's too risky. I'll miss having him home by a few days. And that's …" He swallowed, ground his heels into the doormat inscribed with a calligraphed *S*. He was splicing himself open all over it. He hoped the Sinclairs had stain remover. "I'm just upset, I guess."

"Of course you are." There wasn't a lick of sarcasm or contempt in her tone. Her eyes.

"I still shouldn't have snapped like that."

"You shouldn't have," she agreed, and the back of his neck turned hot. "But I understand why you did." Her brows pinched for a second before smoothing back into two perfect lines. "Do you want to come in?"

Max stepped through the front door and was transported back ten years. Everything was largely the same: professional portraits of Keely and, Max guessed, Vincent on the wall; orderly, impeccably clean shelves and furniture arrangement.

There was one large difference, though.

He toed one of the boxes. "You're moving."

One tight dip of her chin as she called to someone somewhere else in the house that "Max is here." How many times had she screamed those same words? To him, she said, "Byproduct of the divorce. They're splitting the profit."

He followed her to the kitchen, where more labeled boxes stacked neatly in the corner. She took the casserole dish from him, then braced her hands on the counter.

"Do you want a beer or something?" She pulled open the fridge. "I thought we could talk in my room."

He raised an eyebrow, but based on the rigid set of her shoulders, she didn't mean anything by it.

Not that he *wanted* her to mean anything by it. "I'm not drinking right now," he said instead.

Keely paused with her hand extended into the cavern of the refrigerator. "But, at the party—"

"I told you." He shrugged, fingers clenched into fists in pockets. "It was Sprite."

She blinked at him several times, and when she bent back over, a pink flush climbed her neck. She pulled two ginger ales from inside and shut it with her hip. Her shirt was oversized, advertising something called WIS, and hung all the way to her thighs.

He tried very hard not to imagine it without leggings underneath as he followed her upstairs.

There was enough mess in this one room to make his entire house look *tame*. Clothes spewed from the open closet and dresser drawers; papers and books piled so high on the desk, he didn't walk too close in fear of toppling them. The bed was also covered; this would have to be a standing conversation.

To his surprise, Keely went to the window, setting her soda on the sill, to pull it open and slide the screen to the side. The movements were practiced, without noise.

Max feigned a gasp. "Are we *sneaking out?*"

She threw a foot onto the ledge, the corner of her mouth lifting. "Sitting on the roof hardly constitutes sneaking out."

Her room faced the backyard, and Max appreciated the view. There was a large oak tree, though there was a new bench and flower beds around the base, baby blooms sprouting up in polka dots of color. The fence had recently been painted, the yard mowed for likely the first time this year.

She pulled something from her pocket and held it out for him. "Look what I found."

"*Whoa.*" He remembered this picture very well.

This was the day his parents told him they were moving. Away from his life, away from Keely. His dad had found a storefront for his grooming business that was too good to pass up. Three weeks later, he was gone, and Keely wasn't his friend anymore.

"I went to throw it out, but ..." She shrugged.

"But what?" He nudged her with his elbow, hoping to knock loose whatever she was holding back.

It seemed to work. She shuffled around to face him, her breath coming the slightest bit faster. That same pink flush was back near her temples. On the tip of her nose.

He hated that he noticed.

She cracked her soda open, took a dainty sip that still managed to dribble onto her chin, and rested it on her knee. "Where did we go wrong, Max? What happened to those kids?"

"You mean, why did we stop being friends?" When she nodded, his chin dipped. "I moved schools, and we stopped talking."

Her mouth quirked. "That's not exactly how I remember it."

What else was there to remember? He had been showing promise with track, and his parents wanted him in a school with a larger sports program. Combine that with the storefront opportunity and the need for more space, for Max and his brothers and their sports and attitudes, and it was an easy decision.

Her voice pulled him from his thoughts. "I heard what you said."

"I didn't say anything," he said through curled lips.

"Not—not today. Back in middle school. When you were talking with Jackson Crawford. He called me a nerd. And you ... you agreed with him. You *laughed at me* with him because I liked science. That's why our friendship ended."

He almost dropped his soda. "*What?* Keely, are you for real?"

"Yes." Her gaze narrowed. "Just because it's not important to you doesn't mean—"

"No," he interrupted again. "The reason our friendship ended was because I moved schools."

"No," she persisted. "You abandoned me." The words sliced hot through his gut. "We were in all new classes that year, and I didn't have any other friends. Then you got—" she cut herself off and looked down at her hands, clutching her drink "—athletic, and made new friends, but I didn't. Which would have been *fine*, if the one friend I had hadn't made fun of me behind my back."

Her voice was raw, and her eyes looked wet, two things Max didn't care for at all. He lurched closer, the roof's pitch making everything more unstable than it already was.

"I'm not—I'm not dismissing this. I just need to know exactly what you think you heard that day." It was coming back to him in pieces, but something told him he had one chance to get this right.

"It was after third period, the day of the pep rally. We were meeting up so we could walk to the gym together, but by the time I got there, you were already on the way with the cross-country guys. I called out to you. You didn't hear me. I was about to tap you on the shoulder when Jackson said, *Keely's such a nerd*. I heard it clear as day. And you agreed with him."

The memories came faster now, still hazy. He gritted his teeth and tugged them free. "Did you *hear* me agree with him?"

She nodded, but her mouth held a hint of doubt, listing to the side. "You laughed. Said *yeah*." She pitched her voice lower, trying to mimic him.

If he wasn't still so confused, he would have thought it was endearing. Maybe even cute.

"Keely, I wasn't... I was laughing at *Jackson*, not at you." He ran a hand through his hair, using the condensation from his can to slick back the strand that always fell onto his forehead. "I was *embarrassed* for him because he wouldn't ever be as smart as you. Because he thought calling someone a nerd was some great big insult."

"It *was*." She wiped hastily at her face, and Max's stomach dipped like he'd fallen off the roof after all. "To me, it was." She sounded so, so quiet. "Especially if my best friend agreed."

"I ..." He didn't know how to finish that sentence. But if he stared at Keely for one second longer, on the verge of tears with the tip of her nose turning pink, he was going to say something else he'd end up regretting.

So he touched her knee.

A tear clung to her lower lashes, and he pulled his hand back so he wouldn't wipe it away.

"I'm sorry." He pressed a hand to his chest. The cold from his drink seeped through and sent a shiver crawling over his skin. *Good*. Let him focus, let him be acutely aware of his next words. "I didn't think about how my actions would come across. I didn't really think about my actions at all. And I'm sorry if they negatively affected you. If, at any point since then, what I said or laughed at or agreed to made you think you're anything less than fucking *brilliant*, Keely Sinclair."

He was touching her knee again—when had that happened? He peeled his fingers away and wrapped them around his ginger ale so tightly the aluminum dented.

She cleared her throat, delicately, and Max blew out a long, slow breath.

"Thank you," she murmured. "I accept."

"You don't have to."

"I know." She took a sip, so Max did too, and the bubbles, oddly enough, soothed the burn in his throat. "My turn."

"Your ... turn?"

"I'm sorry about your dad," she said. Max's heart ran intermittent sprints in his chest, racing and calming in endless cycles. "And for everything I've done this semester that contributed to any extra stress, either directly or indirectly. I didn't know."

He shrugged, dangling his can between his knees. "I wanted it that way."

Her head tilted as she studied him. He remembered that look, her focused intensity. "Does it bother you? Me knowing now?"

He shook his head, and the truth took him by surprise. "If anything, it probably helps my cause. Now you know why I'm such an asshole."

"What's my excuse, then?" There was a teasing, melodic note to her voice. She licked her lips, leaned a hand behind her and stretched out. She was practically lying on the roof. Her socked foot brushed his tennis shoe.

Carefully, he stretched out too. Coach expressly forbade any and all stupid shenanigans during the season, and roof sitting topped that list. He bumped his shoe to her ankle. "You tell me."

"My parents are—" she rolled her eyes "—not really fun to be around right now. Which is fine. I'm sure I'd be grumpy if I was splitting my life in half too. Nobody gets married thinking divorce is an option."

"You don't have to be cordial with me. You never have before."

"Then it *sucks*," she said. She lifted her hand toward the backyard at large. "It really sucks that they say I can tell them anything and every time I try, they make it about themselves. Or the other person. And before I know it, they've sent me off with a message as a go-between without actually bothering to check what I needed in the first place." Her cheeks flushed, and her voice dropped low enough that he barely heard her. "I ... I told them I already had a loan for grad school, but I got denied, and I haven't had a good opportunity to tell them. They're too busy griping about how their lives are falling apart to notice that mine is too. Pursue Your Passions is, truly, my only shot. And yours."

It was quiet, save for the subtle sounds of spring. Birds tucking in for the night, trees swaying, a dog barking in the distance.

Maybe there wasn't a solution right now, but at least everything was out in the open. She wouldn't need to hide in his locker again to steal his computer, then nearly end up on his lap.

Okay, so everything *wasn't* out in the open. They still hadn't discussed whatever that was.

Before he could decide if he wanted to, Keely tapped his foot again. "Hey. We had an entire conversation and didn't push each other off the roof. Does that mean we're friends or something?"

"Friends," he murmured. "We used to be pretty good at that."

The night was almost entirely indigo now, light spilling out from her bedroom and casting a halo around her silhouette. "We could try it again?" Keely said. "Since we're both so much older and wiser."

"You forgot more attractive."

Her laugh echoed out into the silence. "I said what I said."

Max was having a surprisingly good time, but he needed to head home to prep for yet another night at the hospital. Just because his dad couldn't come home didn't mean they couldn't eke out every possible second together.

They crawled back through Keely's window and, as she replaced the screen, he eyed the mess again with—he could admit now—pure judgment. "You have a lot of crap, Key."

She groaned, latching the window back. "Please don't remind me. I need to get all of this back to campus somehow, but my car was acting weird. I rode the bus here." White-hot panic shot through his bloodstream. *The bus?* She'd taken that crumbling cesspool of public transportation?

"Everything I want to keep," she continued, "I have to take back to campus with me. As far as *getting* it there..." She sighed, flipped one of the cardboard box lids. "How much do you think it'd take to ship all this? A few hundred?"

"I'll give you a ride," he said, and Keely froze with her hand inside the box.

"That sounds like a horrible idea. We'll kill each other before we make it to the highway."

"Friends don't kill their friends, Keely." At least, he didn't think so. It'd been a long time since he'd had one. Maybe the rules had changed. "You said it yourself. I could have just as easily pushed you off the roof, and I didn't. Doesn't that count for something?"

She still didn't look like she trusted him, which, how could he blame her? All they'd done for weeks was figure out ways to sabotage each other.

"I'll let you control the radio," he enticed. "And you can share your location with whoever. Zoey or—or Sam. Whatever you need to feel in control of the situation. I know how much you like control."

Her eyebrows tipped up.

He rolled his eyes. "Not like that." He thought about it for a second, all he'd allow himself. *Okay, maybe a little like that.*

She pressed her lips together, but the color just fled to her temples. Then she crossed her arms, cocking her head to the side. "*Whatever* I need?"

Max already regretted this very, very much.

• • • • •

Max and Keely pulled out of her driveway bright and early the morning they were due back on campus. He'd had a great week spending time with his family, especially his dad. But seeing him so frail made Max anxious to kick his training into gear. Tackle the hurdles again. Act like a teammate for once.

He had to prove to his father that all his sacrifices—the time passed and money spent and dreams tucked away—were worth something to Max. He wouldn't waste the opportunity. The medals were right there. His name was practically already on the inscription.

"Jesus, Max." In the passenger seat, Keely's knuckles were bone white around the handle. "Slow down. Cops are insane through here."

He let off the gas.

"Thank you," she said primly, and in his periphery, her hand fell away. "Where's the fire?"

Max shifted, trying and failing to roll out the tension in his shoulders. "I just—wanna get back to campus, I guess. Every time I see my dad, I . . ."

"He inspires you," she offered.

If he was being honest, he was still getting used to talking with her like this. Having so much of what he usually kept private on full display for her. She had an X-ray view of all the bones that constructed his skeleton. Now she knew exactly how to break him.

"Yeah," he said. "The running stuff I can fix in my sleep—"

"Humble," she blew between her teeth.

"But I'm still worried about my grades. I meant to set up an appointment with the tutoring center before I left but I got, uh, distracted." He left out the part where *she* was the distraction.

A noise of understanding floated to him, and when he spared a glance at his passenger, she was gazing out the window, lost in thought. Figuring she was done being civil, he reached for the volume knob to turn up the music.

Her hand shot out, wrapping around his wrist.

Electricity sparked along his skin and the car jerked to the edge of the lane.

Keely snatched her hand back. "Sorry, I was just—"

"My fault," he grunted.

She let out a soft sound, almost like a moan, and Max resorted to counting the lines on the highway to stop imagining that noise in other scenarios.

"I could—I could tutor you."

He wrenched the wheel, and after a small squeak from Keely, reduced his speed again. Then set the cruise control. Just to be safe.

"*You?* Tutor *me?* What's the catch?" Because there had to be one. He knew her too well by now. Reciprocation and retaliation were how they evened the score between them. He pushed, she pushed back harder. Maybe that's what the shock was whenever they touched: friction.

They were bound to start a fire any day now.

"I need help with my essay," she finally admitted, and there was so much shame coloring her words he thought he'd misheard her for a second. "Dr. Goff says it's what's holding back my application. I can't get it right."

This quirked his eyebrow. "What does she say is wrong with it?"

"Passion," Keely muttered, as flat and monotone as possible. "I don't have it."

He found that difficult to believe. He'd seen her face light up when she was explaining quantum mechanics to first graders.

This was another one of their push-and-pulls. Max was vulnerable; Keely was vulnerable back.

Which meant he really didn't have any other options.

"Sure," he said. "I can help you." Another thought had a smile tugging at his mouth. "Does this mean the prank war is over?"

She ran her hands over her thighs before clasping them politely in her lap. "I'm sure the person most deserving will win fair and square."

Max glanced at her, a grin lifting his mouth. "Do you mean that this time?"

Keely smiled back, and his heart took off in a sprint. "Guess you'll have to wait and see."

From: Max Simmons (mbsimm01@amu.edu)
To: Keely Sinclair (kjsinc01@amu.edu)
Date: Sunday, March 15
Subject: essay

Just ask next time. My locker still smells like peppermints and it's been over a week since you were in there.
  PS: This is too formal. Text me. My number's in my sig.
  Attached: pursueyourpassions_essay

From: Keely Sinclair (kjsinc01@amu.edu)
To: Max Simmons (mbsimm01@amu.edu)

Date: Sunday, March 15
Re: essay

The aroma of peppermint promotes focus and concentration, reduces headaches, and soothes upset stomachs.

PS: thank you for the ride back.

From: Max Simmons (mbsimm01@amu.edu)
To: Keely Sinclair (kjsinc01@amu.edu)
Date: Sunday, March 15
Re: Re: essay

Does your tummy hurt all the time? Might want to get that looked at. www.ashmountain.edu/campus-clinic

PS: you can thank me by TEXTING ME. seriously. I have a big assignment in motor development and I'm totally lost on where to start.

From: Keely Sinclair (kjsinc01@amu.edu)
To: Max Simmons (mbsimm01@amu.edu)
Date: Sunday, March 15
Re: Re: Re: essay

Thank you so much for the link. I went ahead and signed you up for a men's health screening, which should not take the place of your monthly testicular checks, by the way!

PS: texting you now.

Keely

I'll have you know I have a perfectly normal stomach. I mainly use peppermint to stay awake after I've exceeded my daily caffeine limit

Max

And I'll have *you* know I have a perfectly normal prostate

Keely

But how do you actually know, Max? Do a lot of self-exploration?

Max

Don't sound so surprised. Figured you were used to backdoor action, since you usually have that stick up yours

Keely

Keely

What's the assignment?

Max

Meet me at the library. It's easier to explain in person.

Keely

Tomorrow around 3:30?

Max

4? I have physiotherapy until then.

Keely

See you there. with coffee I hope?

Max

...

Max

I'll see what I can do

Chapter Twenty-Three

Keely

Keely's foot bounced wildly under the table. Today, Tuesday, was the first day of her tentative truce with Max. They were going to "work together." Whatever that meant.

They'd managed to make it back to campus okay this past weekend. He didn't leave her stranded, even though she had to pee twice and they stopped for food once. He didn't "accidentally" drop her fries or loosen the lid of her drink.

She was still half convinced it was all an elaborate ruse, that he was planning a bait and switch. That had to have been why, when Max appeared in her line of vision with a Q-branded coffee in his hand, her heartbeat spiked.

His mouth was set in a firm line. "Why the hell do you study in what is essentially the library's attic? There are so many open tables on the first floor." He handed over the coffee, then set the shaker bottle, hanging from his pinkie, on the table before thrusting his hands in his pocket.

She frowned. "Did you get a—?"

He pulled his hand free, revealing not one but two paper straws. "In case you don't finish mainlining your drink before it disintegrates." He pulled out the chair across from her and sat down.

Even she didn't possess that much forethought. Keely unwrapped one straw and stabbed it in. "I like this spot because it's quiet." She eyed him through her lashes. "I can't hear myself think down there."

He wore normal athletic gear in his signature dark, brooding colors. A flush to his cheeks gave him more life than she was used to. It was how he'd looked after his race. And in the locker room.

"You came from physiotherapy?" she said, shutting down the recurring thought of pleasure-filled Max.

He nodded, pulling his laptop from his backpack. "I go twice a week." He slung his bag in the open chair, and his face returned to its hard set.

"Are you still working through the injury from the trials?" Why couldn't she stop asking questions? And why did she keep holding her breath, waiting for his answer?

"It's routine after an in-event accident." He uncapped his protein smoothie, and when Keely eyed it warily, he pulled it closer. "Guided stretching, making sure none of my tendons are too tight or too loose. Checking the cartilage, that sort of thing. Coach has me keeping an eye on it. It makes the idea of hurdles ..." He glared down at his hands—or maybe his legs. "Not something I've been focusing on lately."

"Does it hurt?"

His shrug was too tight. "I'm used to it."

That wasn't an answer.

She took a sip of coffee. The slightly burnt caramel, double espresso, and oat milk made her serotonin soar. Keely blinked. "How did you do this?"

"What?" he said, too casually to not actually know what she was talking about.

"Max," she said through an incredulous laugh. He'd gotten her go-to coffee order *exactly right*.

"I took a guess," he insisted.

She gave him a flat look.

He opened his laptop. "I asked the guy for your usual, alright?" He chicken-pecked around on his keyboard. "I figure you're there enough, they'd know your order by name. I had to get on your good side if you're going to help me with this assignment."

Right. He wouldn't get her coffee order exactly right and bring her extra straws just because they'd had a few charged moments.

She flipped to a fresh page in her Miscellaneous notebook and uncapped her pen, a neutral black. Fitting for him. "What's the assignment? You said it's for your motor development class?"

Max dipped his chin. "We're given a profile of a child at three different stages of their life, plus stressors and outside factors, and asked to diagnose them." He flipped through his singular notebook, pages sticking out and dog-eared seemingly at random, until he found what he was looking for and spun it around.

She skimmed the page. "You're basically playing *The Sims* for a class assignment."

"No wonder I'm struggling. I'm not much of a video game guy." He ran a hand through his hair, and she swore she heard it, the friction of his rough palm over the silky strands. She remembered that hand on her hip, searing through her shirt.

Remembered it in her dreams, in other, more interesting places.

She cleared her throat, focusing on the page until the words blurred. "What's snagging you?"

She'd caught him mid-drink, his throat bobbing, jaw working as he munched on a chunk of ... banana? She picked at a dried-on bit still clinging to her keyboard and waited.

"It feels pass/fail," he said, then swiped his tongue over the corner of his mouth. "Life or death. I know it's an assignment, but I can't get past the thought that these cases are based in reality. They wouldn't be asking if it weren't important for us to know, and there's a lot of pressure to get it right." He scratched his neck.

Keely drew three small boxes, one at the top, middle, and bottom of the page, along with three smaller boxes beneath each. "I have to do this with my thesis sometimes when the picture gets too big. It helps to compartmentalize." A few scribbled words later, she showed him the notebook.

"A checklist," he drolled. "And in black. My favorite color. Thank you so much."

"Write the scenarios in the big boxes, and your possible courses of action in the smaller ones. They'll be your basis for or against your argument."

He tapped a finger against the page, and she felt it at the base of her neck. She shivered and grabbed her sweatshirt.

"Why three boxes?" he said, watching her.

"There's space for more if you need it. It's similar to how we do lab work. You write all possible and expected outcomes, plus what happens if you don't intervene at all, and compare that to your actual results. Which you won't have, but the framework is the same."

Max furrowed his brow, running his top teeth slowly over his bottom lip. "And if I get it wrong?"

"Then it's only wrong on that one paper." She nodded at the notebook. "I've got dozens more."

Drumming his fingers across the page, Max nodded resolutely, picked up the pen, and got to work. She forced herself to focus on her own screen.

She had the email with Max's essay pulled up, but she couldn't bring herself to open it. What if there really was no hope for hers? She'd rescued her own critiqued essay from Dr. Goff yesterday, and there was so much red, Keely still saw the slashes whenever she blinked.

She couldn't exactly read his essay with him *here*, could she? What if she wanted to punch him in the face after she finished?

So she switched to checking AMU's Olympiad email, responding to enquiries and clearing spam. Across from her, Max worked diligently, his tongue poking from the corner of his mouth.

Keely saved another email she hadn't meant to delete. She couldn't focus when he was here.

She couldn't really focus when he *wasn't* here, either, so it was most likely a Keely problem. Maybe Zoey would have a solution.

Keely typed out a text to her: *does coffee stop having an effect after a certain point? my usual is no longer working!!!*

She deleted the entire thing and instead sent: *will you be home later?*

The message displayed read instantly, but no typing bubbles appeared.

Keely's coffee was half gone when Max pushed the notebook back to her side of the table. "Like this?"

Warmth spread through her chest as she read over his first case. "Makes sense to me," she said. "Now do it two more times."

Hours later, after Keely had wrapped up with Max and sent

him on his way with actionable steps for his assignment, she made her way to the lab to work on her thesis. She still hadn't gotten a response from Zoey.

Her latest line of research was aimed at speeding up the reaction to caffeine for her test case, which metabolized caffeine at the "average" rate of three to five hours. She'd seen promising results last week by introducing an extra dose of L-theanine, but that already existed on the market, and if it worked, Keely would know about it by now.

Evening caffeine in hand (a double-bag serving of black tea from the Q, less potent than the drink Max brought her earlier), she settled in at her station and pulled her thesis notebook from her bag.

Her most recent equations stared back at her, swimming on the page, and the stress of this compounded with the stress from her parents, her moving boxes from home shoved in the corner of her otherwise spotless bedroom here.

Max's essay, which still sat unread in her inbox, and Zoey's non-reply.

The words on the page blurred, and she rubbed at her eyes. *Think, Keely.*

She wanted to make the body metabolize the caffeine faster, and safely, without an adrenaline crash or nasty side effects. It couldn't be *that* difficult, could it?

What did she know, at the foundation? The core.

Atoms. Cells.

All life, Keely's included, boiled down to atoms and cells. Her problems—with the scholarship and Max and her parents—would never be bigger than those.

So she focused there now.

Caffeine woke someone up by blocking adenosine receptors,

the parts of the brain that made you tired. It worked a little like a hangover, she now knew, in that there was nothing that dulled the effects of caffeine but time. Some scientists believed boosting the body's metabolism made a difference, though research was still inconclusive. Same thing with drinking a lot of water, though that had more merit.

She doodled a water molecule in the margin of her notebook, the positive and negative ions coded in blue and red. How did the human body produce water?

Hydration, diet, exercise ...

Max exercised. *That* was becoming increasingly clear.

He didn't matter right now, though. She only had, at max (no pun intended), one slot available per day for him, and he'd already used it up.

Zoey would know what specific parts of Keely's brain were pinging with the thoughts of Max's exercise routine. Why things seemed better when he was around.

Better again whenever Max ran his hands all over her.

Better *and* worse, when he took them off.

It was close to eleven when Keely gave up for the night, trudging home. Her nose tickled, and she made a note in her phone to renew her prescription for allergy medicine. This spring was going to be a doozy, if the blooming flowers she passed were any indication.

The apartment was dark when she pushed her front door open, which surprised her. Zoey was usually still awake.

Keely padded down the hall and knocked on Zoey's door when she saw light shining underneath.

"Zoey," Keely whined. "I need you. I was helping Max study earlier and now *I* can't study because I keep thinking about Max. What part of my brain is broken?"

"I'm sorry, Keel." Her voice was strained. "I'm working on the fundraiser."

She frowned at the door. A large wooden "Z" stared back at her, hand painted to mimic the musculoskeletal system. Keely had a matching "K" on her door, painted with a detailed model of DNA. "Oh. Do you want help?"

Zoey hesitated. "Maybe this weekend. I'm almost done for the night, anyway." The door still didn't open. "And I know you're busy."

Keely's eyelids grew heavy, like her body was rebelling at the very thought of doing more work tonight. "Not too busy for you," she said, then yawned.

"Okay," Zoey said on a laugh, and nothing else.

Later, when Keely dragged herself to the bathroom to brush her teeth before bed, Zoey was still up, working in her room.

She'd never texted Keely back.

The wall between them was more than physical. Keely fell asleep facing it, frowning.

At least Max would be at the shelter on Sunday. And maybe she'd see him before then, for another study session.

She was looking forward to it.

Even if she didn't know why.

Chapter Twenty-Four

Max

This weekend was not going to plan.

For starters, Max had to piss before the plane to Philly boarded Friday night, so he missed the boarding lineup and ended up in a middle seat between a businessman who thought the no-calls-in-flight rule didn't apply to him and a grandmotherly woman who threw her all (but mostly her elbows) into the sweater she was knitting.

Secondly, it was *Philly*, one of the largest meets of their season, and the last one Max could realistically afford not to ace. Nationals were a guillotine looming over his neck, waiting for the slightest slip to cut him off from everything he wanted.

Thirdly, it seemed, half of his team was still hungover from spring break. He'd yet to see Jazz without sunglasses, and Alex wasn't much better—during their warm-up lap, he stopped to puke in the grass by the finish line. Coach had been cursing since and threatened to "lock down" training with every other sentence. Max didn't want to know what he meant.

By some miracle, his solo sprints were fine enough. He easily conquered his qualifying heat for the hundred-meter dash and came in the middle of the pack for hurdles.

The relay was a different story. Even from three hundred meters away, he could see Alex turning green. He was slower than average, too, which meant the rest of them needed to pick up the slack. Max had bounced on the balls of his feet, trying to keep off the extra weight perching precariously on his shoulders.

Nolan flew through his leg, but Jazz must have been feeling the effects too, because she'd nearly dropped the baton during the handoff. It had plummeted to earth for a quarter of a second, mimicking Max's heart, before her grip firmed up and she made up for her fumble in the curve.

As she drew closer, Max's mind buzzed, and he heard his dad's voice in his head.

Been better, been worse, here now.

It always helped him focus when the roar of the crowd grew too loud to hear himself think.

He could do this.

For his dad.

His fingers curled around the baton.

He pushed, breath hissing from him in hot pants. With each competitor whizzing by in his periphery, as he moved his team up in ranks by sheer grit, he seemed to get faster, his body settling into the thing it was built to do.

His all was enough—this time. They qualified for finals and went on to place, but Max wondered how long this would last. His best wouldn't be enough forever. Max would lose sooner or later, and then his dad would know for certain Max couldn't handle the pressure. Wasn't built for this, the way his father was.

Now, silver medal tucked in his bag, he waited for the others for their return flight. Coach was discussing something with the employee working the gate, heads bent close together, voices too low to overhear.

The rain streaming onto the windows of the terminal matched Max's mood almost perfectly. He'd wanted gold, dammit.

Unbidden, his mind drifted to another kind of gold.

Campus was hundreds of miles away. So why had his eyes searched the stands before the race and after the finish line, looking for a golden girl he knew wouldn't be there?

And why was he thinking about her *again*, right now?

Her intelligent face, the perpetual smear of ink on her hand, the snarky comments hiding an undertone of something else. Something more.

A bright flash lit the dark sky just as Coach blew a short trill on his whistle. It was enough to get the team's attention and annoy everyone else at the gate.

Max tugged down his headphones.

"Lightning storm," Coach said, crossing his arms over his broad chest. "All planes are grounded for the foreseeable future." The team groaned in unison.

They wouldn't be home until tomorrow at this rate. Which meant there was a chance Max would miss his entire volunteer shift at the shelter.

And Keely.

Not *her* specifically. Just ... the opportunity to see her. The smile she wore when a dog sat a toy at her feet or wagged its tail in her direction.

A large body dropped into the chair next to Max's, and he would have bet the Pursue Your Passions scholarship he knew who it belonged to.

He would have been right. Nolan bumped him on the shoulder and said, "Spring break go okay? I haven't talked you since you got back."

Max lifted an eyebrow. "If you want to know something specific, Nolan, then ask." He didn't have time to read between the lines. Not when he was busy enough side-eyeing the clock and doing mental math on whether they'd make it home tonight.

Nolan hesitated, his gaze bouncing between their teammates and Max.

Max dipped his chin once, succinctly.

Still, Nolan hedged. "How was your week at home?"

"Good," he said too quickly, ready to move on.

"And your ... family?"

"Uh, yeah. They're—hanging in there." His tone was too sharp, but Nolan didn't so much as flinch. Somewhere along the way, he'd gotten used to taking Max's punches. Which was a blow of its own, right to Max's ribcage. He forced out more words, bitter on his tongue. "Dad was supposed to get to come home for it. He usually gets a break between his more intensive therapies, but they wanted him to stay for monitoring this time."

Nolan ran a hand over his head and said, "That really blows." And left it there.

Whereas Nolan seemed content to sit in the silence—as silent as a terminal could be when its flight was delayed—the inequity between them dug under Max's skin and poked sharp nails. Nolan was just *nice*, and Max had only ever been an asshole in return.

It felt a little like the shin splints he used to get in middle school, before Dad taught him proper stretching techniques. A completely avoidable annoyance.

"Have ..." He cleared his throat and looked Nolan straight in the eye. "Have I been a bad friend to you our entire college career?"

"No." Nolan tried and failed not to smile. "Only most of it."

Max laughed, surprised, and shoved him in the shoulder.

"I'm kidding. I thought ... I thought you didn't want friends." Now, Nolan was quieter, and Max leaned in to hear him. "That your focus was on running only, especially after trials last year."

"That's probably part of it," Max admitted. Whatever part wasn't his dad. "I don't usually do things halfway. I need my mind to be right."

Nolan stretched his legs into the aisle, slouching in his chair. "You know I almost quit after the first semester? My mom needed the help at home, and I didn't feel like I measured up to the big boys." Something about the way he said it made Max think he might have been included in that. "I tried to tell Coach I was quitting, and he flat out refused. Said even if I was giving up on myself, he wasn't giving up on me."

Coach was on the phone now, likely talking to the two little girls he had waiting for him at home, if the smile on his face was any indication.

"Sounds like him." Max rubbed at his neck. "He's like that with me, too." A quick cough. "So are you, by the way. And it means ..."

He couldn't find the right words, but it turned out he didn't need to.

Nolan only shrugged, digging in his bag. "I don't like it when people give up on me. So I don't give up on people, either." He held something out. "Gum?"

Just like that, the conversation was finished. And Max, for a change, didn't want to run away.

Until he caught a whiff of peppermint wafting from the stick of gum. Then he *did* want to run.

All the way back to Ash Mountain.

• • • • •

Max was so, so late. Their flight had been postponed until early the next morning, and they didn't touch down until noon. The ride back to campus was two more hours on the rickety team bus that never dared to go over the speed limit.

He navigated to his text thread with Keely. The last thing in there was from her, a gif of a dog wearing a medal around its neck.

Max

Going to be late for my shift

Keely

How late?

Max

We just passed Stanton

Keely

Yikes

Was it okay to ask her for help, or was that something only *friends* did? Did they qualify as friends? Sure, she'd saved his ass with the motor development project, but there was also the locker room, the glide of her skin beneath his hands...

He definitely didn't touch Nolan like that.

He tapped his thumb against the side of his phone, contemplating. Typing bubbles popped up again.

Keely

I can cover you at the shelter until you get here. Farah Pawcett told me to tell you she misses you.

Max

Liar. Farah Pawcett only ever tells me to fuck off. With her teeth.

Outside, a highway sign whizzed by and provided an update. A hundred miles.

Max

Anyone else miss me?

Keely

Obviously.

A picture popped up. Keely sat on the ground in the kennel, peering out and smiling from around Biscuit, perched directly on her lap with his tongue lolling from his mouth. A grin tugged at Max's lips as he zoomed in closer.

He choked on a laugh.

Keely sent a second picture and another text: *does Biscuit have a boner right now??????* Her face was disgusted this time; the hand not holding the phone covered her eyes.

From there, every twenty minutes or so, a new picture would pop up, accompanied by a caption.

Biscuit's boner is gone!!!, with a photo of Biscuit laying in the sun.

One of the new kittens wounded me, after a closeup of the tiniest, most minuscule scratch on the back of her hand.

Georgie said I'm "not allowed" to feed Lottie without also feeding Milo. But Milo steals Lottie's food so who's really at fault here?!

Her messages shrank the distance between them, passing the time until he *finally* pulled into the school parking lot. He sprinted for his car and rushed across town. He didn't bother freshening up or changing out of his rumpled flight clothes.

It was a good thing, too. When he slipped into the main room, it was in desperate need of extra hands.

"What the hell happened?" Max said, fingers still curling around the doorknob.

Georgie looked distraught, up to their elbows in dogs and drool. "*Peanut butter*, Max. Peanut butter happened."

Tricia was no better, pulling Champ back by his collar and kicking the Kong away with her foot. "I've been looking all over for you."

Max winced, searching the rest of the crowded room. "I was—"

"Working in the cat enclosures since it messes with my allergies." Keely's hand brushed his hip as she stepped up next to him. She rearranged her hair in its claw clip—purple today—and warmth hit him square in the chest. "But I still don't get what's wrong with peanut butter?"

"Nothing in theory," he murmured. He needed an antacid. Which had everything to do with the greasy rest stop pizza and nothing to do with Keely's fingers grazing his waist. "But Biscuit loves peanut butter. So much that it gets everywhere. His paws, his neck, his back. I've even found it on his ... unmentionables before."

She grimaced, letting out a disgusted laugh. "No wonder he had a boner."

"We'll have to give him a bath," Tricia said. Her ire manifested in twin lines between her eyebrows. "It's looking like a two-person job."

"I can do it," Keely volunteered, then looked at him. Excitement glowed in her eyes. "Help me?"

How was he supposed to say no to that?

They led Biscuit to the back room, where a few metal basin tubs jutted from the walls. Everything was tile, with drains in the floor for easy clean-up.

"Thanks for covering," Max said, once he was sure the running water would cover his voice from any eavesdropping. "It probably would have been okay, but I'd rather not risk Tricia's wrath, especially on bath day."

"How often does this happen?" Keely unclipped Biscuit's collar, giving him scratches on his neck while Max adjusted the water temperature. "Bulldogs and boxers are short-haired, so I'd think it's more often, right? Or is it different since he's a mix of the two?"

"No, it's more or less the same. He gets a bath whenever we can spare the volunteers. Typically every four months or so, but it should be every three, maybe once a month in the summer. The dogs with thicker coats—"

"Like German shepherds?" she asked as Max turned on the spray nozzle.

He nodded. "And goldens. Those breeds need more brushing than they do bathing."

Keely gawked. "You're telling me I could have volunteered to brush happy dogs all day?"

"Isn't that what you do anyway?"

With an eye roll, she stood and adjusted her claw clip. "I'm wondering if the shelter would get more volunteers if they advertised it instead of the ominous 'other responsibilities as instructed.'"

"But then there'd be no one to clean up the shit."

Her nose wrinkled. "I haven't had to clean up *that* much."

He took the door off the tub and kicked the ramp into place. "Up you go, bud."

Biscuit whimpered, butt planted firmly on the floor.

"Let's be a good boy," Keely tried in her brightest voice, and a hot flash went up Max's spine. It always got so warm in here when the bath ran. "I thought he liked shiny things."

Biscuit, still covered in peanut butter, just sat and stared at them.

"He does, but he's scared of the ramp." Groaning, Max bent down and scooped him up. He grunted under the weight and shifted it to his knees. Coach would kill him if he pulled a muscle.

Once Biscuit was in the tub, Keely slid the door in place. Max slipped the harness on.

They worked in tandem, Keely keeping the dog occupied with neck scratches, cleaning at his face gently, while Max did the muscle work on his back half.

"Dude," Max said. "There are better ways to pull a lady than putting peanut butter on your tail."

Keely choked out a laugh. "I don't know. It might do it for me."

Now was Max's turn to splutter. "Seriously? You have a thing for food play?"

"I said 'might.'" She was *rudely* pretty with embarrassment glowing on her cheeks, turning her face into a watercolor of reds and pinks. "Besides, don't us humans usually go for whipped cream instead?"

He grunted. "Asking the wrong person." He had half a mind to squirt shampoo in his eye to erase the images flitting through them at warp speed. *Down, boy.*

"This isn't working." He grabbed the scrub gloves from the shelf above the tub and pulled them on. He clapped them together like a soccer goalie, and Keely hid a giggle behind her shoulder.

It still took two more rounds of shampoo to get everything out of Biscuit's coat. The only sounds were the running water, Biscuit's tail occasionally thumping the side of the tub, and Keely's soft hum of a song Max didn't recognize. Her tongue poked from her mouth in concentration.

Ready for the conditioning coat, he turned the water down slightly. Sweat prickled at the back of his neck, so after he peeled the gloves off, he pulled up the hem of his hoodie.

His shirt started to go with it, and warm, humid air hit his stomach before he tugged it down.

"What are you doing?" Keely asked faintly.

He tossed the hoodie to a side table and smirked. "Just got a little warm."

She nodded, then went back to scrubbing around Biscuit's neck and ears with that same vigor. He had to be squeaky clean by now. She bit her lip, not meeting Max's eyes.

Was she thinking about the last time he'd been shirtless around her with water involved?

Gah. He needed to shove all thoughts of the locker room firmly from his mind. And set them on fire, for good measure.

He lowered the water temperature again, running it over the pulse point in his wrist to cool his raging blood.

Another, worse idea formed. They were meant to be civil now. Friends, or at least friend*ly*. She'd covered for him today, after all. But he couldn't resist. Part of him wondered if that had to do with Keely, the bright flush of color that crawled up her neck whenever he riled her up, and how he saw it behind his eyelids when he tried to sleep each night.

He jerked his hand.

"Max," she gasped, rearing back as the water he'd flicked dripped down and disappeared beneath the neck of her shirt. She pulled the fabric away from her body. "Stop, it's so cold!"

He looked away, but his gaze crept back. Always. Inevitably.

He couldn't *not* look at her.

Which is how he saw her intention from a mile away when she lunged over, gathering a cupped handful of water and sloshing it in his direction.

"*Whoa*," he spluttered, licking some of the water off his mouth. He pulled the nozzle from its holster. "You're gonna pay for that."

She held up her hands, panic tightening her features. "Wait, no, I'm sorry—"

"Tough luck, buttercup." And he pressed the trigger. Biscuit barked happily, struggling against the confines of his harness to chase the spray.

Max wasn't a complete jerk. He managed to avoid Keely's face and … chest, but her waist was fair game, and he only sprayed in short spurts so she wouldn't get totally—

"Oh my God, Max, I'm so wet," she whimpered.

All of Max's retorts died on his tongue.

"Keely," he rasped, dropping the hose in the tub. Her lips parted. "Please don't say things like that to me."

The water squirted from the nozzle in a fountain, one Biscuit happily nipped and barked at. But Max only focused on Keely as she backtracked to see what, exactly, she'd said.

One of her eyebrows inched upward. "Or what?"

Max took another step.

"What. Is. Happening. In. Here?" Tricia's tone was direct, harsh, and even Max flinched.

He waited to see if Keely would offer an explanation. He figured she'd want to be in control of the situation seconds away from careening off a cliff.

She stayed quiet, and Tricia's eyebrow only kept inching up her forehead.

"We were—" Max started, then tried again. "I was—"

"Max." Tricia shifted her weight, letting out a heavy sigh. "We really don't have time for messing around today. If you're just going to goof off—"

"It was my fault," Keely blurted. "I started it."

Tricia's brows flew up under her daisy-patterned bandana. "Regardless of whose fault it was, you both know better." Disbelief wove through her words, and Max bit his cheek and nodded. Beside him, Keely did the same. Tricia pointed at the floor, where they both stood in small puddles. "Clean this up."

Keely and Max waited for the door to close before they shared a look and burst into hushed, breathless laughter.

Biscuit barked again.

Chapter Twenty-Five

Keely

Keely wasn't one to jump to conclusions. She was a scientist, after all. When she had a hypothesis, she investigated. Gathered data points and waited to see if the pattern indicated she was correct. If there was a pattern at all.

Which was how she knew almost certainly: Zoey was avoiding her.

They were ships in the night; Keely hadn't physically seen her roommate since before spring break.

But she'd heard her moving around behind her closed bedroom door. That was the first red flag. They never shut their doors to each other. Keely had caught Zoey with her hand down her pants—literally—on more than one occasion because of it.

Every time Keely knocked now, Zoey either didn't answer or made an excuse to keep it shut. Sunday after the shelter, it was a headache.

Yesterday morning, Zoey had ducked out before Keely woke and was gone for most of the day, leaving Keely alone with her swirling thoughts. Which was a shame, because Keely really needed to unpack the budding weirdness with Max.

And last night, it was because Zoey had had someone over. (An outlier from her collected data set because it proved true; Keely had had to put in earplugs before bed.)

She'd tried texting Zoey directly. When that didn't work, she'd asked around their friend group, but none of them had answers, either.

By Wednesday evening, Keely had accepted her fate. Zoey would talk when she was ready.

Keely filled in her to-do list, with not nearly enough crossed off for the late hour. The library was all but empty. She kept having to wave her arm to reactivate the motion sensors in the lights.

- ~~Call Matilda to check in (prescriptions ok?)~~
- ~~Research and order kids' science books~~
- Meet with Dr. Goff — Rescheduled until I read Max's essay
- Read Max's essay and take notes
- Class work
- Thesis work
- Make finals study plan
- Finalize to-do list for WIS auction

Nope. *Worry about Zoey* wasn't on there. She was a little mad at herself. If she'd managed to cross off *Read Max's essay* today, instead of carrying it over for the nth time in a row, she'd have room on the list instead of in the margins.

"I love you," a familiar voice said.

She snapped her head up so fast her neck twinged. "Excuse

me?" She was *burning up*. No one had ever said that to her before. Least of all—

Max held up his paper, like that explained everything. "I got an A minus on the assignment. A minus, Keely!" He shook the paper, then smacked it on the desk near her laptop.

She blew out a breath, heart thundering. "I didn't do anything."

"Don't do that." He stared at her, his eyes almost as hard as his jaw.

"Do what?" She was struggling with everything today, especially following Max's line of thinking.

He shook his head, wetting his lips as redness crawled up and over his jaw. "Sell yourself short. Diminish your contributions. You're a really good teacher, and I wouldn't have done this well without you. There's nothing wrong with admitting it, Keely."

Affection bloomed in her chest, and though she'd have to shut it down in a few seconds, she relished the warmth now. She bit her lip to slow the spread of her smile. It pulled free anyway. "Thanks. I think I needed that."

He slid into the seat beside her because, apparently, this was something they did now. Studied together. Like friends. Like … something else.

"Things at home?" he asked.

"Not just that," she said. "Although I don't really have a home anymore, I guess. The house sale was finalized. Another family moved in this weekend." Hopefully the next generation of kids who grew up there would hear laughter more than anger.

"Well, that'd be enough to bum anyone out, but it sounds like there's something else. So what's the most wrong right now?"

He looked so sincere, filling the space in her periphery, ready to listen to whatever she could possibly say.

Which was a problem. Confessing everything on her mind wasn't on her to-do list, either. If she started, she didn't know if she'd stop.

She was beginning to suspect that sentiment applied to a lot of things when it came to Max Simmons.

He shifted in his seat, his foot tapping hers under the table. She moved away, but he chased her, the toe of his shoe brushing her ankle. "Key."

The single syllable scratched across her nerves, leaving them raw and exposed. She was bare wiring when he looked at her this way. Said her name this way.

"That day in the locker room," she said, swiveling in her chair to face him. "The day we almost ..."

He flashed a grin before smoothing out his features. "I have no idea what you're talking about."

She gritted her teeth. This was hard enough as it was. Did he have to make it worse by being so *smug*?

"I was desperate to read your essay," she admitted. His head tilted, and she took it as an invitation to continue. "So desperate I *broke into your locker room*. Into your actual *locker*. And you sent it to me a week ago, and I ..."

"You still haven't read it?" Max laughed, then rubbed a hand over his mouth when she gave him a dirty look he correctly interpreted as *you're being so loud right now*. His voice dropped to a low rumble, one she felt in her chest. "God, Keely, then what was the point of everything?"

She picked at dried banana on her keyboard.

The truth was, she didn't want to know how good it was. How much better and more equipped he was for this. She'd have to face how bad hers was in turn, and she wasn't ready to give up on her dreams just yet.

"For real." He leaned into her personal space and tapped her screen. She tried not to breathe him in, but he was everywhere. He must have showered recently, because spicy sweetness swirled around her. "Pull it up. Or I can read it out loud, if you'd prefer. I don't have any fancy voices like you use with the kids, but—"

She pushed his hand away, and he chuckled as he sat back and crossed his arms.

Her hand hovered over her trackpad, but it still took one more encouraging nod from him to open the document.

Twenty minutes later, she sighed. "That settles it," she said, resting her forehead on the table in front of her computer. "I'm doomed. I'll drop out now."

He placed his phone screen-side down on the table. "You ... liked it?"

Liked it?

She was obsessed with it.

Every single word in Max's essay *bled* running. He talked about growing up with his dad, their family's commitment to fun and fitness. How when his dad got sick, Max had grabbed the baton and picked up where his father had left off.

Keely didn't know if she'd ever been that passionate about anything, not even her first toy microscope set.

Despite the fear that she was absolutely screwed when it came to this scholarship, she was almost ... *happy* for Max, if this was how he really felt.

"I want to go for a run now," she said honestly. "And I don't do that."

Max grinned. "Let's go, then." He stood up and shouldered his bag.

Her brain processed his words slower than normal. His essay was just that good. "Go where?"

"For a run," he said, closing her laptop, and his smile widened. "I'll give you a firsthand account of exactly how passionate I can be."

"Max," she said through a laugh, because it was that or sputter incoherently. "I'm wearing jeans."

"I have extra clothes you can borrow." He lifted the shoulder his backpack was dangling from.

That was a horrible idea, and she told him so. "I'm a foot shorter than you, with a lot less..." *Don't say muscles. Don't think about his muscles.* "Your clothes will be too big," she supplied weakly. "And it's after ten at night."

"I'll keep you safe."

"I meant I'm *tired*."

He fought another smile. "You're coming up with excuses."

A little. "I'm not saying no. I'm just saying not right now. I have too much left to do, anyway." Like figure out how to run in front of Max Simmons without embarrassing herself. She'd taught herself advanced differentials in the summer between freshman and sophomore year. She could surely learn how to jog.

Or speed walk.

Max sighed. "Tomorrow morning, then. At eight? I'll meet you at the track."

She dragged her teeth with her lip, and his gaze dropped there. Darkened.

"Tomorrow morning," she confirmed, wondering where her ability to breathe had wandered off to.

It was a horrible idea.

So why was she so excited?

Keely

What do you wear for something that might be a date but probably isn't but you want to be cute just in case? Exercise will be involved.

Zoey

...

Zoey

Date with whom?

Keely

So you're NOT dead!

Keely

I'm meeting Max at the track. He's going to show me passion

Keely

PASSION FOR RUNNING

> **Keely**
>
> *Forrest Gump Running gif*

> **Zoey**
>
> ...

> **Zoey:**

> **Keely**
>
> Zo?

Of all the things Keely had ever volunteered to do at eight in the morning, this may have been the stupidest. She didn't necessarily hate exercise. She valued it for the natural endorphins, the effects on the immune system and overall health to a person. She just preferred when it fit naturally into her day. Rushing between classes, sprinting up the stairs of Davidson, carrying her laundry to the basement and back up again.

Instead, she was here, in the sliver of time between her pre-class study block and Histology, walking onto the track and tugging up her socks like it was any other Wednesday. Morning practice must have just let out, because athletes walked the *other* way, duffels and backpacks slung over their shoulders.

Max sat at the edge of the track, backlit by the sun. It highlighted the long lines of his legs. His shorts had ridden up his thighs.

Maybe running wasn't *so* bad.

She plopped down next to him.

He stretched out his legs, encroaching on her personal bubble. "Good morning, Keely."

"Don't sound so excited. This is basically going to be torture for me."

He pulled his feet up and pressed the soles of his shoes together into a butterfly. "I have to get back at you somehow for all the pranks." When she didn't respond, he tipped his head at her legs. "What I'm doing, *you* should be doing, by the way."

She scrambled to pull her feet together. "What do you mean, getting back at me for the pranks? I thought we were done keeping score."

Max studied her for a second, dozens of emotions splayed across his face: surprise, amusement, interest. "I don't know if we'll ever be done."

Her heart rocketed so fast and so suddenly, she was sure if she looked down, she'd see it knocking against her ribs.

They continued stretching, and Keely tried not to notice his muscles flexing beneath the fabric of his running gear, a moisture-wicking, AMU-green tank shirt and black athletic shorts. When he shifted, she got a peek of the built-in liner hugging his upper thighs. Was he wearing underwear?

In what world did that matter?

After what seemed like ages but was probably no more than twenty minutes, Max stopped stretching.

Keely popped up next to him and held her hands out, palms up. "Passion, please."

He slapped them in a double high-five, fingers dragging along hers as he drew back. "What's your favorite thing in the world?"

His laugh, her brain supplied.

Oh, no. That was the truth. Max's laugh was her new favorite sound.

Her smile melted into a flat line. "Science," she said instead, tacking on an "obviously" at the end for good measure. Did he hear the lie?

"Obviously," he agreed, and started walking along the track. "And what's your favorite thing about science?"

She rushed to catch up. "The breakthrough."

"And what's your favorite thing about—"

"I *get* it," she said as they fell into step together. "Okay, fine. Do you remember the field trip we went on in fifth grade?"

He grimaced. "The one to the Richmond Science Center? That place was so boring."

"It wasn't, though. Not to me. It made me feel . . . less than—and also somehow bigger than—myself. Bigger than all of it."

It was the first and only field trip her father had ever volunteered to come on, and he was on his phone the whole time, taking hushed calls and answering emails. Usually when a parent chaperoned, that child became *cool* for the day, other kids crowding around during lunch and asking to be in pictures. Keely didn't have any of that.

What she did have, though, was cells.

At Max's confused expression, she kept talking, trying to pull her abstract thoughts and dreams into words that made sense.

"There was this giant cell model. You could walk inside it and see mitochondria—"

"They're the powerhouse of the cell, you know."

At her glare, he mimed zipping his lips and handing her the key.

She pushed his hand away. "The exhibit was nothing spectacular. I've looked at pictures online since, and . . ." She shook her head, struggling to capture the right words from the thousands in her brain at any given time. "I felt so *small*, in a larger-than-life kind of way. I was made up of those little molecules, would only ever be made up of them, but I could do so many things. I could dance and read and sing and laugh. Watch movies, think about boys—"

He hummed behind his zipped-shut lips, but she knew what he wanted to say. She rolled her eyes, and he blew laughter through his nose.

"It's just... miraculous. Billions of years of life, matter, energy, have put us here, with these bodies, on this planet that sustains itself for the most part. I don't think I'll ever know enough about it. About us."

Finally, she inhaled. When Max didn't talk, she glanced over. His cheeks were puffed like he was about to burst.

He was a *child*. She handed back his pretend key, and he exhaled sharply. She wouldn't laugh. She wouldn't.

"That's how I am about running." He shrugged. "I can never know enough, improve enough. The key to passion is always thinking there's more to learn. Going after something with your whole heart until it breaks. Even when it's ugly and leaves bruises."

Keely nodded, Max's earnest words ringing true. "Sometimes I get overwhelmed by how much I don't know," she said. "But it's kind of thrilling to think there's always more."

"*Exactly*." His voice rose a few notches with his excitement. "Each new method or technique unlocks something totally new to work at and master. Every time I'm ready for more, it's there, waiting patiently. It only ever moves as fast as I'm ready to go."

At some point, he'd increased their pace. That had to be why her heart was thrumming so heavily in her ears, why sweat and awareness prickled on the back of her neck.

It had nothing to do with how his words were the same ones written on her soul. How he'd crawled inside her mind and recited her own joy back to her.

This was too much. This was a mistake. Getting closer to Max, asking for his help on her essay. Before the locker room, their trip home, she would have been okay with this. But now, knowing exactly why he needed it, where his passion came from ...

How was she supposed to compete with this, with *him*, when his joy and enthusiasm for his father's legacy seeped from every pore?

There was no real winner in their game, but they still had a finish line. And the closer the calendar crept to the scholarship deadline, the end of the semester, Keely's fear grew that she would lose more than the money.

She'd lose her heart, too.

"Race you," she said, breaking into a sprint and, hopefully, leaving him and those feelings far behind.

"Look at you," Max called, pride coloring each and every word. "You're running."

He zoomed past her, flipping around for a few seconds to run backwards.

"Show-off!" she shouted through a laugh, and he shook his head, spinning back around.

"I'll wait for you," he yelled over his shoulder.

Adrenaline and endorphins flooded her system as she sped up. If he were really trying, there'd be no way, but up ahead, he alternated between glancing back at her, slowing to a jog—was he *whistling?*—and, occasionally, doing his version of a cartwheel.

He fell over on his last one, which gave Keely an opportunity to catch up.

But the harder she went, the farther away he seemed. He was toying with her. She wouldn't ever catch him, would she? Was there any point to this?

Her entire life, she'd been trying to catch up to something, an ambiguous goal she didn't know and couldn't see.

Growing up, there was no space in her house to screw up safely, not when her parents fought so much. She had to time her requests, and her disappointing news. Eventually, it became easier to not disappoint them at all. Instead she stayed in her room, doing her homework, reading textbooks like they held the answers as to why people like Max had families who were happy and perfect.

Then Max moved away, and Keely had to learn how to make new friends. She tried what worked at home—being amenable, being nice, always doing exactly what was expected of her.

What did she expect of herself, though? She had anxiety that never rested, no matter how many colored pens she had or deadlines she met. Zoey was avoiding her, and Keely was spending more time chasing Max around campus playing pranks than she'd spent on her thesis this semester. She—she was just *drowning*.

When would Keely reach the finish line? When would she get to rest?

When would her best finally be enough?

Gasping sounds rent the air, and since she wasn't close enough to hear Max, she had to guess they were coming from her. His footfalls grew softer, and she pushed harder, though she could barely catch her breath.

She *couldn't* catch her breath.

"Max," she said, but it was all hot air. Her knees wobbled.

"Done already?" he yelled back. His amusement was clear, his grin as blinding as the spring sun creeping up into the sky as he looked over his shoulder at her. He slowed to a stop. "Keely?"

"I—" she tried. She shook her head.

Max ran to her. He ducked, and—had he always been fuzzy around the edges like that? And was it getting dark already?

"You're hyperventilating," Max murmured. "Come on, Key. Breathe. In through your nose. Out loud with your mouth. Force it."

She sucked air in through her nose, but it was all hot and humid, and her lungs were burning, screaming at her. She went faster, taking more in. She clawed at her neck. Was there a second part to Max's instructions? She couldn't remember.

"Breathe out now, Keely. Make it messy." He demonstrated, but it just sounded like distant hissing to her. That wasn't helpful. As soon as she could think straight again, she'd tell him so.

"Feel it," Max demanded. If her vision was working properly, she would have sworn he looked nervous, with the way his mouth pinched in at the corners. "I'm going to touch you on your sternum, between your breasts. I want you to breathe deep enough to move my hand. Can you nod to show me that's okay?"

It sounded fine enough, and she needed all the help she could get. She didn't know if she managed the nod she intended, but he let out a sigh her misfiring brain categorized as *relieved*, and he rested his fingers on her chest.

"Breathe, Keely. Move my hand."

The small sliver of space where he touched her re-centered her brain. She leaned into it, closing the distance between them, and her next breath was more of a gasp. Maybe she wasn't going to die, if she could still think about how much she hated this. Hated ... him? That didn't sound right.

And he wasn't looking at her like he hated her.

Her next inhale moved his hand, and he nodded. "That's perfect. Just like that."

Definitely didn't hate her right this moment.

"Touch me, too." He stepped closer and dropped his voice an octave and a few volume notches. "If you want." He tilted his head to catch her gaze. "Hold your hand to my chest to see how it should feel."

She must have nodded again, because warm fingers wrapped around her wrist, bringing her palm up. Then it was splayed across Max Simmons's chest, the way his was on hers.

His heart beats, the blood rushing through his lungs and under his skin, gave her something to count other than all the seconds she wasn't in control, the number of things still on her to-do list today. All the ways she could fail and was *already* failing.

"You're *here*, Keely," Max murmured. After hesitating a second—which stretched wide and endless in front of Keely—he dropped his forehead to hers, his furrowed brow smoothing along her sweaty one. From this close, his jaw looked like her ribs felt, immovable and iron tight. It took up all her vision. "You're here with me, and the only responsibility you have right now is to breathe. To focus on how my chest expands and make yours match. That's all you have to do." His voice was fierce. Commanding. "Just look at me and breathe."

It came back to her in increments. The breeze floating down from the mountains. The sun warming her skin through her black tank top.

Max's hand splayed across that tank top. His heart, slow and steady under her palm, the vein in his forehead pulsing lightly against hers. Her fingers flexed, then curled into a fist around the fabric.

A shockwave of electricity ripped through her. She'd always thought that was a metaphor, how some touches created electricity.

But the buzzing beneath her skin said something different. Her nerves were sparking rapid-fire. They were so *close*. Their bodies were fused, foreheads to chests, the backs of their hands brushing.

Keely tried to step back, put an iota of distance between them so she could unjumble her thoughts. But her legs still weren't working quite right, or maybe her shoelace was untied, or the universe didn't think she'd had enough of Max Simmons's body on hers yet, because something snagged her foot and sent her careening backward toward the asphalt.

Her butt hit first, and she would have smacked her head next if Max hadn't caught it, cradling it and taking the brunt of the hit on his knuckles.

"Oof." Max groaned.

As the dust settled, Keely became hyper aware of their position. Max was on top of her, the hand not cradling her head pressed to the ground near her breast. His thumb was against her bra again. Nerves misfired in her still-fuzzy brain.

Passion. So this was what it felt like.

"Are you okay?" His voice was sandpaper-rough. "Can you still breathe?"

She really couldn't, not with her legs on either side of his hips like this. But she knew what he meant, so she nodded, threaded her fingers through the damp hair at the nape of his neck, and pulled his mouth down to hers.

He grunted, the hand cradling her head tightening around her hair, and she was a scientist, but this was *art*, how he molded her lips with his own and kissed her in earnest.

Max pressed her mouth apart, and she tasted his toothpaste. Peppermint. She grinned, and he used the opportunity to drag her lip with his teeth. The canine was the last to release, and the pinch of pain was followed quickly by delicate pleasure as he sucked her bottom lip into his mouth.

She could work her whole life and not be able to master this the way he had. But she'd try—with enthusiasm.

Her hands weren't in his hair anymore. They were dragging down, down, clawing over his shoulder blades, memorizing the muscles of his waist and back. There were divots just above his waistband, on either side of his spine, and she filled them with her fingers experimentally.

With a groan, Max's tongue shot out, licking up and learning the curve of her lips from the inside out. She met him with her own, and this became a new way they fought and sparred with each other. She pushed and he pulled. He gave and she took, hand over fist, *greedy* for him and his mouth and hands and little noises.

Light burned bright behind her eyes, and she wouldn't have been surprised to open them and find she was glowing. Her entire body was uncomfortably, perfectly warm, buzzing with that potential she'd talked about so many weeks ago. She was the ball before a drop, waiting, waiting, *waiting* for Max to touch her where she ached.

He tore his lips from her with a pained grunt, and she followed him blindly, seeking the softness of his mouth on an otherwise granite body. But his hand was still fisted in her hair, holding her in place.

"I haven't stopped thinking about the locker room," he murmured to the skin of her jaw, his mouth following the same pattern now as it did then. He didn't stop himself this time as he took more sips of her.

"I haven't, either," she admitted, a suck of her neck stealing the last syllable. Stealing her ability to think clearly in any capacity. "*Max*," she breathed.

This was insane. They were in public, in broad daylight. It was the most reckless she'd ever been, and there was a zero percent probability of stopping. She didn't care. All she wanted was this, to quell the desire for Max that had been building since—since longer than she cared to admit. Their bodies hummed with energy; she was sure she felt his heartbeat in the space between them.

With a whimper, she bucked up, seeking relief from his heavy presence there.

Max's hand shot to her hips, stilling her. "*Key*," he said, a warning and a plea. "Stop."

She froze; she'd read this so wrong. Maybe he regretted the moment in the locker room, this moment now, after all, especially now that they were friends.

He was right. It had taken them months to get to this point, this truce, and it still hung precariously in the balance.

Just like the scholarship.

The campus bell tolled, signaling the turn of the hour and breaking the spell.

Keely pulled away with a jolt, and she got to take in the full glory of Max Simmons, post-kiss. Bruised lips, tousled hair, pupils swallowing all but the tiniest sliver of color. She let herself have it for a few seconds, suppressing the ache in her chest.

"I have to go," she said, scrambling out from under him. She rushed for her bag, still back where they'd started.

The back of her neck prickled, which meant he was probably watching as she slung it over her shoulder.

"You okay?" he asked.

"I'm ..." she started, but she didn't know how to finish that sentence. Was she okay? Not really. "Late to class," she supplied instead.

"Ah." He nodded, but a look of confusion crossed his features. His hair was stuck up in wild strands, mussed from her fingers, and his cheeks and the hinge of his jaw were bright red. All of it made him even hotter. Unfair.

He'd shifted to sit on the ground and leaned back on his hands, revealing the lines of his hard body—*all* of his hard body.

She tore her gaze away, turned and ran all the way to class.

Chapter Twenty-Six

Keely

By some miracle, Keely was only five minutes late to Histology. Her professor looked bemused as she took her usual seat in the front row, like she'd been on her deathbed and was checking for signs of life.

She was very alive indeed, with color a near-permanent stain on her cheekbones and across the bridge of her nose. She'd had to finger-comb her hair on the way here because Max's hands had mussed it so thoroughly. And her lips *still* stung. She pressed them together to see if it dissipated, which sent that same warm honey flowing through her veins.

She'd kissed Max. She had kissed *Max Simmons*.

It made concentrating during lecture difficult, to be honest, especially when her phone kept vibrating in her pocket.

During her break between Histology and Biochem, she checked it to find he had texted her no less than three times. Asking to study later. Asking if she'd met with Dr. Goff yet this week.

Asking if she was okay.

She still didn't know the answer to that. She knew the weight of his body on hers now, had learned the shape of his shoulders with her fingernails.

If Max could be normal, then she needed to forget it, too. Nothing good would come of that distraction. Keely didn't have time for romance, anyway. For kissing. For this ... feeling, making her limbs heavy and light all at once. She'd always been too busy with school, studying, extracurriculars.

Even still, Keely couldn't help but press her lips together again one last time as she entered the designated room for the weekly Science Olympiad meeting on her lunch break. The soreness was mostly gone, and she learned firsthand the meaning of *bittersweet*. She hadn't liked it exactly, but she sort of missed the tingling sensation Max had left behind.

Zoey, as expected, was at the table in the front of the empty classroom, hunched over her laptop with stapled packets spread around her. She looked up, clocked Keely in the doorway, and went back to glaring at her screen.

Jeremy sat on the floor beside Maya, her wheelchair pulled up to a table. Both of them were up to their knees in cellophane wrapping, ribbons, and card stock. A giant gold bow glinted on Jeremy's head. They, too, ignored her.

"What is all this? Where is everyone?" Keely slid her backpack from her shoulder and rested it on an empty desk. "Don't we have Olympiad practice?"

Zoey muttered something under her breath that sounded like, "Shouldn't you know?"

Keely halted in her tracks, her mouth agape. She couldn't find any words. Between the kiss this morning and Zoey's attitude now, Keely wondered whether she was dreaming.

"Where have you *been*?" The icy shards in Zoey's words cut into Keely's stomach.

Keely didn't know what Zoey was really asking, so she covered all her bases. "I told you already, I was with Max this morning," she said, willing her cheeks not to flush. "And then class. Same as usual," she added, hoping her tone was nonchalant. Nothing to see here.

Zoey looked away, her jaw ticking. "Not just today, Keely. All semester."

Keely bit her tongue. She'd been with Max—or at the very least, *thinking* of him—for most of that time, too.

Maya pushed back from the table, a piece of cellophane stuck to her knee. "Come on, Jer. We can finish after lab."

Keely almost asked them to stay. She needed something to deflect the thick black ropes of tension stringing between her and Zoey.

"What's going on?" Keely asked again, once they were alone.

Zoey blew a sigh through her nose and slammed her laptop shut. Irritation tightened her jaw, her mouth, her shoulders. "I don't know, Keel. You tell me. Anything on your radar for this weekend?"

Keely's pulse tripped. This weekend was going to be any other weekend, wasn't it? Friday night she'd hole up in the thesis lab until she had to tape her eyes open, Saturday she'd call to check on Matilda and promptly get hung up on, and Sunday she'd be at the shelter with Max.

But if that were true—if it were business as usual—Zoey wouldn't be glaring at her like she was running Keely through with scissors in her mind.

Keely searched the mess of the classroom for clues. The cellophane gift baskets. The papers scattered over the table.

Zoey saved her the trouble, annoyance sharpening the lines around her mouth. "The WIS auction is this weekend. In three days, actually."

"The..." Keely's heart fell through the floor as dates, unchecked boxes, flashed in her mind. Had she really been so wrapped up in this *ridiculous* situation with Max that she'd forgotten one of her biggest responsibilities? "That's impossible. I would have—"

She bit her lip and it tingled, but she ignored it. She could think about Max later. Or never again, if this was the price she paid.

"Would have *what?*" Zoey snorted. "Would have remembered? Obviously, you didn't. You're white as a sheet right now."

Because all the blood had drained from Keely's face to redirect into her heart. It *hurt* inside her chest. How had she let this happen?

"I'm so sorry, Zo. Give me tasks." She pulled the zipper of her backpack so hard it got jammed. The paper caught inside ripped. "Let me get my planner. I'll make a list and we can—"

"Stop with your precious *lists* for a second." Zoey threw her hands up, then crossed her arms over her chest, the WIS logo printed there. Keely's heart lurched again. "It's not just about the auction."

"Then what is it about?" She wanted to collapse into a heap on the floor. Crawl under the table. Get on her knees and *beg*. "Is this why you've been avoiding me?"

This time, when Zoey laughed, it was more of a yelp. An animal, reacting to pain. "I can't believe you noticed."

"Of course I did." Keely frowned. "I've tried to talk to you."

"But all you want to talk about is Max." Zoey spat his name like a curse. "This stupid prank war stole your last semester of college, and mine by association. We haven't talked about grad school or where we're going to live in the fall. Is Caltech even still on your radar? The decision deadline is June first, you know." Her tone had risen in severity, in volume, and it pressed and pressed in from all angles.

Keely's heart was going to explode. More deadlines. More ways to disappoint the people she cared about. "I know," she said feebly. "It's on my list."

"Just like the auction was on your list? The auction I've had to coordinate completely alone?" Behind Keely, the door swung open, and Zoey snapped, "Not now, Christian."

They squeaked an apology and the door thudded shut.

Keely listed against the table. "What can I do?"

For a second, Zoey didn't answer. Just watched Keely's watering eyes and trembling bottom lip. It didn't sting anymore.

"You can leave me alone," Zoey said, flipping her laptop back open in an effective dismissal. "I really need to finish this on my lunch break."

"I want to make this up to you." Keely curled her fingers into her palm.

"Unless you can come up with ten more auction prizes by Saturday morning," Zoey said, "I'm really not interested."

She didn't look up again.

As she exited the classroom, Keely's knees wobbled for an entirely different reason.

Chapter Twenty-Seven

Max

Keely, stretching, her shirt dipping low to reveal the neckline of her sports bra. Her cheeks flushed with exertion as he chased her around the track, his second home.

Her smile pressed to his own. The curve of her neck.

Her.

Max stumbled, then cursed.

"Dude." Nolan pulled away a few paces, wiping at his forehead. "It's no fun if you let me win. At least try a little."

They'd agreed to stay half an hour after their usual practice ended. Max was normally gassed by this point, but kissing Keely this morning had lit a fire under his ass, and he needed something to burn off the excess energy.

Something that wasn't "run to Keely's door and lock it behind them."

The memory of Keely's plush mouth on his own, her hands clutching his back as she squirmed underneath him and moaned against his neck. He'd have her anywhere, anytime, just to hear those sounds again. His chest still reverberated with it, the same way energy lingered in his legs long after a race.

"I *was* trying," Max grumbled under his breath, catching up to Nolan with a few larger strides.

Nolan threw a flat look at him. "I'm patient, not stupid. You want to tell me what's going on sometime today, I'll be right here."

Max still wasn't used to this blind faith. The openness Nolan gifted him—hell, gifted *everyone*. Vulnerability wasn't natural to Max, the way it seemed to be with Nolan. He'd been on his own for so long, head down to focus on his footsteps, working toward his goals. He didn't know how to let someone else in. He'd given his all to one thing; there wasn't usually any left over at the end of the day.

His stomach tugged with the urge to keep it locked in, to shove his feelings down into his legs, convert it to that energy Keely always raved about.

"Any time would be great," Nolan said again.

Growling, Max feigned right like he might trip him. Nolan laughed, jumping out of the way.

"Can I ask you something sort of ..." *Personal* was what Max wanted to say. He settled for, "Different from what we usually talk about?"

Nolan nodded, shoulders tensing before he pressed them down and resumed his stride.

Good form. Max copied him, pushing his own shoulders down. He opened his chest and hips until he settled into a natural groove.

"Do you date?" It wasn't what Max really wanted to ask, but he'd had his head buried in the sand for so long, he didn't know where to start. For all Max knew, the guy just got out of a toxic ten-year relationship.

"Not in a while," Nolan said. His words bounced with his footfalls. "It's been maybe four months."

They had different definitions of "a while." Max hadn't been with anyone seriously since sophomore year. Release had become an obligation to him, something done in the shower each morning to quell energy and flood his system with natural endorphins before practice.

"How do you find time for everything? Practice, homework..."

"Sex?" Nolan tacked on cheekily. "If this is about Keely, you can tell me. It's not like I didn't see her sneaking out of the locker room before break. Or see the two of you after practice this morning."

Max's lungs burned, and he exhaled sharply, hoping to break loose the words he really wanted to say. Why was this so hard?

"It's not ... *not* about Keely."

Nolan hummed, and maybe it was the wind, but Max swore he heard him laugh, too. "Got it. Well. Whoever I want to spend time with, I make sure I'm present with them. Not thinking about racing or schoolwork."

"Can't be that easy," Max huffed.

"You're telling me when you and Keely—sorry, when you and *someone* are doing your thing, you're thinking about how to improve your hurdle stability?" Nolan's eyebrows bounced.

"I..." Hadn't Max just been thinking about kissing Keely again, seconds before this conversation began? "I see your point."

Nolan's head bobbed in time with his steps, which were a hell of a lot faster than when they'd started.

"Isn't it stupid to start something you know has an expiration date?" Max wondered aloud. "The end of the semester is a month away."

"I'm pretty sure it's already started. Locker room, remember?"

"Stop reminding me. Running with a hard-on blows, even at a jog."

"But we're not jogging. We're sprinting."

Max clocked their speed. They were flying, almost at race pace, around the track. The stadium whizzed by in his periphery, bright colors and sharp lines.

A surprised laugh burst from his mouth. "How the hell are you so wise?" Max pegged him in the shoulder. "You're only twenty-two."

Nolan breathed on his fingernails and buffed them where Max had shoved, going faster still. "I'll tell you when you're older."

It was simple, but those words held promise. That Max and Nolan might be friends when they were older and this wasn't some situational, mutual understanding between them.

And for the first time, Max welcomed the feeling instead of shoving it down into the box where he kept all the hard things. His dad being sick. Not living up to the standards and dreams that had been laid at his feet since he was old enough to run.

If he could do it with Nolan, someone he'd wanted virtually nothing to do with at the beginning of the semester, why couldn't he do it with Keely, too?

Max veered off course, heading across the field where the pole vaulters practiced. Maybe he'd get lucky and catch her between classes.

"Where are you going?" Nolan shouted.

On a whim, Max threw the middle finger behind him. "Like you don't already know."

· · · · ·

Keely's now-familiar peppermint scent lit up his brain like a neon sign. It was all he'd tasted during their kiss this morning. Probably all he'd ever taste again.

He'd been on his way to Davidson in search of her and had cut through the Q. He was lucky for a change, because it served up Keely Sinclair on a golden platter, just for him.

"Hey. I was looking for you." He smiled.

Until he looked her in the eye, and the smile slipped right back off.

Keely's eyes were puffy, bloodshot; the tip of her nose was pink and raw. She trembled, and he didn't think it was a good thing this time.

"What happened?" he demanded, ducking his head. She wouldn't look at him.

His question made her shake harder. "I'm fine." She shrugged out of his grip, and his hand fell limply at his side. "It's nothing."

The last time he'd seen her, she was blushing, eyelids fluttering with pleasure as he learned the curve of her neck with his teeth. Had *he* done this? Did she regret what happened this morning? His gut turned to stone.

"Is this ... is this because we kissed?" He took a half step back.

She pursed her lips. They were quivering too, and Max's own foundation shook. Around them, students and staff meandered to their afternoon classes and early dinners. The weather was mild, sunny and mid-sixties, but Max was frozen on the spot.

"No," she breathed.

That was the answer he wanted—so why didn't he feel better? Why was he still panicking, searching for the solution to all her problems?

"I got in a fight with Zoey earlier." She stared at the ground. The tips of their shoes were touching.

It wasn't close enough for his taste. He reached up, wiping at the moisture pooled under her cobalt eyes. Her tears made them glisten like sapphires.

A gem. Keely Sinclair was a goddamn gemstone. "Can I fix it?"

Those gemstone eyes closed, and she leaned her cheek into his hand. "No." She blew out a messy breath, and pride nipped at his heart because she'd let herself be this way with him twice in one day. "Not unless you have a dozen bid-worthy auction prizes tucked in your back pocket."

His brows furrowed. "Auction?"

She pulled her phone from her pocket and groaned at the screen. "I promise, I'm not trying to run away from you again. But I have to pick up my allergy medicine before Campus Health closes or I'm going to start sneezing and never stop."

That explained some of the redness in her face.

Some, but not all.

"I'll walk with you." He nodded in the direction of the health center. "Lead the way."

Their shoes scuffed on the dirt-and-grass paths between the buildings, trodden and packed down with years of use. He wanted to grab her hand but settled for bumping his pinkie against hers a few times. Would the ink transfer?

He sort of hoped so.

"I really dropped the ball with Zoey this semester," Keely said. The congestion clogging her words was more apparent now.

"Zoey's your roommate, right?"

"And my best friend." A wry laugh. "We're also the president and vice president of the Women in Science Society. We founded it together."

She had a T-shirt with WIS on it, didn't she? She wore it to the shelter sometimes.

"We plan a fundraising auction every spring that pours directly into the next year's budget. Since we're graduating, we wanted to go all out, leave them off on a very good note. But I've been a little ... distracted this semester."

The nuance in her words stirred his stomach. "Because of me? Our sabotage games?"

Why was it so much easier for Max to request honesty from other people, but impossible for him to give it himself?

If he *were* being honest, he'd tell Keely he wanted to kiss her again and never stop.

"And the Science Olympiad," she said, lifting a finger and hooking her opposite pointer on it. "And the scholarship work, and my parents' divorce, and moving." She switched hands. "And the new extracurriculars, *and* my thesis, *and*—"

She was going to run out of counting fingers. He hooked her thumb with his pinkie and pulled it down. After this morning, her skin *burned* where it grazed him. She cut off mid word.

"I'm sorry," he said, and dropped her hand.

The claw clip holding her hair back slid down a few inches as she shook her head. "It's not your fault, Max. I should have been able to handle it all. I've gotten pretty good at juggling."

"*Key.*" His heart tugged behind his ribs. "How many things can you juggle when you only have two hands?"

Her steps faltered, and she stared at him for a second before she picked up her pace. "As many as I need to. This ball just slipped. It hasn't hit the ground yet. There's still time to catch it."

"When's the auction?"

"Um." She let out a nervous laugh. "Saturday night?"

Max sucked in air through his teeth.

"I know." She moaned, and his spine tightened.

She must have heard how it sounded, because she cleared her throat. "I'll figure it out." She threw him a blinding smile.

It wasn't her real one, though, the one she'd worn when teaching the children at the school or whenever Biscuit brought her a toy. The one he'd seen glimpses of and savored like his cheat day meals, never quite sure when his next one was coming.

The conversation with Nolan fresh on his mind, an idea sprouted, but he didn't want to bring it up until it was more fully formed. He wanted her to rely on him, and this was an opportunity to show her she could. He could help her juggle some responsibilities. Take something off her plate so she didn't have to work so hard all the damn time.

When they reached Campus Health, Max touched Keely's shoulder, spinning her to face him. "Do you trust me?"

She bit her lip, staring up at him.

Please, he wanted to say. *Please trust me as much as I already trust you.*

Her chin dipped. "Yeah. More than is advisable, probably."

He nodded too, holding her gaze. Tentative hope shined there now. "Let me see what I can do. I'll sell an arm if I have to."

Keely's mouth twisted, and Max's heart did the same inside his chest.

"Now that," she said, wrapping her hand around the door handle, "I'd pay to see."

Chapter Twenty-Eight

Keely

Over the past forty-eight hours, Keely had gotten very good at the one thing she'd never quite mastered: lying.

By some miracle, she'd managed to muscle her way through the rest of classes and make it to her newest favorite part of the week. Reading to the kids gave her the same sense of accomplishment as checking something off her lists early. As getting the lab results she'd expected on the first pass and all subsequent ones. The same burst of endorphins she got from besting Max.

Or kissing him.

It was about the only thing going right for her lately.

Every time she'd bumped into Zoey in their apartment or on campus this week, Keely had plastered on a giant smile, waved her hands in dismissal, and said she had the auction items *handled*. That all Zoey needed to do was handle the other admin tasks and show up.

All lies. The too-big smile didn't fit right on Keely's face and made her cheeks hurt. Her hands were boneless to match the rest of her spineless body, and she absolutely did *not* have the auction items handled.

"We need to leave in ten," Zoey said, banging on the wall.

Keely jumped, then jumped again when her hot curling iron touched her neck.

Now she had a burn mark in the shape of a hickey, but she Still. Didn't. Have. Auction. Prizes.

"I'll be ready!" she called back.

She quickly wrapped another piece of hair around the barrel and swiped her email to refresh it again. She'd called in favors from everyone she'd interacted with during her college career, and all she'd received in turn was a coupon for a year's worth of free Cookout shakes. It would fetch a hefty price at the auction, but one prize alone wouldn't be enough to float WIS. Their guest list was a mix of students, faculty, and AMU alumni, but this was a small Virginia town, not Wall Street or Silicon Valley.

If all else failed—meaning, if a miracle didn't fall from the sky in the next two hours—Keely was planning to offer individualized finals study guides. Or maybe her soul.

"Three minutes." The walls between them didn't dull Zoey's sharp words, and Keely flinched, dabbing mascara on the eyelid she'd just swiped shimmery brown eyeshadow across.

She stared at herself in the mirror. Her olive-green slip dress wasn't anything fancy, but she liked the way it hugged her figure (and namely, her nonexistent chest). The hem hit at her knees, so she'd be able to run around, putting out fires wherever they popped up. Her mental checklist was already a million miles long, and they hadn't even arrived at the venue.

This time, when Zoey rapped a fist against Keely's door, she almost re-pierced her ear trying to slide in her dangling gold earrings, shaped like DNA helixes.

They drove in stilted silence to the alumni center, half a mile west of campus, and Keely's pulse ratcheted up.

"It's going to be great," Keely said through another fake smile as they walked in. She hoped Zoey was still mad enough not to pick up on the uncertainty, the wobble of her words or her ankles.

Failure wasn't an option.

It never was for Keely.

A few of the WIS council members were setting up. The entire room screamed classy, sophisticated, while still paying homage to AMU's green-and-gold color scheme. Maya laid steam-straightened emerald tablecloths over the round tables. Jeremy, ever a faithful tag along, tidied matching bows on the chairs. Lori, dressed in a killer black pantsuit, lit candles in golden votives centered in each table.

It looked great—no thanks to Keely. Guilt shredded her already nervous stomach to confetti, and she pressed a palm there. She could throw up later, after she'd faked her way through having a plan.

"I need to meet the caterer," Zoey said, pushing a gift basket into Keely's arms. "Get the auction table set up." After a second, she tacked on a half-hearted, "Please."

"Absolutely." Keely nodded so aggressively, one of the curls she'd pinned back popped free and landed in her eye.

Twenty minutes later, after multiple trips to the car because she couldn't find a trolley, Keely set the last cellophane basket and wiped gingerly along her hairline, flicking away the beaded sweat. Then she leaned forward, arranging the gifts on the table to make it look fuller than it was. The crinkling was brain-deep, staticky, and too-loud inside her head.

It was no use. Five auction items sat on the table, and one of them was the Cookout coupon. Then again, Jeremy was already eyeing it, and she'd seen him demolish a double quesadilla more than once. Nobody sat close to him when they went as a group, for fear of losing a finger.

She consulted her to-do list, the box in bright red ink next to AUCTION PRIZES??? still overwhelmingly empty. The auction started in an hour; they were going to open the doors to guests in fifteen minutes, and Keely had—

She'd failed. Let down her friends. Her *best* friend, in many more ways than this. Heaviness made a home in her chest as she refreshed her email again. Other than a response from Dr. Goff about Keely's most recent essay draft, sent early yesterday morning after a sleepless night, there was *nothing*.

And she was out of time.

Zoey approached a few minutes before the doors were scheduled to open. A hum of conversational noises filtered in from the lobby now, so they couldn't delay any longer.

"I have a plan," Keeley said, heading off any questions.

"And what is it?" Zoey handed her a name tag, then crossed her arms tightly over her chest. Her own tag was already pinned to her fuchsia dress. *Zoey Lamb, Vice President.*

Keely ran her thumb over the *President* on her own badge. This had meant so much to her. What had happened? Where had she gone wrong?

She owed Zoey honesty, even if it was like ripping out her heart and presenting it alongside the other measly offerings on the table. "Listen. I—"

Noise swelled as the doors burst open.

Not the lobby doors, but the side doors Keely had made sure to close after her last trip to the parking lot.

Nearly a dozen attractive men, all dressed in suits and bowties, filed through. She recognized a few of them: Nolan, with a light blue tux stretching across his chest and thighs. Alex, Keely remembered from the party, with a bright pink pocket square peeking out from the chest of his pristine black tux.

And front and center, wearing a smile only for her—

Max.

His suit was so dark blue it looked black, his shirt bright white and freshly pressed underneath. He'd slicked back his hair, and the lights caught on the waves. She wanted her hands in them again, to see if they were still as soft as she remembered. His smile, too. Her pulse banged an unsteady rhythm against her ribs.

Zoey shifted on her heels as Max made his way over. "What is he doing here?" she grumbled.

Keely didn't know, other than making breathing difficult.

Max jerked a thumb over his shoulder. "We're your auction prizes. Ten of us. Figure we can fetch a few hundred each for a glorified errand boy or personal trainer."

Keely's jaw unhinged. When Keely had imagined what Max would come up with, if anything, she'd never pictured something so *perfect*.

Suspicion narrowed Zoey's kohl-rimmed eyes before giving way to excitement. "*This* is what you were planning?" She nudged Keely in the shoulder. "Why didn't you say something?"

Keely dared a glance at Max, her teeth sunk in her lip. She didn't have instructions for this. How to act around him when there was so much more than gratitude swelling in her heart. She wanted to throttle him for making her think he wouldn't follow through, then shove him to the ground and hike up her dress and thank him—thoroughly—for following through so spectacularly.

"She wanted it to be a surprise," Max jumped in again, holding her eye contact. "For you, Zoey. Since you've worked so hard on everything else."

What the hell? "That's not—" His hand landed on Keely's lower back, and she forgot how to speak for a second. "Not enough to tell you how sorry I am," she finished, trying to concentrate on her words instead of Max's warmth through too-thin silk. "But we can talk more after tonight's over. We'll go to Cookout as a team. My treat."

Zoey's mouth quirked, gaze trailing over the other track and field members hanging out near the doors. She blinked rapidly.

"Um, you can—get the team set up in the back room, and I'll open the doors." Zoey started walking away, then turned back and threw her arms around Keely in a tight hug that nearly knocked them both over. "We're still fighting, by the way."

Keely's knees wobbled, but Max's hand found her lower back again, a steadying presence, reminding her of all he'd done.

Over and over, he kept showing up in her life when she least expected him, pulling her out of her head, her textbooks, her comfort zone.

Keely needed to touch him, to know this was real and *he* was real. Keely smoothed the lapel of his jacket. In turn, he took her hips in his hands.

"You did this." For her. He'd done this for her. How was she ever going to get even with him now? She couldn't repay this. She'd covered for him at the shelter, given him some help on his assignments, but she hadn't reciprocated on an equal level yet. She owed him so much. "I can't ... can't tell you how much this means to me."

He cleared his throat, thumb rubbing the ridge of her hip through her dress. It sent sparks and gooseflesh skittering over her skin, and she would have kissed him again, right here for the whole room to see, if Zoey hadn't let out a warning call that the doors were opening in a minute.

Keely may or may not have whined.

Max laughed under his breath, husky and deep. He squeezed her one last, delicious time before ushering her toward the rest of the group. "Lead the way, boss lady."

Chapter Twenty-Nine

Max

Five minutes later, Max and his teammates were tucked out of sight to the side of the stage, where he assumed the prizes would be announced and auctioned. They were passing the time by drinking a pilfered bottle of champagne Keely had snuck back from the bar. He'd given them strict instructions to (1) take this seriously and (2) not embarrass him. That included not getting smashed, but if Keely thought champagne was okay, he wasn't going to argue.

Especially not when she looked like *that*.

Her dress shimmered from the flickering votives, a warm green that made everything about her glow. Her hair. Her eyes. Her smile.

Her shock when he'd pushed through the doors both excited and saddened him, because he had a distinct feeling she'd only been relying on herself for far too long.

He passed on his own sip of champagne, which Alex was more than happy to drink on his behalf.

Max was gobsmacked when teammate after teammate had

responded to his text late Thursday night, saying he was sure everyone had Saturday evening plans since they didn't have a race, but if they didn't, he could use a favor.

Nolan had been first in line, then Alex. The responses just kept filing in. He'd never helped them in this way—any of them—and yet they'd all shown up in spades for him, dressed to the nines.

He vowed to do better in the future, even if the semester was winding down and he wasn't guaranteed to see any of them after graduation.

With Nolan, especially, who stepped up to Max's side as he peeked through the sliver of curtain to catch another glance at Keely. "Enjoying the show?"

Funnily enough, he was. Keely was on stage now, introducing the Women in Science Society and their mission on campus.

"How am I supposed to know our cues if I'm not watching?" Max murmured.

"I dunno, maybe because we have speakers back here, too?"

"We have a very special treat tonight," Keely said. She commanded the room, made it her own like she did when she was reading to the kids. Every eye in the room was on her. Max was rapt, too. Couldn't look away.

Couldn't ever look away from her.

He was starting to forget why that was a problem.

"In addition to the silent auction prizes located along the lefthand side of the room, donated generously by our sponsors, we will also be having a live auction. The Ash Mountain University track and field team has graciously offered up their best and brightest, and you'll have the opportunity in a few minutes to place your bid for an evening with the athlete of your choosing. The possibilities are endless."

The crowd was eating out of her hand, laughing at all her perfectly timed jokes. Of course everyone here loved her.

It was impossible not to.

Not that Max loved Keely.

He didn't have time for love, not when his focus should solely be on his craft. While he'd seen marginal improvements lately in his PRs and relay splits, he was still a long way off from where he'd been last Olympics season.

Plus Dad was sick. Why would he voluntarily pull someone else into his own misery?

He blew out a slow breath, but his heart jumped harder and faster against his ribs. No, he didn't love Keely.

He just thought she was a gemstone, and effervescent, and absolutely gorgeous when she snarked back at him. He'd only dreamed of her a few times, not every night, and not always explicit. Sometimes he dreamed they were walking Biscuit together, hand in hand. For others, she was asleep in his bed beside him.

Max locked his hands together on the crown of his head, a trick his dad had taught him to steady his breathing. But the longer Max looked at Keely, the tighter his chest squeezed. The distance between them was a vice grip around his heart, growing tighter with every second and every foot between them.

As she called his first teammate to the stage, Max tried to explain away his feelings. He pulled out his phone, navigating to his dad's text chain. The picture he'd sent earlier, an old-fashioned mirror selfie, remained unread.

"It's gonna be okay," Nolan said. Max had forgotten he was standing there. "Whatever thought you're thinking."

Max tugged at the neck of his shirt. If all his teammates could hold out, could keep their ties straight and their pants zipped, then so could Max.

Because it was for Keely.

On stage, she was reading the card of his teammate, who was, supposedly, showing off his cleaning skills by pretending to sweep. She giggled into the microphone, tucked a loose piece of hair behind her ear, and Max's fingers twitched as if to do the same. He groaned under his breath.

Nolan hummed. "I see."

Keely started the bidding, and it was hard to see from this viewpoint, but somehow, he knew, with the excitement splitting her face and her free hand pressed over her heart: this was going to work. They'd raised everything she wanted and *more*.

He grinned back, wide and dumb, even though she couldn't see him.

"Sold!" Keely shouted. "For three hundred dollars."

The antics escalated. His teammates had discovered a pattern: the sillier they were, the more they showed off random skills or their personality, the louder the audience laughed. And the louder the audience laughed, the higher the bidding crept. Four hundred, then six.

Alex, who demonstrated a standing backflip-hip-thrust combo, fetched a flat thousand, and the woman who won him was flushed to her toes. That could have been the alcohol, though. Max hoped he wasn't around to find out for sure.

"This is our next to last athlete for the live auction, and also a reminder that the bar will be closing in five minutes. Up next, we have another member of the same relay team that brought you Alex Dawson—"

"Two hundred!" someone shouted.

"Nolan Aghil was born and raised in southern Mississippi before finding his home here at AMU. Nolan will graduate this semester with a major in exercise science and a minor in early childhood development. He wants to work with children through—"

"*Four* hundred," someone else yelled.

"Primary school fitness programming," Keely finished, ignoring the shouts.

Nolan took to modeling himself over any special abilities, but it worked well enough.

"Five!" Someone yelled over the crowd from the back of the room, and every eye went there.

To his surprise, Zoey Lamb's hand was raised.

Nolan was pretty shocked, too, if his unhinged jaw was any indication.

Once Zoey was on stage to "collect" her prize, Keely pounced. "Any special plans for your athlete, Zoey?"

Zoey stooped down so her mouth was near the microphone. "I'm an anatomy major, and I'm running an experiment that measures electrical impulses to the heart during stressful events. I'm hoping Nolan's expertise as an athlete will help add some complexity to my data."

Max didn't understand half of those words. Nolan must have, though, because he coughed. Zoey handed him the bottled water she'd been holding as they walked off the other side of the stage.

Keely stared at the last card in her hand, reading it over and over. Max's card.

His hand curled around the curtain.

Whoever won him would have him for an entire night. Time he couldn't spend with Keely. But he was her last chance to reach her fundraising goal. He simultaneously wanted to fetch the highest price ever recorded and scoop her under his arm, run and hide.

She looked over again, and he nodded in encouragement.

"I—" she stuttered. What was she thinking right now? Was something wrong? He took a step toward her. He could introduce himself.

His step seemed to spur her into action. "I'm sorry, everyone," she said, crumpling the slip in her hand. "There's been a mistake. The last auction item has already been sold."

A murmur of disappointment flooded the room, but it was only a buzz to Max. He was more confused than anything. What was she doing?

She closed out with parting remarks about the bar closing, rideshare coupons for safe travels home, and queued the DJ—aka Jeremy—to start the background music again.

He couldn't wait any longer.

"Keely," he said, revealing himself in the wings. What had upset her? How did he fix it?

"Max." Her tone, by contrast, was bubbly, her smile rounding out her cheeks. Her dress flowed behind her.

"What changed?" He ran his hands up and over her forearms, holding her elbows gently. "Why'd you stop the auction?"

They were still on stage, and more than a few people stared. Her friends, his teammates. He blocked them all out and focused on the woman in his arms.

She gripped his lapel, wrinkling the fabric he'd gone out and bought a *steamer* for. Her nose scrunched, and he wanted to kiss it smooth again. Wanted to kiss *all* of her and ask if she had enough tissues for her lingering cold. Wanted to drag her to his bed and never let her leave, unless it was to get brunch with her the next morning.

Max wanted a hell of a lot from Keely, and he didn't know what to do about any of it, other than stand here now, completely at her mercy.

"We made triple what we did last year, and that's all because of you. I'll make a donation in lieu of bidding on you." She pressed her forehead to his collarbone, and his hand splayed across her back as he tugged her closer. *Peppermint.* Her ribs expanded with a deep breath, like she was breathing him in too. "I didn't want to share you with anyone else tonight."

He wondered if she felt his heart, knocking against hers, begging to be closer. His nose skimmed her temple. "Just tonight?"

She tilted her head side to side, her little spiral earrings glinting in the candlelight. "Tonight. Tomorrow. Maybe the day after..." A warm glow lit her face, and it took everything in him not to sweep her backstage and show her what exactly he thought of that.

But he'd been learning discipline his entire life; he could wait a few more hours to kiss Keely the way she deserved, without an audience.

Jeremy stepped up and threw an arm around Max's shoulders. "Did someone say something about Cookout?"

Chapter Thirty

Keely

"So." Max fished another fry from his carton. "What are your plans for me?"

Keely nearly choked on her burger. "My *plans* for you?"

He probably didn't mean it to be suggestive. Her mind must still be snagged in that thin loop of time when they'd been stripping linens, breaking down tables, and he'd worked up enough of a sweat to shed his suit jacket.

Roll his shirtsleeves to his elbows.

She was, after all, just a girl.

To Keely's surprise, Max and a few of his teammates had stayed for teardown. She didn't need more instances of Max being completely attractive and charming, but she'd gotten them anyway.

And now he sat beside her inside a regional burger chain, their friends mingling around them like this was something that happened all the time. In the next booth over, Alex and Jeremy raced to see who could finish their milkshake first. Maya gagged, clutching her stomach, filming the whole thing on her phone.

Across from Keely, Zoey sat beside Nolan, discussing the parameters of the experiment Zoey needed help with.

It was another reminder of how far apart she and Zoey had grown this semester, that Keely hadn't even been *aware* of the experiment, and she added a row to her mental checklist that read, simply, *Zoey*.

Keely bounced an eyebrow, hoping it would read as the white flag she intended. Zoey rolled her eyes, but bit her lip to hide a smile as she focused on Nolan again. They weren't sitting any closer than Keely and Max but, on another couple, it looked intimate.

She and Max weren't *good* at intimate.

They were better—safer—as enemies, when their destruction was mutually assured. Somewhere along the line, though, they'd become so entwined that when he'd kissed her neck that first time in the locker room, it felt like an inevitability. *He* did.

She didn't know what their natural state was anymore. Enemies? She enjoyed fighting with Max almost as much as she enjoyed these softer moments.

Lovers?

She'd need to figure out how to do that with him, if it was something he even wanted. Keely wasn't sure she could turn off her brain long enough to enjoy herself. If she'd be able to—

She shifted, and lightning shot up her thigh where it brushed Max's.

That was promising.

"Since you so graciously saved me from the vultures at the auction—" he nudged her again with his knee under the table and, yes, that was *also* too intimate for a public place "—do you know what you want to do with me yet?"

Ignoring the explicit undertones in both his voice and his words, she dragged her strawberry milkshake closer, took a dainty sip, and turned to face him. "We'll be doing an all-night essay-a-thon."

He slow-blinked at her. "I think I missed a few of those words."

"All-night essay-a-thon," Keely repeated. "ANEAT for short."

Max did a terrible job hiding his smile. "And what, exactly, does one do during an ... ANEAT," he said slowly, tasting it.

"Work on our essays, obviously." Her lips curved around her straw as she took another drink, cheeks hollowing as a strawberry lodged at the bottom.

Max's gaze darkened, his throat bobbing. "I thought Dr. Goff said your essay was in better shape." She wasn't sure, but she thought his knee pressed into hers a little harder.

She pressed back. "Better is subjective, and subjective doesn't win scholarships." And Keely did still plan to win.

At the reminder, they both went still, the air between them cooling a few degrees. They had settled into an unspoken agreement not to talk about Pursue Your Passions except when absolutely necessary. Keely tutored Max on his assignments (which he needed less and less; her study techniques were starting to rub off on him), and he'd read over the last draft of her essay. Other times, like when they saw each other at the shelter, or studied at the library, they were friends.

Friends who found ample opportunities to brush hands, smile at each other, walk out to their cars together.

Friends who made out on the track in broad daylight.

A friend who Keely thought of more than was probably healthy. Definitely more than was conducive to her attention span.

Close friends, then.

Max nodded. "Fine. Yeah. Count me in." He grabbed at one of her fries. "When?"

She pushed him away and her fingers skimmed the curve of his thumb. "Next weekend? I can do Friday or Saturday night, whichever works for you."

"I've got a meet Saturday, but I'll be home in the evening. I can start around nine that night?" His hand snuck back, and this time, when she pushed it away, he kept hold of her, setting it on his knee drawn up next to hers in the booth.

"Your place or mine?" she asked, then blushed. It sounded more sexual than it was, which was not at all, thank you very much.

He snorted. "Yours, obviously."

"Why 'obviously?'"

Max cocked his chin. She wanted to pull apart the look on his face. Dissect it, put it under a microscope until she understood it inside and out.

"For starters, my roommate is weird." He shuddered, and Keely didn't even think he was kidding. "And I thought you'd be more comfortable at your place as opposed to staying over at mine."

"Bold of you to assume we're spending the night together."

He arched an eyebrow. That one, she could read as easily as the periodic table. *Is it, Keely? Is it that bold?* "It's an all-night essay-a-thon. Spending the night is implied. Besides, if we do this at yours, you don't need to pack a bag with your extraneous ten-step skincare routine and house slippers or whatever."

"I don't like house slippers," she said primly, but a smile tugged at the corner of her mouth. "They don't have good air circulation."

"So it's a bring-your-own-slippers-all-night-essay-a-thon."

A few booths over, a commotion broke out. Keely snapped her head over in time to see Alex covering his mouth, his shirt dripping with white-yellow goo.

"I think Alex might be lactose intolerant," she mumbled, looking over her shoulder at Max, who was—

Right there, in her periphery, in all she could see and hear and smell. Her gaze dropped to his mouth.

"Jeremy's gonna barf too," someone shouted.

"He just did," Maya bemoaned as Jeremy ducked under the table.

Keely and Max straightened, and her side was instantly chilled from his absence.

She was grateful for the easy out, even if it meant getting banned from the only restaurant in town open after midnight.

Otherwise, she'd have to think about how, in a little over a week, Max would be spending the night.

• • • • •

Keely changed her shirt for the fifth time. She wanted one that said, "I have sleepovers with hot guys all the time" while also saying "I'm focused solely on my essay and not at all on whether said hot guy shows up in gray sweatpants."

The Pursue Your Passions application deadline was just under a month away, and with every day marked off on her calendar, her anxiety ticked up another notch. Was she doing enough?

She'd started looking into alternatives, because Keely wasn't Keely if she didn't have a backup for her backup. Were some of the options a lot more appealing than others? Absolutely. Did one make her stomach flutter? Maybe.

Ideally, she'd get her essay in tip-top shape with Max's help tonight, and spend the last several weeks of the semester studying for finals, all the while pretending she wasn't absolutely terrified of what was happening between her and the guy who was—

Knocking on her door right now.

Max leaned on the frame with his forearm. He was freshly showered, hair damp and curled around his ears. He hiked his bag up his shoulder.

Thankfully, his joggers were black.

She ushered him inside, sliding the deadbolt closed behind him. Her heart thudded clumsily as he took in her apartment for the first time. His attention lingered on the women of science hanging above the TV. The study materials spread on what she'd decided was her half of the coffee table.

"You've got the essay-a-thon part down," he said, slinging his backpack onto the counter, "but it looks like you're missing the all-night portion."

He pulled out a grocery bag and sorted his wares: energy and canned coffee drinks, protein bars, bright bags of sugary candy, and a box of something called Honey Stingers.

She spied a familiar package and laughed, chucking it at him. "You're so unserious for these."

He caught the pre-sliced apples. "What?" He grinned, holding them to his heart. "They're my favorite snack. Matilda turned me onto them."

As Keely stored the cold items in the fridge, he propped a hip against the counter beside her. "Zoey here?"

She shook her head. "I think she's doing that experiment with Nolan tonight." Not that Zoey had *told* Keely where she was going when she left.

"How convenient." Maybe he'd picked up on the strange vibes between their friends, too. "Any other roommates?"

Her cheeks heated, and she debated sticking her head back in the fridge. "Just us."

They each grabbed a drink and settled onto the sofa. Max kicked off his shoes like he'd been here a hundred times. Like he was already comfortable in Keely's space.

And she couldn't tell if she wanted to throw up or throw her books to the floor and have him on the table instead.

He cracked his canned coffee. "So. What's the plan, boss lady?"

This was ... weird. He was so casual about this. Like he wasn't going to still be here when the sun came up. Like Keely wouldn't know how raspy his voice was in the morning, what quirks might surface when he got tired or loopy.

Those doubts from the track crept back into Keely's mind. Maybe she was reading into everything and he *was* just here to study.

As friends.

Which they'd both agreed they were.

Totally casual, platonic friends. Who did not kiss and certainly did not give into the tension stirring in Keely's gut.

She tried to focus.

"Um, right." She sat her own drink on the table and picked up her planner. "I made us checklists. But I didn't know what to put on yours, so I took a guess. I left some space for you to add your own items. If you want."

"You made me a checklist," he mused. He scanned the page, his mouth quirking every so often.

She leaned over to see what was making it do that. "Of course I did. We have to stay on track."

He nodded slowly, an unfamiliar expression lighting up his warm brown eyes. "Can I borrow a pen?"

He didn't cross anything out like she expected. Instead, in one of the blank spaces, he added one single line.

Kiss Key.

Heat thundered between them, and she snatched her planner back, placing it safely on her side of the table. "Okay, enough joking around."

His gaze seared into the side of her face. "I wouldn't make a joke out of something I know you take seriously."

Oh. *Oh.* So he *was* going to kiss her. Maybe they weren't just friends, then. That was ...

That was certainly *something*.

But when she looked over, he was pulling his laptop from his backpack, as nonplussed as ever as he got comfortable on her couch.

Keely tried to focus on her screen for close to a minute before she made sense of the words swimming on the page. Fine. She could *pretend* to focus for a few minutes until he snapped out of this. Until he quit pretending he didn't want this as badly as she did.

Her nerves sparked whenever he shifted. Every time he reached for his drink, she wished he was reaching for her instead.

He stayed completely on his side of the sofa, consulting the list every so often. Once, he even scooped up the green pen and ticked something off.

Not the *right* box, though.

Dammit.

"Max," she whispered, eyes burning from how hard she was trying to focus on her screen.

"Keely?" he stage-whispered back, a laugh right on the edge of her name. He was just *sitting there*, typing on his laptop, and she was going to melt into her couch.

She gave up and looked over. His ears were red tipped. "When are you going to ..."

His head tilted. "Kiss you?"

She nodded, sinking her teeth into her lip so she didn't say anything else incriminating.

Max watched her for a minute, arm splayed behind his head. It pulled his hoodie up his torso, revealing a strip of tight skin and patch of hair she remembered very well from the locker room. It was casual, but unpracticed, and she had a hunch he didn't let himself relax like this often.

So what did it say that he'd done it around her twice now?

He ran his knuckles over his lips, and she licked hers.

"Kissing you is ... a reward," he murmured. "*My* reward. So I'll work hard, and finish strong, the only way I know how. And when we're done with all your checklists, there won't be anything stopping us from what's inevitable. What's been building for months. I can wait a *little* longer for that."

She could have caught fire. Likely would, if she so much as brushed against him. Her nerves sparked, burned, jumped toward his.

Do you know what you want to do with me yet? he'd asked.

She was starting to.

He leaned over and inhaled sharply.

Then he winked, tapped the pen against her screen, and dropped it onto her keyboard. "Better get to work."

Chapter Thirty-One
Keely

Keely understood quantum mechanics now more than ever. Her entire body pulsed with energy, beating in time with her blood. But she was also frozen to her spot, terrified to leap when she wasn't sure he'd catch her. Moving, yet not.

She wasn't going to get any studying done tonight, not when he casually dropped bombs like that.

She slammed her laptop shut, the pen flying out at a wonky angle and landing somewhere beside her on the couch.

"This might be a mistake," she said before she could chicken out. "We're both going out for the scholarship, and the semester is ending soon, and Max, I don't *make* mistakes. I've never been allowed to."

He watched her with preternatural stillness. Sadness twisted the corner of his mouth. "Are you trying to talk yourself out of this, or into it?"

"Neither. Both. I don't know." She shook her head. Keeping her thoughts focused over the last several weeks had been increasingly difficult around Max Simmons. "What I do know is that you feel... safe. To make a mistake with. Like..." She wrung her hands together in her lap before sliding her computer onto the coffee table next to her planner. She itched to pull her beloved to-do list close, but the only thing she'd be capable of scribbling would be the same thing over and over. *Max, Max, Max.* "Like of all the people in the world, you're the only one who understands what it feels like to screw up in the same way I do."

His chest expanded with a deep inhale, nostrils flaring wide. He nodded once, twice, some decision made that Keely wasn't privy to.

"Okay. How about this?" He slid his laptop beside hers. It knocked her planner to the floor.

And then Max grabbed Keely's hips and pulled her onto his lap.

Keely breathed in sharply. "This?"

Her heart relocated between her legs, and she knew that was anatomically impossible, but tell that to the pulsing that only seemed to get stronger as Max enveloped her.

"This." He shrugged, a picture of nonchalance as his fingers tightened around her waist. "Mistake or not, I'll go your pace, Key. Fast or slow or somewhere in the middle. But the choice is yours."

Bracing her hands on his stomach, she leaned in. The muscles contracted under her touch. Their mouths were centimeters apart, and the bridge of his nose caught on hers with delicious friction. "Then I choose fast. Aren't you a sprinter or something?"

Without warning, he splayed his legs wider, making Keely's hips groan in protest before her center aligned with his, and warmth coiled in her belly.

They collided.

If their kiss at the track was exploratory, this was years-long, in-depth *research*. They needed to try it again and again, to prove the points they were creating. Do it not only until they got it right, but until it was impossible to get it wrong.

Max tilted her head, finding the spot that made her whimper as he kissed her harder, nipped at her lips. Keely in turn discovered that when she gripped his shoulders, dug her thumbnails into the space above his collarbones, he took more of her mouth. Max's hips bucked up; Keely's ground down. She bit; he licked.

He slid his fingers up and around the curve of her skull. They met resistance at her claw clip, which he deftly loosened and tossed to the floor. Then he knotted his own fingers there instead, twining together with the strands of her hair.

When his other hand breached the back of her leggings and came to rest on the top curve of her ass, she pulled back. "I—should we—"

"You wanna stop?" He sounded winded, like he'd just finished. Finished *racing*.

She reached down, producing the pen that had been trying to find a home in her kneecap. "I want to not have this inside me before you are. So we should go to my room."

She wanted to stretch out with his body over hers. Or under her—she wasn't opposed to that option.

His throat bobbed as he rose, setting Keely gently down on the floor and twining their fingers together. He tugged her down the hall.

Her gaze jumped up from his backside to narrow on his neck, where score marks from her nails bloomed in bright red. "How do you know which room is mine?"

Max paused, then pushed open the door. "There's a K hanging right here."

"Sure." She shut it behind them, closing them off from her apartment. The world. "Or you could finally admit you brought me home the night of the party."

He took her hands and placed them on his waist. "You want me to admit that, huh?" His own hands found either side of her face, thumbs gentling over her cheekbones, all the way up to her temples. She shivered. "You want me to admit I haven't stopped thinking about you in that little red top?"

The back of her knees hit her mattress, and she fell back. Then he was over her, around her, overtaking every one of her senses. If he was a mistake—if sleeping with him was a mistake—it'd be the best one she ever made.

"You smell like peppermints," he murmured. His nose bumped the pulse point in her neck and made it go wild. "Your skin and your hair and your clothes. And now every time I smell one, I fucking *salivate* for you."

"Pavlov's ... dog," she breathed.

"Please keep talking about science." He sat back on his haunches, then pulled his hoodie off. His T-shirt came with it, and she lent him a helping hand, palms scraping the ridges of his torso. "Gets me hard every time."

Heat erupted in her stomach. "You're so funny."

"*Keely.*" Slowly and so, so carefully, he laid his body atop hers again. Long lines, scorching heat, right over where she ached most. "Does *this* feel like I'm joking?"

Tentatively, she dropped her hand, scraping her nails through the fine dark hair below his belly button, and she delighted when his stomach caved in under her touch.

"Need more data," she murmured. Then she cupped him over his sweats.

The curse that flew from his lips was filthy, ground between gritted teeth, and his head fell forward, thudding against hers. "Please move your hand. *Please.*"

Her grip was clumsy, but he did most of the work anyway, mouth gliding over her lips, chin, throat while his hips rocked.

"Changed my mind." He caught her earlobe with his teeth and tugged her hand away, laying it on the mattress beside her head. Next, he dragged his open lips across the outside of her left pinkie.

Her thighs clenched, then spasmed when his tongue traced the same path. "*Max.*"

"Good?" he mumbled. When she confirmed, he repeated the movements, biting her wrist, sinking his canine into the flesh of her thumb.

She wouldn't come from this—right? She didn't want to find out. Did she? Her brain filled with thick, cloying fog.

Eventually, his mouth wandered up her arm, tracing the lines of her shoulder, down to the collar of her shirt. This was happening. Max Simmons—*Max Simmons*—was in her bed. Was about to take off her clothes.

His hands glided her shirt up her torso.

She shivered.

Max paused, his palm splayed on the skin of her ribs as her shirt bunched at the bottom of her bra. "Have you done this before?"

"Does it matter?" She lost sight of him for a second as she finished pulling off her shirt.

His brow was furrowed when she reemerged. "Not to me. But I'd have to go slower." He sounded like the thought pained him. Or excited him. With the rasp in his throat, it was sort of hard to tell. "Do different things."

He kissed her again, slow and melting, and her hands found a home in *his* hair this time. The soft tendrils glided through her fingers, and she had to knot them, take a fistful to keep from sliding into oblivion.

"You didn't answer my question," he mumbled between a nip and a suck of her bottom lip, pulling back. His pupils were blown, his mouth swollen and deep red.

She tried to tug him closer but he remained immovable. So it was like that.

"I tried, once. Freshman year." She willed her pulse to settle a little so she could get this out. "It wasn't ... wasn't great."

His face shuttered; his arms locked beside her ear. "Did someone—Keely, did—"

"I wanted it," she rushed out, and his shoulders twitched but didn't relax. "I just realized about halfway through that I didn't want him." Her nose scrunched. "So we stopped. He left. Didn't call."

Max's lips parted, his tongue darting out to wet them. "Was that your last time?"

She nodded, sneaking in an open-mouth kiss to his chin. "You?"

"Last spring. Right before Olympic trials."

Before his dad got sick. Before his priorities shifted.

Before her.

His fingers trailed his eyes as a flush climbed his neck like ivy. Crept over the paper-thin skin covering the pulse point in her neck. The chasm between her collarbones. The dip and swell of her breasts. She shivered under his touch.

"We'll give you a do-over, then." Max chuckled softly and licked his lips. "*Yeah*. I'll do those different things I mentioned."

A white-hot spike of pleasure drove into her stomach. Or maybe that was him, hard and thick and notched in the crease of her hip. "What kinds of things?"

"Kissing," he murmured against her mouth. "*Lots* of kissing. In lots of places."

Keely stifled a whimper as he ghosted over her jaw. "Like where?"

"What about here?" His tongue explored the area behind her ear. "Do you like it here?"

"Yeah." Her voice didn't sound like her own.

A noise rumbled in his throat. Small sucks, a graze of teeth. He pulled back, his chest rising and falling in a near pant.

She nodded, again and again, and twined her fingers in the hair at his nape, tugging him back down. This time, he grinned against her skin. His teeth scraped her bra straps.

Then, once that hit the floor, another "here?" That was her favorite of all, if the moan she let out was any indication.

Max, ever the scholar, repeated his experiments many times over here, on one breast, the other. Her nipples pebbled under his mouth, and when his tongue trailed lower, dipped near her belly button, they got harder still.

"And here?" His voice was liquid fire, adding to the blaze along her exposed skin. He trailed a finger along her lower belly, the tops of her thighs. "Do you like to be kissed here?"

"I don't know," she whispered. "I've never—no one has ..." If this was a mistake, she may as well go all in. Keely didn't do anything halfway. "But I'd very much like to try, with you."

He stopped his descent for a second, his breath harsh on her stomach. His fingers curled into the waistband of her leggings.

"Max?"

He rolled his forehead in the space between her hip bones, dragging teeth and lips along her skin, before pulling down her pants and underwear. "Needed a second."

The gruffness of his words scraped over her most sensitive nerves.

"If you don't like it, I'll stop," he promised. "And we'll try something else. Or nothing at all. We can go back to how it was before."

She released a shaky laugh. "No, we can't."

He grinned up at her. "You're probably right about that."

Then, he dipped his head.

The first touch of his mouth was so soft it *tickled*, and he laughed through an apology. He firmed up after that, and pleasure unfurled along her limbs, weighing her down. Making her float.

She gripped the sheets, squirming as he, in short, devoured her. They were the same motions he'd made on her mouth, her neck, so why had her blood pressure spiked, rushing to her cheeks? Why did it feel so *different* there?

Max panted against her, but he was tense. His shoulders were rigid lines where they held her open for him, and the noises—he sounded frustrated.

"Do you like it, Key?" He nuzzled his nose against the crease of her leg, little kisses and nips to the thin, sensitive skin there. "Do you like how I taste you?"

Key. There was that nickname again. "Do *you* like it?" she echoed, nearly jumping off the mattress when he peeled off all his fingers, only to use them to spread her *wider*.

Another slow, languid lick up, centering right on her clit with the flat of his tongue. "You first."

"It's hard not to like—*that*. Like that." It started as an answer and became the *only* answer. That, there, with him.

He groaned, and it got caught in the back of his throat. "Me too. Fuckin' love it. Love—" A strangled moan punctuated that sentence.

Her fingers wound through his hair. "Max."

"Mmm."

"Max," she tried again, planting her heels in the mattress. She wanted to squirm away and burrow closer, chase the sensations and run from them simultaneously. That couldn't be right, could it? Was this supposed to be exhilarating and terrifying all in one go?

"Let's have sex," she blurted after a particularly hard suck. It had to have been ten minutes, maybe fifteen, and she didn't exactly know the mechanics, but it seemed like too long.

His smile took shape against her. "We *are* having sex."

"This doesn't count."

"I promise," he groaned, a noise deep in the back of his throat, "it does."

It reverberated in her *toes*.

"God, look at you," he murmured again. "Keely. *Key*."

She only caught a glimmer of too-wet lips and chin before she squeezed her eyes shut.

He didn't return his mouth to her. She expected the crinkle of a condom. Instead, he said, "Let me—let me just try something?"

She shot straight up. "You are *not* putting your finger in my ass."

His grin was *wicked* around a bark of laughter. "Not what I meant, but noted. I meant this." One of his hands came to rest on her sternum. "Since this worked so well on the track."

When she spiraled too far into her mind. When he brought her back to earth.

He pressed her into the mattress.

"Feel my breath on your skin. Feel my tongue, my lips, my hands. Feel me *here*, Keely. Always here." Max's hand splayed wide enough to reach both her breasts at the same time; his little finger brushed the underside of one as his thumb supported the other. "Your heart is the only place I want to be."

He was already there. It held a lot more space for Max Simmons than Keely Sinclair cared to admit.

His mouth returned to her.

It wasn't immediately different, but his hand—and his words—let her focus instead on the rise and fall of her chest, his fingertips and dull nails biting into her skin. The subtle rock of his hips against the bed. She was *alive*, every drag of Max's mouth over her adding drops of liquid lightning to the heat pooling rapidly in her belly.

"Max," she moaned, and he must have known, somehow, what it meant this time, because he groaned again in turn.

He pressed harder, kissed and sucked more fervently. He might have said something, if his mouth weren't so busy.

She clutched his hair in her fists. "Please—don't stop."

Heat unfurled at the base of her spine, the juncture of her legs where Max worked so diligently. She was already trembling when he shifted, pushing up on an elbow so he could bear down on her more fully. And he *grunted*, a pleased sound, like he was satisfied with himself.

It was her undoing. Fractals of light burst behind her eyelids, and she was falling, falling, honey-sweet warmth flooding her veins. Each cell in her body was a pleasure bomb, bursting apart and fusing back together the slightest bit differently. Just enough room for Max, who worked her over so thoroughly she shook the bed frame with her aftershocks.

She landed back in her body after soaring out of it, above it all. And he was still there, placing little kisses to her clit, cupping her breast, rolling her nipple between his thumb and middle finger.

With a final, sated sigh, her body went still.

Max pulled away, the tip of his nose glistening. "Terrible, right?" He smiled.

She blushed but grinned back. "Worst I've ever had."

It was her turn now, wasn't it? She bit her lip, assessing the physics of the situation.

"What are you—"

He didn't get to finish his question, because, in a feat of strength, she maneuvered him underneath her, pinning his hips with hers. Her fingers found the waistband of his pants.

"You want me like this?" he said. His eyes were all pupil, and *hungry*. "It can be a lot if you're not used to it."

"I'm a quick learner." She tugged at his sweats.

He lifted his hips to help her take them down, and then he was—*oh*.

She imagined that would be a lot in *any* position.

She wrapped her hand around him, tugging lightly at first, then harder, to see what he liked, what made his throat bob or his head roll back.

Turns out that all of it did.

What a horrible experiment.

"*Key*." He grunted. He grabbed her wrist, but she couldn't tell if he was asking her to stop or urging her on. Maybe he didn't know, either. "I won't last like that. I just need to—*fuck*." He sat half up when her thumb ran in small circles, spreading the bead of moisture around. His fingers pressed phantom bruises into her lower back. "Do you have condoms?"

She tipped her chin toward her nightstand drawer. "When I picked up my allergy prescription from campus health, I snagged a few. I'm on birth control, though."

He ripped a package. "We'll be triple protected, then."

She arched a brow. "Triple?"

"Condom, birth control, pulling out. Because I know you," he said. He rolled the condom on. She was *riveted*. "You won't be able to relax if you're worried about anything going wrong."

Keely lifted onto her knees.

"You'll be in control like this," he murmured, swirling designs on her outer thighs. "Which I'm sure you'll love. And I will too. But if you want to give me some of it, just let me know."

And she knew, the same way she knew atoms and cells, that he meant it.

She lined them up, and slowly, *slowly*, sank down.

Her body was still soft from his mouth, but she cinched tight around him, pinches of uncomfortable fullness rocketing down her legs.

Max groaned, low and long in his throat, throwing his head back to her pillow. "You're so tight, *shit*, I can't even—"

Keely braced on his chest, tilting forward to find an angle that would allow him in deeper.

It was a lot like this, he was right. But she threw herself into it the way she would anything else: focusing on her subject, observing for any microscopic difference. The sounds he ground out, the movements that made her insides clench around him. The pace that had them both gasping, gripping each other and the sheets and the headboard.

At one point, Max planted his feet, driving himself deeper, and a spike of pleasure-pain bloomed in her middle. She whimpered.

He must have heard a difference.

"Sorry, Key. I'm gonna—" He wrapped an arm around her, flipping them so she was against the mattress. He caught her head before it hit the pillow and smoothed back damp hair from her temple. "This will be better. I'll make it so good for you this way."

She nodded, but didn't catch his expression. She was too busy lost in this new sensation, the ecstasy of drowning in him. When his forehead lowered to press against hers, she moved his hand to her throat, and she thought she might float away again, even though he covered almost every inch of her body.

He shifted his hips, angling them upward, and pulling Keely down.

"Max," she gasped, eyes flying open.

His jaw locked tight. "There you go. Just like this."

Passion. Chemistry. Words Keely knew by definition, but never by practice.

Never until now, with her body sensitized down to her bones, her heart. Her very cells were screaming his name.

She certainly was.

Max sped up, his movements choppier. He was ripping apart at the seams, the lines of his muscles quivering under her touch. "I'm—I'm not gonna come in you, I promise." His brow furrowed; sweat misted his forehead. "Just a few more—"

The thought tightened her core, and they both made strangled noises at how that changed the sensations. "You can," she said. Begged? "I want you to."

"You're so perfect. Come with me?"

In the haze of her brain, she recognized the cadence was different from what she would have expected. He didn't emphasize *come*, but *with*. The way you'd ask someone to run away with you, to leave everything behind and take only each other forward, forever.

Like he wouldn't go without her.

Her hands dug into his back, nails scoring marks on his shoulders. Holding on so tightly, when everything was so dangerously close to shattering and slipping away. "I can't." A tear slipped from the corner of her eye. He kissed it away.

"Now, Keely," he chided, gruff and grinning. Her name was choppy from his mouth, and the way he spat it, she couldn't tell if it was a curse or a supplication. Both, maybe. "When has that ever stopped you before?"

An ember of pleasure, newer, deeper, went through her center. He understood her so completely. And that thought alone had her tensing, quivering beneath him once again as her hand wound between them to meet his fingers, already fast at work.

It was brighter this time, but softer. Her toes curled as she arched up, lost in the sensations of his body bowed over hers. Push and pull. Give and take.

Keely and Max.

His lips trembled when they touched down in the center of her sternum as he came.

And every single cell in her body pounded in time with their heartbeats.

She was still pulsing when he rolled away. After grabbing a few tissues and wrapping up the condom, he gathered her in his arms, tucking her head beneath his chin.

His heart thundered under her cheek.

He played with the ends of her hair, fanning it across her bare back like a paintbrush. "Are you okay? I didn't mean to go that hard."

"No, it was—" She shook her head into his chest. "I really liked it."

He hummed a sound that was nearly a purr, and for so many minutes, she laid in arms strong enough to carry all her problems.

"Can I ask you something?" she whispered, not wanting to wake him if he'd drifted off.

He nodded, made a noise of agreement. "Anything."

She bit her kiss-stung lips, and a shock of fresh want flooded her system. She tried to focus. "You wrote your to-do as *Kiss Key*. K-e-y. This entire time I thought you were saying 'Kee' with an E, short for Keely. So, Max Simmons." She rested her chin on his chest, stared at him from beneath her lashes. "What am I the key to?"

One long exhale, a shake of his head like he wouldn't answer. And then: "Everything, I think."

Hope buoyed Keely's chest. "What do you mean?"

"For a long time," he said after a minute, drawing stars and shapes on her lower back, "I used running as an escape. I couldn't think about anything—school or home or how long Dad was going to live—if I pushed hard enough. It was restful for me here." A hand atop Keely's, which splayed over his heart. He tangled their fingers together and then lifted them to tap her temple. "And here. Peaceful in a way nothing else has ever been. Until you."

She slow-blinked, memorizing the fan of his eyelashes. The angle of his nose. "What do you think that means?"

"I don't know." Something flashed in his eyes, but before she could think too much about it, he kissed her again. It was softer, this time, unhurried. When he pulled back, he rested his forehead against hers. "I just know my mind is quiet when I'm with you. My mind is quiet, but my heart is so, so loud."

Chapter Thirty-Two

Max

Max's alarm for practice sounded in the quiet the next morning. Keely moaned softly, burrowing her face deeper into his neck.

It was voluntary, but Max had already confirmed on Friday that he'd be there. He'd never viewed practice as optional before, but with Keely's tiny body beside his, warm and naked, he couldn't see any choice *but* staying put. He could run some laps later as penance, right?

He typed out a text: *Sorry, Coach. Can't make it this morning after all.* He thought about adding an excuse, but Coach would see through anything Max tried.

He sent it, dropped it back on the nightstand, and woke Keely up. So much for that all-night essay-a-thon.

They weren't sure if Zoey was home, so Keely told him they had to be quiet. Max fastidiously followed her rules—until he didn't. It was hard, especially when one of her knees was by her head, and the other was hugged to his hip. He was in the middle, of course, pulling noises so deep from Keely's throat that the only way to quiet her was with his mouth.

Which didn't really help, either, especially when Keely smiled up at him and he came unexpectedly. He bit down on his back molars to stifle a groan. It was a chain reaction, and she climaxed seconds later, that smile still rounding out her cheeks.

Breathless, he grazed his thumb across her splotchy cheekbone. "Do you want a dog of your own one day?"

Keely laughed. "What?"

He shrugged, but his heart wouldn't calm. Did he even want it to? "Figured you would. Maybe a laboratory retriever."

She choked and pushed up to her elbow. "Did you—did you just make a *science joke*?"

"Dunno," he murmured. "Was it funny to you?"

"Hilarious." And though she moved to hide her smile in the crook of his neck, he still caught it.

Eventually, she tugged on his hoodie and her underwear and went in search of food. He trailed behind, yesterday's sweats slung low on his hips. He sort of hoped Zoey wasn't home.

The next time he checked his phone, there was one message on the screen.

Coach

> If you find time to pull your head out of your ass, let me know.

· · · · ·

In one single day, Max's priorities shifted.

Or maybe it was quicker. Maybe it'd happened in the instant

Keely put her mouth on his. Her hands, smeared with colored ink from all her little pens.

Even her eyes undid him now.

Every time she looked at him, smiled at him, his heart took off in a sprint. Whenever her name popped up on his phone, his cheeks ached before he realized he was smiling.

Sunday, after he cancelled practice to feed Keely breakfast and watch *Bones* on her couch, they'd ridden *together* to the shelter, her sitting passenger in his car, their hands twined together over the center console. When Keely walked into the back room, Farah Pawcett nearly chewed off his finger because he let his concentration slip.

At least the last few mornings' sprinting sessions were productive. He told himself the faster he ran, harder he pushed, the sooner he'd get to see her again. Nolan stared at him with twin raised eyebrows during their cooldown, but otherwise, he kept his mouth shut. Smart guy.

Max hoped this appointment with Dr. Goff wrapped up quickly, too—the sooner it did, the sooner he could see Keely. Part of him had wanted to cancel with the career counselor completely, but he needed to hear from someone else just how much—or how little—his grades had improved. Other students lined the halls, desperate for a last-minute improvement to their grades or to find out if they would graduate.

Until this semester—until Keely—Max had never been among them. He'd been one of the ones who didn't bother showing up at all.

But he had things to show up for now.

Someone rounded the corner, and his heart jumpstarted in his chest. Worth mentioning to his PT?

"Hey, Key."

She blushed at the nickname and closed the gap between them.

Her flushed skin marked with pleasure. A bitten lip. Nail scrapes on his shoulders. Thighs wrapped around his waist, peppermint-scented sheets and skin. Whimpers for more, harder, there, right there Max—

He gritted his teeth. Now was *not* the time for his dick to get hard. "What are you doing here?"

At his rough tone, her eyes sparkled, and she bit her lip but her smile still slipped through. "I have an appointment with Dr. Goff." She stepped over a student whose legs were stretched across the hallway and tacked on a quiet, "Excuse me."

"Me too," he said. "What time is yours?"

She checked her phone. "Five minutes." She slid it back in the side pocket of her dove-gray bike shorts.

"Only five minutes early?" He nudged her shoulder, then slipped his hand to cup the back of her neck. "Cutting it close, aren't you?"

She peered up at him, a vicious, *delicious* gleam in her cerulean eyes. "My routine was off. Someone disrupted my entire morning."

He grinned. That was him, when he'd rushed to her place after AM practice, asking for five minutes and stealing a full ten, fifteen, twenty, threatening to keep her there forever, her skin sleep-warmed with little creases in her cheek...

Nope. Still not the time.

"Wait..." Max blinked, dropping his hand. "Did you say your appointment's in five minutes?"

She nodded, then fixed the hair clip he'd nudged. "Why?"

"Because mine is, too."

Her hands froze, her head tilting as the smooth skin between her brows wrinkled. "How is that—"

The door opened. Dr. Goff wore a linen set, clearly ready for the end of the semester two weeks away. This was the last full week of classes, and Monday and Tuesday next week were study days, followed by designated finals blocks.

"Hello," Dr. Goff chimed. "How are my best students today?"

Best students? Keely, sure. Max wouldn't go that far for himself.

"A little confused," Keely said. "Are our appointments at the same time?"

Dr. Goff beckoned them in, her loose linen set billowing with the movement. Dark smudges marred her undereyes, and her shoulders drooped. "Just come in together. I don't have another open slot this week." The end of the semester looming closer must be getting to her. "Besides, I think you'll both benefit from this. If you don't mind being in close quarters, that is."

Oh, he and Keely definitely didn't mind close quarters.

"That's fine," Keely said, much more diplomatically than he would've.

How had he ever viewed her kindness as a flaw? It was one of the best things about her. Max's heart squeezed in his chest. And something else, farther south, squeezed in his shorts. He gritted his teeth; he needed to get it together. He was twenty-two, not a quick-triggered teenager.

Once they were all settled, Dr. Goff inhaled deeply. It lasted long enough that Max glanced at Keely, who looked just as lost.

When their counselor's eyes opened again, they were brighter, but no less tired. "Okay. How are you all doing?"

"Fine," Max said, overlapping Keely's own, "Great!"

Dr. Goff's cough sounded suspiciously like a laugh. "Fantastic. Keely, I've got to say, your essay is nearly there. Adding how your reading to children has sparked your love of science again? Brilliant."

"Thank you." Keely beamed. "Ninth time's the charm, I guess.

Teaching has been ..." She sighed dreamily. Max knew, because he'd heard that same sound this morning. "Really great. Seeing their excitement reminded me why we do it, you know?"

Something in Max's chest twisted at her contagious joy.

"And Max." Dr. Goff smiled at him. "Your grades have turned the corner. It's nice to see the tutoring has paid off."

"It has," he confided. "I actually have a session later."

In his periphery, Keely's head whipped toward him.

"I'm planning to work very hard," he continued, wetting his bottom lip. "All night long if I have to."

Oblivious to his innuendo, Dr. Goff nodded, murmuring her approval.

Keely, on the other hand, fiddled with the hem of her shorts as a raspberry red color spread over her cheekbones. She cleared her throat delicately and addressed their counselor. "The last time we talked, you said you were hoping to gain insights into what the scholarship committee is looking for this year."

Damn, that was smart. Why hadn't he thought of that?

"Unfortunately, I still don't know how they'll swing." Dr. Goff clasped her hands on the desk. "I know whichever of you wins will be totally deserving, and whoever loses won't lose for lack of effort."

"And there's ... there's no chance the jury could be hung?" Keely pushed, and the desperation in her voice throbbed through his veins, too. "That we could tie?"

It was the first time someone acknowledged the elephant in the room: there would only be one winner. Extra money wasn't hiding in the woodwork; another scholarship wouldn't randomly appear.

Either Max would fulfill his dreams—his father's dream—or Keely would fulfill hers.

His gut tugged in all directions. What did he want?

He wanted to win, wanted to have his hard work pay off when it never had before. He wanted his dad to see Max win worlds, or nationals. Wanted him to watch Max win gold at the Olympics.

He wanted his dad to be around, period.

But Max wanted Keely, too. As much as he wanted to achieve his dreams, he knew Keely wanted to achieve hers just as badly.

"No. There is only one spot left. One fund to be allocated. Their decision will be clear—and final," Dr Goff clarified, and all remaining hope drained from the room.

Would Keely resent him if he won? Or, more likely, if she won, would he be jealous of her success? He'd probably be too busy scrambling for another option to pay much attention to her. And besides, it wasn't like they were in a relationship. They were graduating in *weeks*, and beyond the hazy refrain of Caltech, he had no idea what her plans were after they walked across the stage and collected their diplomas.

Whether they included him at all.

"I didn't mean to upset you," said Dr. Goff after a stretching silence.

Keely cleared her throat, and Max saw her bottom lip wobble.

"We know," Max said, his voice a lot surer than his heart was. "I just don't think either of us realized the scope of it until now." That was putting it lightly, and Dr. Goff was missing key details.

Keely nodded and gave him a smile she didn't mean. "Exactly."

"There are more important things than scholarships." Dr. Goff's gaze flicked between them. "You know, I didn't graduate with my master's until I was forty?"

Max couldn't wait until he was forty to start chasing his dreams.

Keely shifted in her chair, likely thinking the same thing. "What were you doing instead?" she murmured.

"Living. You've probably heard the saying 'life is what happens when you're busy making other plans'?" When they nodded, she gave them a sad smile. "I like to say that life happens in the space between seconds. Little choices, from one instant to the next, that fill in the gaps of who we're supposed to be. You're allowed to change your mind. To change course or reroute completely. I took a few detours on my way here."

Beside him, Keely was barely breathing. He wanted so badly to reach out for her, to hold her and convince her everything would work out the way it was supposed to. He didn't know that, though, and Keely didn't deserve uncertainty from him.

He swallowed around the glass in his throat and got to his feet, mumbling a weak excuse about practice.

"I should head to the lab, too." Keely shouldered her backpack and thanked their counselor for the both of them.

In the hallway, Keely stepped over the same student as before, who had now fallen asleep.

"It's going to be fine," she mumbled. "Right?"

He ran his index finger along the back of her hand. "Right."

"Text me later?" she said. Her voice shook a little, though, and Max tried to convince himself it was the lingering effects of her allergies.

He nodded, drawing her in for a hug. "Of course."

After Keely had left, he stared at the concrete wall. There had to be a way out of this mess. Maybe they could split the award, or there was a second-place prize that would be enough to tide him over. Dr. Goff would probably know.

He spun back toward her office to ask when he heard someone say Keely's name—talking *about* her, not *to* her. Max's muscles seized, locking him in place. He peeked around the corner. It was that Sam guy, from the party. Keely's friend.

"... barely seen her in months. She's spending all her time with that jock," Sam continued, a bitterness in his tone. "But I don't see it ending well." Max's skin pulsed with the need for oxygen. He didn't dare breathe. "How could it? Both of them can't win, and it's going to cost someone their future."

It wasn't anything Max didn't already know, but hearing it from someone else made the reality of his situation come crashing down onto his shoulders. If there was a solution to this mess, he couldn't see it right now.

· · · · ·

Max made an honest man of himself, heading to the track for a few off-the-clock sprints before his relay team showed up.

His mind wouldn't calm. If it wasn't on his dad, it was racing over his conversation with Dr. Goff, and if not there, then on his scholarship application. Was it the best it could be? Did he have it in him to pull out better grades for finals? He didn't have much more to give, and the only person he would've asked to help him was his direct competition.

Practice went worse than his solo sessions. He tripped off the block in more than one of his heats, and he dropped the baton in the relay. That overheard conversation didn't help, either. Now he had Sam's *and* Dr. Goff's words echoing in his head. *Whoever loses won't lose for lack of effort ... There is only one place left ... It's going to cost someone their future.*

Above it all, he heard his own breath, sawing out of him at an irregular pace.

Focus. Watch your instep—too much. Don't supinate. Steady breaths.

Both of them can't win.

Whoever loses...

His lungs constricted, and he locked it down. *Focus. Don't hyperventilate like Keely—*

His ankle rolled, and while he was able to run it off, Coach still ripped his hat from his head and curled the bill in his fist. "Simmons! Get it together, dammit. Have a trainer look at that."

Max collapsed onto a bench, and a student trainer rushed over with their full kit. Jazz, Alex, and Nolan murmured to themselves from the sidelines, staying limber and stretching while they waited for the verdict.

This is what happened at Olympic trials, wasn't it? He'd been in his head, replaying everything wrong until nothing went right. Ruminating on his mistakes had cost him—and his dad—the trials. He couldn't afford to do that again.

"I'm fine," Max barked, and the trainer reared back. "Sorry," he tacked on, softening his tone.

Whoever loses...

As the trainer wrapped his ankle out of an abundance of caution, Max's brain replayed the memory, over and over until his own name filled in the gaps.

When Max loses...

When Max lost, so would his dad.

And that wasn't an option.

The wrap threw off his times for the rest of the hour. Back in the locker room, head low and shoulders tight, he checked his phone.

Keely

> Did you still want to work hard tonight?

Keely

> On your studying, I mean! We don't have to go all night long

Max

> I'm not sure that worked out well for us last time tbh

Max

> Or it worked too well

He tapped the side of his phone. He should stay here, work on his time splits and do some extra stretching with his ankle to make sure it didn't become a bigger issue. By the time he started on his homework, it'd be too late to hang out with her.

If getting in his head about Dad had cost him the Olympics, what would Keely cost him? The scholarship?

More?

Biting the inside of his cheek, he typed a response.

Max

> I think I should study alone tonight. You're too pretty. It's distracting.

The bubbles appeared and vanished a few times each.

Keely

I can behave

But could *he*? Guilt gnawed at the corners of his empty stomach. He couldn't afford to screw this up again. He was running out of do overs.

Max

Maybe tomorrow?

After another thirty minutes of sprints, he checked his phone again.

Keely

Okay. I have to rerun an assay tonight for my thesis, so I'll be at the lab until late, if you change your mind

He already knew he wouldn't.
He couldn't afford to.

Chapter Thirty-Three

Keely

Keely was ready to be home. She'd driven into town first thing this morning for a children's book she wanted for her weekly visit to Mrs. Kershaw's classroom. The bookstore's website said it was in stock, but neither she nor the employee could find it.

The kids loved the one she'd chosen instead, which was all that mattered, but she still wanted to teach them about unicellular ocean organisms. So after that afternoon's reading, she drove to the next town over, forgoing her self-imposed afternoon study block in place of nabbing the book.

Now, Keely tumbled through her front door, delirious, ravenous, and—

Ran straight into Nolan, still tugging his shirt over his head.

"Whoa," he said, wrapping his hands lightly around her elbows.

He hadn't knocked her off balance physically. It was him here, in this current state of undress and what that implied, that made Keely sway.

Over his shoulder, Zoey popped up from the couch. "What's wrong?" She was fully dressed, but she wiped hastily at her mouth. "Oh. Hey, Keely. I was going to text you."

"I'm sure you were," Keely said. "Busy day?"

"We were working on my final anatomy project."

Keely hooked her keys by the door. She could see how Nolan might need to be shirtless for that.

"I should go." Nolan shot Zoey a look so intimate, Keely had to turn away.

"See you." Zoey waved back and gave him a soft smile. "And thanks again for your help."

"Any time." He reached for the door again.

Keely started forward. "Um, wait. I have a question."

Nolan nodded. "Go for it."

"Have you—have you seen Max recently? Is he okay?" It might have betrayed his trust, and she already knew the answer, but sometimes you learned less from an answer and more from how someone reacted to the question itself.

Nolan's soft mouth fell. "I don't know, Keely. I wish I did." He rubbed at the back of his neck. "If it makes you feel better, he hasn't been ... all there lately. At practice. I think he's going through something. With his—"

He shut his jaw so fast Keely heard his teeth clack together. He glanced toward the door.

"With his dad," she murmured, taking a guess. "It's okay. I know."

Relief relaxed Nolan's shoulders. "Maybe ask him about that?"

Just one problem—she needed to *see* Max to ask him about that. Watch his expression for anger, fear, a tightening of his mouth. Depending on what she saw, she'd most likely want to leave time to wrap him up in a hug, because she wasn't sure anyone had ever done that for him.

Which is exactly why, two days later, she showed up at the track after his morning practice.

Nolan elbowed him in the side, and Max's single-shouldered backpack slipped to the crook of his arm. His face lit up with an eye-crinkling smile, and Nolan nudged him again. Max shoved him back this time, mouth opening on a laugh Keely couldn't hear yet.

Her heart swelled. Butterflies crawled into her throat. Her knees felt the way they had that night in her bed, when they'd squeezed Max's ribcage.

"Oh," she exhaled under her breath. She didn't need that particular reminder.

When she absolutely couldn't stand the distance, she closed it, taking two large strides forward and going in for a hug. She *missed* him, dammit, scholarship or no.

"I'm sweaty," he mumbled, but she was already burying her face in his chest.

It *was* a little gross, but he mostly smelled like *Max*—hard work, diligence, perseverance. His sharp muscles stood out beneath his form-fitting shirt, Abe the ash borer smiling right back at Keely.

He inhaled deeply enough that his ribcage expanded under her palms, and a low sound of satisfaction rumbled under her ear. She clasped her hands behind his back and let out a contented sigh into his chest.

Max laid his chin on top of her head. Wrapped his arms around her shoulders. Tugged her closer like he missed her too.

Which was completely his fault, but she could pick that apart later when she didn't feel like throwing him to the pavement and mounting him.

She tiptoed up to kiss him, but paused. There were other people around, and they hadn't discussed their situation yet, much less whether they were comfortable with PDAs.

His brow dipped below the locks of damp hair on his forehead. He cupped her jaw, bringing his mouth down on hers. A quick peck, but a hard, claiming one. Nolan still managed to squeeze in a wolf whistle.

Max pulled back. "You don't ever have to hesitate to kiss me, Key." He slid his hand from the side of her face all the way down her arm, where he twined their fingers. "What are you doing here?"

She licked her lips—salt and *Max* sang on her tongue. "I wanted to see you. My morning study session got cancelled, so I'm heading to the library and dragging you with me."

They fell into step together, and she didn't know how something so new could be so natural.

"How am I supposed to say no to someone this pretty?"

Nolan cooed. "You say no to me all the time."

Keely and a few others around them laughed.

Max threw up a hand. "I get it. Be nicer to people."

After they ducked inside Athletics so Max could grab his stuff from his locker—*The Locker*, Keely's brain renamed it—Nolan peeled off, and Max and Keely stopped at the Q for sustenance.

She got to see what went into Max's protein shakes, and she grabbed them three eggwiches to split as they walked to the library. It was hard to hold them all, plus eat one, while she was holding Max's hand. But she didn't let go.

She hoped he'd bring up the other day on his own, tell her why he'd canceled, but she'd give him the benefit of the doubt for now. Maybe Nolan was right, and something really was going on with his dad.

At their usual table in the library, Keely had spread out her notebooks and flashcards, plus her detailed finals study guide. Her phone vibrated.

The unknown caller ID made her pulse jump. *It's nothing*, she told herself. There probably wasn't even a real person on the other end, just some automated something that would do more to ratchet her anxiety than anything.

Still. She couldn't let it ring out.

"I need to take this," she said, giving Max a wooden smile.

She tucked herself in the stacks and listened intently, jotting notes on her phone when she needed to.

When she came back, Max's leg bounced wildly under the table, his thumb drumming against the side of his trackpad. He stopped when he noticed her. "Everything okay?"

She nodded, too vigorously, if her hair clip sliding down was any indication. "All good."

"Was that ..." He glared at his screen, but his eyes didn't move. "About the scholarship?"

"What?" Keely sat back in her chair, ice spreading over her skin. "No. I haven't submitted that yet. There's still two weeks."

He nodded once, but his knee still bounced under the table. It shook the water in her bottle.

"Have *you* submitted yours?" she prompted, the thought running rampant through her worst nightmares.

"No," he said.

"Good." She picked at the empty wrapper from her sandwich. "I was sort of hoping we'd submit them together."

He stopped glaring at his screen and his gaze jumped to her instead. He swallowed, his throat bobbing. "Why?"

His face swam with doubt, and she had an overwhelming,

heartbreaking realization that Max had been balancing on one foot his entire life, waiting for the other shoe to drop.

If she could pull this off—if the phone call panned out—he wouldn't need to do that anymore.

Not with her.

"We've done this entire thing together so far, Max." She moved her hand forward, bumping his pinkie beside his laptop. "I figured we'd see it through to the end. Fair and square, like I said from the start."

Her phone lit up again. She slid her hand forward and dimmed the screen.

The corner of his mouth dipped down, but he still nodded. "Fair and square."

His smile didn't touch his eyes.

• • • • •

Max thought Keely was hiding something.

It was in his shoulders whenever her phone buzzed on the table or her email dinged. Whenever she ran late to their study sessions. The casual questions with hidden barbs.

And, well—he wasn't exactly wrong.

It sounded worse than it was.

This had nothing to do with him, and she was still figuring it out for herself.

Turns out, making a spring-semester-senior-year career pivot was really damn hard, more so when she was considering switching disciplines completely.

Keely wanted to teach.

She'd realized it while drafting the latest version of her essay, and the conversation in Dr. Goff's office had confirmed it.

HEART RACER

A tiny ember in Keely's heart glowed like neon every time she let herself think about the "what if." Each Thursday night, she stared at her ceiling, mind racing with anticipation and hope at what new discovery the children would make during her Friday-morning reading session.

It was the exact opposite of her Sunday Scaries. Those filled her stomach with rocks; teaching, witnessing the moment someone understood a concept because of something *she* said? Keely was capable of magic in those moments. Better, she gave other people magic. Even tutoring Max sparked it.

She still couldn't bring herself to open up to anyone about it. She'd drafted no less than four emails to Dr. Goff, only to send them straight to the garbage.

This was one of the first things in life she'd picked for herself, and she was worried the second she spoke it out loud, it would slip through her fingers, dissolve back into her dreams, but she owed it to herself to try. So she'd put out some feelers, reached out to a few nearby schools about their education programs, and had placed some calls about next steps, which she was half-heartedly looking into. It might not even be viable, but she had to do something. Had to convert her thoughts into action, so it didn't feel like she was just ... standing still.

Teaching felt the same way science did: exhilarating and calming at the same time. And if she ever found a way to *combine* them—say, as a science teacher, perhaps—she was pretty sure she'd die of happiness.

"What's that?" Zoey said from behind her.

Scratch that—she was going to die of a heart attack, right here at her kitchen table.

Keely slammed her laptop closed; she hadn't heard Zoey come

out of her bedroom. Usually on Mondays she holed up in there to watch Italian-dubbed, English-captioned reality television. She preferred it over Duolingo.

"*Nothing.*" She blinked. "Just looking at some stuff for the fall."

A stretch, but not a lie.

Zoey pulled a bottled water from the fridge, and Keely stopped vibrating with fear long enough to actually *see* her best friend.

Zoey's raven-black hair bounced in curls around her high bun, and a coral romper lit up her warm bronze skin. Even without the blush on her cheeks or the gloss on her lips, the glow in her eyes would have given her away.

"Hot date?" Keely guessed.

"I'm going to dinner with Nolan." Zoey's response was clipped, but Keely still caught the tail end of a smile.

Their relationship had improved only marginally since the auction. While Keely didn't think Zoey had been faking her gratitude, they hadn't gone back to how they'd been at the beginning of the semester, either. Gone were their weekly grocery runs, the sneaking into the locker rooms.

The grad school housing decision was looming closer, just weeks behind the scholarship deadline, and they all compounded in her head, giving Keely one massive headache, right behind her forehead. She hadn't looked at her planner at all today because there were too many boxes, too much to do, too many people to disappoint.

Keely grinned. "Have fun."

Zoey nodded, eyeing the laptop again. "You too."

"Oh, you know me. Night full of studying!" Keely imbued her voice with as much enthusiasm as she could muster, but when that didn't work, she added a truth. "Max might come over later."

Zoey made a noise in the back of her throat. "Is that so?"

Keely's mind was already too full to parse the subtext.

Her mind had been wandering for hours about what she and Max would get up to tonight. The permutations were endless. They could study—which they both probably needed. Or they could kiss.

Or something in between. A kiss for every page of homework flipped. A graze of teeth for every question answered correctly. A wandering hand because she wanted to.

She was still new at ... at being ... whatever they were. In a relationship? Friends with benefits? Though her thoughts toward Max were the *farthest* thing from friendly.

After Zoey had left, Keely picked up her phone and called him when her eyes glazed over and wouldn't come unstuck. Seemed she wasn't going to be able to focus until he was here anyway, for better or worse.

The line clicked.

"Hey." She grinned at her now-dimmed computer screen. Was there *still* banana smashed in the corner? She picked at it with her thumbnail. "What time are you coming over? Because not to jump to conclusions, but Zoey's going out with Nolan, which means—"

"I have to rain check," he interrupted, then cleared his throat. "I'm sorry. My track times right now are ... not cutting it, so I'm going to put a few extra hours in. Coach offered to stay behind with me."

Her shoulders fell, her hand stilling on the screen. A flake of dried banana fell off and lodged near the escape key. "Oh." She blinked unseeing. "Is, um—is your dad—"

"He's fine."

She nodded feebly. "Are *you* okay?"

"I'm just ... I can't let my training slip, Key. Not now. Not when I'm so close. It—you know what happened last year. I won't let it happen again."

"I understand," she mumbled. She ground her back molars together, and the silence stretched between them like a canyon. She only released her breath when her chest clawed for oxygen, when she realized he didn't have anything else to say. "I'll see you when I see you, I guess."

For the next hour, she stared at the pages of her thesis notebook, but her handwritten equations swam together. She almost made the epinephrine have a delayed-release instead of the melatonin she needed to counteract it. Which would have been fine, a simple mistake, except Keely didn't make those.

Her entire life, she'd bent over backwards to tie herself in knots. Sleepless nights and early mornings, stifling, unending pressure from all sides. From within.

Her eyes watered. If pressure made diamonds, when the hell was Keely going to start shining?

Chapter Thirty-Four

Max

"Again," Coach said.

Max had lost track of how many times he'd heard that word today. He'd been at the track since five this morning, trying to get his head on straight. It wasn't working.

All he could think about was Keely. That phone call at the library had wormed to the center of his consciousness, forming craters and holes of worry and self-doubt.

She said they'd see this through to the end, and he had to trust her on that. But, as Sam so *kindly* pointed out, the end was closer than either of them realized. And the end was going to change everything.

As hard as he tried to run from the endless spiral of negative thoughts, they still caught up with him, no matter how fast he ran.

If his current splits were anything to go by, it wasn't fast enough.

Coach grunted when Max crossed the finish line. "Maybe if you'd quit skipping out on practice, you wouldn't be in this shape right now."

Max's jaw clicked. "I'm in great shape."

"I'm not talking physical, Simmons." Coach tapped the side of his head. "Up here. I can't fix it. Only you can do that. Figure it out and stop letting it affect your game. While you're here, the only thing you should be worried about is your feet."

It echoed Nolan's sentiment from when they were sprinting. Compartmentalization wasn't something Max was ever good at—even less so with Keely. Much as she loved her checklists, she didn't fit neatly in a box for him.

"That girlfriend of yours isn't allowed here anymore, by the way." Coach nodded once, hands on hips, then raised his voice. "No distractions. In fact, as of right now, practice is officially closed."

The entire team groaned.

"You heard me." An angry vein jumped in Coach's neck. And in his forehead. "No girlfriends. No spectators. No pizza deliveries."

Alex whined. "That was one time."

"Twice," Jazz muttered.

"Run it again," Coach said. "Stay focused."

Max wasn't sure how to tell Coach that he could lock down practice all he wanted, but Keely would still be running laps in his head.

· · · · ·

"I'm sorry," Max said when Keely's front door opened. He hadn't seen her in almost a week, and he was crawling out of his skin.

He had his whole speech planned out, the points he needed to lay out and apologize for in a little bulleted list inside his head. Keely would be proud.

Except it wasn't Keely who answered.

Zoey rolled her eyes, stepping out around him with her bag

over her shoulder. She then closed the door in his face, and locked it, leaving Max staring after her for a few dumbfounded seconds before he was forced to knock again.

The entire process repeated when Keely answered the door.

"Key, wait, *no*—" His head fell onto the wood, narrowly missing the metal peephole. He sighed. "I deserve this," he muttered to the empty hallway.

"I agree," Keely said from the other side of the door. After another beat, he heard a sound that might have been her clearing her throat. "But tell me why *you* think you do."

Okay. The list. "I canceled on you twice with no explanation."

The lock unlatched, and Keely's face appeared through the sliver. Despite being a foot shorter than he was, she somehow managed to look down her nose at him. "I'll accept one now, if you're offering."

"I owe you an apology, for starters. The dinner I canceled." He hefted the bag of takeout. "All the study sessions. A thank you for the grades you've helped me rescue. Not to mention the incredible, spine-twisting org—"

She clapped a hand over his mouth and, with her other, pulled him through her door by his collar. "That's enough of that."

Only when the lock was engaged, sealing them in, did she turn back to him.

"What are you doing here, Max?" She crossed her arms. "And no excuses this time. Or funny business." Her cheeks glowed pink, and he wondered if she was thinking about his truncated thought like he was. He hadn't been sleeping well since this weird tension had sprouted between them, and when he did sleep it was to dream of Keely over him, under him, in front of him ...

He willed his blood to remain in his brain. He needed all his mental faculties to save face like this.

"Apologizing, honestly." He scratched the back of his neck. "I'm sorry I've been so flaky. I think our meeting with Dr. Goff got in my head, and I heard Sam talking—"

"Sam?" Keely reared back. "What does Sam have to do with this?"

"Nothing. Forget I said that." He shook his head. "I started seeing stuff that wasn't there."

Her lips parted, but he needed to get all of this out before she stopped him.

"I won't cancel on you again without ample notice or an honest explanation. And I just ... missed you." His brow furrowed. Was he rambling? So what. Maybe she liked to hear him talk as much as he did her.

"I know things are coming down to the wire," he continued, "but I wanted—needed a night with you all to myself. Before we get too busy with finals or theses or qualifying for divisionals. Outside of school or practice or any other obligations. For the next twelve hours, I only want to be obligated to you."

She eyed the takeout bag with a steely gaze, crossing her arms over her chest. "*Twelve* hours?"

"We have a lot of making out—I mean, making up—to do." He took a chance and winked. Then moved the takeout bag in front of his balls in case she decided to kick him there.

Thankfully, she let out a light, airy laugh, one that Max had missed tremendously over the last few days. "You're ridiculous."

He slid the food onto the counter, then took her face in his hands instead. "I'm ridiculously attracted to the way you look when you're mad at me."

"That's so unfair." Her breath hitched when he moved closer. "I want to look indomitable. Fierce."

He leaned in. "And you do, Key. Completely. But you also look so—" he pressed his lips to her forehead "—so—" another to her jaw "—kissable."

He waited, though, giving her the choice.

She closed the distance. Her lips were pillow soft, impossibly sweet despite the bite of peppermint just behind them. She tasted like the first warm sunny day after a bitter winter, coming home after vacation.

She tasted like Keely.

She tasted like ... *his*.

Max grinned against her lips at the whimper that slipped out. He'd missed that, too, and if all went according to plan, he'd be hearing that later. Preferably as soon as she was fed.

Which reminded him.

"Come on," he said, pulling back to turn toward the food. "I've gotta feed you. I know how you forget to eat when you're busy."

He unpacked the burgers and fries, remembering her order from the night of the auction. The shakes were well on their way to melted, the cherry sinking down through semisolid whipped cream, but Keely's face lit up at the first sip all the same.

They took their food to the couch, and Keely threw on a random show as background noise.

He'd *really* missed her. All the negative thoughts and spirals didn't exist when she was around. The restlessness in his body disappeared. He felt ... stretched out, relaxed in a way his honed athlete's body rarely was. She put him at ease.

He hadn't known anyone—or anything outside of running, for that matter—could do that for him.

"How's your dad?" Keely asked, licking a glob of ketchup off her thumb.

His bite went down roughly for more than one reason. "He's decent right now. He's basically reached his med tolerance, so they're giving him a few weeks to recover. Lots of scans, PT, bloodwork in the meantime."

"Will he be here for graduation?" She coughed and took a large swallow of her shake. "I mean, physically able to attend."

"That's the plan," he said quietly, "but it's a game time decision. He has an appointment the day before with the doctor to make sure things are good to go."

Her eyes glistened, and his heart chose to call it something other than pity.

"Is he ..." Keely shook her head violently, ducked her head to focus on the food in front of her. "Never mind."

"Is he going to die?" he asked when she wouldn't, the words burning but familiar. It was the same question he asked himself every single day. What drove him harder at practice. What put one foot in front of the other when all he wanted was to give up. "Is that what you mean?"

She looked up at him through wet lashes. Her nod was so small he almost missed it.

"I don't know," he rasped. "One doctor says a few years, another says eight months. There's really nothing to do but wait and see."

A drop of water hit his face, and he looked up, sure Keely's ceiling was about to cave in. But it was normal, smooth, off-white, and Max's face only grew wetter. It slid down his neck in hot rivers, and he wiped it away with a groan that broke open on the end.

He would have cracked completely down the middle if not for the arms that appeared in his periphery, wrapping around him, holding him together.

"I'm so sorry, Max."

He buried his face into golden hair, hoping some of her warmth would rub off on his suddenly frigid soul. He was *shaking*.

She pulled the food from his lap and placed it on the coffee table before taking up its spot, throwing her legs on either side of his hips and winding her arms under his.

"There." Keely was soft, barely a whisper. Her heart raced against his. "That's better. Go ahead. Continue."

"Thanks," he croaked through a laugh. Then, more seriously, "This might be the best hug I've ever had." He held her hips, supple and warm through her leggings, and the exact right size for his hands.

He didn't deserve her gentleness, not after he'd made an ass of himself this week. He wasn't strong enough to pull away, no matter how much he should.

Instead, he burrowed closer.

She tensed, just for a second, before melting.

"When you get sad ..." Her breath was hot on his neck, her mouth close enough that her lips brushed his skin with every word. "Do you want to stay that way?"

Peppermint flooded his senses; if it was so great for concentration, why was his mind so blurry? "What do you mean?"

"Do you want to sit in the sadness," she repeated, silk now blanketing her words, "or do you want to be distracted?"

A stronger man could resist.

But Max had been strong for too long, for too many other people and, dammit, Keely made him weak.

His fingers dug into her lower back. "Distract me."

A satisfied hum rumbled through her chest, her lips curling into a smile. Then, in a move that proved she would always have the upper hand over him, she dropped her weight, settling her center over the growing bulge in his jeans.

"Keely," he hissed.

She ground her hips down again. He threw his head back and she licked the pulsing vein in his neck. It elicited a wanton moan that she echoed.

She liked this, he realized. Liked being in control.

Or maybe she liked *him*.

Which was fine, because Max was already half in l—

Her phone's ringtone blared.

"Sorry," she said, dragging herself along Max as she reached for it on the coffee table.

"Let it ring out." He thrust up, his cock rubbing the seam of her leggings.

She jerked, squirming in his lap. "Max."

If she kept doing that, he'd bend her over right here, screw anyone who might walk by out in the hall. He tightened his grip. "Key, please. Can't you call them back later?"

She grabbed it anyway, scrambling to her feet. "I'm sorry," she mouthed. "This is important. Two minutes."

He threw his head back so far it missed the couch and hit the wall instead. At least it gave him something else to focus on aside from his raging hard-on and the roller coaster of his emotions. The fear of losing his father, the lust still thrumming in his veins for the girl taking a private phone call in another room.

Why *did* she keep slinking off? He'd believed her when she'd said it wasn't about the scholarship, that they'd see it through to the end, but what else would she need to keep from him like this? He was opening his heart and she was shutting him out just when he'd realized he needed her there. *Wanted* her there.

He grabbed his phone and scrolled mindlessly through his socials as a distraction, but it wasn't enough. Eventually he stood and walked the hall, half in search of her and half in need of the toilet.

The bathroom was empty, but he did pee, wash his hands, and poke around a little.

He finally found the source of his deepest desires. A little roll-on bottle of peppermint oil sat on the vanity next to a red hairbrush with a claw clip around the handle.

He rolled some onto his neck, hoping it'd help calm him the way it did Keely. The way *Keely* herself calmed him.

She still wasn't back when he re-entered the living room.

Maybe she'd laid down on her bed to take the call and fallen asleep? Or maybe it had been bad news—or something had happened with her parents. If it was as important as it seemed to be, she'd probably be crushed if it didn't work out in her favor. Whatever it was, he needed to make sure she was okay.

He padded down the hall to her bedroom and grabbed the handle.

"I'm very honored," Keely said, her voice brimming with excitement.

Max's stomach sank.

Chapter Thirty-Five

Keely

Keely opened her bedroom door to find Max leaning on the wall opposite it.

"I guess I owe you some congratulations," he said in a wry, cutting tone before she could corral her thoughts into a semblance of working order.

"What?" She blinked. How much had he heard? "Were you—were you *listening* to my phone call?" Dread, slimy and thick, curled through her stomach and wound out to her veins, turning her simultaneously ice cold and fire hot. "A phone call I wanted to take in private?"

His jaw ticked. "I got worried. I came to check on you and ..." He blew air through his nose. "I heard the last part, about you being 'very honored.' It sounding like you were accepting something. When did you submit your application? So much for seeing it through to the end together."

She reared back, catching herself on the door frame. Where was this anger coming from? "I told you, I haven't yet."

His laugh sliced through her skin and stuck her in the heart. "Sure you have. You just won the scholarship. Which doesn't feel great, if I'm being honest."

"I didn't win the scholarship, Max." She ran a hand through her hair. The claw clip slid down, and she ripped it out, taking a few strands with it. "The phone call had nothing to do with that."

"Right." Max's gaze narrowed as his weight shifted. "So what *did* it have to do with?"

Fear pressed her lips together, and she shook her head. "I can't tell you. I don't want to jinx it."

His gaze darkened. "Keely, I'm sorry, but I need a little more than that."

She wrapped her arms around her torso, some of the ice in Max's glare having dropped onto her skin. "Why can't you trust me?"

"Trust should go both ways," he countered. "And you're clearly hiding something. Something to do with the scholarship that we're *both* going for. I'm an open book here, Key—I *sent* you the essay you tried to take."

"What does that have to do with this?"

"Because all I've been trying to do is help you, and you're shutting me out."

"That's not fair." And Keely was proud of herself for a second, because despite how badly her knees were shaking, her voice was resolute. "You're the one who went AWOL these last few weeks. And I've been helping you too, with studying, with your grades—"

"Oh, were you 'helping me study—'" he threw up lazy fingers around the words "—when you emailed me and told me class was canceled? Or when you tried to take my laptop?"

As if he didn't give it back tenfold. "I thought we were . . ." *in love, or on the way there.* "Past that," she finished weakly.

"And I thought," he ground out, blinking hard. His brows gathered on his forehead and he stared down at her. "That we were in this together, going to see it through to the end. Which means you trusting me with whatever and *who*ever was on the other end of that phone call. *Please.*" He jerked his chin at her phone, tucked in her fist.

"I ... I'm ..."

He looked so *earnest*. And he, loath as she was to admit it, did have a point. If they were supposed to be together—to have a shot with each other after graduation in a few weeks—she needed to tell him.

The call hadn't been anything, not really. She'd just been invited to formally apply. She still had so far to go, and it might not work out. What if this was the complete wrong decision?

She *wanted* to talk it through with him, ask his advice, but she couldn't do that. Couldn't ask him to give her reasons *for* and *against* pulling out of the scholarship when his own dreams were so entwined with it.

It all spun around in her head, and the words lodged in her throat. The harder she tried to push them, the bigger they swelled. Her entire life, she'd worked toward one thing, and now she was trapped in a current she'd made herself. She didn't know how to get out. She couldn't fight it.

Could she? What if the only reason she and Max worked so well was because of the Keely she was right now? If she changed, would they? Would they survive this fallout? She already felt like there was shrapnel in her heart whenever he looked at her lately.

And what would her parents say? Would her dad twist it around somehow to point the blame at her mom's influence on Keely? *Keely's giving up on her future, just like Veronica had given up on him.* Would her mom tell her dad it was his fault Keely was feeling so unstable, that she'd learned to make careless life decisions from him?

What about Zoey? Zoey, her very best friend, who Keely had already let down so many times this semester. Could she really say goodbye to their shared dream of Caltech?

She just needed a few more days to wrap her head around it all.

Days she didn't have.

Teeth sunk into her bottom lip, she shook her head.

His face fell, and Keely's body ached like she'd taken the plunge instead.

"I, uh ..." His jaw clicked as he ground his teeth together. "I don't think this is working."

Pinpricks of pain shot through her heart. More of that shrapnel, digging deep. Her brain worked overtime making sense of his words, but it was tired. *She* was tired. "This, as in—"

"Us." Max expelled air in a quick, rough burst. "Being together."

Keely's chest caved in like her ribs had collapsed, but when she glanced down, she was still whole. "If you give me a little more time to work this out, I'll—"

"A few more days won't change the fact that we both can't win the scholarship." A garbled, strangling sort of noise escaped his throat. "One of us is going to lose. Are you prepared for that to be you?"

Her heart beat an odd rhythm in her chest. She pressed a hand there, grounding herself the way he'd taught her to on the track. In this very bedroom. "You're so sure you're going to win?"

He threw up a hand, let loose a sharp laugh. "It doesn't matter who wins, Keely. We're going to lose something either way."

That didn't make sense. What would she lose if she won? She

searched every valley and crest of his face for the answers. The downturn of his mouth. The harsh angles of his jaw.

He wouldn't lift his gaze, and that was answer enough.

Him. She'd lose Max.

"Oh," she whispered. She didn't trust herself to speak any louder. "You'd rather ... stop now?"

The corners of his eyes were glassy, his dark eyelashes fluttering as he blinked. "It's easier this way." Raw pain seeped under the cracks in his voice. "You're moving to California at the end of the summer anyway, aren't you? And I'll be traveling with the team for most of that."

She inhaled once, twice, quicker.

"Breathe," he reminded her, gruff and reluctant.

Keely forced out her air, messy, like he'd taught her. Max was the only person she'd ever let herself be messy around. "Is now the time where we say we're going to try and still be friends?"

"I don't think I can be friends with you," he muttered.

The slight stung more than she'd expected. Of course he couldn't. She didn't have anything to offer him, now that his grades were better. Now that he'd gotten what he wanted from her. The hurt compounded with the pain already in her chest and set off a chemical reaction.

Her nose, face, everything *burned*. "Silly me, I forgot. You don't *have* friends." She threw up a hand. "You have teammates you push away over and over. Tell me, Max, what's going to happen in a few weeks? Who's going to be there for you after you graduate, and you're not all trapped in a locker room together anymore?"

His jaw unhinged, and he finally turned his amber eyes on her. They were molten, hardened, on *fire*. Anguish sharpened his features into blades, designed specifically to cut her. "I don't need them. Running is a solo sport. And I'm *damn* good at it. I have a legacy. I'm *building* a legacy, something my family will be proud of. Something my father—" his voice cracked as he pointed a finger at his heart "—will be proud of. And at least I'm honest about who I am. You think you're so much nicer than me, that you have all these amazing friends, but if you looked up from your precious checklists once in a while, you'd realize that all you have is a network of people to use when it's convenient. Who are *you* taking with you to your shiny new life in California except someone who, last I heard, still isn't talking to you?"

Her chest caved in around the dagger he'd shoved there. Was he right? "That's not ..." A tear slipped down her cheek.

Max reached for her for a split second, his hand suspended between them, before he curled his fingers into a fist. He blinked several times in succession.

"So," she tried again. Her voice was just as shaky. She collected her stray tears with shaking fingers. "This is it."

His throat bobbed, and he went back to staring at the wall instead of her. "It was always going to end up here one way or another."

He didn't slam the door when he left. She wished he had, because then she would have been able to blame the crackling, broken sound on something other than her heart, shredding to pieces in her chest.

Chapter Thirty-Six

Max

No distractions.

Don't think about Keely.

Watch your instep—ouch, a little lighter on the balls of your feet next time.

Don't think about Keely, how she laughs, how she smiles at you different from how she smiles at anyone else. At everyone else.

Tighten your core. Remember to breathe. Like how you taught Keely.

Don't think about her. Don't think about how you broke each other's hearts.

"Simmons!" Coach's voice snapped him out of his head. "It's like you don't even want to be here."

Max slowed to a stop, hands splayed on his head. Truth was, he *didn't* want to be here.

It'd been nearly a week since he'd left Keely's apartment, both of them crying and pretending they weren't, his chest on fire. A week of sleepless nights, his mind playing tug-of-war on what went wrong, whose fault it was, whether it truly was inevitable like he'd claimed.

All he'd wanted was for Keely to be *open* with him, and his fear had overtaken his tongue, his insecurities running the show.

Like everything else in his life, he'd imploded them. Imploded the best thing that had ever happened to him.

Maybe Max wasn't meant to have good things. He was supposed to shoulder his hurt and carry his burdens on his own.

He was the anchor, after all. He only existed to drag others down with him.

Like Keely.

Don't think about Keely, he chastised as he jogged back to his position. They'd been running relays this afternoon, and where normally Max settled in the longer he ran, today he was clumsy. Messing up strides, straining his calves, going slow, slow, too slow to win like he needed.

If he didn't win, he'd lose everything.

His dreams.

His dad's dreams.

His dad.

Keely.

Max fumbled the baton at the handoff, then his left foot dragged, catching on his opposite ankle.

"Damn," Jazz said, trying to save it. They tumbled over each other, and Max's knee skidded across the track, bright pain manifesting alongside drops of blood.

By the time Alex and Nolan showed up, Jazz was already on her feet, shaking out her muscles.

All of Max's were tight, closing him in while out in the open. He was supposed to be better than this. He wasn't allowed to stumble, to mess up. He'd been surefooted his entire life. He wouldn't let himself mess it all up because of—what? Because of a girl?

Nolan nudged Max's shoe with his own. "You good?"

Max grunted, wiping at his bloody knee. "I will be once we do that again."

It didn't get better. During the next heat, the wind blew too strongly and Max caught a whiff of peppermint from one of the passing teammates, which was a problem because (1) his head jerked in that direction, taking his eyes off the finish line and (2) it meant someone had *passed* him.

Coach took pity on them and had Max switch to hurdles. But he couldn't get in the rhythm there, either, and his movements were too slow, his foot clipping again. Fall after fall after fall.

Max hadn't fallen all semester.

Or maybe he had, and that was the real problem.

He'd fallen for Keely, but he'd never learned how to fall safely. No wonder he was so bruised and bloodied.

After four more abysmal attempts, Coach ended their practice twenty minutes early. "I'm done looking at you four today."

They trudged in silence to the locker room, and Max checked his phone. Nothing. Why should he expect anything when they'd left things like they had? *His fault.* Everything was his fault lately.

Guilt slugged him in the stomach around the same time Alex slugged him in the shoulder.

"Dude. What happened out there?"

Max reared back. "Nothing *happened*, Alex. It's called a bad day." He tossed his phone into his locker, aiming for the towel at the bottom. It missed, cracking against the metal with an ominous thud. That's what his heart had done the day he'd found Keely in there. "Thought you knew all about those from the way your splits look. So what's your excuse?"

Alex's face went slack for a second, then morphed into reddened rage. "Oh, really? We're doing this? What's *your* excuse for being an absolute asshole, then?"

Movement blurred in his periphery, and Nolan pressed a firm hand to the gaping hole where Max's heart used to sit. He'd thought it would have hurt, but he was numb. Did Nolan think Max would—what? *Fight* Alex?

It shocked him. He ran a hand over his sweat-dampened hair. "Do you really think that? Does *everyone*?"

Nolan and Alex shared a look, and Nolan spoke for both of them. "Kinda, yeah. You're not a total asshole, but you sure as hell don't let anyone close. Isn't that lonely?"

Max sucked in air through his teeth.

"I know you've been going through it this semester, and I'm here for you. Or I've tried to be, anyway," Nolan continued, voice steady. Max didn't remember what *steady* felt like. "But we all have stuff going on. You wouldn't know that, though, because you don't ask."

"I—"

"There is no 'I.'" Nolan's hand, still on Max's chest, gave a tiny shove to emphasize his words. "We're a relay *team*. We win or we lose. Together."

"Speak for yourself. I've got two other events where I don't have to put up with this."

"Dude. Take a walk," Nolan said.

Alex mumbled something under his breath Max chose to ignore. It didn't matter anyway. He spun back around to his locker, grabbing his bag and his phone.

Max caught another whiff of peppermint and slammed the door. It echoed, bounced back at him from all angles. He hiked his bag over his shoulder and stared at Nolan. His chest pulled tight; his knee ached; his heart squeezed.

He blew a humorless laugh through his nose. "I thought you didn't give up on people."

Something like hurt flashed in Nolan's eyes before a shutter came down over them. Then, all Max could see was himself, standing alone while surrounded by people.

"This isn't me giving up on you." Nolan swallowed, his jaw tight. "This is me giving you space not to give up on yourself. And I'm sorry you can't recognize the difference."

What the hell did that mean?

Max left the locker room, left the athletics building and the stadium altogether. He didn't look back.

Spring had fully arrived now, so daylight lingered, casting everything in shades of Keely—golden light spilling over blooming flowerbeds, warmth hitting his bare skin, joy knocking at his heart, begging, just *begging* to be let in.

He wasn't sure he knew how anymore.

He pulled his phone from his pocket and smoothed his thumb over the new ding in the corner. A souvenir from his little tantrum in the locker room. Something else he'd messed up.

Gritting his teeth, he dialed a familiar number and let it ring through his headphones.

His mom's voice filtered in, and Max's heart picked up pace. It was unusual for his dad not to answer.

"Max?" His mom's voice was pinched, tired. "You there?"

"Hi, Mom. Is Dad okay?"

The silence stretched before him in a chasm, and he felt like he was free falling on flat land. Like he'd always be moving, never quite reaching the finish line.

"He's ... having a rough day."

So was Max. That was the whole problem. All the days since his blowup with Keely were rough.

"Do I need to come home?" he asked.

"No." His mom sighed. It was shaky—or Max was. Everything blurred together.

They caught up for a few minutes, but Max's fear stretched before him, and he only half heard everything.

What was all this for if his dad wasn't going to see him win?

If he didn't win the scholarship, he had no chance of racing.

And if he won the scholarship, he still lost Keely.

Which was worse than all of it combined.

Chapter Thirty-Seven

Keely

Keely called in sick to her shift at the shelter that Sunday. In her head, three things would have happened.

She'd show up, and Max wouldn't, which—fair.

She'd show up, and Max would too, but he'd look devastated, which—ouch.

Or she'd show up, and Max would too, but he'd be fine.

That last one did her in. The idea that he wasn't as destroyed as she was, that he could continue with his days like his entire world hadn't been upended the ways hers had.

The only thing propelling Keely forward was the end of the semester, the looming deadlines, the absolute necessity of not failing. She simply couldn't, not when so many people depended on her.

Like the smiling, shining faces of her students the following Friday. April thirtieth. It was her last day here. The scholarship was due tomorrow at midnight, and it was a compounding fracture, a one-two punch.

She knew these children by name, by voice, by face, and had prepared individualized print-outs for each of them, a take-home list of children's science books geared at their individual interests. Dinosaurs for Mateo, animals for Evelyn. Weird facts about bodily functions for Dallas. There was a whole chapter on boogers.

She stifled tears, but the kids didn't, because they were kids and they hadn't mastered emotional regulation yet. Keely hoped they never would. It really hurt, holding everything in.

She handed her visitor's badge in for the last time and sobbed all the way home.

Which was sort of how she existed all the time now.

If she wasn't crying, she was checking her email. The last thing Keely needed while prepping for finals was to be on her phone, but it was the only thing her brain would focus on with any regularity. She was a machine: refresh email, check texts, repeat.

Both apps remained empty, echoing Keely's stomach, and bed, and heart.

She missed Max. Missed him filling the chair across from her at the library or sitting on the couch in her living room. Texting her bad science puns, texting her how pretty she'd looked earlier in the day.

All of this over a damn scholarship she didn't know if she wanted anymore. Not even the thought of new school supplies or grad school-level textbooks sparked her passion the way teaching did.

More than that, if she won the scholarship, it meant Max had *lost*, and his shot at racing toward the finish for his dad was over. Him losing his dreams hurt almost as much—honestly, probably more—as losing her own, and it was the last sign she needed that she'd gone and fallen headfirst into love with him.

She hadn't expected it to hurt so much. Then again, he hadn't been here to catch her this time.

She toggled between her thesis paper and the Pursue Your Passions essay. Every line bled passion now—especially the ones Max had helped with.

She still hadn't submitted it, and she didn't know why. It didn't matter now, did it? She could just ... send it out into the ether, forget about it and hopefully focus on something important. Like her finals, mere days away.

But something was holding her back. Her dreams and responsibilities were at war in her chest, her heart, her mind. The dream she'd always planned, the new one she wanted now. Teaching or Caltech.

She'd sent that teaching application through on a whim a few days ago, mostly to keep her options open. She wasn't Keely Sinclair without a contingency plan or two. But she could have all the contingencies in the world and she still wouldn't know what to do.

More than anything, Keely wanted to talk to Max, work through the what ifs with him. She could half-imagine exactly how he'd guide her, the low rasp of his voice, the little furrow in his brow he always got when he was wholly focused on something, like running. Like her.

Max wasn't an option anymore.

She sighed, picking her phone up from the table and starting her refresh cycle again.

To her surprise, it vibrated in her hand, an incoming call dimming her still-empty inbox.

"Hello?" Keely didn't sound like herself. Was she smiling? She couldn't remember the last time she'd meant one of her smiles.

"This is Jordan with the Virginia Teachers' Association. I'm calling to speak with Keely Sinclair."

"Yes?" She physically tasted her heartbeat, iron flooding her tongue and throat.

"I was calling about your application. Is now a good time to talk?"

They needed time to talk; a rejection would have been an email. She agreed, flipping to a random blank page in her planner and grabbing a pen. Red for *SUPER IMPORTANT, FUTURE-DEFINING NOTES*.

And then the woman on the other end of the line decimated Keely's dreams with three simple words. "I'm so sorry."

If there was more to that sentence, it was drowned out by a high-pitched ringing deep in Keely's brain. She let out a soft, *oh*, but the woman on the other end heard anyway.

"Your application was very strong," she continued. "Unfortunately it came down to timing, and we're unable to offer you a spot this fall."

Capping her pen, Keely blinked away tears. "Right. Of course."

"We encourage you to reapply next year. If you'd like, I can send some application tips and guidelines? Or I can refer you to some other programs that may still be accepting applicants. Whichever you prefer. Are you sold on staying in Virginia?"

"I ..."

This had to be a sign. Grad school was her only option. Caltech with Zoey, and vitamins, and hiding her true self away to appease everyone else, always everyone else, never herself.

She'd just tuck those dreams deep in her heart, right next to the ones she'd cultivated with Max. She'd pull them out when she wanted a shot of pain to keep her grounded, the way you couldn't help but press on a fading bruise.

This was the ideal scenario for everyone involved: Zoey, her parents... Max, who had made it crystal clear he wanted to stay as far away from her as possible.

Hopefully California was far enough for him.

Chapter Thirty-Eight

Max

By sheer luck, divisionals were only forty minutes outside of Max and Keely's hometown. He'd been to this track so many times growing up, watching races with his dad. He knew it as well as the AMU track at this point, which might have made a difference a week ago.

But today, his teammates hadn't talked to him the entire ride here, Nolan included. Even Coach had given him distance.

He was used to it. Everyone in Max's life pulled away when he got prickly. Which was fine. Running—outside of the relay—was a solo sport. He shouldn't have to rely on others to succeed.

From here it was another few weeks to regional qualifiers, then nationals, if they made it that far.

He'd know his future by then.

It was May first. The scholarship application was due at midnight, and his was still a draft on his laptop, waiting for him to press *submit*.

And he would.

Later. Currently, he was doing his best just to focus on the ground in front of him. His knee still ached from busting it at practice Tuesday.

No more than his heart, but still.

Max bounced on his toes and kept his core loose in the staging area until it was his heat for the hundred-meter-dash. He eyed the runners, clocked their builds and strides as they lined up on the blocks. Max had drawn lane three, which wasn't his favorite, but he much preferred it to one of the outside positions.

He'd breezed through the qualifying heat earlier, but now the stands were fuller. More people to watch him fail. Or fall. They were the same thing in his mind.

The hairs on the back of his neck prickled. He scanned the stands, hoping for a glimpse of a certain golden girl. Something that proved he was being watched like he suspected.

He shook his head. *Of course* he was being watched—upwards of five hundred people waved pom-poms, hoisted banners painted with their schools' colors. He caught flashes of emerald and gold throughout, and a larger blob of them closer to the finish line he was sure hadn't been there earlier, but no one was close enough to make out.

Max needed to focus on what was in front of him: the track, wide open, his for the taking.

He centered his right foot on the back block, stretched his left knee once more, and took position. The sun-warmed pavement bit at his palms, grounding him. One deep breath right after the warning tone, and—

Go.

Max burst from the starting block, his heels digging in to find purchase as he hit his rhythm. The stadium blurred. Or maybe he was the blur, the only thing in motion while everything around him stood still.

This was flying.

The runner to his right tucked in closer, edging Max out. So he dug harder, leading with his chest. It was almost over, twenty or so meters until the end now.

He was going to lose, and what would this all be for?

Disappointment thundered through him, rattling his bones.

Then he heard his name from a familiar voice, clear through the haze of focus. "Go, Max! Bring it home!"

He twinged a neck muscle forcing himself not to look. It was *impossible*.

But the mere thought propelled Max farther, faster, and he edged in front of the runner on his right again.

Bring it home, Max, that voice echoed. It dug into his muscles, lengthened and strengthened his strides. His shoes ate the pavement. Nothing existed but the track and his mind and his body and his heart, all perfectly synchronized for the first time in weeks. In months. In his entire life.

Bring it home.

And he did.

When he'd slowed on the other side of the finish line, hands atop his head to press him back down to earth after flying so far above it, he gave into the urge to crane his neck and see who'd shouted.

His hands slipped right off his head, his entire body jolting.

That emerald-and-gold blob he'd seen from the starting block was right in front of him now. He recognized every single face.

His brother Thomas with his wife, Max's nephew tucked

between them on the row and wearing massively oversized headphones. His other brothers Henry and Jacob. Max's mom, her face wet, hands clutched together beneath her trembling chin.

Nolan, who must have snuck over between his own heats to sit with the rest of the AMU cheer squad. Zoey, tucked into his side. Max resisted raising an eyebrow at that.

Front and center, wearing a smile that outshone the sun—

"Dad?"

Max leapt over the barrier, not caring whether he was impeding the races, the medal ceremony. He didn't care about any of it anymore. "What are you doing here?"

He didn't wait for an answer before throwing his arms around him, crushing him in a probably-too-intense hug.

"I couldn't miss the chance to watch my son doing what he loves in one of his final college meets, could I?"

The back of Max's neck *burned*. His brothers stifled laughter. Zoey hid a smile in Nolan's arm.

"Doing what *we* love, Dad." Max nodded, his breath coming both harder and easier. "It's your sport, really. My win is your win. This one, the next ... the Olympics. It's all for you. So you can finally achieve your dreams."

Dad's eyes shone. This was it. Regardless of the scholarship, *this* was Max's goal. Giving back to his dad everything he'd given up. Proving the sacrifice served a purpose.

His father's face twisted, his jaw dropping half an inch. "My ... dreams?"

"Winning gold," Max went on. He gestured vaguely to his chest, where a medal might lie. "You don't have to regret giving it up anymore."

Dad shook his head, his mouth opening and closing a few times.

Max lurched forward, ready to help him through a coughing fit or find the nearest sip of water and force it down his throat. But his dad only blinked up at him, and the longer he didn't say anything, the more Max felt like maybe he'd messed something up. Something *else*.

"What?" he said when the silence had stretched on long enough.

His father stroked his chin. "What is it, exactly," Dad said, "that you think I gave up?"

What? The bleachers jolted under Max's feet. He grabbed the railing. Somewhere, distantly, someone called his name. "Your ... your whole life."

Another slow blink from Wade. "And what might that be?"

Max stared ... and stared. "Your athletics career. Running. Track. Competitive sprinting. Going for gold. Everything."

"I didn't give it up, Max. That implies ..." Dad scratched his neck, looking for the right words. "A sacrifice, when it really wasn't a decision to be made at all. My entire life was you. You, and your brothers, and your mother." He turned his pensive gaze on each of them. Max followed behind, slogging to catch up.

His dad slipped a thin, wiry arm around his mom, who had buried her face in his neck. "As long as I had that—as long as I *have* this, I will be the happiest man on the planet."

Max's head pulsed, and he sucked in air. More distant shouts of his name. Down on the track, the next event was due to start, and Coach was waving his hat at Max, trying to get his ass back to where he belonged.

But Max was already there. He blocked out all the other noise. "My entire life, I thought you'd sacrificed so much."

Dad grinned, wan but happy. "Just because you didn't see me running doesn't mean I didn't. Sometimes I woke up at four in the morning to get in laps around the neighborhood. I'd strap you all into strollers and take you with me. You don't give up what you love for *who* you love. If it's meant to be, you won't ever have to pick between the two. You just ... figure it out as you go."

Max laughed, hands on his hips. "I'm not sure if I know how to do that."

Dad chuckled, and his eyes crinkled so much Max could have sworn he winked instead. "You'll figure that out, too."

Somehow, without ever having explicitly discussed it, Max's dad knew the root of the problem. Why this was tripping Max up so much. Maybe he'd known since their phone call earlier this year. Or over spring break.

The announcer called the event on deck.

"I've gotta go," Max said. He touched his dad's shoe with his own. "You sure you're okay out here?"

"Been better, been worse, here now, Max." Dad nodded. "So be here now."

Max's eyes stung—sweat, probably. He'd have to mainline electrolytes to make it to the starting line. Or the finish line. He wanted to win this for himself this time, since that was an option now.

Max turned to Nolan then, whose arm was around Zoey. Her curls were going wild in the wind, and some of them kept hitting Nolan in the face. He didn't seem to mind. They looked good together.

"What are you doing over here?" Max asked. Last he'd seen, Nolan was still busy ignoring him over by the race tents.

"Had a few minutes." Nolan shrugged. "And I told you, friends show up for each other. Even when things get rough." His head tilted. "Even when they're still mad at each other."

Max tipped his chin, a smile taking him by surprise. "Yeah, that's fair." He swallowed. "I appreciate it. I guess friendship is something you show, not just say." He made a mental note to fix what he'd screwed up, sooner rather than later.

"Maybe when Coach isn't turning purple yelling our names," Nolan offered, and Max was grateful all over again.

As they went to leave, Max searched the bleachers again for golden hair, a hint of peppermint, a wide smile aimed only at him.

"She's not here," Zoey said, throwing a sad smile Max's way.

He'd known that, but it still pulled at a stitch near his heart.

As he and Nolan walked down to the track and over to their team, Max tried to focus.

Be here now. Why was that so hard?

He loved running, would always love running and what it did for his body and mind, but he'd missed out on so much this semester by putting his all into dreams that—surprise—weren't legit to begin with. He'd worked himself to the bone, missed out on time with his dad he wouldn't ever get back. Time at the shelter with the dogs, time with Nolan and the team.

Time with Keely.

Don't think about—

Why the hell shouldn't he?

Dad said you don't give up what you love for who you love, and if Max wasn't in love with Keely, he'd never known love at all.

He'd messed everything up. She probably hated him.

He didn't hate her—the opposite, actually—but he wasn't sure they could come back from where they'd left it. They'd thrown punches intended to hurt, and they did. And if nothing else, Max was very good at running from his problems.

So he put his head down and did exactly that.

Chapter Thirty-Nine
Max

Later that night, the entire Simmons family filtered in through their front door, raucous laughter following in their wake. They'd grabbed pizza on the way home, and Jacob had already told Max no less than five times he had plans to decimate him at Madden tonight.

Max's relay team had snagged the bronze medal, easily securing their place at regionals. He'd pulled out a silver for the hundred-meter dash, and didn't medal for hurdles but still snagged a qualifying slot.

And he was *fine* with all of that. Dad got to see him race. To watch his sacrifices pay off in real time.

"Max," his mom said while she helped his dad get settled in his chair, a prime viewing spot for the video game tournament which would ultimately end in a broken piece of furniture. "Get the paper plates down, please."

"Just a second." Max hefted his new medal. Like his dad said, this one was for Max. "Wanna add this to my wall."

He took the stairs two at a time. If he didn't hurry, Henry would eat all the pepperoni pizza and Thomas would take the good controller.

Max added this newest medal to the collection hanging from the wall above his bed. A horrible design choice, because on the off chance he ever had a girl in here, the headboard would rattle them together.

His gut bottomed out. He didn't want any girls but Keely in his bed, and there was a subzero chance of that happening now.

God, he'd really screwed up. How was he supposed to shift his priorities so late in the game? He'd been programmed his entire career to view success as being first. Sacrifice, discipline, work ethic.

Somewhere, though, he'd let his insecurities come through and ruin his relationship with Keely. At first he thought if he'd worked harder, he would still have her, because that's how winning worked.

You couldn't put rules like that around people, though, and that's all Max had been trying to do. First with his relay team, then with Keely. Even with himself.

Laughter erupted downstairs. He wanted to be there, with them.

He breezed toward his door when something flapped in his periphery.

The picture from spring break, the one of him and Keely when they were kids, sat atop his dresser. He thumbed the edge. He remembered slipping it in his pocket before he'd left her house that day.

God, he'd wanted to kiss her so badly on that roof. She'd looked so pretty with the setting sun glowing in a halo around her face.

Then her voice had broken around the words "Keely's such a nerd." He'd put tears in her eyes—and he'd wanted to kiss them away.

Keely *was* a nerd. She had atom earrings. A framed picture of Marie Curie on her living room wall. She enjoyed *reading textbooks and* reading him to filth because he didn't.

He regretted upsetting her, but he didn't want to take the words back. Keely with science at her fingertips was unstoppable, and sexy as hell. She made him want to be a better runner, devote himself to his craft the way she had hers.

The edge of the picture bent around his grip.

He might not have his priorities completely straightened, but he could start.

He eyed the clock. Six thirty.

Could he still save this? Was there enough time to turn it around?

Max ran out to his car, ignoring the questions from his family. His backpack was still stuffed in his trunk from after the meet. It was possible he left a trail of old clothes, a tennis shoe or sweat towel, as he tornadoed through the house and back up to his room.

He flung his laptop lid open and cracked his neck.

It was going to be a long night, writing an essay from scratch with no outline. He'd be fine. He'd—what had his dad said? *Figure it out?* Hell, maybe it'd be easier, since it was about Keely.

As the hours ticked by, Max hunched over his computer, pulling passion from all the new places Keely had touched.

His grades, which she'd completely turned around despite only having a few solid weeks to do it. The study methods and compartmentalization, breaking things down to a granular level when the picture became too big.

The enthusiasm of the children at school, her ability to not only hold their attention but to get them asking thoughtful, intelligent questions that had Max himself wondering, leaning into the quest for more knowledge.

She'd even made life better at the best place on earth. At the shelter, she improved their surrender process and paperwork. Built it from the ground up, really, and now the rescue had maximum information when choosing proper care for a new animal. She made bath time more efficient. She had Farah Pawcett eating out of her hand.

Max knew the feeling.

At some point, his dad came up and dropped off half a pizza, knocked on the door frame twice with a shake of his head, and shut the door behind him.

Max ate straight from the box as he chicken-pecked the new essay.

He knew she didn't need him to do this; he'd read her most recent essay, and she'd always been the better student anyway. She was probably going to win regardless of his interference. But *he* needed to do this. Needed her to know how he felt, what he'd learned from her.

It might not even work, which was okay. And, if by some miracle he *did* win, he'd help her find another, better scholarship for grad school. Reach out to a few sports agents for himself and see if there were any low-hanging sponsorship opportunities he hadn't thought of before. Get a job, pay her rent, wash her ... laundry? Her dishes? Her hair?

Whatever he could do, however he could prove this to her. Starting with this.

He looked at the photo of their younger selves again, now taped to the wall behind his computer for him to look at whenever he needed an extra boost.

Finally, at 11:52 p.m., he sat back and made one final click on his computer.

The screen changed; a new message was displayed. *Your application has been submitted.*

Max grinned from ear to ear.

Chapter Forty

Keely

It worked.

Her endless refresh cycle had miraculously produced an email in the minutes between apps.

More than that, the email it produced had been positive.

> Dear Miss Keely Sinclair ... pleased to offer you the Pursue Your Passions scholarship ... Extracurriculars and academic resumé, in addition to your essays ... Field was extremely competitive ...

She finished reading the email and burst into tears, right in the middle of the library, and not for the reason she ever would have guessed.

Max.

Max had *lost* and Keely had *won*, and it wasn't supposed to feel like this. None of it was right. His dreams, the dreams of his dad and his family, had turned to dust because of her.

She still sat at their table in the library. Still held her breath every time footsteps came up the stairs. Still looked for him around every corner, on every square inch of this campus.

They'd made it three and a half years without running into each other; no wonder it was so easy for him to pretend she didn't exist now.

Keely wasn't that skilled yet. Wasn't ready to pretend they hadn't happened in the first place. Her heart—something she rarely let take the lead—wouldn't let her.

Wiping her face on her shoulder, she pulled her Finals Week To-Do List in front of her.

- *Pick up cap and gown*
- *~~Histology Final Tuesday @ 9:00 a.m.~~*
- *TACC Final Wednesday @ 12:00 p.m.*
- *~~Submit thesis paper~~*
- *Results of PYP submission*

With a shaky hand, holding her breath until her eyeballs pulsed, she crossed off the last item with a green pen.

This was everything she'd wanted. It was all going exactly as she'd planned.

So why was there a nagging tug in her gut that told her something was horribly, massively wrong?

She skimmed the email again.

> In addition to your essays...

Keely blinked, a tear dripping onto the page of her planner as her head tilted. She hadn't caught that the other dozen times. Essays, plural?

It must have been a typo. Academic professionals: they were people too. Lord knows Dr. Goff's recent emails were riddled with extra punctuation and grammar mistakes. The one Keely had received this morning had no body text, and the subject line simply read COM C ME ASP!

It wasn't sinking in yet that she had won. Maybe when she told someone? But who did she have left to tell? She and Zoey were barely speaking. Sam, Maya, and Jeremy all had their own finals to study for, and their plans had *been* sorted. There was no sympathy to be had in the scientific field. She was used to that by now.

She couldn't tell her parents, even though this entire convoluted scheme was for them. She hadn't ever told them her funding was in jeopardy. Bringing this up now—*days* before graduation—would open Keely up for more worries, criticism she wasn't sure she'd ever harden to.

And Max was, obviously, out of the question.

She pictured his face, the exact opposite of how he'd been in her bed. Waking her up with slow kisses down her spine or putting her to sleep with tender ones on her forehead.

He'd get the crimp between his eyebrows the way he did when she wasn't explaining something well enough. His mouth would pinch, his strong shoulders would hunch. Let out a little puff of air from between his rosy lips.

Keely wanted to stand in the sun and see if it touched the chill that settled in when Max had walked out her front door.

She'd just walk by the track. If he was there, she'd apologize for how it had ended. Offer him luck at his upcoming races, well health for his dad. A more natural conclusion than the jagged edges and unanswered questions that existed there now.

The sunshine warmed her face but little else, and she tugged her sweatshirt sleeves over her hands. Max's sweatshirt sleeves. He'd left it bundled at the foot of her bed the night of the essay-a-thon and had ignored all her attempts to return it.

She pulled it up to her nose now, inhaling the scent that had, at some point this year, started soothing her more than mints or coffee.

She hadn't planned for it. For *anything* that had happened to her this semester—Max, most of all.

So what did it mean that she got the same swoop in her stomach when Max looked at her as when she nailed a convoluted equation, or when one of her students at school got the answer she'd been leading them toward?

Was there room in her plan for surprises?

Keely came to a crossroads in the winding paths across campus. She'd walked them hundreds of times now, could draw a map in her sleep.

Davidson was to the left, labs and lecture halls as familiar to her as her own mind. She'd *honed* her mind in those very walls, decided the path that would please and help the most people.

Other parts of campus, like the athletics buildings, the *education* building, hadn't existed on her radar until this semester.

Once again, she had Max to thank for that.

As Keely stood in the middle of the path, a student rushing to a final bumped into her. The breeze blew her hair in that new, unknown direction.

She'd almost secured the teaching position. *A matter of timing*, the woman on the phone had said.

Keely could do it, right? Completely change course and rewrite the rest of her life, with no instruction manual, no to-do lists?

Who was she kidding—she was Keely Sinclair. The founder of the Mid-Atlantic Regional Science Olympiad, President of AMU's Women in Science Society, total biochem badass. Of course she could change paths.

She turned away from the gym and went to pick up her cap and gown instead.

• • • • •

The admin building crawled with students either squeezing in last-minute counseling appointments or picking up graduation regalia. Everywhere Keely looked, green and gold fought for dominance. She had a headache.

The gowns were deep emerald, AMU's seal in gold stitching. Keely would have several cords, a few each for participating in and being leadership for WIS and the Olympiad, plus a gold stole, an outward reflection of all Keely's hard work. Graduating with honors—in the wrong major.

She bit her lip, because despite the horrible prospects of her post-grad life, she kind of wanted to laugh.

A few administrative faculty members stood to the side, answering questions already answered in the dozens of mass emails sent over the previous two weeks.

Dr. Goff stood behind the table for students with last names P–S, and she waved as Keely riffled through the cellophane bags.

"How are finals going for you?" Dr. Goff sipped out of a Q-branded disposable coffee cup.

Keely noted the tea bag pinned under the rim. Huh. Maybe Keely should switch to tea.

"They're fine." She threw a smile up as her fingers skipped over Price, Ruiz, Simmons—

Simmons, Maxwell.

A little breathless laugh slipped from her mouth. It was probably for the best that she'd forgotten his full name this time around. She'd have been thinking about Maxwell's equations the entire time. No wonder she was magnetized to him.

She lingered for longer than was wise. Her pinkie snagged on the tag and left a little smear of ink behind.

"Great, actually," Keely amended, plucking her own bag from behind Max's with hot cheeks. "I submitted my thesis paper a few days ago."

"Did you solve the world's problems?"

"No, Linda." Keely gave a one-shoulder shrug and a sad, tight smile. "Not even close."

Dr. Goff spun her tea in her hands. "I heard the scholarship committee sent out their acceptance. It's unprecedented how fast they decided. Apparently, there was a clear winner."

Keely's heart knocked against her chest. Right beneath the spot where Max had touched her so sweetly on the track. Where he'd kissed her as he came.

"Have you checked your email lately, Keely?" Based on the gleam in her counselor's eye, she already knew the answer.

"Actually, I—"

"There you are." A voice came from behind Keely, and she spun.

"Tricia?" Shelter Tricia. Dog-print-bandana Tricia. Total hardass for everything with two legs Tricia. "What are you doing here?"

"Well." Tricia grinned and held up a travel coffee container. "I thought I'd bring my wife some caffeine, but it looks like she couldn't wait."

They shared an intimate look. Keely's gaze ping-ponged between them. Had she known this? There were the photos on Dr. Goff's windowsill with that amorphous other person, but they'd been too far away to make out clearly.

She must not have hidden her shock well.

"I told you." Dr. Goff slipped an arm around Tricia's waist. "You have to let life surprise you, Keely. See where you end up."

Shining black hair at the other end of the hall stole Keely's attention.

Zoey.

"I have to go," she blurted, hustling after her best friend. Former best friend? Future, forever best friend, if Keely had anything to say about it. "I'm really sorry."

Up ahead, Zoey ducked around the corner.

Keely took off after her, catching up as the admin building spit them out into the blinding sunlight.

"Zo!"

Zoey looked over shoulder, saw it was Keely, and kept on walking.

"Wait, Zoey, please!"

With a frustrated sigh Keely only usually heard in the context of a K-drama cliffhanger, Zoey adjusted her backpack on her shoulder and checked her phone.

"I can't talk long. I'm supposed to meet—" She cut herself off, but by the flushing of her cheekbones, Keely had a *highly* educated guess.

"You're with Nolan." She brushed her fingertips over the outside hem of her shorts. "If it's supposed to be a secret, you're not doing a great job."

It was a testament to their friendship that Keely still recognized

Zoey's tugged earlobe as hidden excitement—and a sign of how far they'd drifted that the frown returned with a vengeance.

"Do you have time for coffee?" Keely said.

Zoey's jaw slackened. "Do *you*? Since when do you get spontaneous beverages?"

"Since I spectacularly screwed up." Keely went to spread her hands, but she still clutched her graduation garb. She hefted the clear garment bag between them. "And I'm running out of time to fix everything."

Zoey shifted on her feet, chewing her lip. She sighed. "Coffee *and* a Danish. Nolan was going to feed me."

"A good man," Keely murmured. She knew because *Max* was a good man. He wouldn't keep bad company.

The Q was less crowded than usual, so after they got their coffee and snacks, Keely followed Zoey to her table of choice, a round two-seater in the corner. The plastic was sun-warmed. Keely's thighs would stick to the vinyl.

She stabbed her paper straw through the lid, slushing her ice. "How ... how have you been?"

"Fine." Zoey's words were as breezy as the trees outside, raining magnolia blossoms onto the sidewalks and against the glass walls.

Then, holding direct eye contact, Zoey tore her Danish in half.

Keely gulped.

She must have swallowed an ice cube, because her throat closed around her next words. "I'm so sorry, Zo."

Zoey's lips pressed from one side to the other. "For?"

"This entire semester. I slacked on my responsibilities and left you alone to organize everything."

"For a man, no less," Zoey mumbled around her Danish.

Keely gave her a sad smile. "I got wrapped up in all the wrong things. It was supposed to be the two of us."

A quiet hum. "Was he worth it, at least?"

She still didn't know, so she changed the subject. "You should take the women of science posters with you to California."

A tight, confused expression pinched Zoey's brows together. "You're not coming with me?"

They must have been in a vacuum, because Keely couldn't hear anything beyond the panicked beat of her heart against her eardrums.

But her gut was quiet, settled despite the ill-advised afternoon shot of caffeine. Even though it was scary, this was right.

"Not for biochem," she whispered. "Maybe not at all."

When she dared to look up again, fire lit her friend's face. "Well." Zoey dropped her Danish back in its paper wrapper, dusted her hands over it, and sat back in her chair. "It's about damn time."

Keely choked on air. "*What?*"

Zoey's nose scrunched. "Be honest, Keel. Would you have done *half* the stuff you did in college if it didn't go on your resumé? Or if you weren't trying to avoid driving a wedge between your parents? A wedge that you had nothing to do with, by the way."

A drop of condensation slid down Keely's cup, and it splattered on the table alongside the truth. "No." Her shoulders slumped.

Zoey nudged her foot under the table. "That's because it wasn't for you. You were awesome at all that stuff, yeah, but that was because *you* are awesome. At whatever you do. You succeeded at science, but it was only what you tried first. And I love that about you. You inspired me to be better at anatomy." Her gaze dropped to the floor. The bag with Zoey's graduation garb had slumped over on top of Keely's, knocking them both over. "Your work ethic is the whole reason I have a gold stole too."

"That's not true." Keely jolted forward. "I didn't do the work for you, Zo. You're amazing at it all on your own."

"I am," she said, "and I proved that this semester. But I learned it from someone, Keel, and that was you."

Keely opened her mouth but closed it when she realized she couldn't tell if she was talking Zoey into or out of forgiving her.

"What do you want to do?" Zoey said instead. "Gut instinct."

"Teach." The word was out before Keely had even considered holding it back, but the unfiltered truth was so much stronger on her tongue than coffee. Sweeter, even, than any kiss from Max. "I want to teach science to elementary school kids. Like how I've been reading to them at school. It's my favorite day of the week."

That and Sundays.

Well, Sundays when Max was still a part of them.

Zoey nodded, giving a small smile. "So you'll teach. And be awesome at it. And we'll get together once a month to commiserate and eat Cup Noodles because I'm choosing academia and you're choosing education and, I'm sorry, babe, but Nolan can't support us both and I've already called dibs."

A laugh lifted Keely's spirits. "Maybe we can room together in a year or two if I end up at a program near yours. I still have a lot to figure out, but I want you in my future. As my friend."

Zoey slid the torn half of the Danish across the table. "I've always considered us more like sisters. Fight like hell and still show up when we need each other."

Keely picked up her half and dinked it to Zoey's. "You're so right. I can't believe I forgot you were a genius."

Her best friend laughed. "Don't let it happen again."

Chapter Forty-One

Max

Max did two things he swore he'd never do.

He washed Yoon's dishes. Rather, he texted Yoon five times to do it, and when those messages went unread, Max bit the bullet and did it himself. The smell was atrocious, and he bathed his hands in bleach afterward, but it was done.

And then, after the kitchen was clean for probably the first time all semester, he invited someone over.

Not Keely. Not yet. He figured he'd hear from her once she found out about the scholarship—because in his mind she was the only possible winner—but Max had some things to take care of before he sought her out. If she wanted to see him at all.

Nolan looked around Max's living room with a keen eye. There wasn't art on the walls, and his gaming system was a few years outdated, but Max hadn't ever needed much when his entire life was running. Could it still be that?

Could it be running *and* something else?

He really wanted to find out.

"Nice view," Nolan said, eyeing the stadium outside the window.

"I dunno." Max shrugged. "Makes it hard to get out of my head sometimes."

"Ah." Nolan nodded slowly. "I can imagine."

Max scratched the back of his neck. "Yeah."

Best to do this now while he still had the balls.

"I'm sorry," he said.

Nolan, who'd leaned against the side of his couch, straightened. "For?"

Where did Max even begin? "For being a selfish jerk the entire semester. Maybe our whole college career." He sat on the couch, rested his elbows on his knees and his head in his hands. "Mostly for being an asshole to you, when you've only ever been kind to me."

With the grace of a bull in a china shop, Nolan hopped over the armrest and took up the other end of the couch. "Finally, the Max Simmons Apology Tour. Let's hear it. Am I your first stop?"

"First of many," Max muttered. "Or second." He wasn't sure what to call rewriting his essay for Keely. "One-B."

"I'll take it." Nolan kicked his feet up to the coffee table. "Anything else?"

Max scoffed. "You're not supposed to let me off this easy, dude."

"Sorry." Nolan twisted his features into something sterner, drawing his dark eyebrows together over his forehead. But he only held it for a few seconds before his face relaxed and he chuckled. "I think you're harder on yourself than anyone else could ever be on you. You've pushed some really good people away because of it. Alex and Jazz, Coach. You're lucky I'm stubborn."

Max's chest ached. "I just added the entire team roster to my Apology Tour."

"As you should." Nolan was always serious, but his voice held more weight now. Which made sense, based on what he said next. "You might be the best of us, but you're not *better* than us. They put in the work, same as you."

Max's throat burned. So did his eyes. "I know."

"We're good, then. Now we can focus on getting gold at regionals and running laps around Rutherford."

Max chuckled. "Damn straight." He wanted to keep reciprocating, trying, putting himself out there. Returning the energy Nolan had thrown his way their entire college career. "What's next for you? Moving home, staying here?"

Nolan looked away, and the color on his cheeks deepened. "Gotta figure a few things out first. Mostly Zoey."

"Good for you, but..." Max shuddered. "She kinda scares me."

"Hell, me too," Nolan said with a laugh.

The conversation fizzled, but Max wasn't ready to be done. Afternoon practices started earlier now that finals were over, but they still had a few hours to kill.

"I've got GTA." Max cleared his throat. "It's not the new one, but I remember you said you liked it."

"You're going down, Simmons." Nolan kicked his shoes off, then went to the fridge and made himself at home with grabbing them both bottles of water.

Max gave Nolan all he had, and Nolan, as always, gave it right back.

Chapter Forty-Two

Keely

The call connected, and Keely's dad's face appeared on her laptop screen. This was a computer activity, like buying plane tickets or making a spreadsheet.

She didn't recognize his background; this must be his new apartment. The one where she'd have to share a room with her little brother if she ever visited, because two bedrooms were cheaper than three.

Her stomach churned. "Hey, Dad."

He grinned. "I'm glad we could talk. I had a question about the graduation ceremony. Do people with tickets have to sit together, because I don't—"

The line clicked as her mom jumped on the call, a bright smile in place. "Hi, sweetheart."

Her dad's grin, however, faded. "Veronica? What are you doing here? Keely, what's she doing here?"

Keely's mother's angry flush spread one pixel at a time. "Good question. I've got better things to do than listen to your—"

"Mom, just stop. Actually, *both* of you stop!" Keely shouted.

Judging from the way her parents froze, it might have been the first time ever.

"I have to talk to you." She wished for a second she'd taken up Zoey's offer to be here for this, but Keely needed to start figuring things out by herself. Lay out *her* expectations.

"And I need you to focus on me instead of tearing pieces off each other. It's important," she added, because they couldn't see her strangling the edge of the couch.

Her parents managed to share a look, even though they were separated by a screen and a divorce. "Is everything okay?" Dad said.

"I'm not going to grad school," Keely said before she lost the nerve. She'd made up her mind. Knew what she wanted, mess and uncertainty and all. "At least, not right away."

"*What?*" Mom laughed, but it was her panicked one that pinched at the edges.

"Mom, please listen. I've wanted to say this for a while."

Her mother fell silent, and Keely had the floor.

She started from the beginning. Her grad school application, how she didn't want to ask them to co-sign because they'd already incurred so much of their own debt going through the divorce. Pursue Your Passions and the subsequent volunteering at the school. Realizing she wanted to teach instead.

Once she cracked the safe, everything spilled out. She told them about Max, their reconnection, their stupid prank war. Their falling in love.

Keely's falling in love. She couldn't say the same of Max. She wiped the skin beneath her eyes until it was raw.

"I know it sounds like it, but I'm not throwing away my future for—for Max or anything," Keely repeated, firmer, clearly, even though his name scraped over her tongue like sandpaper. "I'm closer to finding myself now more than ever. And I know you're still figuring out how to coexist. But I'm going to need you both to—to swallow your egos and be on my side while I do that."

Dad rubbed at his jaw, and Mom pressed her lips together into a tight line. Another look between them on the screen. Keely wondered if they'd always be able to do that, even if they weren't in love.

It gave Keely a little hope that one day she'd see Max, hear his name, and it wouldn't feel like her heart was being hole punched.

Her mom shifted. "Why wouldn't you tell us any of this, Keely? This is a lot to carry on your own."

Keely stared at the women of science hanging over the television and prayed for an ounce of their wisdom. "I tried so many times, but you both found a way to bring it back to the divorce. There wasn't any room for my problems."

A thick beat of silence before Dad cupped his neck. "How long have you felt this way, punk?"

Keely's parents blurred on the screen. Silly tears. She blinked them back and tried to answer honestly. "At least since you told us about the divorce. Probably longer. Whenever you were fighting, basically, for as long as I can remember."

Mom wiped at her own face. "I—I'm so sorry, sweetheart. Of course there's space for you. I feel absolutely terrible you didn't feel like you could come to us. And I'm mad that we didn't see that you were hurting."

Keely shrugged, staring at the last remaining fleck of banana, dried and stuck between the M and K on her keyboard. "You were hurting, too."

"Hurting or not, we shouldn't have done that." Dad chuckled, but it was raw, wet, and Keely wasn't surprised when he wiped at his own eyes. "I'm sorry. I'm—*we're* going to do better."

"For Vince, too," Keely said. "He's getting more of it than I am. Just because he's quiet doesn't mean he doesn't need support."

"Oh, honey." Mom threw another look at Dad. "You really are so, so smart. You've got so much—"

"Please don't say 'potential,'" Keely blurted. "I love that you think so, but if I hear that one more time I might throw up."

"I was going to say *passion*," Mom mumbled, and Dad's mouth quirked like he was fighting a smile.

He gave a small nod. "So I guess you'll be moving home after graduation, after all? How about we sit down together—all of us—and work your next steps out face to face?"

"Can you be cordial for that?" Keely said without thinking.

"We'll figure it out for you," Dad said, looking a little sheepish, and her mom nodded emphatically.

"And for Vince," Keely reminded them.

Her parents weren't okay—but maybe they *could* be. If not all the time, then at least when she and her baby brother were around.

"So ... Max Simmons, huh? We always joked you two were a love story waiting to happen." Keely's mom winked, and yeah, Keely's heart still ached at his name.

"Max and I aren't—I don't think we—" She had no words. None that didn't tear her wide open. She settled for, "If it was a love story, then I didn't like the ending very much."

· · · · ·

Later that afternoon, a soft voice welcomed her into the office that had, for the last four years, become sort of a home base for her.

The pictures in the windowsill, stale coffee permeating the air, the woman smiling at her from behind the desk.

"Hi, Dr. Goff. Sorry for running off the other day. I had something important to handle." She held out the envelope. "This is for you ... and Tricia. A note of appreciation. And a gift card for the health spa in town. To counteract all the stress I've caused you over the last four years."

Dr. Goff stood, rounding the desk. She pulled Keely into a warm hug. "Thank you. This is very thoughtful."

To Keely's surprise, Dr. Goff took the seat behind the desk, next to her.

"So." Dr. Goff smiled widely. "Excited for Caltech?"

Keely ducked her chin. The more people she told, the realer it became. Guilt gnawed at the edges of her stomach; Dr. Goff had done so much for her, had stuck her neck out for Keely and answered frantic 2 a.m. emails for the last four years. She was throwing away all that hard work.

But she had to be true to herself.

"I'm not going. I didn't accept the scholarship," Keely mumbled down at her lap. She was secretly thrilled. This was, all things considered, the best-case scenario. She knew what she wanted; she had her parents' tentative buy-in for her new plan.

And Max won the scholarship by default.

This way, they both got to live their dreams.

Dr. Goff studied Keely, her mouth tipping up at the corner. "I had a feeling." She rummaged on her desk and produced a stapled packet. "This is what I wanted to tell you the other day. I *really* think you should read this."

Brows pinched, Keely hefted the paper and skimmed the title lines.

Pursue Your Passions, Max Simmons

What...? Her gaze snapped up to Dr. Goff.

The counselor sat back in her chair, sipping her tea with a knowing gleam in her eye.

Keely started reading.

```
At the beginning of this semester, I was selfish,
rude, and would rather shut myself off from
everything to avoid hurt, than allow the tiniest
joy to filter in. Through necessity and fear, I was
forced to let sunshine into my life.
    That sunshine's name is Keely Sinclair, the true
winner of the Pursue Your Passions scholarship.
She gives her heart openly, honestly, the way
everyone should strive to. Her enthusiasm for
teaching, for learning, has inspired my own
passion toward my craft, the mark of a true leader.
    Keely is a testament not only to Ash Mountain
University, but to the science community in general.
Anyone who knows her loves her—myself included.
```

Keely kept reading, kept holding her breath. *This* was the essay he submitted? But what about the one that poured out his dedication to running and his family legacy? This was...

For the first time in her life, Keely couldn't find any words.

He'd put her heart on paper, more succinctly and beautifully than she'd ever managed, with dozens of drafts and red lines.

Max knew her. Understood her.

Loved her.

She stood so swiftly, she knocked her backpack over. A rainbow of pens and highlighters scattered onto the floor and across the carpet. Her planner splayed open, the corners bending, coil resting at an odd angle.

She dropped to her knees, scooping supplies into her backpack. She clutched Max's essay so tightly in her other hand that some of the ink rubbed off on her skin.

She had to find him. Had to tell him how *stupid* it was for him to risk his shot for her.

Then kiss him forever.

Pens mostly gathered—but honestly, she didn't care if they weren't—Keely rounded the chair and made for the hallway.

"You forgot your planner," Dr. Goff called after her.

With a smile, Keely planted her foot directly into the smoothie stain on the hallway carpet. "Keep it!"

• • • • •

God, she hated running. There was a reason she'd had the same pair of gently used trainers since high school. Her preferred exercise was strolling the aisles of Barnes & Noble. She'd never so much as thought of running a 5k, and up until this moment believed she physically *couldn't*.

What had Max whispered against her mouth, though? When has "can't" ever stopped her before?

She ran through his schedule in her head as she sprinted—a modest jog, really—to the track. It was the first place she knew to look for him, especially if he was practicing for regionals. Which he *should*, because she didn't give up the scholarship for him to squander his shot at his own dreams.

To her relief, the visitor's gate was unlocked, the track populated.

Sweat stuck her shirt to her torso; her hair clip bobbed and pinched at her hair.

But none of that mattered, because he was *right there.*

Max.

He was bent over, adjusting his shoe. His unitard, not the one she'd stolen and shrunk, pulled taut over his delicious muscles. His skin had developed a natural tan now that the days were longer. He needed a haircut. Needed nine hours of sleep and a giant hug.

And he needed to not look at her like that, because she had Things to Say.

I'm in love with you, she thought.

"I hate running!" she yelled instead.

It bounced back at her, and she heard her desperation in the echo.

Oh well. Might as well go for broke.

Max's head cocked to the side as he threw a glance at Nolan. "Good to know."

She closed the distance. Her thighs *burned*, but it was nothing compared to what her heart was doing right now. God, she'd missed him.

"You," she wheezed, shoving the essay into his chest. "Why would you *do* this?"

He didn't look away, even though Keely was pretty sure the staple was digging into his nipple. His throat bobbed. Jaw tensed.

"Because you needed to win, Keely." His eyes were bright as they stared straight into Keely's soul. "*I* needed you to win."

He wasn't supposed to say that. And he definitely wasn't supposed to look so devastating while he did it. His hand came up, holding the paper, holding her, in place directly over his heart.

"Well." She inhaled. Held it. Let it out in a single, slow gust. "I needed you to win more."

"Since when?" Max licked his lips, his brow slashed across his forehead as he stared down at her.

She shook her head as she spoke her new core truth. "Since I fell in love with you."

Max gawked at her, and his hand slipped off her wrist, falling limply back to his side. She missed him instantly, the feeling that she was safe. Anchored.

"I..." He chuckled under his breath, stared at their feet mere inches apart. Then he looked up at her from beneath his lashes, and Keely witnessed alchemy in real time as his eyes turned to gold. "Was this on your checklist?"

Her checklist? What was that supposed to mean? Confused, she shook her head. "What are you—"

"Was it on your checklist," he repeated, drawing out the words until Keely's hope hung on each and every one, "to make me fall in love with you back?"

Her throat closed. "No," she whispered.

"Shame." The gold from his eyes melted over her skin, turning the moment languid and viscous. Malleable. They could make this whatever they wanted. "You could have crossed it off."

A surprised laugh escaped her lips, but she couldn't stop it.

Max rested his hand on her hips, fingers digging in to keep her still. As if she wanted to be anywhere else. "I love you," he said again, but firmer, in different words. "And I'm so sorry for what I said to you, Key. If I could go back..."

She shook her head, then let it fall to his chest. "The things I said to you were equally as terrible."

"They were true, though. What I said was not. Being nice isn't a character flaw. It's one of the reasons I fell for you. Seeing you give so much to others and still have some leftover for yourself. For someone like me, no less." He hummed softly, deep in his chest. She felt it everywhere. "I'm working on being more like that. So I don't make any more mistakes."

"Mistakes aren't so bad," Keely said. Over Max's shoulder, Nolan and the other track members watched them. "I make them all the time." She reached up, smoothing over the harsh lines of his jaw. Let her hand trail down, ghost over the vein in his neck, throbbing wildly beneath her touch. She came to rest over his heart again. "But loving you is not one of them."

His chin dipped once, a deep nod that nearly touched his chest. The corner of his mouth tilted up. "No?"

Her heart was suspended in her throat. Her backpack slid off her shoulder, and she let go of her essay. It fluttered to the ground. "Loving you feels like first place."

Max's tongue darted out, and his lips spread in a slow smile. "And loving *you* feels like the biggest trophy at the science fair."

"They actually gave us ribbons," she murmured. Now was probably not the time to be correcting him, but she couldn't change who she was. Not completely.

"The brightest, bluest, biggest ribbon, then." He stepped forward, then she did, and each of their toes was on a corner of the paper. "Loving you is ... it's peace, I think. And it's trouble. And it's fun, and *maddening*, and ..."

He let out a small laugh under his breath, and his hand came up to brush her cheekbone. "Loving you is everything, Keely."

"Max," she murmured.

His other palm slid around her waist to span her lower back.

"Have any hypotheses up there in that big brain of yours that predict what we're supposed to do now?"

"I think," Keely said, her gaze trained on his mouth, "we start with a kiss. We might need to do it a few times, though. To prove it. For science."

"For science." He nodded, brows furrowed in concentration. In understanding.

Max grinned, scooping her up until only her toes skimmed the track he loved.

This time, when he kissed her, she didn't know. She didn't know what tomorrow would look like, what their future held. Where she'd end up.

But she knew Max, his body pressed in strong lines against her. His hands, tangling in the hair at the back of her head. His smile, and his smell, and his heart.

"You won the scholarship." He pulled back, then surged forward again like he couldn't quite help himself. And he kissed and kissed and kissed her. Hot, searing brands of his mouth and hands. "I'm so proud of you."

"I didn't," she said as her toes touched the asphalt again.

Max's head tilted, an errant curl popping down over his forehead. "What do you mean?"

Keely shifted her weight. The essay ripped beneath her sole. "I didn't accept."

Max tilted his head. "And why the hell not, Key?"

She beamed. "I—I want to be a teacher." It was still scary as hell to admit out loud, but easier with him. It always had been. From the beginning, he'd seen the girl hiding behind the planner. The fire under her blue-tipped fingers. "I applied for a teaching program. That's the call you heard me take, why I was so secretive.

I couldn't tell anyone about it because I was so terrified it wasn't going to work. And it didn't. I didn't get in."

Sadness discolored his features, and she didn't want that look on his face. Not now, not ever.

"But I talked to my parents. Told them everything. We're still figuring some things out, but I'll apply again next year. And when the time is right, I'll have my own classroom full of kids to teach science to."

"That's perfect for you, Key." He blinked hard. Color crept up from his neck, climbed his throat like ivy. "And the scholarship?"

"I heard it deferred to the runner up. Which ..." She trailed off, trying and failing not to smile. "I guess you haven't checked your email this morning, what with all this hard work you're doing." She patted his sternum.

Max's eyes narrowed for a split second, then blew wide open. Same as his mouth, which let out a surprised, choked sound. "*Keely*. You didn't."

She surged up to kiss him again. She couldn't help it.

"I told you. The best person was going to win, fair and square."

He wound his arms around her waist, pulling her up so her toes grazed the ground. "God, you're so smart. Tell me more."

They leaned in for a kiss when Coach blew the whistle behind them. Keely shrieked, stumbling, but Max held steady.

He was so good at that.

Epilogue
Keely

One Year Later

A nacho, dripping with fluorescent neon cheese, bobbed in front of Keely's eyes.

"Move, please," she said, pushing Zoey's hand down at the wrist, then snagging the chip before it was too far away. "They're lining up."

Keely wouldn't let anything block her view. Not that there was much that could. Even as a spectator, she'd always be a front-row girl at heart.

Charleston sun broke through the clouds, dappling the stadium in warm, polka-dotted light. Her nose tickled as the trees outside rustled with the breeze, but it was nothing her weekly allergy shot wouldn't fix.

Max's mom leaned over Keely's lap, grabbing a nacho for herself. "It will still be another few minutes." Her lips pursed as she glanced at the bottom of the bleachers. "But if Jacob and Thomas don't come back from the beer stand soon, they're going to miss it. Max is certainly fast enough."

Keely smiled at Virginia, bumping her shoulder. "Don't say that too loud. It'll go straight to his head."

Virginia nudged her back. "Wonder where he gets that from."

A sweet sadness passed between them, and Keely sought Max's now-familiar form down on the track, wondering if he carried the same sense of bittersweet melancholy on his shoulders today.

Max's dad had passed away in his sleep right before Thanksgiving last year, and it had been a long six months since then. Black clothes, sleepless nights, Max pulling Keely close in bed because he didn't want to be alone.

After Max had found the right people, surprisingly, he preferred company.

On Zoey's other side, Nolan echoed Virginia's sentiment. "They've got another two minutes, at *least*."

Nolan was another reason Max had made it here. He'd done just as much heart work on Max as Keely had, training with him, late nights and early mornings and sprint after sprint after sprint. She wondered if it bothered him, not being down there. Nolan hadn't gone pro the way Max had. Didn't have a closet full of Team USA gear edging out Zoey's clothes the way Max's did to Keely's. Wasn't getting his passport renewed and travel documents ready for Worlds in Beijing this fall, the way Max was.

Nolan still looked pretty content, though, snuggled up next to Keely's best friend. Then again, a well-functioning long-distance relationship didn't usually leave space for anything other than contentment when they were together physically. The California sun had done wonders for Zoey's warm brown skin. She was *glowing*.

When Keely had visited her at Caltech a month ago, all she'd got was a sunburn.

The stadium quieted as the announcer called the runners to the starting blocks.

Keely's muscles strained like she was down there with him. Her heart certainly raced like she was.

"Sorry, Mom." Jacob slid in behind Keely, and Thomas muttered under his breath as he passed his mom a freshly poured beer, the top inch still filled with foam.

Virginia downed it in three thick swallows.

As he walked to his block, Max craned his neck. The sun illuminated every facet of him. This unitard featured stripes of navy, white, and red. The colors of the national team.

Keely stood and waved to make sure he spotted her.

He pointed back at her, then pointed at the space between his ribs. His heart.

Feel me here.

She did. Every day.

Max pointed again, at the sky this time, before he crouched into his starting position. Keely knew he was thinking about his dad, asking for any last-minute bits of wisdom. It had become a ritual of his—they still raced together, even now.

The tone sounded.

She wasn't sure she breathed the entire time. She never did when she watched him sprint. He looked so natural, his chest proud and strong and upright, the way he'd taught her was correct. His strides ate up the asphalt, and she tried to count them but got dizzy.

Also a regular occurrence around Max.

He passed one runner, then another, pulling ahead. *Farther* ahead.

She shot to her feet, gripping Virginia's hand. She heard what might have been the nachos tumbling onto the bleacher floor.

He's going to win. Keely knew it, in a space in her brain reserved for the most essential scientific equations. Knew it in her heart, the way she knew Max would always have ended up here, scholarship or not.

She was already crying when he crossed the finish line.

Keely was enveloped in arms; she couldn't tell who they belonged to or whose toes were under her feet.

She grabbed the bar in front of her, screaming, rattling the rail. *"You did it!"*

And then he was running again—this time, straight for her.

She leaned over the railing and would have jumped it herself if he wasn't so damn fast.

Max wrapped his arms around her waist, and she clutched at his shoulders as he buried his nose in her hair. Her toes left the ground.

"Key."

She *felt* her name on his body. His heart knocked against hers, begging to be let in. He was already there.

He pulled back far enough to plant a searing kiss on her open mouth, his hands cradling her head, moving her effortlessly in his arms.

She wanted this so badly, but kissing in front of Max's mom was one thing, and Keely was pretty sure the jumbotron camera was on them right now.

She rested her forehead on his. "Fair and square," she whispered, a promise, a reminder.

Then he was kissing her again, this time so *passionate* she forgot to care about his mom or the cameras altogether.

After they'd managed to break apart, Max was passed between loved ones, and Keely watched on, pride shining in her eyes. She had to be effervescent with it. It oozed from her pores.

Later, she walked hand in hand with Max out of the stadium, his gold medal hanging from her neck.

She lifted it, letting it wink at her in the sun. "We'll have to hide this as soon as we get home."

Biscuit hadn't changed either in the last year. He still loved shiny things, just as much as the day Keely had met him. He was waiting for her at home, a little two-bedroom apartment right outside their hometown.

For *both* of them. Turns out, when they tried to pick favorites, the stubborn dog absolutely refused. So they both adopted him. Tricia cried that day.

Max kissed the side of her head. "Add it to the list."

She mimed pulling her phone from her back pocket, the one Max's hand wasn't occupying. Truth was, she hadn't looked at her planner in weeks.

Well, days. She hadn't changed completely.

She still loved Max. Loved how he challenged her. The pranks they played on each other, with much lower stakes. Like when she picked out her outfit for her first day of education classes, set to start in a few weeks with an accelerated summer program. He somehow found a child-size version of the same outfit and swapped it from her dresser, a direct reminder of the time she shrank his uniform. Or this winter, when he'd lost his gloves and she'd replaced them with a Smurfs-branded pair.

Beyond that, beyond Max, she didn't know.

Her future was completely uncertain.

She couldn't wait.

Acknowledgments

It's weird to start book acknowledgments with thanking a thing or an institution instead of a person, but I promise, it's relevant.

So.

I'd like to thank the Summer 2024 Olympics, which bore the clips of many top-tier athletes—Mondo Duplantis, Tara Davis-Woodhall, and Hunter Woodhall, to name a few—achieving their wildest dreams and running straight to the loves of their lives. Those ten-second clips set to "The Alchemy" by Taylor Swift were the seeds that sprouted this entire wild ride. That's sort of what this book feels like to me, too.

Some books are nightmares to write, and some are fever dreams. This book came together so easily that, somehow, I blinked and missed it. This little (thique) book with a little (accidentally a lot of) angst has (so many) little chunks of my heart. Keely's perfectionism and fear of the unknown. Max's tendency to shut down and push people away when the hurt gets too big for your chest.

So I want to thank my younger self too, for showing me we can get through the hard parts. If this book helps one person feel known or seen, it will be enough. Even if that person is me.

To Ethan, my husband, my number-one fan and biggest supporter. It's been fifteen years of love and laughter, yet somehow you still make it both harder and easier to breathe. Thank you for being my safe space.

For my IRL besties, Michelle, Grace, Casey, Katrina, and Ashley, who were here from the inception of this book and will be here long after the last page. And to Christine, Callie, and Melanie, my fangirls and critique partners. My excitement is made even better because I can share it with all of you.

To Isabelle, my absolute ride or die. I can't wait to support you the way you have me and scream about your talent from the highest rooftops. Your turn next—and I mean it this time.

To my Book Train girlies. Particular thanks go out to Allissa and Isabelle (again), for your contributions to Chapter 18. The world will thank you, but never louder than I will. TRAIN GANG STAYS WINNING!!!

My parents, who have always given me space to fail. Please enjoy my tamest book. Here's hoping the locker room makes you forget about the laundry room.

My agent Rebeka Finch. You know what you did. I love you for it, and for much more than can ever fit into the space allotted here. You are a publishing warrior, and I'm so glad you're fighting for me. And to the support system at Darley Anderson: my career shines brighter because of you.

To my editor, Molly Walker-Sharp. Max and Keely were always meant for you. And the fantastic team at Sphere, who helped shepherd this book into its final form. I'd also love to thank my cover artist, Meg Shepherd, who brought Keely, Max, and AMU to life in a way that exceeded my highest expectations.

To my teachers, for introducing me to books that made me love worlds beyond my own. For all the teachers, everywhere. And always, endlessly, to booksellers and librarians.

To the readers who have followed me from a small town in Indiana all the way to a fictional college in Virginia, and the ones I gained along the way. To the readers who picked this up just because of the cover. To the readers who burn the midnight oil and shamelessly recommend books to their friends. To the readers, period. Never stop.

And lastly, to the women who paved the way, and the ones who have yet to walk it.

RAISING READERS
Books Build Bright Futures

Dear Reader,

We'd love your attention for one more page to tell you about the crisis in children's reading, and what we can all do.

Studies have shown that reading for fun is the **single biggest predictor of a child's future life chances** – more than family circumstance, parents' educational background or income. It improves academic results, mental health, wealth, communication skills, ambition and happiness.[1]

The number of children reading for fun is in rapid decline. Young people have a lot of competition for their time. In 2024, 1 in 10 children and young people in the UK aged 5 to 18 did not own a single book at home.[2]

Hachette works extensively with schools, libraries and literacy charities, but here are some ways we can all raise more readers:

- Reading to children for just 10 minutes a day makes a difference
- Don't give up if children aren't regular readers – there will be books for them!
- Visit bookshops and libraries to get recommendations
- Encourage them to listen to audiobooks
- Support school libraries
- Give books as gifts

There's a lot more information about how to encourage children to read on our website: **www.RaisingReaders.co.uk**

Thank you for reading.

hachette UK

---

[1] OECD, '21st-Century Readers: Developing Literacy Skills in a Digital World', 2021, https://www.oecd.org/en/publications/21st-century-readers_a83d84cb-en.html

[2] National Literacy Trust, 'Book Ownership in 2024', November 2024, https://literacytrust.org.uk/research-services/research-reports/book-ownership-in-2024